THE
PUPPETEER

TAMSEN SCHULTZ

*everafter*ROMANCE

EverAfter Romance
A Division of Diversion Publishing Corp.
443 Park Avenue South, Suite 1008
New York, New York 10016
www.EverAfterRomance.com

Cover Design by Greg Simanson and Sian Foulkes
Edited by Julie Molinari

This is a work of fiction. Names, characters, places and incidents either are the
product of the author's imagination or are used fictitiously. Any resemblance to
actual persons, living or dead, events or locales is entirely coincidental.

For more information, email info@everafterromance.com

First EverAfter Romance edition March 2017.
Print ISBN: 978-1-63576-034-7

To Nav, even though you don't read fiction

CHAPTER 1

AGENT DANIELLE "DANI" WILLIAMSON EXAMINED the picture lying in front of her. The subject wasn't the man she was looking for. None of the other twenty or so photos she'd looked at were any closer. The subjects were either too young, too old, not the right race, not the right build, not the right gender. She sighed and slid them back into the envelope the courier had dropped off earlier.

Rising from the non-descript hotel bed, she walked to the window. The room was a hotel version of her utilitarian apartment in Washington, DC, and a far cry from her more luxurious apartment overlooking Central Park in New York. But she'd picked this hotel for a reason. It was seven blocks from the police headquarters, where she would be giving a briefing to the local vice department in the morning. And it was also three blocks from a bar owned by a family friend—a place she knew she could rack a few games of pool to help clear her head if she needed. And she needed.

Dani's hand jerked as she pushed the curtain further aside. Her body was as unsettled as her mind. She knew that until she was physically with her team, working their case, she wouldn't feel at ease. But, compliments of the team director, she was stuck here for a night, twiddling her thumbs. She was pretty sure he'd given the briefing assignment to her as warning not to go off half-cocked.

Pool, she thought, moving toward her bag.

Grabbing a top that was more "woman" than "agent" she changed. Sliding on a pair of heels that were anything but sensible, she didn't fool herself into thinking that a game or two, even if accompanied with a glass of wine, would take her mind off of the case at hand. But, glancing at her weapon in its holster on the bedside table, she could at least try to act like a normal person for a night, clothes and all.

Pulling out her gun safe, she placed her weapon inside, put the whole thing in her bag, locked the zippers together, and slid it under the bed. No, a couple of games of pool wouldn't take away the images in her mind, imprinted there for over half her life, and she didn't want them to. A game wouldn't erase her excitement about this case or the healthy anxiety she felt in believing she was *this* close to getting the answers she'd been seeking. But what a few games would do, what she was counting on them to do, was focus her mind on something else for a short time. If she didn't calm her mind down, she wouldn't be able to calm her body down. And if she didn't do that, she would never sleep tonight. And, though she could go hours without sleep, knowing she was giving the briefing tomorrow, knowing she would stand in front of a room full of alpha males and feed them half-truths, a little rest couldn't hurt.

Grabbing her key and her purse, she took one last glance at the room. The envelope lay on her bed. Since, out of context, there was nothing incriminating in the photos, she left it there. Everything else looked nice and normal, just like it should. Sliding her key into her clutch, Dani turned and headed into the night.

CHAPTER 2

NOT A FLICKER OF RECOGNITION.

Ty Fuller was impressed. Annoyed, but impressed. But, being honest with himself, he wasn't sure what irritated him more: the fact that, as good as he was at hiding his reactions, Agent Dani Williamson—or, "Ella," as she had introduced herself last night—was better, or the fact that she was hiding hers at all.

"Nice to meet you Detective Fuller." She shook his hand, as professional and as cool as the briefing room where they all sat, tucked away like errant children, on the fourth floor of the police headquarters.

"And you, Agent Williamson," he responded, pleased that only a miniscule amount of sarcasm laced his voice. He wasn't being fair, and it wasn't as though he expected her to admit they'd already met, or that, not more than three hours ago they'd been "meeting" each other in every conceivable way. But it didn't sit well on his wide shoulders that she'd no more than glanced at him when they were introduced. That she'd just given him the same perfunctory handshake she'd given all the other detectives in the room. Not even a smile.

"And this is Detective Warren, Fuller's partner." Captain Jefferies continued the introductions by indicating the man standing to Ty's left.

"Detective." She turned to the left and shook Warren's hand.

Ty pushed aside his personal bias—and let's face it, ego—and focused objectively on the person in front of him, not on the woman he'd met last night and taken home, but on the agent working the

7

room. Her tone didn't change from one officer to the next; she was seasoned and sure. Both her words and the way she said them were matter-of-fact and neither condescending nor nervous. Her demeanor was confident, free of any apprehension she might feel as a DEA agent stepping into local territory. She knew her job well.

As she moved about the room meeting the other detectives, he noted that her language, both verbal and body, was subtly different than other federal agents who had visited the department in his six-year tenure. Ty frowned. She was here to give the obligatory, one-big-happy-family-that-is-law-enforcement talk like most feds. Or in other words, she and her team intended to play nice only as long as everyone played *their* game by *their* rules.

And there was nothing unusual about the approach. What was different was that she didn't seem to care much one way or the other as she made her way around the room. The feds were usually either very clear about wanting vice out or very clear about what they needed from the locals. In the former instance, they didn't bother meeting the team. In the latter, they tended to go overboard.

Dani wasn't doing either. She was making the rounds and taking the time to meet and greet everyone. Her sincerity each time she smiled at someone was the easy kind—the kind a person uses when making promises they know they'll never have to deliver on. And if Ty had to guess, since collaboration of any sort didn't seem to be on her mind, he'd bet she was going to share some information, make them feel like they were part of the investigation, then walk away as soon as she had reason to.

Watching her shake hands with yet another detective, it occurred to him that she probably even hoped they wouldn't play along. If they didn't, it would be easier to sever the tie between the two agencies. And she could place any claims of lack of cooperation squarely on their shoulders. It made Ty wonder what would happen if they cooperated, if no one ever gave her a reason to sever the tie.

He watched her move down the line, toward the last of the detectives from his department. Whatever the DEA was up to, they'd been up to it long enough to believe they had all the information they needed—or had the resources to get it. And whatever it was, he would know soon enough. Or, he conceded to himself, he would know at least what she wanted them to know.

"Now that you've met everyone, why don't we get started?" Captain Jefferies directed, as he stepped aside and let Dani move to the front and center of the room.

She moved into place without a single hint of unease or self-consciousness. She faced six of Portland's top vice detectives, all of whom were men, and many of whom were ex-military of some sort, himself included, without batting a single one of her long eyelashes. It was more than most men accomplished. And she did it with style.

"Thank you, Captain," she began. "Thank you all for meeting with me this morning." She continued the pleasantries with a businesslike nod to the men. He could feel the tension creeping up in the room and he could sense, if not see, that all eyes were focused on Agent Williamson. He wondered if they were fooling Dani but he doubted it. Yes, they were interested in what she had to say but, these alpha males were much more interested given the messenger, a five foot eleven blonde who carried a gun. Her conservative black suit and slicked-back hair did nothing to hide the fact that she looked like she'd stepped straight off of the set of *Faster, Pussy Cat! Kill! Kill!* She had all the curves and confidence that made a man look a time, or three. Sexist? Yes, but true. His men would listen a whole lot closer to words coming out of a mouth like hers. Whether or not they would hear anything was up for grabs, but they would listen. Hell, he was no different. Yes, he was as interested as the rest of his men—probably more so—in what came out of that beautiful, familiar mouth.

• • •

Dani had almost laughed aloud when she walked into the non-descript briefing room—and it wouldn't have been the good kind. The room itself was the approximate temperature of the Antarctic, and about as gray and somber. But Dani was pretty sure that, despite the dreary environment, someone somewhere was yukking it up, and at her expense—someone with a twisted enough sense of humor to throw a man like Ty Fuller at her on this case.

After shaking hands with him, she slipped into autopilot, going through the mechanics of introductions, as she had hundreds of times before, with the rest of the team. Knowing she knew her stuff well enough that no one would suspect a thing, she let her mind linger on Ty, wondering what he thought about this turn of events. He must have been surprised at meeting her here, in this room, in this role. She certainly was. But he was good at hiding his reaction. Almost as good as she was.

Her thoughts ventured to the night before, even as she made her way down the line of vice detectives. A couple of games of pool had taken her mind off of things for a short while. But then Ty had walked in. Dark hair, strong jaw, and a way of moving that had caught her eye. And so the night had unfolded in a very different stress-reducing way. She would give credit where credit was due. Ty had done the job and done it well. Never before had she spent the night with a man she'd just met. And never, in all her adult years, had she wanted to. But when the bartender, an acquaintance of hers, had vouched for him, she had gone where her hormones had urged her to go since the first moment she'd laid eyes on him. No last names, no shop talk or small talk, and no expectations of seeing each other ever again. It had seemed so easy, so perfect. And now, thanks to the preceding hours, she was relaxed, with her body still lingering in the memory of their night together.

Maybe the twinge of regret she'd felt when she'd left his place in the early hours of the morning—regret at thinking she would never see him again, would never really know him—was enough to tempt the fates. Whatever it was, he was here, in Technicolor, and they were now officially working together. For the moment anyway—as soon as her appointed liaison gave her cause, she would drop the pretense of collaboration.

Dani pulled out a half dozen folders from her briefcase, then handed them to Ty in the front row to pass around. She caught his eye for a split second. Irritation lurked there but she chose to ignore it. She could see his point. Given what had happened between them, he had a right to at least be acknowledged. And she regretted she couldn't, she really did. The problem was she couldn't do that without the rest of the room jumping to conclusions. That they would be the right conclusions didn't matter. If it were a different situation, maybe she wouldn't mind as much. But not now, not with this case.

"These folders contain information on the investigation that brings us to your fair city," Dani began the presentation. "Ramon Getz, resident of Portland, is the primary focus. The first page has his photo and general stats." She called up his image on a projector the captain had prepared for her at her request. The face looking back at them was that of a forty-five-year-old man in a well-cut suit and silk tie. His first name was Hispanic, but Getz's features, like most Americans, were mixed enough that it was impossible to tell his heritage.

"Over the years, he's been making his way up the drug distributor food chain." Dani clicked to the next slide showing a picture of younger Getz standing on the tarmac of an airstrip in Colombia. "He got his start over thirty years ago as a transporter for one of the South American cartels. He made enough contacts and enough money that he went into business for himself about ten years ago." The slide she clicked to next showed a map of the United States with cities color coded to dates.

"At first his influence was pretty much limited to the Portland area but in the last year or so, through various avenues of information, we've been hearing his name crop up in places like Miami, Seattle, and LA." She paused, studying the map. "He's getting big and we'd like to make sure he doesn't get any bigger."

"His cartel buddies just let him go into business for himself?" one of the vice detectives asked, not bothering to hide his cynicism.

Dani smiled to herself, it had been her first reaction too, when she heard about Getz. Drug cartels tended to hold tight to their markets and their members. Getz was an enigma in more ways than one. "They were—lucky for Getz—short sighted," she explained, turning back toward the room. "Portland just wasn't on their radar. The cartel was focused on the big cities: New York, LA, Miami. Maine was too remote, not wealthy enough, you name it."

She pulled out the third page from the folder and held it up. "The intelligence we've collected suggests that Getz made a deal with them. He'd stay out of their territories and they would leave him alone. In exchange, he would do a certain percent of his business with them. At the time, it was a standard high-risk investment for him. He took on all the risk of obtaining and distributing the drugs in newer, untested markets while there was only an upside for the cartel.

"By the time they realized how short sighted the deal was, Getz had already built himself quite an empire and it was easier and less costly to keep the status quo than for the cartel to try to change the arrangement."

"Convenient for Getz," Ty interjected.

She glanced at him and saw a hint of amusement flash across his features. It almost made her smile. Almost, but not quite.

"He's a nasty son of a bitch. But, unfortunately for all of us, he's not dumb," Dani responded in acknowledgement. "He has no formal education beyond tenth grade, but he grew up in South Boston in one of the toughest neighborhoods on the Eastern Seaboard. He knows how to move drugs through a community— he lived it firsthand. He learned what drugs can do to people and he's used this knowledge to pit people against each other in ways that leave him on top. He manipulated his former employer in a way that would almost be admirable, if it weren't so dirty."

"So now that he's a big dog, the DEA is sweeping in to clean up the mess?" Detective Warren asked.

Dani saw Ty slide his partner a look. It was a subtle show of support that was both surprising and welcome. Warren's comment echoed the cries of local agencies all over the US—that the DEA didn't really care about the drug situation until it got big enough that resolving the problem would earn them congressional kudos, and more budget, of course. In the meantime, the locals were left to do all the dirty work.

She couldn't blame Warren for thinking the way he did—hell, she'd thought that way more than once herself. But the reality was, Getz was much more than just a kingpin.

"I wish that were the case, Detective," Dani started, surprising the man with her acceptance of his implied criticism. "But the truth is, Ramon Getz is involved in a lot more than drugs and *that's* why we're here."

"That begs the question then…" Ty met her gaze straight on. It wasn't a lascivious comment, but somehow, for a moment, they were back in his loft, just the two of them.

He was the first to break eye contact as he looked back down at the file. "If it's about more than the drugs, why are you here and why are you involving vice?"

When he looked back up she kept her expression neutral, careful not to give him or anyone else in the room any reason to suspect the truth about what she was thinking—about Ty or the investigation.

"Because the drugs are the start of the trail," she leveled her eyes on Ty. "We're coordinating with other agencies, but this is where it starts. This is why we're here. Why we're involving you."

And once this briefing was over, she expected to have minimal contact with them. She just needed to get through it without giving any of them a reason to think this was anything other than what was in the files, not that it wasn't enough.

"Where what starts?" Ty pushed. It was a question she expected and was prepared for, and it gave her a reason to turn away from him.

"Turn to page four and have a look for yourself." Other than the rustling of paper, the room was silent for a long moment. Then someone let out a low whistle.

"Terrorists?" one of the younger detectives from the back row commented.

Dani couldn't help but offer a jaded half smile. "Cliché, I

know," she acquiesced with a shrug. "But in this case, it does look like Getz is going to be buying his next big shipment of drugs from a group of folks who aren't very fond of our government. And he's not paying in cash."

"So for once, TV advertising isn't lying. Drugs really do put money in the hands of terrorists," the young detective grinned.

"That's what our intelligence is saying," she confirmed. "The difference is that the ads like to imply it's foreign terrorists."

"And these are homegrown," the same detective commented, flipping through the papers in his folder.

"Born and bred in the good ol' US of A," Dani nodded.

Ty raised his head, even as his eyes stayed fixed on the pages he was skimming. "So this militia group, a group that claims to want to protect the American people from its own government, doesn't see a problem with selling drugs to a man who will distribute them to the very people they claim to want to protect?"

"If you ever come across a rational militia group, let me know, Detective. I'd be fascinated."

Ty's focus went from the file to her. His eyes searched hers, and then his lips quirked with a hint of a smile. "So who else are you coordinating with?"

"FBI, ATF, Homeland Security. All the usual suspects," she answered. "For the purposes of your involvement in the case, you only need to liaise with us. We'll handle distribution of information to and from."

Ty studied her for a long moment. She sensed he wasn't satisfied with her answers and was grateful when he nodded, glanced at the folder again and then closed it.

"So that's the deal, gentlemen." Dani snapped off the projector and faced the men. "To make a long story short, we believe Ramon Getz will be trading a number of weapons and questionable equipment to the Eagle's Wing Militia in exchange for a large shipment of high-grade cocaine. With your help, we hope to stop the transfer and apprehend the men involved from both parties," she hoped she sounded convincing. "We will, of course, coordinate the details with your liaison," she tossed the file back in her briefcase and snapped it shut to signal she was done.

She'd done her part and briefed the department; not everyone in the room needed to know all the details. "Do you know where the militia is getting the drugs?" Ty asked, not letting the meeting end yet. "It's not their usual stock in trade."

"We have a couple of leads—we're working on it," Dani answered. Too fast, she noted with a reminder to watch her step with Ty. His eyes narrowed a fraction and he opened his mouth to say something but she cut him off.

"That's all I have today, gentlemen." Dani didn't want to give him time to ask the likely follow up question: "Where are the weapons from?"

She turned, "Who would you like us to liaise with, Captain?"

"Fuller," he answered, with no hesitation.

Of course.

"Great," she said, forcing a smile and turning toward Ty. He watched her with a subtle and very personal look. *Good lord, the man was attractive*. The thought flew into her head before she had the presence of mind to stop it. And she wasn't sure if it was a good or bad thing that she now knew he was smart and, judging by the way his teammates reacted to him, capable.

"I have a few things to take care of at my hotel," she said, grabbing her bag. "Can you meet me there in forty-five minutes? We can head to the house where we're set up and I'll introduce you to the rest of my team."

For one heart-stopping moment she thought he might say something about just where they could meet, but then he took a step away and nodded. "What hotel?"

She told him, though he already knew from their brief—very brief—discussion about where to go when they'd left the bar the night before.

"I'll meet you there."

And to her relief, he turned and left the room with the rest of his team.

CHAPTER 3

Ty GLANCED UP FROM HIS desk and, as casually as he could, let his gaze follow Agent Williamson as she exited the building. Instinct and experience told him there was more to what she and her team where doing in Portland than she let on. That alone wasn't surprising—most agencies held information back. But what did surprise him was that it was more than a healthy dose of skepticism that made him think that. It was something about Dani herself.

He would be the first to admit he didn't know her well. Yes, they'd spent an intense night together, but it had been more physical than anything else. There was no reason he should feel like he knew her on a deeper level. But when her intelligent gaze had met and held his in the conference room, the feeling that he *knew* her settled in his gut. And, in turn, he knew there was a reason she was here other than Getz or Eagle's Wing. As if that wasn't enough.

"You'll have a hell of a job dealing with her, if you know what I mean." Marty Warren said from the opposite desk.

Ty swiveled toward his partner.

"She's a hell of a looker, Ty, but she's got that look to her."

Knowing his partner well, Ty waited for him to continue. Marty, like the stereotypical cop he liked to portray, obliged. "She's got that look that says if you so much as think of thinking about her as just a pretty blonde, she'll nail your balls to the wall so fast you won't have any idea what hit you."

Ty laughed out loud at this assessment. He had first-hand knowledge of how physical Dani could be. And, after witnessing her iron-clad control during the briefing, he had no doubt his partner's characterization was spot on.

"I guess I'll have to be careful what I focus on," Ty responded.

"Yeah, like that's gonna be easy," Marty rolled his eyes. "You'd have to be dead not to notice she's built for sinnin'," he added, thickening his usually toned-down southern accent. "I'm an old fart and even I can see it."

"You're fifty-two, Marty. I know your still sinnin' away with the best of them."

"Tryin' anyway," Marty grinned and winked.

"And besides, I didn't say I wouldn't notice, I said I wouldn't focus," Ty conceded.

"So you think it's how she says?" Marty's accent lightened up again. "You think Getz is that big a dog? Kinda gets your goat knowing he's been right under our noses the whole time," he thought out loud.

"We've known about Getz for a long time," Ty reminded him. "Hell, I even knew of him when I was here in high school. We just haven't been able to get anything on him and haven't had the resources to pursue anything."

"And now we got us a whole team of grade-A DEA agents."

"Yep, that we do," Ty responded, with the same level of enthusiasm.

"Good luck with that," Marty said, swinging his feet off his desk and rising. "That filly is going to be a firecracker. Let me know if you need help handling her." He winked again and cast Ty a lascivious grin. "Of course, a young buck like you might be just what she's looking for."

"I think all she's 'looking for' is a way to bring Getz down," Ty said, despite his own belief otherwise. But he was speaking to empty air; Marty had already disappeared. No doubt to prepare for his favorite activity: interviewing trainees. Or, as Marty liked to refer to it, "scarin'-the-shit-out-of-young-people-who-should-know-better-thanto-want-to-work-vice."

• • •

Dani came to a stop a few buildings down from the police head-quarters. She took a moment to let the tension drain from her body. A woman paused at the curb beside her with a woolly, goofy-looking St. Bernard in tow. Dani smiled and gave the dog a good rub. He drooled in appreciation. She watched them cross the street as she reflected on the meeting. For the most part, it had gone well. And aside from seeing Ty again later, which was something she decided not to think about for a few minutes, she was now free to focus on her job. On this case.

Pulling out her cell, she speed-dialed a number. "Marmie, it's Dani." She stopped at a light and waited for it to turn green.

"Mack!" Marmie said, referring to Dani by her handle "Are you headed out now?"

"Yes, just finished the meeting with Portland Vice. I'm walk-ing back to the hotel and will be out to the house in about an hour." The light changed and she proceeded across the street.

"How did it go?"

"Fine. Seems like a good group. They seem fine with us."

"And our liaison? Will he be easy?" Easy to manage, easy to manipulate, was the translation.

"Easy" was not a word she would use to describe Ty Fuller. Even though she didn't know him that well, words like "smart," "capable," and "confident" came to mind. "Easy" did not. She got the sense they would be able to manipulate him only if he let them. Whether or not he would let them remained to be seen. "You ever meet an easy SEAL?"

"Not intellectually." Marmie's smile shined through in the comment and Dani laughed. Marmie was their sifter; she dug and scraped and gathered information for the team, sifted through it all, and then gave the agents what they needed. She would develop her own intel on Ty, but Dani wasn't surprised she'd asked.

"Be that as it may, he won't be as easy as we would have liked."

Dani commented, visualizing his focused look and remembering the intelligence that radiated from him. She glanced around the street, noting the few people nearby as she proceeded past several shops. "We might be able to use him. He's sharp, he might be an asset."

There was long, silent pause on the other side of the line. "That would be Drew's call," Marmie answered, giving no indication of her own opinion.

"Yeah," Dani agreed. "Unfortunately, we might not have a choice."

She sighed. She had a sinking sensation Ty was not the type to smile and nod at the half-truths and non-information they would give him.

He'd figure it out—or rather he would figure out something else was going on. If they could trust him, they could let him into the full scope of the investigation and he could be an asset. If not, he could prove to be a real liability. But either way, Marmie was right. As team leader, it was Drew's call.

"Anything new?" Dani asked, changing the subject as she waited at another light.

"A couple of interesting items have popped up. We can go over them when you get here, nothing to make or break us. Drew's on his way here. He called and said he was getting on a plane."

Which meant he would get to Portland any time between three hours and three days. No one ever knew where the director was at any given time, unless he was standing right next to them.

"Sounds good," Dani said. "I'll be in soon. Anything you want from the real world?" she asked as she pushed through the hotel doors.

"No, we're good. Your sister, bless her, had a huge basket of goodies waiting for us when we arrived yesterday. Thank god, too, because all Spanky bought was a box of mini donuts. I'll eat them, but only when I'm desperate."

Dani smiled into the phone as the two hung up. Her sister was good like that. She didn't know the team, other than Drew, and didn't have a clue what they did, but they were her guests and she would damn well treat them that way.

She headed up to her room, ignoring the memories of the night before that played on the edges of her mind. She had thirty minutes to pack and get ready before Ty showed up. She needed focus.

Twenty minutes later there was a knock on her door. She opened it, leaned against the frame, and regarded the man in front of her.

CHAPTER 4

"I'M EARLY," TY OFFERED. AN unrepentant smile played on his lips.

Dani eyed him for a long moment before deciding to let him in. She stepped away and turned back to the room. As she placed her duffel bag on the bed and gathered up the last of her belongings, she heard him enter and close the door.

"So, how'd you get the name Ella?" he asked. The lock on the door clicked into place. Her eyes flickered toward him as he leaned against the wall.

"Danielle Gabriella Williamson." Turning her back to him, she grabbed a pair of shoes—the very same pair she'd worn to the bar. She didn't look at him as she tossed them into the bag, but she could feel his gaze follow their trajectory as they landed atop the sage green top he'd peeled off of her less than twenty-four hours ago.

Dani reached for a sweater she'd brought and shoved it into the bag, pushing down both the shoes and the shirt. Without a word, she zipped the bag and then reached for her gun and holster which were lying on the side table. She strapped on the holster and removed the gun.

"So," Ty said from across the room. "How long are you going to ignore what happened last night?"

Once again, she let her eyes flicker to his. His tone was a mixture of curiosity and good-humored mockery. She held her gun up and checked the clip. It wasn't pointed anywhere near him, and the safety was on, but she hoped he got the message.

"Forever?" he prompted.

"Pretty much," she replied. The crispness in her voice was punctuated by the sound of the clip snapping into place. To her surprise, he said nothing. She slid the gun back into her holster and pulled a zip-up sweatshirt over the t-shirt she'd changed into. She didn't so much need the warmth, but it hid her weapon. Closing her case and grabbing her duffel, she gave him another measured look. And reminded herself that he didn't create the situation any more or less than she did. But she did need to be clear that, from here on out, they were professional associates only. Nothing more. This was the first time she had ever had to deal with this kind of situation and now, on this case, well, the fates really were a bitch.

She allowed herself a smile as she walked toward him. "Although you have to admit it is rather ironic, don't you think?" He raised a brow in question.

"My guess is that you were out last night looking to release a little tension after hearing the feds were coming to town," she stopped in front of him and searched his eyes. He didn't bother to answer, so she continued. "I was looking to do the same. The fates must have been laughing when they threw us together." She meant to close the door on the conversation, but standing there, looking into his eyes, for a moment she slipped back to a few hours earlier. The same eyes that had held hers as they lay tangled in his sheets, catching their breath, held hers now.

The tension in the room was so thick Dani had to remind herself to breathe and, in an instant, it wasn't funny anymore. Her pulse kicked up, but it wasn't out of desire. She'd been in enough situations to recognize her own reaction to fear. Why she was afraid, she didn't know. But now was not the time or place to sort it out. She pushed past him, breaking the contact.

"Ready?" she asked moving toward the door. "For everything," he replied.

• • •

He should be more pissed, Ty thought as he followed Dani out of the hotel. He *had* been irritated less than an hour ago. Her willingness and ability to ignore what had been a pretty incredible night should put a damper on his ego. But somehow it didn't. Or maybe it did, but the feeling was replaced by an altogether different feeling when he watched her check and handle her gun. He must be sick in the head. There was something just plain wrong with being turned on by watching a woman handle a gun. Then again, confidence was always seductive. And Dani was nothing if not confident.

They entered the parking lot and he led her to his car. He put the duffel in the trunk then opened the passenger door and motioned her in. As she folded her long legs inside he flashed back to last night when those legs had been wrapped around him. His eyes caught hers as she pulled the door shut. Even her frown didn't dampen his attraction.

He slid into the driver's seat. "So, where to, *Agent Williamson*?"

"Take a left. Head to Highway 1, then turn north. And you can call me Dani," she added.

"Not Ella?"

She shook her head. "Not many people call me that."

He could see the minute the words left her mouth, she regretted saying them. She had given him leverage. And it just might be worth it to call her Ella every now and then—in private—to see what kind of reaction he might get. If it was anything like the night before when he'd called her name, it would be worth it.

"So, how long have you been working this case?" Ty asked, pulling his mind away from the gutter, or bed, as the case may be, or kitchen table, or elevator.

Dani stared out the window for a long moment. "About a year, more or less." Her voice held a weary tone that suggested more. But her voice shifted back to "agent" with the next comment. "Take 88 North toward Broad Cove. Then take the third right."

"And he's big enough to warrant the interest of an entire team of DEA agents?"

"Getz is a man of interest to a great number of people," she answered. "But yes, he is of interest to us, for all the reasons I mentioned today. The network is big enough now that it's showing up on the radar in a number of cities. That and the apparent tie to the Eagle's Wing group upped the priority to bring him in. Or down, whichever works."

"So how long do you think this will take?" he asked, following her directions. It was early still, so as he turned east toward the water, the sun hit them full in the face and they both reached up and flipped down their visors. With brilliant blue skies, cool temperatures, and calm winds, it was Ty's favorite kind of day. But a storm somewhere out at sea caused waves to crash against the rocky coast, throwing spray high into the air. The juxtaposition between the peace and violence of nature, in his mind, defined Maine. Defined a lot of things.

To his right, he caught Dani lifting her shoulder in response to his question. "Hard to say. Our intelligence indicates the transfer is going to occur at his place, here in Portland, sometime in the next few weeks. Of course, we all know how reliable dealers are, so that could mean tomorrow or it could mean two months from now."

"And you're here for the duration?"

Dani hesitated for a second before answering. "It's likely, yes. But where I go and how long I stay is up to the team director."

"But it's unlikely the director is going to reassign you."

Ty felt her gaze fix on his face as he focused on the road. From the corner of his eye, he saw her big brown eyes narrow in calculation. Not a coy, catty calculation, but a professional, agent-to-detective assessment. He'd wager her mind was firing in rapid sequence.

"What makes you say that?" she asked, turning her body back around and transferring her eyes to the side mirror outside her window. Her nonchalance surprised him given the intensity of her focus seconds ago. And then he recalled her control earlier in the day. She had moments when it looked like she thought about letting her guard down—like that one, brief moment in the hotel room—but he would do well to remember she was a trained federal agent. He would be able to read her only when she wanted him to.

"Just a guess."

He glanced over in time to see her take a quick study of him before turning again to the window. For a while she remained silent, except for telling him the turns he needed to make. After a few moments dragged on, she seemed to come to some conclusion.

"It's unlikely my director will reassign me," was all she said.

"And why are you so adamant about ignoring what happened last night?"

The only indication that she'd heard him at all was her sudden stillness. And then she spoke. "Last night was personal."

"Very personal," he said.

She ignored him and continued, "And work is work. They have nothing to do with each other."

"Personal is personal and professional is professional and never the twain shall meet," he offered.

"I hope that's not a problem for you."

It was, but he wasn't going to tell her that. He understood the situation. It wasn't that he was blind to the problems that could happen when colleagues became romantically involved. But depending on how things progressed, he also wasn't one to use the "problem" as an escape hatch.

"Here," Dani interrupted his thoughts by pointing to a driveway all but hidden by landscaping. He pulled in and stopped at the gate. Dani gave him a code to punch in.

"If you're alone, use the code we just used," she directed. "If you're traveling with someone authorized to be here, add a one at the beginning. If you happen to be traveling with someone who isn't authorized to be here, add a one to the end, before you press the pound sign."

He glanced at her to make sure she wasn't joking with him, hazing the new guy. Between the gate and the four cameras he saw hidden along the shrub-covered fence, it was a hell of a security system for a DEA sting.

"The house is a private home that has been loaned to us," she explained. "The system was a standard, code-based system but the two additional features were added by our team. We've got good people and expensive government technology on this case, we want to make sure we protect all the assets."

"And everyone is based here?"

"It's a big house."

He wanted to ask how the DEA managed to get the wealthy owner of a prime, ocean-view estate to "loan" the house out but, as they made their way up the winding drive, he just closed his mouth and stared.

Ty had a few investments and had done well for himself over the years. His salary wasn't much, but his investments more than made up for it. He considered himself a fairly wealthy man with a nice loft and a few small properties scattered around the country, but he had never seen anything quite like the house looming in front of them.

The place—the grounds and the building—was huge. The house itself was a combination of traditional Colonial, with an Italian influence, and easily over ten thousand square feet. With a façade of white, painted brick, it was more along the style of the Hamptons or Newport than the cute summer cottages of Southern Maine. Long, black shutters lay open and lined each of the tall and numerous first floor windows. Matching shutters lined the windows on the second floor and half of the third. The other half of the third floor was all glass and looked to be some sort of sun room. In a more traditional Maine house it would be a widow's walk where, in days past, a sea captain's wife would sit and watch for her husband's ship to come in. But this was unlike any widow's walk Ty had ever seen.

"Park in the garage around the corner," Dani directed, pointing the way.

He pulled to the side of the house and saw a discreet five-car garage. From the front of the house, the garage looked like another room on the first floor. Modern convenience meets old-world charm. He pulled into an empty bay and killed the engine. Dani moved to exit the car but he held her back with a hand on her arm.

"Is this your usual boondoggle? Whose house is this?"

Dani laughed. He'd heard her laugh last night, but this was the first time he had heard it since they had met this morning. Maybe because the genuineness of it was such a juxtaposition to her cool control, or maybe because it reminded him of last night—either way, he liked it. A lot.

"No," she said shaking her head. "It's not our usual boondoggle. Usually we cram into a couple of dirty hotel rooms in the parts of town most normal people like to pretend don't even exist. But none of us are complaining now, that's for sure." She smiled again, slid out of her seat, and headed for the trunk.

"Wait," he said as she grabbed her duffel and headed toward a door. "Whose house is it?" It was public record, he could look it up, but he was more interested in hearing the story behind how the DEA ended up using it, which the public records wouldn't be able to tell him.

"Oh, the house?" she turned, looking around the cavernous garage. "It's my sister's."

CHAPTER 5

"Hey, Spanky," Dani said, dumping her bag in the small hall next to the butler's pantry.

"Hey, Mack," he called back from the kitchen.

Dani strode in, leaned her hip against the kitchen island, and surveyed the scene. Spanky, one of the skinniest people Dani knew, was making a sandwich stuffed with some sort of meat. Mustard, mayonnaise, and horseradish jars were scattered around him. It wasn't even ten in the morning.

"I'm not backing you up if you get heartburn or die of a heart attack." She made a face at him.

He grinned and took a bite of his sandwich. Then his eyes moved to a point behind her.

"Ty," she said motioning him forward. "This is Conner James. Conner, this is Detective Ty Fuller." Ty stepped forward and the two men shook hands. Dani didn't miss the quick assessment Spanky gave Ty. She wondered what he saw.

Ty was an imposing man. At well over six feet, he wasn't quite muscularly bulky, but not lean either. He was built solid and, even with clothes on, it was easy to see he kept in shape. Aside from his physique, his eyes were dark and flashed with a combination of intelligence and a healthy dose of wariness. He was the kind of man who watched, observed, and took stock. Though it might make her job harder, she had a certain amount of respect for that.

"Call me Ty, please," he said.

Conner smiled. "You can call me Spanky, everyone does."

Spanky was one of Dani's favorite people to work with. At

a few years younger than her, his off-color and irreverent humor, coupled with his intense focus and intelligence, balanced the team well. Just seeing his goofy grin could cut any escalating tension in the group, whether it was from an external source or from frustration with a colleague.

"Spanky is in charge of audio and tech surveillance. He's got a couple of people working with him. Some may be around, but most likely they're out now. If you have any questions about the audio, talk to Spanky."

"What are you using?" Ty asked, propping his hip on the kitchen island too.

Spanky finished his bite before answering. "Phones, satellite, electronic ears, the usual."

"Electronic ears?" Ty smiled at the term.

"Not quite as cool as the eavesdropping devices from *Harry Potter*, but much stronger and you can't see 'em." Spanky took another bite.

"I can't imagine you're dropping them down stairwells. Where do you set them up?" Ty asked, genuine curiosity clear in his voice.

"Cars usually but, Getz is too isolated and it would be too obvious to use mobile surveillance for this job. So, little does he know, but his trees, and his walls, have ears," Spanky gave them a dramatic, conspiratorial wink.

"Trees?" Ty responded with surprise. "Aren't they visible?"

"If we'd been here two months ago, when none of the trees had leaves, yeah, that would have sucked. But, there are enough leaves now that, unless his goons are building a tree house, they aren't going to see a thing. And believe me, from what little we've seen, his goons don't carry anything heavier than a Glock."

"How big are they?"

"The goons? I've seen bigger," Spanky shrugged and smiled. Ty's mouth curled into a half grin. "The ears." Spanky held up half his sandwich in response.

"And they're good?"

Spanky's eyes glittered with admiration. "They are fabulous.

We've picked up some interesting things in the last few days. Come see when you're done with the meet and greet. I'm housed in the parlor," he winked at Dani. "Oh, wait," he paused for dramatic effect. "Maybe it's the morning room, or the blue room, I just can't keep them all straight."

Ty chuckled. Dani rolled her eyes. "It's the third door on the left from the center hall."

"Come by, I'll show you my toys," Spanky added, as he waltzed out of the kitchen.

"Interesting character," Ty commented.

"Yeah, don't let the grin fool you though, he's one of the best surveillance guys I've ever worked with. It's frightening the things he can pick up."

Ty's expression turned thoughtful as he watched the empty doorway. Then his eyes swung toward hers. She sensed he was about to say something about their night together. She remembered how vocal they'd been and it wasn't hard to come up with a few things herself. She cleared her throat.

"Come on," she motioned for him to follow. "I'll introduce you to the rest of the team so you can then forget their names."

Marmie looked up as they entered and pushed to her feet. "Mack," she said holding her arms out. Dani stepped into the hug without hesitation. Marmie was stick thin with no figure to speak of, with black hair pulled back into a low bun and glasses hanging around her neck. Her clothes, always gray or black, hung off her body at least a size too big. But, despite her somber and somewhat stern appearance, she had a heart of gold. And, truth be told, Marmie was the only one capable of keeping her teammates sane— capable of keeping them out the black abyss of helplessness that tempted them with every new mission.

When Ty shifted behind her, Dani remembered she and Marmie were not alone. "Ty, this is Rose Davies, also known as Marmie. Marmie, this is Detective Ty Fuller." Ty stepped forward and shook hands with Marmie.

"Marmie is our sifter." Dani took a few seconds to explain

what that meant. "She also has a couple of folks downstairs who focus on finding patterns and connections. You might meet them but my guess is they don't come up very often?" She added this last bit with a confirming look at Marmie who nodded her head.

"They're kind of a unique breed," Marmie shrugged. "There's a kitchen down there, bedrooms and tons of space. When I have my meetings, which is twice a day, you'll see them dragging themselves upstairs. If you need something or have any questions, come to me." Marmie paused, glanced at Dani, and then nodded to the door behind them. "Or Adam."

Adam Francey stepped into the room and then smiled when he saw Dani.

"Dani!" he exclaimed stepping forward and giving her an enthusiastic handshake. Dani liked Adam, but he was a little like a puppy dog. He was the new kid on the block and a little over-the-top enthusiastic, but he also showed an incredible ability to absorb and sift through intelligence. Marmie had spotted him early in his training and snatched him up.

"Adam, good to see you again. This is Detective Ty Fuller, Portland Vice. He's our liaison on the case," she added, indicating the man who had somehow managed to move a little closer to her without her even noticing—which was a bit disconcerting.

"Detective, it's good to meet you," Adam pumped Ty's hand, sharing his trademark enthusiasm. Dani hadn't noticed the tension in Ty's body until she saw his shoulders relax with Adam's effusiveness. She glanced at his face and wondered if it was tension related to meeting new people, or related to her. She frowned, wondering if it was a mistake to not address the night before. Ty had given her no indication so far that he had any serious issue with her insistence on leaving the personal out of the investigation. But he hadn't said he agreed either.

"How long you been with vice?" Adam asked, still smiling.

"A few years. I was a SEAL before that, though," Ty answered, much like he would if he were talking to a young boy.

"A SEAL? Really? Wow." Adam eyed Ty again.

Dani smiled to herself. Ty might think the young man was looking at him in awe. Adam's voice *was* a pretty good imitation of admiration. But Dani knew the real Adam. The enthusiasm was real, but he was not naïve or easily impressed. Knowing Ty was a SEAL, that he was more than just the average, small city detective would change the filter Adam used when talking to Ty. She had no doubt his brain was sifting through information right now, breaking it down into categories—information he could share and information he could not, or would not, share.

"So, Dani filled you in?" Adam asked, clearing a spot on the desk across from Marmie's and leaning against the edge. Ty wagged his head, "More or less." Adam's eyes sought hers.

A twitch of her brow communicated her answer. *Just the bare minimum.* Adam's acknowledgment was even smaller. Spanky and Marmie had both done an excellent job of giving Ty information without *actually* giving him information on the case.

"Good, glad to hear it. If you need any information or have any questions, I'll be happy to help as much as I can."

Ty's look of mild amusement was becoming very familiar. The last part of that sentence hadn't gone unnoticed.

"Thanks, I appreciate it. I do have some questions. Where can I find you later?" Ty continued. Again, Adam cast a glance in Dani's direction. She gave him an almost imperceptible nod. She trusted Adam.

"Here or downstairs. If you can't find me, ask Marmie. She always knows where I am." Adam rose from his perch, thumbed through some papers and then straightened. "Well, we're running some numbers downstairs so I guess I'll see you around. Good to see you Dani," he added as he disappeared down the hall.

"Nice meeting you Detective Fuller," Marmie said as she turned back to her computer, dismissing them.

"We have a couple more people to meet," Dani said.

While her team had been a team for a long time, they didn't usually work in the same proximity. It did happen on occasion, but much of what they did could be done from remote locations, leaving just the field agents on the ground. But that wasn't the way the DEA operated, so here they all were. Keeping up appearances. It made for long introductions, but if Dani were pressed, she'd admit it was kind of nice to be surrounded by everyone. Especially on this case. They weren't all personally friendly, but she didn't doubt for a second that everyone in the house would have her back if needed.

"This way." As Dani ushered Ty out of the room, she recognized the look of interest in his expression. His eyes were sweeping the room, taking it all in. And judging by his wry comments, her unspoken communication with Marmie and Adam hadn't gone unnoticed either.

She walked ahead of him through the enormous main hall of the house in silence, cursing the fates again, whatever their names were, for throwing a man like Ty onto this case. He wasn't going to miss a thing.

"What was that look about?" he asked, as if to prove her point.

"Nothing," she responded, climbing the stairs to the second floor.

"Liar."

"I wouldn't want to disappoint you. I *am* a federal agent."

"So federal agents lie?"

"Doesn't matter if we do or don't, the locals always think we do anyway. Right?"

"Just as often as you feds think the locals are backward yokels unable to grasp simple concepts—like the fact that there is more to this case than you're letting on. *Agent*," he added.

Dani could argue with him, but it wasn't worth the effort. If he'd already figured out there was more to it than Getz and Eagle's Wing, she was better off not saying much of anything at all. That there was a chance the investigation might surface some facts about the weapons everyone in the broader US intelligence world would want to keep a lid on was paramount. As for her, this case was the case she'd been waiting for her whole career, it was her reason for joining the CIA in the first place. She wasn't going to let anyone or anything interfere with it—including Ty. And neither of those aspects of the investigation were anything she or the team wanted to share with anyone.

Under normal circumstances, it wouldn't have been an issue. Jurisdictional courtesy between the DEA and the local law enforcement was encouraged but not required. And sharing wasn't all that big with the CIA either. But, in this situation, they didn't have a choice. Playing nice with the locals was the price her team paid to the DEA team who would have handled the case if CIA hadn't taken over. If they weren't going to get the credit, Drew had to at least agree to preserve their relationship with Portland PD.

With a renewed focus and plan, Dani sighed. Glancing at her watch, she wondered how long she'd have to shuffle him around before he settled somewhere and she could get away from him. And it didn't escape her that this sentiment was a far cry from less than twenty-four hours ago, when she couldn't seem to get enough of him. If she let herself, she might even start to feel a bit schizophrenic about it.

"Earth to Dani," Ty's voice came from behind her.

"Hmm?" she turned and looked at him over her shoulder.

"I asked where we're going? Since you don't seem interested in telling me what's going on inside that head of yours, I might as well meet everyone and see if someone might find me useful."

She wanted to say, "Don't count on it," but held her tongue. Her team was top notch and didn't tend to take to outsiders. Trusting someone from the outside, even if they were trustworthy, added a layer of complexity to the investigation no one wanted. As far as Ty was concerned, the less said, the fewer opportunities he would have to question them or their actions.

"We're going to meet Cotter, who runs visual surveillance, then I'll take you up to the sunroom to have a look at Getz's compound. After that, if there's anything you want to follow up on before you leave, feel free."

"Aw shucks, you're just saying that."

She turned and caught his eye. And laughed. He knew there

wasn't a snowball's chance in hell he would be *free* to follow up on anything. At least he had a sense of humor about it.

As they climbed the stairs to the second floor, Ty changed modes. "Since you're not going to tell me anything interesting, explain the handles to me." It was an easy topic. A safe one. And one that would keep him from thinking about the case, and what she wasn't saying.

"Where should I start?" she glanced back at him over her shoulder.

"Marmie."

"Marmie looks like the quintessential school Marm, don't you think? She's an amazing woman. I've worked with her a long time and not a single thing has changed about her. Not her hair, not her clothes, not her glasses. She could be anywhere from forty to sixty. I have no idea."

"You mentioned a Cotter?"

"Cotter's handle followed him from the Army and he refuses to tell anyone the origin. Adam's too new to the team, he doesn't have one yet. And Spanky, well," she paused, searching for the right words. "Let's just say that when he was in training, he spent a lot longer in the shower than most of the other guys."

Ty chuckled. "Hell of a stigma to carry around. Though, of course, he didn't seem to mind," he added. "And what about yours, Mack?"

Dani winced to herself. She knew the origin of her name and had always thought it sounded more sarcastic than true. But in the confines of the stairwell, walking so close to Ty and refusing to acknowledge anything about the night before, she heard a ring of truth in it, and it didn't feel good. So she hedged.

"Long story," she shrugged. "But it's short for Mack Truck."

That earned another small, knowing laugh. "Let me guess, you run your investigations like one?"

She did, that was true, but that wasn't where the name came from. They hit the landing and she moved to look out one of the tall windows. The peninsula where Ramon Getz's house sat was visible over the bluff, but she pointed it out.

"We can start to see his property from here," she explained. "After we meet Cotter, I'll take you up to the sunroom where we have a great view of his place."

"You have people set up in the sunroom?" Ty asked.

"Not full time. Most of them are set up closer, but Cotter sends people up every now and then. It's a convenient site, but doesn't add to what we're seeing from some of the other locations."

Ty nodded and she moved away from the window.

"So the name. Mack," he repeated. "Was I right? Are you a Mack Truck?"

"When it comes to men, according to Spanky and Adam, I am," she answered, figuring honesty was the best route.

"Men?" His head drew back and an eyebrow arched.

"Yes," she said. "The team teases me about my dating practices. Or lack thereof, since I don't date often," she added. "Anyway, they claim, that I'm like a Mack Truck when it comes to men—I barrel in and barrel on, leaving men emotionally flattened behind me."

"Emotionally flattened." Ty repeated the words, testing them. They were silent for a few minutes, and then Ty made a little "huh" sound.

She stopped and turned to face him.

"Was that a warning?" he asked. He didn't look warned off.

"Just a fact. You asked about handles, now you know," she lied. She wanted him warned off. For her sake probably more than his.

"For the record," he said. "I wouldn't agree with the assessment. To emotionally flatten someone, you'd have to get emotionally involved, and I'd wager that's something you don't do, is it, Agent Williamson?"

The comment unsettled her, even as her eyes held his. There was no challenge, no judgment in his voice, nothing she could respond to. And when she realized he wasn't going to push, he wasn't going to demand an answer, her heart rate kicked up and she could feel the sudden rush of blood course through her body. He wasn't going to give her an easy out. Whatever she did or however she responded would rest on her shoulders.

She pulled her gaze from his and moved toward a closed door. "I think it's time to meet Cotter." She directed him to a room toward the back of the house and made the introductions. While the two men talked, Dani stepped away and took a deep breath. It was no surprise to her that what she wanted most at that moment was to be with her team. The familiar, the safe. But it wasn't an option, at least not right now.

She glanced at Ty, talking with Cotter. To be fair, he hadn't crossed a line, just made an observation. And she couldn't muster any self-righteous anger because he was right *or* because he was wrong. Introspection was not her strong point. And that, she realized, was the real problem. She didn't know the answer to the question—hadn't ever considered it. Was pretty sure she didn't want to either.

Sex, she thought. It would be much easier to spar and parry with him if he kept the personal comments on the topic of their physical encounter, or encounters to be precise. Lord knows there was enough to comment on, even though they'd only spent about eight hours together in his loft.

Pushing the emotional "stuff" from her mind, she deliberately remembered the way he touched her, the way he felt against her hands—the physical, the easy—and a satisfied smile touched her lips.

After leaving Cotter, Dani led the way to the sunroom. The final stop of the tour. Though she'd dismissed the subject of "feelings" from her mind, she didn't like the way his presence set her on edge. He wasn't doing anything but his job, but she wanted to be away from him. She wanted to be holed up with Marmie and the rest of the team digging into Getz, the Eagle's Wing, and their two primary suspects for drug sources, Sonny Carlyle and Joseph Savendra.

Shaking her head at herself, Dani stepped into the sun room. "Here," she said, handing Ty a pair of high-powered binoculars.

"That's his house, out there on the point." She took up her own set of binoculars. For a few minutes, they were both silent, lost in the surveillance of Getz's house.

"I never thought I'd see the front of his house," Ty commented, eyes still glued to the binoculars.

"But you've seen the back?"

"From the ocean. I've gone by a couple of times in a friend's boat. It's a hell of a compound, even from a mile out in the ocean."

Dani gave a little laugh of agreement. "Yeah, no kidding. His private peninsula, a huge house, clinging to the hill, almost camouflaged. There's a boathouse on the other side with mooring for his eighty-foot yacht and a couple of empty bays."

"Is that how you think the shipment is going to come in? By boat?"

Dani lowered her binoculars and looked at the area, taking in the larger details. "Yeah, I do. We don't know for certain but I think it's going to come down the coast."

"Down the coast? Why not up the coast?" Ty asked, lowering his binoculars and turning to Dani.

It was a legitimate question, and one she didn't have a solid answer for, just a couple of hunches. "All I can say is it's a hunch. Bradley Taylor, the head of the Eagle's Wing group has a cousin from his mother's side living in New Brunswick. We don't have any definite communications between the two, but the cousin, Martin Cassidy, has been known to share some of the same ideals as Bradley."

"A Canadian? You don't meet too many anti-government Canadians."

"He lives in Canada, but he's not Canadian. Cassidy grew up on the Texas plains. Has a girlfriend who inherited some property in Nova Scotia so they took off to live somewhere they didn't have to pay for."

"Any problems with him?"

"Standard stuff you'd expect. Some poaching violations, some gaming violations. A couple of drunk and disorderly citations, but nothing to suggest he's helping to plan a terrorist attack on the US."

"Then again, nobody suspected Timothy McVeigh, either," he said. She could feel Ty studying her before turning back to the window. "Does Getz have any cousins in Boston or New York or New Haven?"

Dani knew what he was asking, wasn't it just as possible the drugs could come from another direction? With a connection as tenuous as a distant cousin, his doubt was reasonable.

"Like I said, a hunch."

"But you're watching? You've got surveillance on the water."

Dani sighed. It was the one sticking point of their surveillance, the one area where she wasn't satisfied with their resources or capabilities. "Not as much as we'd like. We've got the Coast Guard on the alert, but since we can't tell them what to look for and don't want to raise a lot of noise, they'll be as helpful as they can. As for our own, we have a couple of boats we send out a few times a day to get a lay of the land, so to speak. They aren't set up for serious marine surveillance."

"Too bad," Ty commented. It wasn't a judgmental statement, just commiseration on the lack of resources from one branch of law enforcement to another.

Dani shrugged in agreement and then swung around in surprise as the door opened behind them.

"Drew!" Dani exclaimed. They took a few steps toward each other and within seconds, she was enveloped in a huge hug. She pulled back and kissed him on the cheek. "What are you doing here so soon?"

"It's nice to see you, too, Danielle," he smiled down at her, one arm still wrapped around her shoulder.

"Did you see the family?" she demanded. "How's our new nephew?"

"Yes and he's great. Just like my brother. We can hope he gets your sister's looks," he answered and Dani laughed as a gentle cough came from behind her.

"Oh," Dani stepped away from Drew. "Ty, this is our team director, Andrew Carmichael. He's the lead on this case. His brother also happens to be married to my sister, Sammy," she explained. It probably wasn't necessary, but by now she knew it would have piqued his interest when she asked Drew about "our nephew," and their association wasn't a secret. "Drew, this is our local liaison, Detective Ty Fuller."

"Nice to meet you, sir," Ty stepped forward and shook Drew's hand.

"Dani showing you around?"

"Yes, sir."

"Then you've met the team."

"Yes, sir."

"Call me Drew," he said.

Ty nodded.

Dani watched the two men take stock of each other. They were about the same height and had the same air of confidence, but beyond that, they were about as opposite in looks as two men could get. Drew was lean and lanky, like a swimmer, and, even at the age of thirty-eight, his blond hair and smile made him look like a frat boy or member of a Hamptons yacht club. Ty, on the other hand, was dark—black hair, dark eyes, and mixed heritage. Drew looked like the product of years of breeding amongst the social elite of the East Coast. Ty looked like a mix of different races, bred to survive and thrive. Maybe some Asian or Native American, mixed with something of Celtic origin, Irish or perhaps Scottish.

"What are your thoughts?" Drew asked with a nod in the general direction of Getz's domain.

Ty picked up his binoculars again and turned to have another look. "Tactically, it's well positioned. Hard to plan a stealth attack on a place surrounded on three sides by water. Then again, that's old thinking. Not as true as it used to be with the developments in underwater surveillance. I assume he has underwater security?" he asked, turning back to face Drew.

"We're working on the details," Drew answered. Ty turned

thoughtful for a moment, not really looking at her or Drew, but focused more on the empty space between them.

"And your visual surveillance?" he asked, picking up the glasses again.

"Cotter can go through that with you if you want the details. It would be good for your team to know where we are."

Ty nodded. "Dani thinks the shipment is going to come from the north. Do you agree?" Ty asked.

"It's a hunch, we're not certain one way or the other right now. For all we know it could be coming by seaplane."

"But you don't think it is, and you agree with Dani," Ty commented.

Dani cast Drew a quick look and caught him studying the detective. A second later he flicked his gaze to Dani and she confirmed his snap observation with small nod. Ty wasn't the average cop.

"Yes, I do. I've known Dani long enough to know her hunches are more likely than not to be true."

"So I see," Ty replied.

Dani frowned at Ty's tone and then turned away when her cell phone buzzed in her pocket.

She took the call, keeping her eyes on Drew who was keeping his eyes on Ty. A few seconds later she ended the conversation and slid her cell back into her pocket.

"That was Marmie," she said to Drew, whose eyes had flickered back to her when her phone snapped shut. "She says the house is too big to bother trying to find me," she smiled and shrugged. She glanced at Ty then at Drew.

"I'll take Detective Fuller back down to Cotter when we're finished up here." Drew's eyes held hers. Drew had picked up on the tension between her and Ty and his silent disapproval was clear—casting a shadow over their initial pleasure of seeing one another. He was the team director, she reminded herself. He had reason to disapprove. They—she—couldn't afford to have any slip-ups on this one. Dismissing the urge to make excuses, she nodded before leaving the two men in silence.

CHAPTER 6

Drew studied the man whose back was to him. Christ, he was going to be yet another victim of the Mack Truck that was Danielle Gabriella Williamson. He could see it already, the tension, the interest, Dani's refusal to acknowledge it. It was the last thing Drew needed on this case—hell, it was the last thing *Dani* needed on this case.

Of course, it wasn't Dani that Drew had to worry about—it was never Dani. She was too tough for her own good. Whatever interest the detective had in her she would ignore. And while she was one of Drew's top agents, and had a scary ability to remember details, she was very good at ignoring anything she didn't want to deal with on a personal level.

Drew could handle her, but he wasn't so sure about the detective. His interest in Dani was about as obvious as the sun hanging high in the sky. Would he pursue it? Drew knew it wouldn't matter if he did. But how would he handle the rejection?

"What made you leave, soldier?" Drew found himself asking, curious about the man's character. Ty turned from his examination of the compound, his eyebrows raised. "The SEALs," Drew clarified, as if Ty didn't know what he was talking about. "What made you leave the team?"

Ty studied him for a moment. "It was time."

"You don't strike me as the kind of man to leave before it's time," Drew pressed. "So what made it the right time?"

Ty regarded him for a long moment before placing the glasses on a nearby table. "I imagine you've seen my file, Sir. It should tell you everything you need to know."

Drew *had* read the file and it did give a reason, a bullet had caught him in the leg and almost killed Ty when it went through an artery.

"Most SEALs I know wouldn't have let that end their careers," Drew said.

Ty was debating telling him the real reason, Drew could see it in his eyes. And, because he was more interested in letting Ty come to his own decision than forcing him to answer, Drew used the time to focus on the man in front of him, again.

He was similar in many ways to all the other men that had come and gone through Dani's life. Tall, well built, confident, and at the top of his game as a professional—Dani never did have good taste in men. Oh, they were all good men, but they were more like robots than humans. Most of them seemed to have some sort of checklist for life that included graduating from an ivy league school; entering either the CIA, FBI, or any of the other intelligence units; being top of the profession; and finding a wife who was the same so they could be a power couple together—which was why Drew never liked many of them, since they seemed more interested in how Dani made them appear, than in Dani herself.

"Are you going to tell me the real reason for this investigation?" Ty asked, interrupting Drew's train of thought. From most, the question would have sounded like a petulant demand. But there was nothing ill-tempered in it coming from Ty. His voice held too much experience. And his eyes conveyed a familiarity with secrecy that Drew recognized.

Drew had to respect the spirit. Tit for tat. Quid pro quo. But both men knew it didn't work that way.

"It's my investigation," he answered. "I need to know if there's something we should know about you," he added. The unspoken option he laid on the table didn't go unnoticed. Ty could tell him the story of why he left the SEALs and continue working on the team, or keep it to himself and kiss any ideas he had about being part of the investigation goodbye. It was true, Drew had promised the DEA he'd play nice, but not at any cost.

Ty's eyes narrowed as he leaned against the wall and crossed his arms. The room was silent, the air heavy with humidity from the sun glaring down through the glass.

And something shifted in Drew's assessment of the detective. Ty was like the others, but there was something a bit different, too. There was a quiet intensity about him, not like the frantic concentration of the others. He looked like a man who wasn't out to prove anything. He wouldn't have a life checklist; the thought had probably never even crossed his mind. Drew had seen Ty's type before, worked with a lot of them. He was the kind of man who wouldn't do anything because it was expected of him; he would do it because it was the right thing to do. Which meant that any interest he showed in Dani was genuine. He would be interested in *her*.

"Tell me, Sir, have you ever heard the sound of a mother's voice when she's just watched her child get blown to pieces?" Ty let his arms fall to his sides.

Drew blinked. He wasn't sure what kind of answer he'd expected, but it wasn't this. The rhetorical question went unanswered.

"I have," Ty continued, looking a lot older than his thirty-six years. "Over and over again," he added.

He took a deep breath and stared at something beyond Drew's shoulder. "I entered the service right out of college and left eight years later. Do you have any idea how many dead bodies I saw?" His eyes sought Drew's. "It was the kids that got to me the most. I know some people can compartmentalize," he paused and shook his head. "I'm just not one of them."

Ty shoved himself off the wall and paced to the other end of the sunroom. "And then, when we were blamed over and over for all the devastation," he paused, searching for the right words, his eyes fixed on the sea. "Well, there is only so much hate I could take. I wasn't effective anymore, I started to identify with people

I shouldn't have. The lines became too blurry for me. I needed to leave before I put myself, or my men, at risk."

Drew found himself more than interested in the answer. It wasn't an unusual situation, but still, he knew there had to be more.

Ty shook his head and picked up the binoculars again. He didn't look through them, but rather adjusted the settings, again and again, giving his hands something to do. "I knew who the enemy was, don't get me wrong. But it was the innocents that I started to identify with, the parents who'd lost their children, the wives who'd lost their husbands. I couldn't stop thinking about how what we were doing played a role in so much pain." He paused again and then gave another shake of his head, unable to explain everything.

"I know the difference between right and wrong. I guess I wasn't sure if what we were doing was always falling into the right category."

Drew considered this, considered the man in front of him. No, he was not a bit like the other men in Dani's life. And Drew wasn't sure if this was a good thing or not.

• • •

Ty wasn't surprised when he spent the next four hours without so much as a glance from Dani. Rather than moon over it, he'd spent over an hour with Cotter learning the details of the visual surveillance and about the same amount of time with Spanky. The fourth time he walked into the room where she sat, oblivious to everyone around her, he considered taking it personally, but the intense energy surrounding her, the way she talked to her team-mates, the way she focused on the information before her, all told him that her concentration on her job was absolute.

And he had no doubt the information she was reviewing, the pieces of the puzzle she was playing with, were significant. Both the team and the equipment appeared to be top notch. Almost too good for the DEA. Granted, he didn't know all that much about the inner workings of the DEA, but there was something about the quality of the equipment that raised red flags—front, back, left, and right— about its origin. But, putting aside those thoughts, he felt confident that any information floating around the house was relevant to the task at hand, or would become relevant, which is why he opted to give Dani the benefit of the doubt.

Deciding to let the DEA team do their thing without him looking over their shoulders, Ty made his excuses and left to do a little digging on his own. He made a quick call and, thirty minutes later, steered his car into a parking spot outside Pete's Place, the local watering hole.

"Hey, Jay," Ty said as he slid onto an empty stool.

Jay turned his head, studied Ty, then turned back and took a sip of his beer. Jay had no use for niceties, or anything else that suggested form over substance. His slipshod appearance, grungy clothes, and too-long hair, were a cover for one of the greatest strategic minds Ty had ever encountered. Jay's private security company was one of the best in the country, and the only reason he was not a rich man was because he chose not to be, picking and choosing clients by whatever whim interested him on any particular day. He wasn't an easy man to get along with, but they'd been friends long enough to consider each other almost brothers.

"Late lunch," Ty nodded to the empty plate in front of Jay.

"God, I hate primadonnas," Jay started without pretense. "I got called to do a job down on the point. Some local girl who made it big in the movies and wants to come back and flaunt it. Big house, lots of cars, the whole nine yards." Jay's opinion of the woman, and her choices, was clear in the tone of his voice. "Anyway, she hears about my company, demands I come out to set up her security. No 'Hi, Mr. Alexander, could you find a time to come and look at my place? I heard you were good,'" he mimicked. "No, it was more like 'You will show up at eleven a.m. or suffer my wrath, which is worse than god's.' I should have known then to stay away."

Ty chuckled. Jay was a sucker for women, always had been,

always would be. He'd never *been* suckered by one, his natural sense of preservation tended to kick in within about the first ten minutes. But the next time a woman called with some sob story about her security, he'd rush right over. He had what some people referred to as overly-developed protection instincts. Whether they were well placed or not was a constant source of debate between the two men.

"So I get up there," he continued. "And she starts screaming when she sees me. I mean, shrieking her fucking head off. Who would have guessed such a little thing had such a mouth on her?

God, I don't know how she made her money but two-to-one says it was in some horror flick. She had a screech that could peel paint."

Jay shook his head and took another sip. "She thought I was some stalker or freaky fan or something like that. So her personal security comes out and tries to take me down. What a sorry bunch of mother fuckers. It took me all of about two minutes to put them on the ground." He sighed in resignation. "So there we are, four downed security, one shrieking movie star and me."

Ty was laughing now. "So what did you do?"

"I crossed my arms and leaned against my truck until the little banshee quit. I figured she'd either figure out I wasn't a stalker or run out of breath and pass out. To be honest, I was kind of hoping for the latter," a ghost of a smile appeared. "After about thirty seconds she must have figured out I wasn't there to rape or kill her. She stops screaming, but then starts yelling at me, 'Who the hell are you?' and 'Get the hell off my property!' and all that kind of shit.

"So I wait again until she's quiet and then I tell her who I am. For one second, the expression on her face almost made the whole ordeal worth it," he did smile now. "But then she got pissed again and started yelling at me about her security, who were starting to move around. They weren't hurt, but she didn't know that. She started yelling about lawsuits and assault and all those things.

None of which would have held up, since they attacked me first, but the little spit didn't think of that."

"And…?" Ty prompted when Jay stopped and took another sip.

Jay shrugged. "After about thirty seconds my ears couldn't take it anymore. I got in my truck and drove away. I figured, no way was I interested in working for a crazy woman like that."

Ty smiled and shook his head. "Let me guess, she called you back, apologized, maybe even cried a little, and swore it would never happen again. Then claimed that she *needed* you to do her security because you're the best in the state, possibly the country. And you rushed right back up there and finished the system," Ty goaded.

"Fuck you, Fuller."

Ty let out a bark of laughter—he couldn't help it.

"What the hell brings you down here at this time of day?" Jay demanded. The same thing that took Jay back out to the movie star's house, Ty thought. His friend had more integrity than any man he knew. Jay never, not once, backed down from doing the right thing—even when he hated doing it. Which is why Ty had thought long and hard about coming to Jay. He didn't want to back his friend into a corner, but he knew Jay would have the information he needed.

"You ever design or install a little system for a certain kind of house that sits out on its own little peninsula?" Ty asked. A direct question might have been best, but he wanted to keep it vague and give Jay some breathing room to answer how he thought best.

"Maybe," Jay drained his glass and signaled the bartender.

"It's an interesting piece of land. Surrounded by water on three sides. I was wondering how a person might secure that kind of frontage."

Jay thought about it for a minute before answering. "There's a special, very expensive, acoustic monitoring system called the Hunley. It would do the job. But if I used the Hunley, I would use a secondary system for visual surveillance as well."

"What would you suggest?" Ty asked.

"Hard to say, I'd have to look into it," Jay answered.

"Let me know." Ty said as the bartender set another beer in front of Jay. "And where can I find some information on the Hunley?"

"I'll let you know," Jay nodded. "I'll send it to you, along with some ideas as to where, if it were me, I'd install the monitors."

"Thanks, I'd appreciate that," Ty nodded back, and then slid from his seat.

"Hey Ty," Jay called as Ty made his way toward the door.

"Yeah," he responded, turning back.

"I knew a nasty son of a bitch who had a set up like that. Dealing with him made me watch my back for a long while."

Ty studied his friend. Jay was about the last person on this planet Ty could envision worried about his own safety. Well warned, he nodded in acknowledgment.

● ● ●

Back at the house, Dani stared at yet another photo. Only this one wasn't one of her special pictures. It was a legitimate part of the investigation.

"No one is this dumb," she said.

"You ever meet Jonathan Smythe?" Drew countered.

"At a reception at the Tate Gallery in London a few years ago. Before his political appointment as the British Ambassador to the US." She paused and scanned the other faces in the picture. "He isn't the brightest bulb, but still, you would think his handlers would try to keep him from meeting with Michael Keogh, arms dealer extraordinaire. At least in public." But they hadn't, and the CIA had a picture to prove it.

"Here's Michael Keogh's movements for the past few weeks," Marmie said, handing her a set of papers.

Dani gave them a cursory perusal. "Well, he hasn't been anywhere unexpected, at least that we know of. Iraq, Saudi Arabia, various former Soviet republics." She placed the papers on her desk and sat back. She'd analyze them more later.

"Okay, so what do we know, Adam?" Dani asked.

Adam looked up from his computer at the sound of his name, then rose from his seat. Adam always paced when he talked. "Michael Keogh, international arms dealer, met last night with the British Ambassador to the US." He nodded to the picture.

"How did they first meet?" she asked, leaning forward and placing her elbows on the desk.

"We still don't know. It's possible they met while both were in Jordan a few months ago. We don't have any intel placing them in close proximity, but it's still possible, since we do have some unaccounted for time for both men. It's also possible their meeting last night was their first meeting."

"Closing a deal?" Marmie offered.

"What do you think, Adam? You worked in Europe before joining this team. What's your take on Keogh and Smythe?" Dani asked.

Adam frowned then walked toward a board they'd hung in the room. It was covered with pictures of Getz and various Eagle's Wing members. But when Adam flipped it around, the faces of Smythe and others in their circle came into view. Adam tacked the picture of Keogh up. This side of the board was the real reason her team was here, why the CIA was running a drug bust in Portland, Maine. Having a diplomat from an ally country suspected of being involved in arms dealing was something they'd prefer to keep close to the vest. And this was a board Ty would never see.

At the thought of Ty, Dani glanced around. She knew he wasn't at the house, knew he'd left earlier, but she still couldn't help but look. For a fleeting moment, she wished he were there—his watchful eyes taking everything in, his physical presence solid and sure. She had thought she'd be glad when he was gone. But now she wasn't so sure. Now that she was with her team, working the investigation, she felt his absence. Had felt it the moment he'd left. She wondered what he was doing and when he would be back.

Giving herself a mental head shake she turned her attention back to Adam, who was still studying the board.

"Smythe has a daughter that has, well, let's just say she has a reputation," Adam said.

"What kind of reputation?" Marmie asked, handing off a set of papers to Drew.

"She likes fast cars and older men. Lots of them. Lots of both," Adam answered.

Dani looked at the picture of Jonathan Smythe. He didn't look much older than fifty. "How old is his daughter?"

"Twenty-two, I believe. She lives with her mother, Smythe's first wife. Doesn't have much to do with her father other than his money and connections."

"But there is a reason you're mentioning her," Dani prompted. Adam ran a hand through his hair. "Maybe. I don't know."

"Lay it on us Adam. It's got to be more than what we have right now." Dani identified with the frustration she heard in Drew's voice. The more they seemed to uncover, the less they seemed to know.

"Well, we know Ambassador Smythe shipped a cargo-load full of personal belongings to the embassy in the US six weeks ago. And we know that shipment contained a single crate of unregistered weapons," Adam started.

"Which is why we were called in in the first place." Dani sat forward in her chair, interested in hearing where Adam was going with this. That they found the shipment at all was a complete fluke, pure luck. Customs for diplomats was more lax than for regular people and if it hadn't been for the sniffing dog that happened to be walking by Ambassador Smythe's crates when they were being unloaded from the plane, they never would have known. But as it was, Homeland Security was called in and then, when they discovered who owned the crates, Drew and the team were contacted. They had tagged the weapons with locators and put them back in the crate. The tags had led them to Getz, which had then led them to their current situation. But they had yet to figure out how Ambassador Smythe was involved, if at all.

"We know Ambassador Smythe is more interested in appearance than substance. Being an Ambassador, especially to the US, is a big deal for him." Adam continued, moving a few of the pictures around.

"Why? Other than the obvious perks," Marmie asked.

"He grew up wealthy, but in a very dysfunctional household. His grandfather made the money, his father expanded the empire. But Jonathan didn't get any of those genes." He held up a picture of Ambassador Smythe in his younger days, at a polo match. A vacuous grin on his face and a glass of champagne in his hand.

"That's an understatement," Drew interjected, not looking up from the report he was reviewing.

Adam continued, "And his father was very vocal about it. Jonathan tried, but couldn't live up to his dad's expectations."

"And being appointed Ambassador is a way he can try to prove his worth," Dani stated.

Adam nodded. "It is. But there are two ways this can go. Either he is using his political position to get into the arms trade as a way to make money and show his father he has balls—"

"Or, given his background, he wouldn't risk losing the position, in which case someone else is involved," Dani interjected as she rose from her chair and approached the board. "Do we have any real intel on the daughter? Other than her reputation?"

"No," Adam shook his head.

"And why her?" she pressed.

"If Keogh is involved, he is just the kind of man she would go for. Older, distinguished, rich, and a man who likes to have a good time."

Dani studied the board, examining the faces. Wondering who, if any, might be illegally shipping weapons into the United States.

"Drew?" she said, turning for confirmation that they should follow up on the newest Smythe to enter the equation. He nodded.

Dani stood and spoke as she collected the photos. "Let's take a closer look at the daughter, Adam. See what you can find. And let's keeping digging on Keogh."

CHAPTER 7

AFTER LEAVING PETE'S PLACE, TY headed back to the station, thinking about what Jay had told him. If there were two levels of security, was there a third or a fourth? Chances were, two levels were probably it. There weren't that many firms in the US that worked with underwater security systems. Of course, that assumed Getz hired local, and Ty wasn't about to make that assumption.

He tried to finish up some lingering paperwork, but his head was focused on what advantage Jay's information might give him. And when it arrived, it made for interesting reading. By the time he scrolled through the email, he knew all the benefits of the system and all the potential pitfalls—pitfalls intended to be covered by other, equally expensive systems.

Ty leaned back in his chair and absorbed what he'd read. He knew what the Hunley protected and what it didn't, but he didn't know if there was a way around it, a way to get through it. No doubt Getz's secondary set up would cover the holes the Hunley left open, creating the semblance of an impenetrable wall. So, working on the assumption that the holes would be plugged, the only way through would be to find some weakness in the system itself, some way to get around it.

Ty picked up the phone and dialed. "Cam," he said when the line picked up.

"Ty," a voice answered. "How's my baby brother?"

"Ready for a little one-on-one," Ty smiled as he answered.

"My computer or yours?" his brother shot back. Cameron was three years older, but about half a foot shorter and whole lot lighter. He'd made a bundle in a computer start-up that went big, and then quit because he got bored. Cam was a genius with no talent for anything more physical than rapid-fire keyboarding. On the other hand, he could hack a computer like nobody's business. Legally, of course. Companies hired him to find the faults in their software and billionaires hired him to test entire systems. And his brother was going to tap him for information.

"What's up?" Cam asked.

"I need some information and I was hoping you might be able to help me out? Are you familiar with an underwater security system called the Hunley?"

"I live in the Northwest which is nothing but water and billionaires." Ty could imagine Cam's eyes roll. "Yes, I'm familiar with the product."

"Exactly what I was counting on, old man," Ty grinned, knowing the name-calling would goad his brother. "I'm looking for a weakness."

There was a pause on the other end of the line. Ty knew his brother was obsessive about the confidentiality of his findings—as was everyone who worked for him. The only people entitled to know were the people who paid to know. And the people who paid to know went through an extensive background check to ensure the information they were asking for was being requested in good faith.

"Are you asking in an official capacity?"

"I don't have a warrant for the information, but yes, it is for a case. I can't say more than that." Ty understood his brother's hesitation, and wouldn't hold it against him if he decided not to share the information, but he had to ask anyway.

"A drug case?" his brother pushed.

"Seeing as I work for vice, that's a pretty good assumption."

"But there's more, isn't there?" Cam asked, knowing the answer.

Ty wasn't at all surprised at the question. He had been with vice for six years, and this was the first time he'd ever asked his brother for information.

"Yes." Ty knew he didn't need to say more. Cam would sort through the scary maze that was his brain, start making connections, and figure that if Ty was asking for help, the case had to pose a substantial risk.

"9/11 or Oklahoma City?" Cam said. He was talking more to himself than to Ty, but Ty knew that when he remained silent, Cam would know he was right.

"OK." Cam drew the word out. "I'll see what I can get you."

"Thanks. You're the best." Ty breathed a sigh of relief.

"Tell that to mom," Cam rejoined, lightening the conversation. They chatted for a few more minutes and, when Ty looked up after putting the phone back in the cradle, Marty stood across the desk.

"How's the girl?" he asked.

"Girl?" Ty pretended to not understand.

"The hot little filly," Marty demanded, taking his seat across from Ty.

Ty rolled his eyes. "The *woman* is a federal agent, and she's fine."

"How fine?" Marty waggled his eyebrows.

Ty shook his head and decided to change the subject. "They've got quite a set up out there. Big house, lots of equipment."

"Good stuff?" Marty asked.

"Best I've seen. Some of it I couldn't even have conceived of. But there it was, functioning like a dream."

"Kind of like the filly," Marty grinned.

"How did the terror tactics work this morning?" Ty tried to change the subject again.

Marty made a face. "Interviewing a bunch of upstarts who want to be undercover. Why the hell they'd want to give up their nice clean lives to go play at being the scum of the earth is beyond me."

"Anyone good?" There had been a couple of open positions in the division for a while now and everyone was starting to lose hope they'd ever get filled, despite the near constant inflow of candidates.

Marty hemmed and hawed a bit before answering. "Yeah. A

girl. A *woman*," he corrected at Ty's raised brows. "Looks like a girl though, barely sixteen. Would be perfect for the high school scene."

"How old is she, really?" Ty asked, curious. The cops who could go undercover as high school kids always sort of fascinated him. By the time he'd come into law enforcement he knew he wore a weary, wary, and jaded look. He couldn't remember ever looking as young as the kids in school these days.

"Twenty-three," Marty replied. Ty wasn't sure of the reason for the disgust he heard in Marty's voice. Marty had a whole host of things he believed justified his aversion to almost everything. Thank god most of them were about as superficial as Marty's feelings. At heart, he was a good guy, just hard to get used to.

"On that note, I'm out of here," Ty said, rising from his seat.

Marty roused. "Going to see the filly?"

"Nope, going rock climbing. See you tomorrow," Ty called over his shoulder.

Marty grumbled as Ty headed out the door, "You young 'uns have no respect."

• • •

Dani lay crosswise on the bed and thumbed through a stack of grisly photos. A man shot execution style the subject of all but a few of them. "He's involved, Drew. I know it."

Drew cast her a look before returning to the suitcase he was unpacking. "Maybe," he said.

"Not maybe, Drew. I *know* it."

"I'm glad you know it. I think I'll wait for more evidence," he replied, turning to the closet to hang a suit.

"Sarcasm does not become you, Andrew," she grinned up at him.

He rolled his eyes. "Yes, mother," he drawled. Dani smiled to herself, she was *nothing* like his mother.

She turned her head and looked out the window, it wasn't dark yet, but it would be in a few hours. The team had spent most of the afternoon looking into Smythe and his family. Adam still was. But Dani was taking a few minutes to catch up with Drew and try her hand, yet again, at convincing him that the man she was looking for was involved in this case.

She opened her mouth to say something else, then closed it, cocking her head to the sound of footsteps on the stairs.

"Come in," Drew called after a sharp knock echoed in the room. The door opened and Ty stood in the doorway.

Dani's eyes, of their own free will, swept over him in an appreciative glance. Until she looked at his face. His eyes darted from her, fully clothed, but lounging on the bed, to Drew, also fully clothed, but in different clothes than he'd worn earlier.

"Sir," he said to Drew holding out a file.

"What's this?" Drew said, taking it from Ty.

"Getz's underwater security system. Or a part of it anyway," Ty answered.

Drew's brow shot up as he flipped the folder open and perused the pages. Dani didn't often see Drew impressed, but he was impressed now.

"Good work, Detective," he said, handing the folder to Dani who opened it to find information on the Hunley monitors as well as a map with the location of each monitor and marks indicating possible secondary monitors.

"And the secondary system?" Drew asked.

"I'm working on it. I should have something to you in a day or so." Drew nodded in approval.

"I'm also obtaining information on the weaknesses of the Hunley. Once we know the make and model of the secondary monitor, I'll do the same for it."

"Fast work, Detective," Drew commented.

"We locals are sometimes good for something," Ty responded. Dani glanced up to see Drew's reaction to intentional provocation. To her surprise, he seemed more amused than anything. And then his eyes flickered to her.

"I'm sure you locals are good for quite a few things," he commented.

Ty's mouth hinted at a smile. Only it wasn't the warm fuzzy kind. "I also have a couple of visual surveillance spots I think Cotter should know about. They wouldn't have shown up on his radar."

Dani watched as the two men assessed each other. No doubt, Drew was pleased with Ty's information and action-oriented characteristics but, to her, he looked as if he was withholding his final judgment.

"Cotter's busy, take Dani," Drew said as he turned back to his task of unpacking.

To anyone else, the words would sound like any other order handed down from the team leader. But to Dani, they held a hint of something else. Her eyes narrowed as she tried to gauge him, tried to read his intent. Never had Drew asked her to take a visual surveillance lead when Cotter's team was at full capacity.

"You own a leather jacket?" Ty interrupted her thoughts.

She turned to look at him.

"A leather jacket?" he prompted. "We'll take my bike."

"Of course I have a leather jacket," she replied.

"Fine," he answered. And waited, holding her gaze.

"Fine," she said, pulling her eyes from his. "I need a few minutes to finish something and then I'll go grab it. I'll meet you downstairs in five minutes." She had dismissed him. And with one last glance at Drew, Ty complied and disappeared down the stairs.

"Jesus, Dani. What the hell is up with you and the detective? He looks like he wants to kick my ass when he sees the two of us together." Drew took a pair of shoes from his bag and set them in a line in the closet.

"You could take him," she interjected with a nonchalant shrug.

Drew raised a brow. "I'd suspect something happened between the two of you, but you just met this morning—so what the hell is going on?"

She was silent.

"Shit," he said on a breath, acknowledging her unspoken confession.

She'd never been able to hide anything from Drew. And until now, it had never bothered her. "It's nothing."

"Like hell, it's nothing, Dani."

"I went out last night to blow off some steam and happened to meet him." She sounded blasé, even to her own ears. But he knew her better.

Drew stared at her for a long time.

"What?" she demanded, on the defense. "I'm a grown woman."

"Who is stupid enough to go home with some guy she just met. Jesus, Dani what were you thinking? You weren't," he answered himself. "He could have been a psychopath. And even though he turned out not to be, didn't you at least talk enough to find out he was a cop?"

Dani opened her mouth to answer but Drew interrupted. "Never mind, I *don't* want to know."

"The bartender is a friend of Sammy's. I know her from a few years back. She vouched for him." Even to her ears, this logic sounded lame. It *was* stupid to go home with a guy after meeting him at a bar, but even knowing that, she was hard pressed to feel bad about it. Whatever it was that sparked between them last night was stronger than anything she'd ever felt before.

"Great," Drew grunted. "I'm glad you had your fun. The Mack Truck strikes again. I'm surprised he could walk this morning."

Dani felt like she'd been slapped in the face. Why did everyone insist on likening her relationships with men to them being flattened by a truck? As far as she knew, everyone walked away unscarred and unscathed. Her relationships never included any emotion deep enough that would warrant that kind of analogy. On that point, Ty had been spot on. As far as she was concerned, every man she'd ever been with knew the score.

Didn't they?

The little niggling doubt that had been lingering since earlier in the day crept back into her brain and settled uncomfortably.

"Maybe you should be surprised that *I* can walk this morning," she tried to joke, but it fell flat when Drew leveled his gaze on her.

"That's the problem, Dani. You can always walk. No matter what happens, what you ignore or leave behind, you can always walk. For as smart as you are, Dani, sometimes you don't have a clue." She opened her mouth to protest but Drew stopped her with his next question. "What happens, Dani, when you find him?"

She didn't need to clarify who "him" was, but the abrupt shift caught her off guard.

"What do you mean what happens?" She was confused. Was Drew asking or was he trying to tell her something?

"I mean just that, Dani. When we find this man—the man who killed your parents—what will you do? And I don't mean at that moment, or even a week later. I mean *with your life.*"

Her heart rate kicked up at the question. She took a deep breath and willed the rising panic to subside. Panic because, truth be told, she hadn't *ever* thought beyond tracking and catching the man responsible for her parents' murders. It had been her singular goal since the day the fog cleared from her mind after their deaths. She'd been lost for so long after they died and finding the man with the blue eyes—the man she'd watched assassinate her parents in their own living room—became her reason to live. What *would* happen after she found him? And why was Drew bringing it up *now*?

She frowned. "I...I don't—" she searched Drew's eyes for a hint of what he was looking for. She didn't like the sadness staring back at her.

He raised his hand to stop her and shook his head. "Think about it, Dani. If you're as close as you think you are to finding him, I suggest you figure it out soon."

She tilted her head and studied him. His unusual request that she go on the surveillance field trip, tumbled through her mind. "What does this have to do with Ty?" she asked.

His sigh irritated her, like he knew something she didn't. "Maybe something, maybe nothing."

"Maybe something? I told you it's fine, there's nothing to worry about." The words were confident. Thank god she knew how to lie.

Drew made an annoyed, dismissive gesture with his hands as he turned back to the closet and adjusted his shirts. "Sure, fine, whatever, Dani. Just make sure it stays that way."

Now he was starting to piss her off. "Meaning?" she demanded.

He spun around and stared hard. When he spoke next, his words were deliberate. "We need Getz in order to close in on Smythe and we need to know if we're going to have a major international incident, not to mention a possible terrorist attack. Whatever the hell is or is not going on between you and the detective, deal with it and make damn sure it doesn't interfere with this investigation. In any way."

Dani leaned back, stunned by the intensity of Drew's warning, by the fact that he issued the warning at all. Then, something shifted in the room.

"Dani," he said and took a conciliatory step toward her.

She vaulted off the bed and took a step backward, toward the door, as he took another toward her.

"Fuck you, Drew," she replied, hoping he didn't hear the quiver in her voice.

Down the hall, Dani slammed the door to her own room behind her. She felt like an unruly teenager, which pissed her off even more. Drew was out of line. He had no right to think her personal life would *ever* interfere with an investigation. It never had before, and it never would. And that Drew thought it might on *this particular* investigation *really* pissed her off. He knew how personal this case was to her, how it might give her a chance for some closure after all these years. *He knew.*

And yet he still felt justified in insinuating she'd let anything interfere with that.

Drew was supposed to be *her* friend. That he seemed more worried about Ty—that she would hurt Ty or do something that might make his working with the team difficult—made her furious.

Catching a glimpse of herself in the mirror as she tugged on her jacket, she paused. Looking at her reflection, she forced herself to be honest. That Drew seemed more worried about Ty didn't make her angry. No, she felt betrayed. She didn't like that he seemed to think she could hurt someone else without a second thought, like she was some kind of machine. And it was clear in Drew's voice that he assumed it would be her fault if things did go wrong. Why didn't he consider that Ty might hurt her? Did he think she wasn't capable of being hurt or worthy of his concern? Did he think she was incapable of emotions, period?

Why?

Dani stilled, and then swallowed as she studied herself in the mirror. She reached out and placed a hand on the dresser, steadying herself and taking a deep breath. Because she knew the answer to that last question. Up until a few moments ago, even she herself wondered if she was capable of having true emotions of any kind. Yes, she loved her sister and her family and yes, she was passionate about her work. But, aside from her family, she'd never been emotionally involved with *anyone*. Ever.

It was possible that Drew and Spanky and all the others didn't think she had it in her to be emotional over anything or anyone for one simple reason. Up until now, she never had.

CHAPTER 8

TY WATCHED DANI JOG DOWN the front stairs of the house. Her hair was pulled back into a tight ponytail, her fists jammed into her pockets. Her expression was closed. She looked damn good in her leather jacket, but judging by the way she moved, he would guess she was pissed at something.

Good, he thought, as he smiled to himself. She was too pragmatic to hold a grudge so, when he pushed her, and he intended to push her, if she exploded on him, which he hoped she would, she wouldn't stay mad at him for too long.

It wasn't a very nice plan but he was tired of her ignoring him, ignoring what had happened last night. He wanted more than her professional persona. He wasn't sure how much more. Oh, he wouldn't turn down another night like the one they'd spent together, but he would settle for at least blowing through her professional cool. He didn't think he was asking much, he just wanted her to see him as a person, maybe even a friend—hell, anything other than a cog in her investigation.

"Have you ridden a bike before?" he asked as she came to a stop a few feet away. She fixed him with a look.

"Right, of course you have." He tossed her a helmet. "There's a voice activated radio system so we can talk during ride," he explained.

"Great." She slid the helmet on. Ignoring her mumbled sarcasm, he straddled the bike and she climbed on behind him. He almost laughed when she put her hands behind her rather than wrap her arms around him. Shaking his head, he started the bike up and headed down the drive.

"So what are you so pissed about?" he asked, knowing it would get her back up even more. He shouldn't have fun doing this, but he was. He knew how she reacted physically to him—which was a stark contrast to how she reacted professionally. And the contradiction was intriguing. He wasn't the kind of guy that was interested in being a woman's doormat, but he sensed her quasi-split personality was more a result of the case they were working than a reflection of her. And given how she *had* responded physically to him, he couldn't help but wonder what might unfold if they actually got to know one another.

"Nothing," she replied.

"Liar."

"I wouldn't push if I were you, Detective," she snapped. "Where are we going?"

Ty weighed whether or not to answer or keep pushing. He opted for playing nice, at least for the moment. "Your team is high tech and good, but there are a few things we locals can contribute," he started explaining. "Getz's peninsula is located in a bay. It's about a mile and a half from the northern tip to the southern tip, and hard to see, but it is a bay. There are a couple of spots where, with a pair of high powered glasses, you should be able to get a good view of Getz's compound." He leaned into a curve, her body moving with his.

"So what's the deal with you and Drew?" He knew he'd caught her off guard when he heard her let out a little huff. She didn't answer for a long minute and then her voice came through.

"Nothing is going on with me and Drew. Though he does think you want to kick his ass," she answered. "So what makes you think we haven't already checked out the spots you're taking me to?"

"Because one is on private property and the other is a spot only the locals know, trust me. So you two aren't sleeping together?" he asked, taking heart from the fact that she answered his first question. He didn't think she was the type of woman who would have done the things they'd done last night if she was seeing someone else, but wanted to hear it from her.

She paused again before answering. "That's rather personal, Detective," she drawled.

"And yet, I ask."

"No we are not, have never, and never will sleep together," she answered. "How do you know we haven't been on the private property?"

He breathed a sigh of relief. Not that he and Dani were going anywhere, but if they did, it was nice to know Drew wouldn't be an obstacle.

"Because in order to go on it, you'd have to ask permission from the owner. You haven't done that. Besides, I was up there today after doing a little rock climbing. I'd have known if you were there. So, if you aren't sleeping together, what's the story? You're obviously close."

"I've known Drew all my life. How do you know we haven't asked permission?"

"Because it's my land, and what do you mean you've known him all your life?"

"I mean just that. Our parents were best friends. When we were born, Drew and his brother were almost the next people to hold us. I told you, his brother and my sister are married. We couldn't get away from each other if we tried. Are you on the take?"

Ty almost lost his grip on the bike. "Why would you ask that? And who is 'we'?"

"You have an amazing loft and own a tract of waterfront land. It's not something your average cop could do."

Her failure to answer his second question didn't go unnoticed, but Ty decided to come back to that. After all, she'd admitted to liking his apartment—it was a start wasn't it?

"So you like my place?" he couldn't help the teasing tone.

She sighed. "Answer the question."

"No," he laughed. "I'm not on the take, and I wouldn't tell

you even if I was. I own a couple of patents that don't bring a ton of money but did give me enough to buy my place."

"What kind of patents?" she asked.

"So suspicious, Agent," he clucked at her tone. "Mostly gun safety advances. Some patents that relate to the way a clip moves inside a handgun and a couple that apply only to rifles. Now tell me who 'we' is?"

Dani didn't speak for a while and he sensed she was letting this new information sink in. A lot of people were surprised to hear he owned a few patents, not that he talked about it a lot. But during his time in the Navy, he developed a lot of opinions on what would make a gun better, safer. When he got out, he played around with a couple of ideas, patented them, and then, before he knew it, a couple of gun companies bought licenses. It wasn't big money by any stretch, but having enough to outright buy a place to live was nothing to scoff at, and it made living on a cop's salary a little easier.

"Okay," she said, almost to herself.

"So who is 'we'?" he prompted again.

"We?"

"You said 'when *we* were born.' I assume you mean your sister?"

"I do mean my sister, but I'm not going to say anything else about her," Dani replied.

Her answer was final but it seemed more protective of her sister than dismissive of him. He could live with that, god knows he knew what it was like to feel protective of family.

"We're here," he said, pulling onto a gravel drive and maneuvering around the side of a closed and locked gate that was meant to keep cars—not motorcycles—out. He shifted down as they headed up a hill. The driveway was lined with trees and other brush. It was getting cool and the air was crisp.

"It's beautiful," Dani sighed. Ty had the distinct impression she'd forgotten he could hear her so he didn't respond.

They pulled to a stop and both climbed off the bike. Dani

looked around, curious, but Ty knew she would never ask. So he offered.

"I bought it about ten years ago. I was in the military and was deployed so often that I could never spend the money and combat pay I made, so I bought this, thinking I might settle down here. Turns out that didn't work out. If you go another little bit up the road, you'll see a small house. My folks stay there when they're in town."

Dani glanced up the road and stared for a while before turning back to study him. "So why did you decide not to settle here?"

The question was expected, but still he was surprised Dani ventured into the personal. "Long story," he replied with what he hoped was a careless shrug.

"Let me guess," she half smiled at him. "Some girl broke your heart? Shattered your dreams of settling down?" she teased. As clichéd as it was, it was also the truth.

"More or less," he responded.

Her eyes studied his face. Then her eyebrows raised in curiosity, prompting him.

"I was engaged to a woman I grew up with," he complied. "We planned to marry when I discharged. A couple of months after I got out, she died."

Dani's head drew back in surprise and, for the first time, he saw her expression soften.

"I'm sorry…I didn't," she paused, shook her head and gave a small, self-deprecating smile. "I was going to say I didn't know, but that's a pretty dumb thing to say. Of course I didn't know," she paused again and Ty sensed that her statement meant more than what she was saying. "I am sorry though, Ty. It must have been difficult."

Ty hadn't come here to rehash the events of five years ago, but he found himself wanting to talk about it. He wasn't sure if it was because it had been a while since he had done that or because he and Dani were actually *talking*. Her dark eyes fixed on him and he held her gaze as he continued.

"It was. It's not uncommon for military spouses and significant others to need a stress outlet. The leaves are so long, the tension is always high. Many turn to people outside of the relationship to make things better.

"She sought out distractions and entertainment from her friends. She looked to them to help her deal with the stress. I didn't even know the crowd she was spending time with," he turned away from Dani and stared out toward the trees, which were starting to bud in the mid-May weather.

"I don't know that it would have made much of a difference even if I did know them. I think, by that point, she probably wouldn't have listened to me anyway." He glanced back at Dani who was standing with her hands resting in the pockets of her jacket, her expression thoughtful, not pitying.

"Anyway," he sighed, turned, and continued. "One night she got in a car with a couple of friends who were both drunk and high. I don't know if Carrie ever partook of the drugs, but I do know that the night she died, she didn't have a thing in her system that would have impaired her. A couple minutes after leaving a bar, the driver wrapped the car around a tree. No one survived."

"Jesus, Ty. I'm sorry," Dani said. They were quiet for a few minutes and then Dani asked, "Is that why you went into vice?"

He shook his head. "No, I'd planned that long before coming here. I'd seen enough dead bodies during my tours that I knew I didn't want to go into homicide. I figured vice was the best way to try and help save people." He knew his grin was an uncomfortable one, but he'd never admitted this to anyone before. Not even his parents. "I figured if I could help keep the drugs off the street, then maybe that would mean one less OD, one less body, one less family with one less member."

"I like that reason," she replied. Her voice was soft and personal.

Ty felt a wave of tension leave his body and his breath fall back into rhythm. After such a short time, not even twenty-four hours, her acceptance, her approval shouldn't mean much. But it did.

They were quiet for a few more minutes and then Dani asked, "You don't blame yourself do you?"

Surprised at the question, Ty turned and searched her eyes. There was an odd expression on her face, maybe a little sympathetic, maybe a little worried, and maybe a little something like curiosity.

Ty frowned and shook his head. "I did, but I got over it."

Dani muttered something that sounded like "good for you," but she wasn't looking at him so it was hard to tell.

"Strange enough," he continued, his brow furrowed in thought. "It was her parents who absolved me. For a long time I wondered if there was something I could have done to change things, or if there was something I should be doing to fix things. What I could 'fix,' wasn't ever really clear even in my own mind. But it seemed like I should have been doing *something* to make things right." His voice trailed off remembering the pain of doubt in those first few years after Carrie's death. He looked down at his feet as the sounds of the ocean nearby filtered through the trees.

"But," he continued. "Carrie's parents helped me remember that she was an adult and she made an adult decision. Granted, we all wished like hell it hadn't happened, it was such a waste of life, but the truth is, Carrie could have made a different decision that night. She could have made a whole lot of different choices. She didn't and she paid the ultimate price. It wasn't my decision or her parents' or her friends' to make for her, but hers alone."

Ty looked up at Dani again, standing there, in her jeans and black leather jacket. The end of her ponytail was lifting with the breeze and she looked nothing like the woman he'd seen all day. Gone was the trained agent, gone was the intense passion and focus. Standing there, with her hands hanging loose in her pockets, her head cocked to the side, she looked almost like a lost child, confused and scared.

Ty didn't take his eyes off of her. Whether she sensed his thoughts or not, she turned and made a pretense of looking up the road, toward where the house lay, unseen from where they stood.

"Want to go see the site?" he asked. His heart was pounding

and, even though he had bared his soul, he felt an inexplicable urge to reach out and comfort her. To run his fingers down her cheek and pull her close. But whatever it was that was going through her mind, he sensed she needed to let it settle before she would let him near her personal side again. He was beginning to realize that Dani was not a woman comfortable with emotions. And he'd just laid a lot on her.

When she nodded, he grabbed a bag from his bike and motioned toward a small path in the woods. They walked in silence for about ten minutes and then, as they neared the edge of the woods, he held an arm out to stop her.

"The view is from the cliff. If we walk out there, we might as well have a flare and a homing beacon. We can either crawl on our bellies to the edge or climb the tree and get a little higher. Both work."

Dani scanned the landscape then nodded toward the tree. Then she surprised him with a little smile. "I haven't climbed a tree since I was twelve." And she was off.

Before he could offer to help, she'd swung up, hooked her legs, and pulled herself into a sitting position. Her butt planted on a lower branch while her arms hooked over a branch above her.

Ty chuckled and, not quite as gracefully, clambered up a branch on the other side. Once they were both seated, he pulled out two pairs of high-powered glasses and handed one to her. She took them without a word. For a few minutes they absorbed the view.

Dani let out a low whistle. "It's gorgeous, Ty." And they both knew she wasn't talking about the house. The view from the tree was a clutch recon position. From their perch they could see the entire south side of the house and all the south-facing windows. The windows were mirrored which made things a little more difficult, but they had a clear view of the pool, the terraced yard, and most of this side of the peninsula.

"With the equipment you guys brought, we should be able

to get some prime photos. Confirm who's in the compound with him, and how many guards."

"You do know how to make a girl's heart go aflutter," Dani murmured from behind her glasses.

Ty chuckled, if she thought this was good, he couldn't wait to show her the next site. And then he laughed aloud. It was a sad day when he was wooing a woman by showing her surveillance locations.

"You can't see the boathouse from here," Dani commented, ignoring his laughter.

"No, it's on the north side of the peninsula. But, we've got it covered," he answered. Dani lowered her glasses and looked at him from around the tree's trunk.

"You have a location where we can watch the boathouse?" she asked, her voice as close to incredulous as it probably ever got.

Ty grinned. "Stick with me, kid, I'll show you places."

"I will truly love you forever if you can get us good surveillance of the boathouse. It's our weakest point."

"Then I hope you're ready to commit," he teased. "I think you're going to like what you see."

Dani swung down from the tree and surveyed the surrounding area. "We'll have better visibility of the water from here, too," she noted.

Ty nodded. "It should be pretty good, and could be very good, depending on the equipment Cotter has."

"He has the best," Dani said.

"The recon team will have to watch each other's sixes, but other than that, it should be a good spot," he commented. It was true, whoever took recon on the south end of the bay would have to watch the back of the man, or woman, on the north side, and vice versa. But it wasn't anything anyone hadn't done before, so it would be duly noted, but not a concern.

"This is great, Ty," Dani smiled as she took her GPS unit out of her pocket and noted the location. "When we get back, I'll give this info to Cotter and walk through the locale with him. So, I take it you're granting us permission to use your land?"

He made a grand gesture with his arms that encompassed the woods and water. "It's all yours, but try to be kind to the trees. My mom likes to gather the sap from the maples in early spring." Dani smiled at the comment and glanced around. "The picture is more charming than the reality," Ty continued, "though I can't complain with the results; there's nothing quite like the taste of homemade maple syrup. Come on, we've got one more place to go and it's getting late."

They'd just turned onto the road when Dani surprised Ty once again. "Do you have any siblings?" she asked through the radio headset.

Ty paused, wondering if he'd heard right—if he'd really just heard her ask another personal question. "Yes. I have a brother who is three years older than me and a sister who is a year older."

"So you're the baby."

"Yes, but I'm the biggest." He could almost feel her smile.

"Do you see them often?" she asked.

"As much as I can. My brother lives in Seattle. He's a tech guy but he runs his own security company."

"As in personal security?"

"No, as in testing the reliability of security systems, which may or may not include people, machines, robots, computers, phones, and a whole host of things I can't even begin to imagine."

"Hunley," Dani said, making the connection.

Ty nodded as they passed through the quiet neighborhoods heading from the south point of the bay to the north.

"And your sister?" she asked.

He took a tricky curve before answering. "She's a social worker. She lives in Taos, New Mexico, where my parents are."

"I thought you were from here?"

"We moved here when I was twelve. My dad got a job, and my mom thought we'd get a better education here. We loved it, but after I moved out and my dad retired they decided they missed

New Mexico, so they moved back." They were clipping along the coastal road, the ocean to their side, the breeze against their bodies. Almost like a real date with real conversation.

."Do you see them often?"

"They come in the spring and then again for a couple months in the fall, and I make it out as often as I can. It usually ends up being a couple of times a year," he answered.

"Sounds nice."

"It is. What about you? Do you see your sister often?"

"Like you, as much as I can, which isn't as often as I would like. We're close though, we talk at least once a day when I'm not on assignment."

"Once a day?" Ty asked with mild incredulity. In his mind the phone was pretty much good for making business calls or ordering food for dinner, beyond that, it was a nuisance.

Dani laughed. "We're identical twins, we've got that twin connection thing. I talked to her yesterday when I landed in Portland and I'll probably call her tonight, even though I'm working and she knows it. With my work schedule and her travel and family schedule, we can't always talk, but we try."

This little insight hit Ty from way out of left field. "Wow," he managed. "You have a twin." He couldn't imagine another woman looking like Dani and had an image of them wreaking havoc on teenage boys everywhere in their younger years. But what was just as interesting was how much Dani's voice changed when she talked about her sister.

"Other than looks, are you two alike?" he asked.

Dani laughed again. "Don't worry, she isn't a thing like me. She's sweet and naïve and almost always content with life. I think I've heard her complain about twice in the last year and one of those was when she was dilated ten centimeters with her third baby and the doctor refused to give her an epidural. He claimed it was too late. I think he wanted to hear my sweet baby sister cuss a blue streak."

He knew she wasn't as cool as she seemed at the briefing,

and Ty liked these revelations and glimpses into Dani's life. They made her seem more real, more *her*. "So you are an aunt? Three times over?"

"Two girls and a boy. Sammy and Jason, Drew's brother, decided at the ripe old age of six and eight that they would get married. It stuck. They are about as in love with each other now as they were then. The kids are adorable but a handful. My sister has the patience of a saint."

"She sounds great," Ty commented.

"She is," Dani responded. "She's nothing like me."

Ty thought about asking Dani what she meant about that ambiguous statement. Did she think she wasn't a good person? Or did she think her sister was great and recognized the differences for what they were, just differences? He was pretty sure Dani wouldn't be interested in hearing his opinion of her, interested in hearing that he thought she was pretty great too. Not to mention that he'd come off sounding like a seventh grader. She was smart and capable and confident and sexier than a woman had a right to be. But she wouldn't want to hear that from him, so he decided to change the subject.

"So what about your parents? Do you see them often?" He felt Dani stiffen on the seat behind him and, though his rational mind knew it wasn't possible, he had a very tactile sense of her pulling away from him.

"They're both dead," she said. Her voice was rote and flat. "They died about twenty years ago."

And just like that, the conversation died, too.

In silence, they pulled up to an empty parking lot that hosted a beautiful view of the Atlantic Ocean. A short distance from the lot was a fence that protected the tourists and sightseers from the sheer cliff that plunged into the sea below. Other than that, it was about as exposed as it could get.

"Maybe if we dressed in bright orange or sent up a flare, they could see us better," Dani commented the minute their helmets were off. Her jaw was tight and her arms crossed rigid over her middle.

Ty held her gaze for a brief second before turning to the saddlebags on his bike. He pulled out two pairs of fingerless gloves, a blanket, and the glasses. No way would he push her further. The mention of her parents had not only brought back her professional wall, but also seemed to make her edgier and more aggressive. It was there—in the way she moved, in the tone of her voice. He'd go back to the professional playing field, but he wasn't about to cater to anything else.

"Have you rock climbed before?" he asked tossing her a pair of gloves as he moved toward the fence. She managed to peel her arms off her middle in time to catch them.

When she didn't answer, he turned back. Her eyes were going from him to the ocean behind his back. She met his gaze. "Of course I've rocked climbed, but I'm *not* climbing over a hundred foot cliff without gear. And no, these gloves," she said holding them up to make her point, "do not constitute gear."

Ty smiled. He had to admit he loved that she didn't bat an eye at scaling a cliff. It was only at the lack of equipment that she protested. He winked once and then swung himself over the fence.

"Ty," her voice raised in reluctant concern as he approached the ledge. He turned back again and damn, if she didn't look a little pale. He walked back to the fence but stayed on the other side as he motioned her forward. She paused for a second then moved closer.

He studied her face as she watched him.

"Heights?" he asked.

"Not my favorite, but I'll get over it," she replied taking a few deep breaths.

Ty slipped a hand behind her neck, tugged her toward him, and leaned forward. Her mouth opened in surprise and he moved in, covering it with his. And she kissed him back. It was a brief, sweet moment and just long enough that, when he pulled away, her face was full of color again.

"What the hell was that for?" she demanded, sounding more astonished than mad.

Ty shrugged and turned back to the cliff. "I figured it would give you something to occupy your mind rather than thinking about the height. And it's only about fifteen feet," he added with a nod down the cliff side.

"Come, take a look," he said, holding out his hand to her. She searched his face for a minute and then put her hand in his and climbed over the fence. The only sign of her discomfort was her hold on his hand. Her color was good; her breathing was fine. Her grip was strong, but not terrified.

"Holy shit," she said looking over the edge. "There's some kind of shelf there. And is that a cave I see?" she asked, her voice taking on an excited pitch.

Just what Ty had hoped.

"It's a tunnel, and you're going to love the view from the other side," he said, tugging on his gloves. "I'll go down first. I was here earlier today and found some good footholds on my climb. Once I'm down, you come over and I'll direct you."

Before Dani could answer, he'd lowered himself over the edge and was down, back on solid footing in less than three minutes. He called out for her to come down. She took one more look down the cliff side and then lowered her body over the edge. He guided her down and, in no time, they were standing on a ledge, about five feet deep, staring out at the ocean again.

"Here," Ty directed as they made their way toward the tunnel. It was an odd piece of land he and his buddies had found in high school one crazy night. He wasn't sure how it happened, but once they found it, it had become the place where they "got away from it all" in their years of teenage angst. He hadn't been back in years, but when he and Cotter had gone over the maps of the location, his brain had stirred with the memory of the place.

Years had reduced the fallen stones to gravel and what was left was a wall that ascended from the floor of the shelf to the top of the cave entrance. From the ocean, it looked like just another jag in the ragged coast of southern Maine.

"Cozy," Dani spoke.

"Wait until you get into the tunnel," he said, handing her a pair of binoculars. "Not that you're squeamish, but I did clean it out a little bit when I was here earlier."

That earned him a smile. "I'm never one to look a gift horse in the mouth, especially when it involves cleaning."

"Go on through," he nodded to the tunnel. He was looking forward to hearing her reaction. She took one last look at him before getting down on her belly and crawling into the tunnel. It was big enough to move in but not big enough to stand in, but Ty was pretty sure the view would far outweigh the discomfort.

CHAPTER 9

DANI ELBOWED HER WAY THROUGH the tunnel. She could see the light at the far end; it wasn't more than twenty feet away. Still, twenty feet on your belly wasn't as much fun as it sounded. It took a few minutes longer than she thought; she was out of practice. But when she reached the end, pulled out the glasses, and had a look, it almost took her breath away.

She laughed at herself. Most women needed gold or diamonds to gasp in delight—all she needed was a clean, unobstructed view of her target's private domain.

"Happy?" Ty called from the opening of the tunnel.

"Very."

She couldn't have had a better view without being on the property. The house was more exposed on the north side than the south. Getz hadn't bothered with the mirrored windows, he must have figured the trees and foliage protected him enough. There weren't as many windows on this side, but those she could see gave her a clean view into the house. Even without the equipment, she could see people moving around. Once Cotter and his folks got up here it would be like having a video camera inside.

After a long look at the house, she moved her focus to the boathouse. Surveillance of the boathouse wasn't going to make the case for them. And with the two new recon positions, if the drugs were going to come in by boat, they'd have plenty of advance warning. But the boathouse was the Achilles' heel of the compound. She had no doubt it was well protected, that Getz knew it was a vulnerable point, but no matter what he did, the fact remained, the boathouse would never be as fortified as the house or the land. And if the transfer were to take place out at sea, having a view of the boathouse would give them a heads-up to any activity that might indicate movement.

"Enjoying yourself?" Ty's amused voice echoed through the tunnel.

Dani glanced at her watch; she'd been in the tunnel for over twenty minutes already. "Immensely, now be quiet, I'm focusing."

"Fine," Ty laughed. "I'm going up to my bike to grab something, I'll be right back." A few seconds later Dani heard the sound of his feet on the rock and then silence. Her eyes stayed focused on the house, even as she wondered what he was getting from his bike.

She felt bad for snapping at him earlier. She knew her attitude was out of line, he'd done nothing but help her and her team since she'd dropped the bombshell on his department that morning. In fact, he'd gone above and beyond the call of duty. She had a fleeting thought that his actions were because of her, but she dismissed it just as fast. Ty would have done it anyway, he would have gone out of his way to help because that was the kind of guy he was. When he saw a job that needed to be done, that he knew he could do, he went ahead and did it.

He was different than other men who had passed in and out of her life. In the few hours she'd spent with Ty, she realized that not only could she *like* the man, she might even *respect* him. Not that she'd disrespected the others, but nothing in those relationships had ever inspired her to offer anything more than the basic respect a person should hold for another human being. But with Ty, it was more.

He went about his job with quiet confidence and she got the sense he was a team player—as long as the team was doing the right thing. But even as Dani acknowledged this aspect of Ty's character, she knew it wasn't the only, or even the main reason, she found herself wanting to really *talk* to Ty. That she'd asked about his family, or, even more startling, that she'd told him about hers, was as much of a surprise to her as she knew it was to Ty.

It was a strange tug inside her. On the one hand, she wanted to ask, she wanted to hear about his life and his family. But she was out of practice and it felt awkward. Then again, if she was being honest with herself, which seemed to be a growing trend in the last twelve hours, it wasn't the talking that was awkward, it was the wanting. The wanting to know more, to hear more. And the more she thought about it, the more she knew her discomfort wasn't because she was out of practice, it was because the wanting was a new thing all together.

"You didn't pass out or anything?" Ty's voice filled the cave. Startled, Dani bumped her head on the low ceiling of the tunnel.

"Christ, that hurt," she complained, rubbing her head. "Give me a minute," she grumbled.

"A real minute or are you going to spend another twenty minutes?" he chided. Dani looked at her watch and chastised herself. She'd been in the tunnel for over forty minutes and over half of that had been spent thinking about Ty and her confusing reaction to him. Yes, the time had come to admit that she was pathetic; she grimaced.

She wiggled back out of the tunnel, stood, stretched, and turned. "Whoa, hey," she all but sputtered and then frowned. "Please tell me I didn't just sound like an extra out of *Bill and Ted's Excellent Adventure?*" she asked, her hand pressed to her chest in concern.

Ty laughed, and handed her a glass of wine. Well, it wasn't a real glass but a little plastic cup. It went with the little picnic he must have set up while she was hiding from him in the tunnel. Dani glanced at the blanket, now spread out and covered with various foods. Nothing heavy, but Ty had managed to bring down a few cheeses, some bread, some fruit, and a few of what Dani suspected were lobster rolls, though it had been years since she'd had one.

"Wow," she said, taking the cup from Ty's outstretched hand. He was sitting with his back against the cliff wall, legs outstretched and ankles crossed.

"It's just dinner, Dani," Ty said when she didn't move to sit. "Everyone has to eat some time. And drink. I assume one glass won't get you any demerits with Drew?" he teased.

It was so obviously *not* "just dinner" that Dani took a long moment to search Ty's face. He didn't seem concerned with her scrutiny. He sat back, closed his eyes against the fading light, and enjoyed a sip of wine. He didn't look like he had any plans other than to sit and enjoy the coming evening and the food. He didn't look like he expected anything else from her other than to join him. So, she brushed herself off, sat, and took a sip of her own wine. Unlike the military, the CIA was way more lax in its drinking policy. In fact, whatever an agent needed to do to get the job done was actively encouraged—not always beneficial to the agent, but encouraged nonetheless.

They ate in companionable silence for a while, until Dani's guilt got to her. "I apologize for the attitude earlier," she said.

Ty glanced at her and shrugged. "Apology accepted. Why does Drew think I can kick his ass?"

Dani laughed. "He thinks you *want* to kick his ass. I'm the one who thinks you *could*."

"Thanks for the vote of confidence, but those tall wiry guys are quicker than they look."

"Yeah," Dani gave him a rueful grin. "Tell me about it."

Ty shook his head. "You've sparred with him haven't you?" He didn't wait for her to answer. "Of course you have. Have you ever won?"

"Yeah, but it took me a while to get there," she grinned.

"So what did he say to piss you off earlier?" Ty asked.

Dani's first reaction was to answer the question with a glib "nothing" but she bit her tongue and took a few deep breaths before deciding how to answer. That she was going to answer at all surprised her, but her conversation with Drew earlier, and the subsequent revelations about herself were lurking in her mind. Nausea roiled in her stomach. Fear. Fear of maybe offering a little bit more of herself. She took another breath and looked at Ty. And even more powerful than her fear was her desire to overcome it. Maybe it was a control issue, or maybe it was Ty. Either way, she answered.

"He figured out something had happened between the two of us. He was concerned."

Ty's eyebrows shot up. "Don't tell me he thought you might let it compromise the investigation?"

Dani shrugged, still not comfortable having this conversation, but wanting to have it anyway. "Something like that."

Ty's eyes narrowed. "Something like that?" he repeated and then paused in thought. "I can't believe he would think you would let anything interfere with an investigation. I've known you less than twenty-four hours and even *I* know you wouldn't do that. Wait," he paused. And then his eyes narrowed. "Is he afraid *I'm* going to do something to screw it up?" he asked in dawning recognition.

Dani glanced up and shook her head. "I don't know what brought it on. I have some ideas but I'm just…" she paused, thinking. There was more than one reason Drew might be concerned, although, at this point, she was pretty sure it was because he was worried she would hurt Ty and Ty would retaliate by becoming difficult. By now she knew this wasn't a fair assessment of Ty so she didn't want to share it with him.

"He's like a big brother to me. And kind of like a father figure, too. I'm sure he has his reasons, and I'm sure none of them are based on his professional knowledge of you or me," she said.

"Father figure?" A hint of a teasing grin curled his mouth. "He's what, three years older than you?"

Dani, thankful to him for not pursuing the personal conversation, gave him a cheeky smile. "He's five years older, but don't let those boyish good looks fool you. Underneath all that baby skin is an old man."

"You mean, old soul," Ty corrected.

Dani's smiled widened, "Maybe that, too."

• • •

Several hours later, Dani jogged up the steps to the second floor of the house, hoping to avoid Drew. But the fates weren't that kind.

"Dani," he called from the bottom of the stairs. She hesitated for a split second before turning to look down at him. "It's late, where have you been?"

Dani glanced at her watch, surprised to see it was close to ten p.m. "I got hungry. We stopped for dinner." The lie came easy. The truth was that she and Ty had stayed on the little shelf talking. Nothing too serious, just chatting about life. He talked about how he went from being a Navy SEAL to a vice detective. He talked about his family, his life in Portland. She talked about Sammy and the kids. They even spent a bit of time talking about Getz and Ty's recollections of him—of things he'd heard, over the past several years.

Drew didn't look like he believed her, but for the first time in a long time, she didn't care what Drew thought of her. She felt a sense of calm that she hadn't experienced since the investigation started, probably even long before that.

"How were the sites?" he asked, sounding like he wanted to ask something else.

"Better than we could have hoped for," she replied with a telltale glance down the hall toward Cotter's set up. "You going to tell Cotter?"

Dani nodded and made to move away, but Drew stopped her. "Dani," he spoke, the regret clear in his voice. Dani turned to looked at him, studying his face. After a moment, she shook her head in resignation.

"Forget it, Drew."

"I was out of line," he continued.

"Yes, you were." She refused to make him feel better, but she wasn't interested in pushing back or fighting about it either. "I want to catch Cotter before he closes up shop for the night, and then I need to go to bed. It's been a long day."

Drew studied her face. He knew as well as she did that Cotter wasn't going to close up shop for the night. Cotter wasn't going to close up anything until the investigation was long complete. But he was searching her face, looking for something. Whether or not he was satisfied with what he saw, she didn't know. But he gave her a sharp nod. "Stop by the library when you're done. I have a new stack of pictures for you."

It was as close to an apology as she was going to get, which was fine with her since she didn't want an apology—didn't know if she deserved one anyway. "Thanks, I will," she responded, as she turned and headed toward Cotter.

An hour later, she dropped into the library to pick up the promised photos. She'd hoped that her extra-long detour would mean the room would be empty—that she wouldn't have to see Drew again. She was disappointed to find both Spanky and Drew there, looking like they wanted to talk to her about something. But she wasn't interested in having any conversations, so she gave them a brief nod and picked up the tidy folder resting on the edge of the big, teak desk. She slid out of the room before either man could stop her and headed for her bedroom.

She'd gotten only a few hours of sleep over the past three days—her eyes felt gritty and her limbs heavy. But even as she tossed the folder onto her bed and headed for the adjoining bathroom, she knew she wouldn't rest until after she looked at the new set of photos.

Ten minutes later, showered and dressed in one of the old tshirts she'd found in the dresser, Dani sat cross-legged on her bed and opened the folder on her lap. This stack of photos, like all the other photos he had given her over the years, was something Drew did for her—something that, if pressed, would be considered inappropriate. Many of the photos had nothing to do with her assignments and the agency wouldn't take kindly to her studying them. But Drew had made a promise to her over fifteen years ago, and he'd stuck by it.

Focusing on the task at hand, Dani began to review the first photo in the stack. It was easy to dismiss. The single form in the picture was a woman, dark hair, young, wearing sunglasses. She looked like a journalist, ambitious but weary. The picture was taken in the desert somewhere; judging by the colorless beige background Dani would place it in the Middle East. It wasn't the face she was looking for.

Setting it aside, she looked at the second photo. A single form was in focus, a young man, not the man she was looking for. But the photo was taken at a café so she pulled out her magnifying glass and scanned all the other faces. No traces of the blue-eyed man whose face was burned in her memory.

Methodically, Dani went through all thirty-six photos before sagging against the headboard, closing her eyes, and admitting defeat. One day, it might be different. One day, she might see the man who haunted her nightmares. She had to hope that, one day, in some photo, she would see the face of the man who had killed her parents.

CHAPTER 10

"I MADE BLUEBERRY SCONES," DANI announced as Marmie walked into the kitchen the next morning. "Want one?" she asked. Dani saw Marmie glance at the clock and didn't miss the look of concern that passed over her colleague's face.

"Everything okay?" Marmie asked, reaching for a pastry.

"Fine. Did Adam find anything on Smythe's daughter?" Dani poured a cup of coffee, offered it to Marmie, then poured another cup for herself.

"He did. We have some evidence she might have met with Keogh a few months ago in Morocco."

"Some evidence? Might have met? How close are we to getting anything more definite?"

"Close," Adam said, entering the kitchen followed by Spanky.

"God, that smells good." Spanky sidestepped Adam and went straight for the scones.

"How close?" Dani asked, leaning back in her chair. The two men joined her at the table after filling their own mugs and loading up on scones. If she didn't know better, she'd think they looked like a group of old friends enjoying breakfast together.

"I know they were in Morocco together." Adam said, catching a falling blueberry. "I even know they attended the same party. But I'm waiting for a contact to send me his surveillance data to see if I can get a photo of the two of them together."

"Can we sketch this whole thing out?" Dani asked Spanky, their resident artist. "We have a lot of players and having to divide up the board and keep our investigation into the drugs separate from the investigation into the weapons is making me crazy."

"Sure." Spanky rose from his chair, grabbed a pen and paper from the counter, snagged another scone, then sat down again. Flipping over a clean sheet of paper, he wrote "Drugs" on the lefthand side. Under it he wrote "Savendra" and "Sonny." On the righthand side he wrote "Weapons" with Smythe's name under it.

"We need Getz's name on there somewhere," Dani pointed out. "He's a key player in all this."

"More than the others?" Marmie prompted, even as Spanky added the name in the middle of the sheet.

"He's the place where everyone meets." Dani paused and took a sip of coffee. "I can understand how Smythe might come in contact with Keogh, given their similar circles. And since Sonny has lived in most of the major drug producing countries and Savendra has family connections to the Colombian cartel, I can understand how Sonny and Savendra might be the drug contacts. But what I can't figure out is how Sonny and Savendra got hooked up with Eagle's Wing and how both Eagle's Wing and Smythe got hooked up with Getz."

Dani took a sip as she leaned forward to study the paper. Next to her, Adam did the same, while Spanky tapped the pen on the table.

"Something smells good." Drew walked into the kitchen. Dani glanced up. He caught and held her eye for a moment.

"Blueberry scones," she said, turning back to the paper.

"Did you make them?"

"If you consider 'making' adding water and an egg," she replied without raising her eyes.

"Good enough." Scone and coffee in hand, Drew dropped into a seat beside Marmie. "What are we doing?"

"We're trying to figure out the connection each of these parties has to Getz," Adam answered.

"What more did you find out last night?" Dani asked Marmie.

"I spent my time on the weapons piece of this case. I figured we can do the other part, researching Sonny and Savendra, any-time," Marmie said.

Across from her, Drew gave a tight nod. No one on the team liked operating this way—breaking the investigation up into sev-eral parts. It obscured connections and relationships and made it harder to find patterns or links between parties. But, given the sensitivity of the possible Smythe connection, they didn't have a choice. They couldn't lay everything on the table at the same time.

"We did receive confirmation that Keogh and Smythe did not meet in Jordan a few months ago. Yes, they were both there, but they didn't meet. Smythe's two unaccounted for days are now accounted for. He was staying at a resort with a very married woman," Spanky added.

"How reliable is the confirmation?" Dani asked.

"I have photos if you'd like to see," Spanky said, offering her his cell with a mischievous smile.

Dani shook her head. "No thanks. If Smythe looked like David Beckham, maybe, but since he doesn't, I think I'll skip confirming the gross visual I already have."

"So what about the daughter?" Drew asked.

"Cornelia Elizabeth Smythe. Goes by Nelly." Adam proceeded to tell Drew the information he'd already shared with the rest of the group. As if on cue, Adam's cell buzzed.

"And we have confirmation they met." Adam held up the phone that revealed a picture of Nelly and Keogh dancing much closer than the couples around them. Adam scrolled to the next picture. Nelly and Keogh slipping out a door, holding hands.

"Okay, let's assume Keogh is involved and he uses Nelly to get the weapons into the country. But do either Smythe or Nelly know? Does he ask either, or both, to help? Or does he use his connections to broker the deal on his own, using info he learned from pillow talk with the daughter?" Spanky posited.

Dani rose from her seat, mulling over the possibilities, as she headed to the coffee pot.

"It's empty," Drew said.

"Thanks, Drew. I figured that one out." She held up the empty pot and made a face at him.

"You do make good coffee. Better than mine." He smiled. Things were righting themselves between the two of them.

"Glad I can be of service." She filled the water and added the grounds and soon the kitchen was filled, again, with the smell of fresh coffee. When enough was in the pot, she dumped it into her cup and leaned against the counter.

"Can we take another look at the paperwork on Smythe's shipment that contained the crate of weapons? Maybe cross-check the names on the forms with any known persons of interest? If we have any footage of the crates being loaded, we might want to run some facial recognition on those folks, too."

"Smythe doesn't have any cameras at his house," Spanky interjected.

Adam stood as he spoke. "No, but London is filled with CCTV cameras. We can get an idea of when the goods were packed and see what we can find in the surrounding area."

"It might be a needle in a haystack," Drew said. Sighing, he added, "Then again, we don't have anything else. Adam and Marmie, why don't you coordinate that with your team." Both nodded in response.

"Even if Smythe is involved as only a mule, we still have no idea how Keogh, assuming he is involved, and Eagle's Wing got connected with Getz," Dani pointed out.

"Then take a closer look at Keogh," Drew directed. "We have more files than we know what to do with on the man, we just didn't suspect he was involved until that photo of him and Smythe came through yesterday."

Dani opened her mouth to say something then snapped it shut. She wanted to focus on the drug connection, on Sonny Carlyle. But she'd opened her big mouth and given Drew a perfect opening to redirect her. With their fight the night before still fresh in her mind, she decided not to push. Nodding, she followed Adam and Marmie to the study.

...

The sun was hanging high in the sky when Dani sat back from her review of Keogh's files. The man had been to every country any self-respecting arms dealer traveled to. And judging by the photos and information, he liked his women young, his cars fast, and his parties lavish. A lot like Nelly Smythe. Not a thing like Ramon Getz.

"I was talking with Ty last night and he said that, as far as he knows, Getz doesn't leave his compound very often." Marmie and Adam raised their eyes as Dani spoke.

"As far as we know, he's only left the country a few times. At least under his own name," Marmie confirmed.

"And our surveillance hasn't been set up long enough to know who comes to visit him," Dani thought out loud. "He's so different from Keogh. How would they have connected?"

"We probably won't know until we get into Getz's place and see what else he has there. Assuming he has more than the one crate of weapons, once we can get some forensics, we should be able to trace where they came from and then do a geographic profile to confirm Keogh's involvement and figure out where they might have met," Adam said.

Dani frowned. The wait-and-see approach wasn't one of her favorite options. Unfortunately, sometimes it was their only option.

"So what about the drugs? Do you think it's Sonny or Savendra supplying them to Eagle's Wing?" Dani changed the subject, taking a little break from Michael Keogh. Her team was more interested in Getz and how he was involved with Smythe, if at all, than either Sonny or Savendra. But, they'd promised the DEA they'd give them not just Getz but the drug channels, including the two boys. Which also happened to align with Dani's personal interest in the case.

"Well, they both joined the group within the past year and both have connections to drug producing countries. But if you were to push, I'd put my money on Savendra," Marmie offered.

"Why?"

Marmie took off her glasses and sat back. "Don't get me wrong, I'm still keeping my eye on Sonny, but Savendra has the most direct connection, the most stable connection, to a known middleman."

Dani acknowledged this with a small nod. "Yeah, that's true, but other than that one summer, do we have any other intelligence showing that Savendra spent time with his uncle in Colombia?"

Adam rose from his seat and adjusted the shades as he joined the conversation. "He's an interesting guy. Born in the US to an immigrant mother and US-born father—his life is solid middle class."

"Until he went to spend a few months with his uncle in Colombia," Dani pointed out.

"Yeah, that does raise a few red flags," Adam grinned as he handed her a file.

She glanced at the file then tossed it on the table, more information on Savendra. "Especially when he returned to the US and joined the Eagle's Wing." Pausing, she drummed her fingers on her thighs. "But that's what we need to figure out. Militias don't typically form alliances, of any sort, with foreign groups. So why would Savendra join one after leaving his uncle? And it makes even less sense to think about his uncle supplying drugs to the militia."

Marmie lifted a shoulder and replaced her glasses on the tip of her nose. "Which is why we're still watching Sonny. You seem to have an opinion, Dani. What's your take?"

Dani stood and paced toward the window. "I'm not getting a good feel on this. I'm hung up on how everyone is connected to Getz. But, boiling it down to just the drugs, I *want* it to be Sonny. But wanting it doesn't make it so."

"Why Sonny?" Marmie asked.

Dani paused, debating whether or not to move forward. She pushed the shades aside and stared down the long lawn and out toward the sea. Like the previous day, the weather was clear and the sky an intense blue. But all was not as calm as the sky would have her believe, as waves from another off-shore storm crashed along the rocky coast with spray high enough to be visible from the house. Without turning, she spoke.

"The murder of Sonny's father is similar to another murder I've looked into—a couple of murders I've looked into," she corrected herself. "I'd like there to be a connection. I'd like for Sonny to lead us to the man who killed his father so we can figure out if he was responsible for the other murders as well."

A moment of silence followed her pronouncement. Then Adam spoke. "What is the connection, Dani?"

Dani shrugged. "Maybe there isn't one," she admitted. "But Sonny's father was in the same line of business as the victims in the other case, and he was killed in the same way. Maybe it has nothing to do with why Sonny joined the Eagle's Wing, or maybe it does.

But either way, I'd like to talk to him. See if he can point us toward the murderer."

"What murderer?" Ty's voice echoed through the room. Dani spared a quick look at her teammates, who had both gone back to whatever it was they were looking at before she had interrupted them.

"Just talking about an old case. What have you been up to today?"

He studied her face for a long moment before answering. "Paperwork. A little bit of this. A little bit of that. Can I see you for a minute?" He motioned toward the hallway with his head.

She thought about telling him she was busy. But, with his arms crossed over his chest and his feet planted apart, he wasn't a man who was going to go away. And looking at him standing there, looking back at her, she wasn't sure she wanted him to. She wasn't about to go running into his arms. But she could do with a little bit of the calm he'd brought her when they were out on the ledge the night before.

She inclined her head and he followed her out.

When they were alone, he spoke. "I'd like to get a better idea of how you think the drugs are going to be coming in. Not the physical way they'll be arriving, but who the players are. You've mentioned a couple of names and I want to get a better sense of who they are, maybe see if we've seen them up here before."

Dani found it a bit ironic that, as she looked to him to satisfy a personal need, he was all business. A hundred thoughts tumbled through her head as her eyes searched his. Like her, he had a job to do and, like her, he was going to do it. He took his responsibilities and position seriously and, despite any awkwardness between them, he wasn't going to let things slip. He wasn't going to back away to make things easier.

The same sense of calm from the night before washed over her. Ty was the man he portrayed himself to be. And to Dani, a woman used to living lies and half-truths, there was a measure of comfort in that—a measure she found herself taking. Again.

She recognized her own desire to trust him, as a man and a teammate. She wasn't going to spill her heart out to him in the hallway—if she was even capable of that—but she did want to treat him as a colleague, as a partner. Because he was who he was and he wasn't going to change on her, or for her.

Accepting more than his request for information, she spoke. "Of course. Come with me, I'll show you what we have."

They grabbed a couple of boxes and extra files from the study and headed to the front sitting room.

"There's not much of a table in here." She flicked on the lights and surveyed the room. "We weren't intending on using this room, but I think it's the best place for us spread out for a few hours."

Ty placed his box on the coffee table and went to the windows. "Mind if I open things up a bit?"

Dani shook her head and, as she began to sort through her box, Ty pulled the drapes and opened some windows. The cool, May air flowed into the room, bringing with it the smell of the ocean and fresh cut grass. Dani inhaled. Those scents reminded her of her childhood—the good parts.

"It's beautiful here," Ty said.

"We used to spend our summers in the Hamptons. This place is a lot like it but more relaxed and less, well, Hampton-y."

Ty turned from his position at the window even as she wondered why she had shared that bit of information. Only certain kinds of families spent their summers in the Hamptons. She was one of those families, as were the Carmichaels, but it wasn't anything either she or Drew talked about. It was helpful in that their official CIA covers were that they both ran family businesses and their wealth wasn't exactly a secret. Still, it felt awkward at times like this. She sank to the floor beside the coffee table that held the boxes and began laying files out.

"So tell me what we have." Ty left the window and came to sit across from her.

She handed him a couple of files. "Sonny Carlyle and Joe Savendra are our primary leads for the drugs. These files will give you some good background."

"How did they show up on your radar to begin with?" He opened the top file and began to scan the contents.

"Like I said in the briefing, Getz's name started to crop up here and there. We had a warrant to monitor his communications, but not to tap them. Pretty easy work since he doesn't get many calls. But, about a month ago, he made four phone calls to this number." She handed him another open file showing a list of numbers and pointed to one.

"It's the number for the Eagle's Wing compound," she continued. "Once we had that, we started looking at them and, once we started to find things, we were able to get authorization for this operation."

"And Getz?"

"We have a number of files on him, but these will have most of what we know," she said patting one of the boxes. It wouldn't have any of the information on the weapons, but Ty wasn't asking for it. Yet.

Dani rose. "I haven't had lunch yet. Have you eaten?"

Ty looked up, "No." He started to rise but Dani held up her hand to stop him.

"Stay here, look through the files. I've been reading for hours already and could use the break. Turkey and Swiss okay?"

Again his gaze held steady, a question lingering there. After a moment, he nodded. "Sounds great, thanks."

Dani made her way to the kitchen and started pulling out the sandwich fixings. It was such a mundane chore, it felt nice.

"Make me one?" Drew said, entering the room.

"After you disparaged my cooking this morning?"

"Your cooking is awful. But putting sandwiches together doesn't constitute 'cooking.'"

Dani made a face at him, but pulled out enough bread for three. "Ty's here."

"I heard. I heard you set him up in the front room with some of the files. Any updates on Keogh from your research this morning?" Dani tuned her ear to listen for any hint of disapproval. She didn't hear any.

"Keogh has done some business in Nicaragua." She laid out the bread and started making the sandwiches as she spoke.

"Same country as Getz's supplier."

"It's possible they met that way. Adam is seeing what he can find. We're cross-checking Keogh's visits to the region with Getz's, to see if they were ever there at the same time."

"But even if they weren't, it's still possible that's the connection," Drew said, handing her a jar of mustard.

"Yeah, it's possible. Probable, even." Dani finished off the sandwiches and grabbed some glasses from the cupboard.

"But you're still hung up on the Sonny/Savendra/Eagle's Wing connection aren't you?"

Dani could take exception to the "hung up" phrase, but didn't. Filling two glasses with water, she spoke. "I am. I want to know how Sonny and Savendra got hooked up with Eagle's Wing, why the group is selling drugs, and how they got connected to Getz."

"And why Getz is suddenly dealing in weapons."

"A sixty-four thousand dollar question."

"Maybe Ty will have some insight."

Dani turned at the comment. Drew was leaning against the counter, arms crossed, watching her. She picked up the plates and glasses. "Maybe. I'll let you know."

She made her way back to the front room contemplating the interaction. No doubt it was a test. But he wasn't revisiting their argument from the night before. He seemed more curious than anything. Frowning to herself, she pushed open the door to the front room. Ty looked up from his position on the floor, then held out his hands to take some of the dishes from her.

A few minutes later they were situated on the floor, files and food scattered across the coffee table. "Any questions?" she asked.

He frowned and shook his head. "No, not yet. I'm still reading the background on Sonny Carlyle. I don't think I'll have much to offer on him or Savendra, but it's still good to know the players."

Dani passed the time flipping through files and watching the shadows on the floor shorten as the sun moved west. Every now and then Ty would ask a question. At one point she got up to get them another snack. It was heading into the evening when Ty closed the last file and looked up.

"Thanks for sharing."

"Not a problem." Dani rose and stretched. Ty did the same. "So, have any insights? Find any magic words that tell us where the drugs are coming from and when?"

"I could pull my magic eight ball out for you." A smile tugged at his lips. Dani gave him a rueful smile back as she walked to the window. The lawn was cast in shadows now as the sun had moved far into the western part of the sky. She could still hear the ocean. And she could feel Ty approaching. She looked up when he was just a few feet away.

"We don't know how Eagle's Wing and Getz got connected in the first place, do we?"

Dani shook her head.

"Or why Getz is suddenly expanding into weapons?" Ty took

a step closer. Looking lost in thought, he stared at a point over her head for a long moment before meeting her gaze again. They were alone and now just inches apart. He must have recognized it at the same moment she did. His pupils dilated and his jaw twitched.

For what felt like forever, Dani stood stock-still. The breeze from the window slid over her face and her bare neck. And Ty's eyes stayed locked on hers. He raised his hand, brushed a thumb across her lips and cupped her face with the palm of his hand. Without taking his eyes from hers—giving her every chance to turn away— he lowered his lips to hers.

This was a test. She could feel it in the tension of his body, in the deliberateness of his actions. He was waiting for her to turn away, to pull back, to slam the emotional wall back up between them.

He brushed his lips across hers once. Then again. This was not the flaming passion from their one night together. This was soft and gentle. About the present. The future. When he raised his head, his eyes searched hers. She stood, accepting his touch. She still wasn't sure it was the right thing to do. It was too new. It was too different. And it was coming at a really bad time. But she wanted it anyway.

And then he moved away. Turned his back on her and faced the window. Dani blinked then ducked her chin. Turning away, toward the door, she searched her mind for an excuse. Then she saw Drew enter the room.

She glanced back at Ty, who met her gaze. Understanding dawned on her. She hadn't heard a thing, but he must have. He'd moved away to save them from being found by Drew.

"Drew," Ty said in greeting.

"Ty." Drew nodded then scanned the room. "Find anything interesting?"

Ty moved back to the coffee table and began picking up files. "A lot of interesting parties involved in this."

"You could say that again."

"Like I told Dani, Sonny and Savendra are outside my jurisdiction and the reach of my intel, way outside. As is Eagle's Wing.

But I can focus on Getz. Maybe see if I can find out how he got connected to the militia, or why he's moving into weapons."

"That would be good. Any insight you can dig up will be appreciated."

"No problem. Dani, do you need help with these boxes?"

She shook her head. "No we've got them."

"Then I'll be leaving. I'll put some feelers out tonight. See what might pop up. I'll come back here tomorrow morning."

Dani and Drew both nodded. Ty gave her one last look on his way out.

"You good?" Drew asked. She turned and faced her boss and friend.

"Yeah. I'm good."

CHAPTER 11

"ALUMINUM FOIL?" TY ASKED. HIS brother's laugh carried over the phone. Coffee in hand and back in his office after a long night putting out feelers on Getz, he couldn't quite believe what he was hearing.

"Confuses the hell out of the system," Cam commented.

"A million dollar system thwarted by *aluminum foil*. Shit, I don't even know what to say about that," Ty shook his head, setting his cup, none too gently, on his desk.

"I'd pay a million bucks to see you and your SEAL buddies decked out in full gear and foil," Cam teased.

"It would cost twice that, I guarantee," Ty shot back, still not accepting the fact that the best underwater audio surveillance system, the Hunley, could be thwarted by a common household product. And it was even better than that. The system didn't even recognize it as an error. So you could swim right up to the monitor and scream your head off but, if you were surrounded by enough foil, the monitor wouldn't pick up a thing, not even an error in the system.

Ty shook his head again and closed the folder that contained a printout of the email his brother had sent about the Hunley. "What about the Abram system? The visual monitor?" he asked, picking up another folder. This folder held an email from Jay with info about the secondary system set up around Getz's peninsula.

"The good news is that it's not that reliable. We don't use it much around here because of that."

"What's the bad news?"

"Bad news is that, because it's not used that often, the only information we have on it is a couple of years old. I'll send it right over, though," he added, and Ty could hear him clicking away on the keyboard as they spoke.

"Well hot damn, imagine that," Cam murmured, catching Ty's attention.

"Something I should know about?" Ty asked. Cam was silent for a while but the keyboard was now clicking away at rapid speed.

"You didn't tell me you were working with the CIA," Cam commented, more curious than anything.

CIA? Ty's feet hit the floor and he cursed under his breath. He *knew* there was something Dani and her team were hiding. Silly him for thinking it might be something minor, not the fact that they worked for the fucking CIA—and they were working inside the United States.

"They claim they're DEA," Ty commented.

"Hm, probably are, for now anyway," Cam responded.

"Meaning?" Ty asked. After ten years in the military, he knew a thing or two about intelligence agencies all over the world, but he wasn't as savvy as his brother, who worked with them more often than not.

"Agencies loan agents out to other agencies, or in this case, the CIA probably directed the DEA to bring on the team so that there aren't any questions about their operating in the US. Unless of course this is a counterintelligence operation, that might confuse things a bit more."

Counterintelligence? Ty frowned in thought. He didn't think so. He didn't think Dani and the team were lying to him about their objective when it came to Getz and the Eagle's Wing. But knowing they didn't work for the DEA, knowing they'd lied to him once— well, anything was possible.

"Are you sure?" Ty asked.

"Sure they're CIA or sure you're working with them? Well, let's just say the same information I'm faxing you has already gone out today to another number in the Portland area, attention: Dani

Williamson. What are the odds that you and Agent Williamson would be working on the same system in the same town? I put two and two together, but if you want to be sure, I can describe her to you. Tall, blonde, looks like a playmate that carries a gun? Sound familiar?"

"Shit," Ty sighed. "You know Dani?"

Cam paused. "Dani?" he asked with a laugh, not missing the subtle shift in his brother's tone of voice. "Yeah, I know Dani, and Drew, and the whole team. We've done some work with them over the years. Probably why they contacted us for information about the Hunley."

"I thought the CIA wasn't allowed to operate in the United States? And why would an intelligence agency be running an investigation?" Ty asked, relying on his brother's knowledge of the intelligence world.

"As to the first, it's a common misperception, perpetrated by poor research. The CIA is generally not allowed to gather intelligence information directed against *US citizens*. But collecting intelligence information directed against foreign citizens or governments can happen anywhere, even here in the US."

"You said 'generally not allowed.' Does that mean, in some circumstances, they can?" Ty asked, thinking about the players involved in the Getz bust—as far as he knew, they were all US citizens.

"With proper authorization, under some circumstances, they can gather intelligence about US citizens. But, it's pretty limited to things like espionage and international terrorism. And as to your second question, the CIA runs investigations all the time. But most don't require law enforcement or pop up in a court of law. There is very little public record on them."

"Okay, so given we've got some potential international arms dealing going on and we don't know the target of the Eagle's Wing, Drew's team might have been authorized."

"They might have been but, based on what I've heard, the information they have probably isn't enough to justify the authorization, which is why they are there as DEA. Mind you, that's just a guess," Cam added.

"Hmm, well, hot damn," Ty murmured. "This bit of information opens a whole new realm of possibilities."

"You going to call them on it?" Cam asked.

"Do you think I should?" Forcing himself to be fair and logical, he knew that if the CIA was running an operation in his town, chances were he didn't need to know everything—even if they agreed to tell him. And chances were, whatever they were doing was way above his pay grade.

And, in all fairness, focusing on Getz and the drugs *was* his area. Ty was going to be glad to see the end of him. One less drug distributor on the streets meant fewer lives at risks. Part of him wanted to let the CIA do their thing and accept the good fortune in having help with Getz. But another part of him wanted in. A part of him wanted Dani to tell him.

"It's bigger than you or the Portland Vice," Cam answered, echoing his own thoughts. "And if you bring it up, they have two options. Read you in, or—"

"Or push me out."

But still, it would be interesting to see Dani's reaction if he told her he knew the truth. Something had changed with her yesterday afternoon. She'd treated him more like a partner. Her rough edges were softer and she'd been less guarded, more open. And she had let him kiss her.

Would calling her on it bring back her walls? Would it be better to let sleeping dogs lie to ensure he stayed part of the investigation? Ty let out a huff of air.

"No, I won't say anything. I think it will be a whole lot more interesting if I let them continue to think I think they're DEA." Interesting in more ways than one, he thought.

"Of course by now, they probably know you know," Cam responded. Then he added, "Drew's team is top notch, Ty. Keep your eyes open but remember, it's their operation. If they've gone to the trouble of using another agency, I'd say let them."

It was a fair warning from his big brother. Ty appreciated the sentiment and insight from a man who probably knew more about Dani and the team than he did.

"Thanks, I'll keep that in mind," he answered. "Thanks for the information," he added.

"Anytime. And, Ty?" he paused, "Watch out for Agent Williamson. I've seen her make grown men cry."

Whether or not Cam was kidding was a toss-up. Ty could well believe it. In the few hours they'd shared, she'd made him all but beg.

• • •

"What's this?" Drew asked picking up the file Ty tossed down on the desk.

"Information on the Hunley's weaknesses and more specifics on the Abram system," Ty answered.

Drew picked up the folder, flicked through it, and put it down. Confirming what Ty suspected, the director didn't need to study the information—he already had it.

"Thanks, Ty. I'll hand that to Cotter," Drew responded with a nod to the documents. "Thanks again for showing us those sites. Dani and Cotter have already set up shop. We wouldn't have known about them if you hadn't offered."

It was an interesting compliment. A bit forced—as if he wouldn't have bothered had Ty been part of his team, but he was trying to play nice.

"Oh, hi Ty," Dani said, entering the room.

"Dani," he acknowledged. She gave him a second, curious look, then frowned. He wasn't quite at peace with the fact she and her team were keeping things from him.

Breaking the awkward moment, Marmie's voice carried across the room. "We've got movement." Her eyes stayed locked on her computer screen as all three moved toward her.

Other team members materialized as Marmie's fingers flew

across the keyboard. The text scrolled so fast that Ty had to look away for a second. "Sonny's headed for," she paused, hit a few more keys and then announced. "He's headed for Miami."

The team began moving into action but Marmie stopped them by adding, "And Savendra is headed home to San Diego. Both are scheduled for flights leaving tomorrow."

Everyone paused and Ty watched as all eyes swiveled to Drew. After a split second of clear concentration, he turned to Adam.

"Adam, you'll go to Miami. Dani, you're going to San Diego. Cotter, Spanky, get them what they need. Marmie, arrange the transport."

"Done," Marmie answered.

"Done," echoed Spanky and Cotter, already halfway out the door.

"Drew, Adam's never been in the field. Savendra is going home. Sonny is being sent somewhere he has no known ties. Let me go to Miami," Dani spoke in a quiet measured tone.

"Adam's been in the field, just not as much as you. He needs the experience," Drew responded. Even Ty could see Drew's patience was running thin.

"Let me go to Miami, please. I'll blend in better than Adam, and you know it."

Dani had added a "please," but her jaw was set and her hands were balled into fists at her sides. And, Drew didn't care.

"Dani, get your ass on the plane to San Diego," he snapped. Then giving her a level look, he added, "Do not even think about breaking rank on this one."

And Ty sensed if she broke rank Drew would do more than toss her nice little behind to the wolves—he would serve it up himself. Why Drew was so set and why Dani so insistent, Ty wasn't sure, but he suspected it might have something to do with why they were masquerading as DEA in the first place.

After a long, still moment, with the tension still high in the room, Dani conceded. Her body rigid and her movements jerky, she gave Ty a look, daring him to say something, then left. Ty turned his attention to Drew who slammed a file on the desk and planted a fist on his hip. Running a hand through his hair, the team director let out a litany of curses. Ty's lips tilted into a smile—no wonder everyone else vacated the room as soon as Drew first issued his order.

"Anything I can do, sir?" Ty asked. He should have kept the half smile to himself but he couldn't help it. It's not that the situation was funny, but the way Dani could set Drew off *was* comical—from the outside. Maybe it was a good thing they hadn't brought him into their little circle.

Drew whipped his head up, ready for a fight, and glared at Ty. When Ty didn't so much as bat an eyelash or twitch a muscle, Drew's shoulders sagged and he took a deep breath. "I swear to god, if this job doesn't kill her, one of these days I will," he said with a rueful shake of his head. "But I imagine you have a good idea how difficult Dani can be," he added with a glance at Ty.

Ty opted not to respond. "Let me know if there is anything I can do," he offered again, as he reached for his files.

"Yeah, go make sure she gets on the plane to San Diego, will you?" Drew responded. Ty stilled, mid-reach. Was Drew kidding?

"And if you tell her I sent you, you'll regret it. Trust me," Drew gave him a pointed look.

Well, shit. He wasn't kidding. Drew wanted him to "handle" Dani. He studied Drew's face, wondering if he'd done this before, if he'd asked any of her lovers—not that he fit that profile at the moment—to "handle" her. Something about the bald honesty in Drew's expression answered his question. No, Drew had never asked anyone else to do something like this. That he thought Ty would be able to was an interesting development.

Ty nodded, dropped the file and headed to Dani's room.

• • •

Dani grabbed her duffel and tossed it on her bed. Flinging open her closet door, she took out her frustration on the clothes she grabbed at random and threw on the bed. Damn him. While everything Drew said about Adam was true, he did have field experience, good field experience, she also knew that wasn't the reason Adam was going to Miami. Adam was going to Miami because Drew didn't want to send her.

Rummaging through the pile of clothes, Dani grabbed a few tshirts and shoved them into her bag. She wanted to throw something—something more substantial than a pair of pants. It was the second time in the past two days that Drew had hinted she might screw up the investigation. First with Ty and now with not letting her go to Miami to follow Sonny—the man she believed might, just might, be able to give her a lead on who killed her parents.

She grabbed a book off the bedside table and a photo slid to the ground. Bending to pick it up, she glanced at the scene. It was familiar. Too familiar.

It was a photo taken of Sonny's father. The man had been shot execution-style and was lying face down on a blood-stained carpet. Dani sank onto her bed and stared at the photo. The picture was gruesome but it wasn't the picture that made Dani deflate—it was the memories it conjured.

What would she do if Sonny *was* the link to her own past? What would she do if she went to Miami and found out Sonny knew the man who killed her parents, the man she believed also killed Sonny's father? What would she do if she saw him?

Christ, she realized Drew was right and her heart slammed in her chest at the thought. She'd be down there with no backup, no support. It would be bad, not for the investigation but for her. Drew was protecting her. Like he always did. Since those days when she'd relived her parents' murders, crying on Drew's shoulder, he'd always looked out for her. It should bug her; she knew she should insist she could take care of everything, but Dani wasn't one to lie to herself. If she saw the man again, she didn't know how she would react, how she would hold up. It wasn't worth it to her or the investigation to risk it.

Calmer now, Dani stood and went back to packing. Drew

was right, she knew it—she didn't have to like it, but she couldn't disagree.

"Come in," she called, expecting Drew when a knock sounded at the door. She was feeling better but still wasn't over her pique. To her surprise, Ty entered, shutting the door behind him.

"Hand me your cell phone," he said moving toward her.

"My what?" she asked.

"Your cell," he repeated.

Dani arched her brow, debating whether or not to ask why. Deciding against it, she picked it up from the bedside table, entered her password, and tossed it to him. He caught it one-handed and began entering numbers.

"My contact info," he said in explanation. "In case you get bored or need to bitch about your boss," he added with a smile. Turning the phone off, he tossed it back to her.

She shook her head and gave him a conciliatory look. "Drew's right," she said on a sigh as she tucked a skirt into the bag.

"Doesn't mean you have to like it though," Ty responded and moved closer to her.

"No, I don't," she agreed. "What are you doing up here?"

"At the risk of losing my *cojones*, Drew sent me. Although I would have come up anyway. He wants me to make sure you get on the plane. The *right* plane, to San Diego," he added.

Dani glanced at him. His honesty surprised her, as did his easy tone. He also didn't look all that concerned about her temper. "I have to say this is the first time Drew has willingly sent a man to my room to handle me," she responded with a self-deprecating smile.

"Has he *unwillingly* sent a man to your room?" Ty asked, his brow arched in interest, even as he took a step toward her.

"Ha ha, you know what I mean," she rolled her eyes and turned toward her closet.

"Is he trying to protect your virtue?" Ty teased, reaching her. His hands made contact with her shoulders and she turned to face him.

"He may be trying to protect someone, but it sure isn't me,"

Dani answered. They were standing less than a foot apart and his hands had moved from her shoulders to her neck, with one making its way gently into her hair. His expression had changed again to a more familiar one. And she breathed a small sigh of relief. Whatever had been bothering him earlier, when she'd seen him talking to Drew, wasn't bothering him now.

"I wouldn't be so sure about that," Ty said before he kissed her.

She responded and accepted his contact. Her hands came up to his chest and he deepened the kiss. Just as she started to curl her fists into his clothes and lean into him he pulled back enough to look at her.

Dani blinked, bringing herself back into the here and now. "What was that for?" *And why did you stop?* Even she heard the yearning in her own voice. She wanted more. Maybe not the whole thing quite yet, but more.

He smiled. "It's a tradition between people who like each other and aren't going to see each for a few days. It's called a goodbye kiss. I'm sure you've heard of them."

She looked at him from beneath her eyelashes, letting him know what she thought of that reasoning, but stepped back and resumed packing. "You kiss everyone goodbye like that?"

"Just you, sweetheart." He moved away, making it easier for her to focus.

"So, tell me the plan then," Dani prompted switching back to work mode.

"Marmie gave me the details before I came up. There's a military transport leaving at around noon."

That would explain his stepping away, Dani acknowledged. Her flight left in less than an hour.

"It will get you to San Diego before four," he continued. "I'll check out the potential sites Savendra might go to and find a hotel somewhere convenient. We'll call you when you land and give you the details."

"That's right, it's your old stomping ground," Dani commented, remembering the SEAL training facility in San Diego.

"As long as the hotel doesn't have fleas, I'll be happy," she added, shoving one more pair of shoes into her bag and zipping it shut.

"We'll find you something nice. I might even toss in a couple of good food recommendations," he offered as she hefted her bag over her shoulder.

"Ah," she sighed. "A man after my own heart." And, as she said it, she wondered if there was more truth to it than even she would credit.

CHAPTER 12

SHE KNEW SHE WAS BIASED, but Savendra felt *wrong*. Even his friends were unremarkable. There was just *nothing*. And that was what Dani couldn't wrap her mind around. Dani was feeling grumpy. If Savendra stuck to his usual haunts and friends, her trip to San Diego would be extremely uneventful.

The wheels hit the tarmac and she gathered her things. She needed to remember her primary objectives. The weapons and the drugs. *Not* Sonny Carlyle. If Smythe was involved in arms dealing, they'd be due for some very long paperwork when this whole thing wrapped up. And if Eagle's Wing got ahold of the arsenal they believed Getz had stored in his seaside fortress—well, *ugly* wouldn't even begin to cover what it would be like.

Knowing how the drugs were coming into the country, and through whom, would make it easier to build the case against Getz once the bust was over. And the more they had against Getz, the more he might give up about the weapons. But maybe when Sonny was in custody, just maybe, she could get some answers.

Her phone rang as she walked down the stairs onto the tarmac and into the hot Southern California spring air. "Williamson," she said.

"It's me," Ty's voice responded.

"Good timing, I just stepped out of the plane. Christ, it's hot. Hold on, I need to take my jacket off." Dani moved the phone away without waiting for an answer.

"Can I help you with your bag ma'am?" a young soldier appeared. "Thanks, I have a car in the parking lot," she said. "I do have a car in the parking lot, right?" she asked Ty, bringing the phone back to her ear. He told her the make, model, and color, which she repeated to the young man who headed off to find it for her. It would have been chivalrous, but Dani knew it was more about security than anything else.

"Who was that?" Ty asked.

"Some sweet, young soldier. A cutie, too," she couldn't help but add.

"How young?" Ty asked, a tad more interested.

"It's quite possible he's still nursing," she answered. "God, I hate flying into military bases. It makes me realize how *old* I am," she added, following the young man at enough distance so he couldn't hear her.

"I'm not old, and you're younger than me," Ty responded.

"Yeah, well I feel old when I come to these places."

"If it makes you feel any better, you don't look old."

Dani could hear the smile in Ty's voice. "So says the man I'm having sex with," she responded.

"We had sex one night, I'm not sure that qualifies me as the man you're 'having sex with.'"

Dani stopped mid-step. "Please tell me you didn't just say that in front of anyone," she demanded. She knew it was her fault, she'd baited him. But that was before she'd remembered he wasn't the kind of guy to refrain from responding just because he was surrounded by colleagues. Even if they were her colleagues. Of course, very little got by any of her teammates, and while she'd like to think she and Ty weren't obvious about whatever was going on between them, some things were too hard, if not impossible, to hide completely. She would have preferred it if Ty hadn't announced their personal connection, but in all honesty, she doubted he'd said anything that shocked anyone.

"Marmie's here, doing her best to pretend she's not listening. She's not doing a very good job of hiding her laughter though," he added, not at all contrite. "Oh, and Spanky is here, too. What's that Spanky?" he asked, and Dani could hear her colleague saying something. Ty let out a bark of laughter. "Spanky wants to know if you're going to come through the phone and emasculate me now, or if you're going to wait until you get back here? Either way, he wants a heads up so he can take bets."

"Later. Definitely later," she muttered as she reached the car. The keys were inside and she popped the trunk. The soldier placed her duffel in the back, closed it, and gave her one last look. He was very cute, in an Opie Taylor kind of way.

"Stop smiling at the private, you'll make him blush," Ty commanded.

"Too late," Dani answered, as the young man murmured his goodbye, blushed, and walked away.

"You in the car now?" Ty asked, bringing her back to the task at hand.

"Yes, now you can give me the specs."

And he did. Ty rattled off the name of the hotel they'd reserved for her, the names of local DEA agents she'd be working with for the next few days, and a few pieces of intelligence that had come in during her flight. The only surprise was the fact that Sonny's trip to Miami had been delayed by four days. He'd leave the militia compound the same day Savendra was scheduled to return. Maybe they didn't like too many people to be off the compound at the same time.

"So, what's the plan?" Ty asked when he finished giving her the details.

"I'll go to the regional office, meet the agents, and then scout the area. Savendra doesn't come in until this time tomorrow, so I have plenty of time to check things out."

"Go to Mamarita's for dinner, if you have a chance," Ty suggested. "It's the best Mexican in town."

As far as Dani was concerned, good Mexican food was the best thing Southern California had to offer.

"What's the address?"

"It's in your email already," he answered. "Marmie told me

how much you like Mexican food—figured we'd toss it into the reports we sent."

"I have high standards, so don't get offended if I don't like it."

She was only partly teasing. After spending a couple of months in Mexico on three separate occasions, her standards were high. But, outside of Mexico, she was pretty easy to please.

"Well then, when this is all over, I'll take you to a little place near my parents' home in Taos. You'll love it." Dani almost drove off the road.

"Ty," she half-warned.

"Gotta go, Drew's giving me the stink eye. I think I blew my chance to give you any more updates. I'll talk to you later." Ty ended the call. Dani pulled the phone from her ear, looked at like it might bite her, sighed, and tossed it onto the empty seat.

• • •

An hour and a half later, most of which was spent in traffic, Dani was sitting across from Agent Alicia Gordon in the San Diego field office of the DEA. Both women were watching the figure of Agent Jeffery Diamond disappear down the hallway in a huff.

"Whose puppy did you kick to get him for a partner?" Dani asked.

"Just another day in the life of a pregnant DEA agent," Agent Gordon replied with good-humored resignation—which was more than Dani would have been able to muster.

Dani turned her attention back to the woman sitting at the table. Agent Gordon was a few years older than her, and about six months pregnant. True, Dani wouldn't want her on a high-risk stake out or other physically demanding assignment, but Agent Gordon's attractive face held eyes that were intelligent and sharp. Dani would bet, hands down, that even six months pregnant, Alicia Gordon was the better agent.

"I'm not sure about the wisdom of partnering up a misogynistic SOB with a pregnant woman. What did they think that would accomplish?" Dani asked. Agent Diamond had done nothing but insult her intelligence and ogle her breasts for the past thirty minutes. Well, to be fair, he also ogled her legs. She wished Ty was there. It would be funny to watch Ty do his he-man thing.

"Yeah well, I have to stick to desk work or—" she added with a nod to the Savendra file, "low risk surveillance. Diamond is already skating on thin ice, that's why we're assigned together; they needed to get him off the streets for a while. He has no idea what a bad move it is to go complain to the captain right now."

As if on cue, Dani and Agent Gordon heard the captain yelling, a short scuffle that sounded like a chair being knocked over, and then a door slamming. Dani cast Alicia a look and they both burst out laughing.

"So what'd he do? Do I need to worry about him?" Dani asked, before Diamond made it back to the room.

"Nah, not like that. He's good at surveillance. He's not a loose cannon or anything like that—he won't go cowboy on you. In fact, it's more like the opposite. He's a bit terrified of guns, so try not to get in his line of fire if it ever comes to that."

"Did I miss any makeup secrets?" The man in question sneered as he walked into the room. Dani glanced at Alicia who shrugged.

"No, but I have a report I'd like you to run," Dani replied, off the cuff. She didn't want to spend a second more with this man than she had to.

He looked at her, waiting for her to continue. His eyes drooped with age as his jaw set in furious resignation. Dani had to admit, after a long career in the DEA, he might be entitled to be a bit grumpy.

"What? Did the air suddenly leave that little blonde head of yours?" he barked.

But it did not entitle him to be an asshole.

"Savendra's mother is a real estate agent. I want the addresses of all the houses she's listed as a seller or worked on as the buying agent. I also want a list of the buyers and sellers of all the properties and I want that cross-checked with the names on this list," she slid a sheet of paper across to him. A list that held the names of a bunch of men in Savendra's uncle's cartel. "Go two degrees deep on all of them for the past three years," she ordered. Out of the corner of her eye Dani saw Alicia bite her lip to keep from grinning.

"Bullshit," Diamond exploded.

"There a problem, Dani?" Captain Young stuck his head in. Dani turned and smiled. She'd known Craig "Buster" Young for several years. He was the only person, outside her team, who knew who her real employer was.

"I don't think so, Buster," she responded with a nod toward Diamond. "Agent Diamond, is there a problem?"

Diamond opened his mouth to protest, saw the warning look on the captain's face, and closed his mouth. "Nope, no problem at all," he muttered, pushing away from the table.

"Two more months, Alicia," Buster said apologetically after Diamond was out of earshot. "Two more months until he retires and I promise you'll get some sort of combat reward."

Alicia smiled and rolled her eyes. "It's fine, Captain. I appreciate the thought, and wouldn't say no to a bonus, but we're all just doing our jobs."

Buster looked at the two women again and gave a quick smile. "You two will work well together. I take it you gave Diamond a long and solo assignment?"

"It should take him a few days." Dani grinned as Buster turned and left.

"You know the captain?" Alicia's eyes were bright with interest.

"We've worked together in the past," Dani replied. She could see the thoughts bouncing around in the agent's eyes but discretion won out and Alicia let it drop.

"So have you been by the house yet? Done any recon?" Alicia asked.

Dani shook her head. "No, I will in the morning." It was heading on toward six in the evening and Dani didn't need to keep anyone late when the morning would be fine. "Is it okay for a pregnant woman to ride around in a car? I'd love the company."

"As long as you don't mind stopping for bathroom breaks, I'd like nothing better than not to have to hear Diamond bitching about everything all day."

• • •

After making plans to pick up Agent Gordon in the morning, Dani checked into her hotel and then headed for Mamarita's. With a little sigh of contentment, she tipped back in her chair on the restaurant's deck and took a sip out of her long-neck bottle, enjoying the taste of the cold, crisp beer and the soothing feel of the setting sun on her face. Judging by the clientele, it was a popular dinner locale—with the military crowd. The place was full of them, both in and out of uniform.

But lost in her own thoughts about the investigation, Dani didn't mind the curious looks pointed in her direction. Taking another bite of her empanada, she stretched out her legs, feeling the night air wash over her bare skin.

"She's gotta belong to someone," she heard a voice to her right say. He was speaking to a table of four other guys. Dani had noticed the group in her quick survey of the patio when she first sat down. There were two men, probably a couple of years older than she was, and three men several years younger. They were definitely from the nearby base, even though not one of them was in uniform—they just had that look.

"Girls like that don't come here without belonging to someone from the base, or hunting for someone from the base," another one of the young men agreed. Dani had to bite back a grin and stop herself from rolling her eyes at his use of the word "girl."

"She doesn't look like she's hunting anything," another pointed out.

Dani knew exactly what they were talking about. Other than talking about her, they were talking about the military groupies. Women that looked for men in uniform for the sole purpose of putting another notch in their bedposts with someone they see as *dangerous*. And she never could figure out why some women found killing to be sexy, anyway—even sanctioned killing. Having done her fair share, she could say with complete honesty that there was nothing sexy about it. The men and women in the military who did it, did it for a living and, she was pretty sure, most didn't enjoy it— understood it yes, but enjoyed it, no.

She cocked her ear toward the table of men, wondering what they would say next. For a while they said nothing, so she sat back and stretched again, propping her feet on the empty plastic chair on the other side of her table. She took another sip of beer and closed her eyes.

"Shit, I'm going to ask," she heard one of the men mutter and she couldn't help the grin that stole across her face.

"Excuse me, ma'am," the man said as he came to stand next to her. Dani looked up into his face. It was one of the two older men from the table. He was tall and handsome and hid his eyes behind a pair of sunglasses. His brown hair was military short and his chest was defined under a gray t-shirt. Baggy shorts hid what Dani guessed was a lower half that was a perfect match with his upper half.

"Yes?" Dani said, tilting back her bottle for another sip.

"I was wondering what brings you to town?" he asked. His question was direct, nothing subtle about it, but there was an underlying hesitation that Dani found endearing—like he was trying to be more nonchalant than he was—which was difficult, coming from this six-foot-plus man.

"Work," she replied, knowing he hoped for more of an answer, but not willing to give one yet. This was probably the most fun she would have in San Diego.

"Uh huh," he said, crossing his arms over his chest. "At the base? I mean, I'm just curious. We don't usually see…well, let's just say that you—"

The sound of Dani's phone cut him off. "Excuse me for a minute," she said, taking out her phone.

"It's me," came Ty's voice.

"Drew gave you phone privileges again?"

"Yeah, well," he cleared his throat. "What are you doing?"

"Eating at Mamarita's and chatting with another handsome SEAL," she replied. The man standing next to her straightened and, behind his glasses, she felt his eyes snap to hers in surprise. And suspicion. "You are a SEAL right? Or used to be?" she asked him.

His brows disappeared behind his sunglasses. "Yes, ma'am."

"And he's going to *ma'am* me to death even though he's older than I am," she added, speaking back to Ty.

"What's his name?" Ty demanded.

"What's your name?" she repeated the question. For a second it looked like the SEAL might not answer, and then he spoke.

"Dan Fowler. Fawkes," he answered, adding what she assumed was his handle.

"Like a little, red, furry fox?" she asked.

"No, like Guy Fawkes. I like to blow shit up," he added.

That didn't surprise Dani; he looked the sort. After repeating what he'd said into the phone, she laughed, then listened to what Ty had to say.

"I'm supposed to tell you that if you even think about trying to pick me up, Ty, who I am supposed to refer to as Folsom Fuller," she added with a smile, "will make you wish you never even had balls."

Shock registered on Fawkes's face for a split second, and then he rocked back in laughter. "Ty Fuller?" he laughed.

Dani nodded. "Big guy, scar on his right knee, bullet bite on his butt," she added for clarification. Fawkes laughed again.

"Hey Roddy," he called to one of the other men. "She's Folsom's girl, that lucky son of a bitch. I told you she belonged to somebody." Dani opted to ignore his use of the word "girl," again, and turned to look at Roddy, who was rising from his seat.

"No shit? Folsom?" he said, as he walked toward them, leaving the younger men at the table, brows furrowed, trying to put pieces together. "Well, I'll be damned," he added stepping close enough to shake Dani's hand as she introduced herself to the two.

"That him on the phone?" Fawkes asked. Dani nodded and handed the phone to him. He took it, stepped away and started talking trash with Ty.

"So what brings you to town?" Roddy asked, taking a seat across from her. "Last I heard, Fuller was working vice. Are you vice?"

"DEA," Dani answered, the lie rolling easily off her tongue. "We're working on a case together."

"Here in San Diego? That's a long way from Maine."

"We have a suspect on the move, so they sent me," Dani shrugged.

"Alone?"

Dani smiled at the disbelief in his voice and shook her head. "No, I've got backup from the local office. Not much, but enough. I don't think he's our guy but, hey, how could I turn down an opportunity for Mexican food and the chance to track down some of Ty's dirty little secrets? So, you got anything good on him?" she asked, steering the conversation away from her assignment. Neither of them was fooled.

"Yeah, right. He was my lieutenant before he left, but I have no doubt he'll still come kick my ass if I tell you any of his exploits."

"And he had a lot?" She knew Ty would tell her if she ever asked. He had told her about his team and some of his friends that night on the ledge—he'd even told her about that last bullet he took.

"Nice try, Agent Williamson," Roddy smiled but refused to elaborate. "Why don't you tell us a little something about yourself instead? You and Ty a real thing? How long have you been together? Is it driving him crazy to have you out here without him at your back?"

"Maybe, not long, and yes, probably," she said.

Roddy looked at her, then at Dan Fowler—or Fawkes, as Dani had already started to think of him—who had removed his sunglasses. Fawkes's eyes kept darting to her, even as he stayed focused on a conversation that had turned serious. Dani could see Roddy putting two and two together.

"I'd say that both the 'maybe' and the 'yes' are probably both 'hell, yeses,'" he offered.

"Maybe," was all she said.

"Here," Fawkes said, walking back toward them and handing her the phone. "He wants to talk to you."

"I hope you've picked up *The Care and Feeding of a DEA Agent*," she spoke after taking the phone back. "Because by some weird little twist of reality that occurred the minute I set foot in your SEAL-infested Mexican restaurant—which is good by the way—I now 'belong to you.' Even though I outrank you and I can probably outshoot you," she added, knowing he would hear the smile in her voice.

Ty was silent for a long pause and then he chuckled. "Ah, Dani, in case you hadn't figured it out, you belonged to me long before you set foot in Mamarita's. Probably from the moment I saw you in that bar in Portland. And again, just in case you didn't know, I'm as much yours. Even if you haven't accepted it yet."

Before Dani could respond to his blunt assessment of their new relationship, he continued. "So what are your plans for the rest of the weekend? Drew had a conversation with someone named Buster. Says you're still the same ballbuster," his voice was laced with amusement.

"Such a nice image, don't you think?" Dani replied. "I'm headed back to the hotel now. Tomorrow, Agent Gordon and I will do some scouting and then pick up the target when he arrives. She and I will be on day watch. I'll be on night watch with Agent Diamond, the agent with the now-busted balls, in case you were wondering."

"And when are you going to sleep?" It wasn't actually a question, just Ty's way of looking out for her.

"Alicia, that's Agent Gordon, and I will be on from nine to seven. Diamond and I will be on from seven to midnight. Diamond and another agent, Buster is going to let me know who tomorrow, will be on from midnight until nine. Make you feel better, *Dad*?"

"Dear god, don't call me that, it makes me feel dirty," Ty replied.

"Yeah, well, don't worry about me," Dani protested. But it was halfhearted at best. Though the glare she turned on Roddy and Fawkes, who'd burst out laughing at her last comment, was genuine.

"Your friends aren't endearing themselves to me," she said.

"Fawkes is going to walk you home," Ty spoke.

"First of all, how do you know I walked, and second of all, no."

"First all," Ty mimicked. "Your hotel is less than a mile from the restaurant. You've been sitting down all day. I'd bet my pension you walked just to use your legs. And second, yes he is—whether you want him to or not—so smile and nod at the nice man."

Dani glanced over at Fawkes. Standing there watching her— feet apart, arms crossed over his chest—he knew full well he was the topic of conversation.

"I could probably take him," Dani said. Fawkes raised a single eyebrow at the statement. She reassessed him. "Okay, maybe not," she conceded. "But, seeing as it's unlikely someone more skilled than me would attempt to attack me between here and the hotel, I think I should be okay on my own."

"Hand to hand isn't the only way to ambush," Ty pointed out.

"Last time I checked, SEALs weren't bullet proof either," Dani snapped.

Ty took a deep breath, paused and then spoke. "Dani, please," was all he said.

Dani bit her lip. The tone of Ty's voice was like a breeze clearing the fog and the clouds. They weren't talking about whether or not SEAL Fawkes would walk her home. They were talking about her letting Ty into her life—letting him care, letting him be a part of her.

She stood, knocking the chair back against the wall, and moved away from the watchful eyes of Fawkes and Roddy. She didn't harbor any doubts that moving ten feet away would make her conversation any more private. But she hoped, by turning her back on them, they would give her a measure of privacy.

"I'm sorry, Ty. This is all new to me," she said. And it was. She had people in her life she'd let in, she'd let care, but she could count them on one hand and they were all related by blood or marriage. And in truth, Drew was the only one who she ever really let "take care" of her. She hadn't been kidding when she'd told Ty that Drew was almost like a father figure to her. But what Ty wanted was different and they both knew it.

"I know, Ella," he answered, using the name he'd whispered across her skin as they'd moved together in the dark of his bedroom.

He didn't push, he didn't demand or get angry. He didn't say another word as Dani stood staring out at the ocean. *I belong to you* floated through her mind. How could he be so sure? Her breathing was shallow, her pulse erratic. It was her reaction to fear. Again. At least she knew what she was afraid of now—letting someone get close in a way she never had before. She'd turned and walked away from Ty the first time it had happened, just a few days ago in her hotel room. She could walk away again.

She swallowed. "Yeah, okay," she said, almost to herself. But she knew Ty heard her when he let out a deep breath.

"I'll call you tomorrow?" he asked. He was giving her some space and time to absorb the decision she'd made.

"Yeah, sounds good," she said, hanging up the phone.

"I find it a bit unusual meeting a DEA agent who thinks she can outshoot and out-spar a SEAL," Fawkes commented when she returned to the table. His voice was light but his eyes were assessing her, as she had assessed him earlier. His insinuation—that she was more than a rank and file DEA agent—was accurate. There weren't many DEA agents who would tangle with a SEAL and think they could win.

She glanced his way and blinded him with a smile. "Honey, there's a lot that's unusual about me." She gave him a wink and walked away, okay with the fact that he would follow.

CHAPTER 13

"So, TELL ME AGAIN WHY we think this kid is the link between Eagle's Wing and a shitload of drugs?" Alicia Gordon asked from the passenger seat. Doubt laced her voice, but she never took her eyes from the high-powered glasses she had trained on Savendra's house several blocks away.

"I could but since we've gone over this six times already, I think I'll pass," Dani said from her position behind the wheel.

"God, I'm being annoying aren't I?" Alicia acknowledged.

"Believe me, it's nothing I haven't done or said at least as many times to my team director. He won't listen. Well, that's not really true. He listens, I think he even agrees, but he can't really run the investigation on my intuition. And wouldn't we all look stupid if it turned out the kid fooled us."

"At least you'll see some action tonight when he meets his friends," Alicia offered.

"Yeah, we'll get to go to the bowling alley," Dani said. All of Savendra's friends had jobs—like good little college graduates. Savendra was the odd one out, so if he wanted to play with his friends, he had to play on their schedules.

"Yeah, well at least it will be cool," Alicia pointed out as she tugged at her shirt trying to get some air flowing over her body.

"Wrong. Buster is putting two other agents inside. He wants me and Diamond in the van," Dani countered.

Alicia laughed and Dani cast her a look. "I'm sorry," she said. "I just can't get used to you calling the captain 'Buster,' though,

I admit, he does kind of look like one," she conceded with another smile.

"So, if it's not Savendra. Who do you think it is?" Alicia asked, turning serious. Dani kept her eyes on the street, debating how much to tell the other agent. She liked Alicia Gordon, and her instinct said to trust her, but Dani's training said not to. She decided to hell with training; she had a niggling sense Alicia might be able to help in some way.

"We've got another potential. His name is Sonny Carlyle. We refer to him as Sonny. Sonny and Savendra has a better ring than Carlyle and Savendra or Sonny and Joe." Dani explained conversationally why they referred to one suspect by his first name and the other by his last.

"And you think Sonny is the man—or rather, boy, I take it?"

"I do," Dani answered.

Alicia took her eyes away from the glasses and glanced at Dani. But before she could ask why, Dani's phone rang. Glancing at the screen and seeing Drew's name, she hopped out of the car and walked several feet away.

"Dani. We have some news on Keogh I wanted to pass on." Drew spoke the moment she answered, also explaining why Ty wasn't calling. "The crate with the weapons was already in the hanger at the airport when Smythe's belongings were prepped for shipping."

"So they were never at his house?" She walked a little further away.

"It's looking that way. Adam is searching for footage in the storage area to see if we can either figure out who dropped the crate, or at least a time frame of when it was dropped."

"I would think the hanger would have twenty-four-hour security footage." As she commented, Dani's gaze caught on a little girl riding a tricycle in a driveway, her mom watching from the porch.

"They do, but it's not reliable. As in, there are several key hours missing at interesting times."

"So is Smythe still on our list?" It would make things a hell of a lot easier if they could strike the ambassador off the list of potential arms dealers.

"Despite the fact that we can't find any additional intel linking the two together, none of us like those missing hours so we're all leaning that way."

"And the daughter? Nelly?"

"Her father is on the list because we can't find any reason to take him off, but Nelly is a different story. Given her background and behavior, if either Smythe is involved most of us here would place our bets on her." Drew's voice fell flat.

"So, we're not out of the woods?" It would be better if it was Smythe's daughter who was involved, but it would still be an interesting negotiation between the intelligence organizations of the US and the UK.

Dani sighed and looked away from the little girl. The valley sprawled below her, bleeding into the ocean beyond. "I know I sound like a broken record, Drew, but we're missing something. There are too many pieces moving with too much precision. It's almost as if there is someone pulling strings somewhere, orchestrating the whole thing. How else can we account for a drug dealer and militia hooking up, or Getz getting into arms dealing?" Her voice trailed off.

Both she and Drew were silent for a long moment. She was conscious of the heat radiating up from the sidewalk, the sounds of birds and children's laughter, but her mind was mulling over what she had just said. It wasn't anything that had formed in her mind before she'd spoken. But now that she'd vocalized it, it felt right. There had to be someone manipulating the whole mess. Who and why was a whole other question.

Drew sighed. "I think you might be right on this. Which is fucked up. The last thing we need is one more player, but without a central person, someone calling all the shots and making the connections, there's no way this level of operation, with this many players, would get off the ground."

Dani didn't answer, knowing Drew was figuring out next steps.

"Fuck," he swore.

"You want me to come home?"

"No," he said after a pause. "Stay there, do your thing. If someone is orchestrating this whole thing, we need to at least keep up the pretense of going along with it. I'll talk to Marmie and Adam. We'll have some changes to discuss when you get back."

And, once again, she knew he was right. Even though she didn't like it. They hung up after she agreed to stay put, as planned. She took a few minutes to breathe before heading back to the car.

Alicia gave her a quick glance when she slid back into her seat. "So why do you want Sonny to be the one?" she asked, returning to the conversation they were having before the call.

Dani stared out the window and didn't answer for a long while. With the idea that someone was manipulating the whole web of events, she forced herself to accept what she had always known. She had wanted Sonny to be the drug source as an excuse to get to him. But whether or not he was didn't matter. In her focus on him, she'd lost sight of the bigger picture. And now that they were considering the possibility of a conspiracy, a conspiracy on the scale of what they were looking at—one that involved European diplomats and South American drug cartels—it put things in perspective. Yes, she'd like to have her chance to talk to Sonny. But what they needed to do was find the person who had the level of power, influence, and access required to pull this off.

Dani sighed. "It's a long story. But not as relevant as it was when we first started this investigation. I'll have my chance to talk to him when the time comes." She picked up her glasses and looked at Savendra's house. She could feel Alicia's gaze on her. Already unsettled by her conversation with Drew, Dani didn't want the extra scrutiny.

"So," she said, changing the subject with a pointed look at Alicia's belly. "Do you know if it's a boy or girl?"

"Girl. I'm going to name her Carolina," Alicia replied, going along after a moment of hesitation.

"That's a good name. I have two nieces and a nephew. Kids are great, but I don't know how my sister does it."

"You don't have any kids," Alicia commented.

Dani shook her head. "Nope, not married either."

"You and me both." Alicia's tone suggested she'd long ago accepted this fact, but didn't necessarily like it.

"I'm prying, I know. So don't feel the need to answer if you don't want to, but is there a reason the baby's father doesn't want to get married? Or do you not want to get married?"

"The father doesn't even know. And before you judge—not that you would," she added as Dani opened her mouth to protest just that. "I would tell him, but I don't know how to find him. We worked together six months ago. I was undercover with the LAPD at the time and I have no idea who he worked for, other than knowing he was definitely a government man. It was a classic cliché. We were riding the high of an extremely successful bust and we ended up in bed. At first I attributed it to the adrenaline but then—" Alicia paused and looked out the window.

"But then you thought it might be something more," Dani suggested, sympathizing with the woman's confusion. She was just beginning to understand what it meant to have that kind thing sneak up on a person.

"Yeah, maybe. It was an amazing night but in the morning he was gone, so then again, maybe it wasn't as amazing as I thought. I just…well, I thought there was more. But, we never bothered exchanging names. I figured it would be easier to go at this myself than to try to track him down only to find out he wouldn't want the baby anyway. And that's the one thing I do know for certain—I want this baby. I already love her and can't wait to meet her."

Dani smiled at the affection in Alicia's voice. She had a long road ahead of her but Dani had to admire the way she was embracing the challenge. Doing what she did for a living, the thought of having a family had never really crossed Dani's mind. But looking at Alicia's smile and thinking of Ty, for the first time in her life, Dani began to let herself wonder what it might be like.

• • •

"You're going to get skin cancer," Fawkes said as he lounged next to her on a big beach blanket two days later.

Dani didn't bother turning around. "I'm not letting you rub more sunblock on me. Besides, we're sitting under an umbrella."

"Okay," Fawkes continued, sounding way too cheery. "Maybe you could rub some on me."

The comment earned him a look. "I've already done that. Twice," Dani replied.

"Yeah but you like having those lovely hands on this hot body. Admit it," he grinned at her. His outrageous flirting was nothing but an act and she had no doubt Fawkes would be on the phone to Ty as soon as the day ended, telling him all about how he'd rubbed sunblock on "Folsom's girl."

"If you really want to get your ass kicked, we don't have to wait for Ty. I could do it," she offered with a laugh and shake of her head.

"You are a girl after my own heart. Come on," he pleaded with her. "Forget Fuller and run away with me."

"You need to shut up. I *am* on a job," she reminded him, her smile taking the sting out of the rebuke. "I have no idea what Ty was thinking when he recommended I bring you with me today," she added as she pulled out her phone and, looking like every other tourist on this stretch of beach, began taking some pictures.

She snapped a couple more photos of Savendra and his friends surfing. She was sure to capture a good facial picture of each of his friends. Marmie probably had them all identified by now but she took a few more for the sake of it. The phone rang just as she decided to take a break and watch the surfing. She'd take more photos when they left the water.

"Hey," Ty said.

"Hi," she replied with a smile.

"The beach looks nice. Fawkes with you?"

"It is and yes, you want to talk to him? He wants me to run away with him, by the way. I think he's thinking Vegas."

"Give him the damn phone," Ty snapped with an irritated resignation.

Dani handed Fawkes the phone; he winked at her and took it. "Hey Folsom. Your girl looks hot in a bikini, by the way," he taunted. Dani rolled her eyes at his shameless teasing.

"You mean, I can't do this?" Fawkes asked as he placed his hand Dani's shoulder. She glanced around at him and he clicked a picture. She could imagine the shot that appeared on Marmie's screen and she had no doubt Ty was watching it download in real time.

Dani assumed the photo had come through when Fawkes covered the phone and doubled over laughing. "You should hear him," he finally said to her.

"Dear god, I bet you were a menace to have as a report," Dani replied as she swiped the phone back with a quickness that left Fawkes surprised.

"No wonder you're so good at dealing with me," Dani interrupted Ty's tirade. He stopped as soon as he heard her voice. "How many years did you have to deal with Fawkes?"

Ty sighed. "Four. Four long years."

"Oh, you poor baby," she crooned as Fawkes made little kissy noises in the background. She smacked him on the arm like she used to smack Jason and Drew. When she was six.

"Ouch," he made a show of rubbing his arm.

"You hit him?" Ty asked.

"Yes, but not hard enough, he's still waggling his eyebrows at me."

"Tell him you'll rip them off," Ty suggested.

"I think not," Dani laughed. "Is there something going on?"

"Nope, just checking in."

"It's boring here, in case you didn't figure that one out. The best part of this whole trip has been getting your friends to rat you out." They both knew this wasn't true. "Savendra hasn't done anything but sleep, watch TV, bowl, and surf. He's on vacation; this little trip has nothing to do with business." And sitting on the beach with Fawkes was heaven compared to the hours she'd spent the two previous nights in the van at the bowling alley with Agent Diamond. It was sheer force of will that had prevented her from pulling her own gun on him.

"Drew agrees. Good thing Savendra is going home the day after tomorrow, you can come back and be bored here. Nothing new is developing on our side of the country, if that makes you feel better," he offered, probably knowing it wouldn't, and it didn't. But she also knew a lot more was going on than Ty was privy to.

Dani sighed. "It doesn't, but I will be glad to be back home. Maybe something will crop up during Adam's trip to Florida. Is Marmie getting anything from the pictures I'm sending?"

"It's the usual suspects. Wait—" Dani heard Ty say something to Marmie but it was too muffled to hear.

"There's a new guy in the group," Ty came back on the line.

"Yeah, the tall blond guy." Dani had noticed him earlier. She hadn't gotten a good face shot until a few minutes ago, which is the picture she assumed Ty and Marmie were looking at. "I haven't seen him before; he looks a bit older than the others," Dani added. Stylewise, the man looked like the other kids—dressed in a wet suit with sun bleached hair, carrying a long board. She was too far away to see how much older he was than the others, but by the way he moved, she'd put him a few years older.

"He is," Ty responded, having the benefit of being able to see the photo in zoom. "By at least eight or ten years, I'd say."

Dani frowned and watched the man chatting with one of Savendra's friends, straddling his board about thirty feet from shore. "You want me to follow him?" she asked. More muffled talk came through the phone and she picked up Drew's voice as well.

"No, Drew wants you to stick with Savendra. He'll call Buster and have him put someone on the blond."

Dani sighed. "I was kind of hoping for a little excitement here, guys," she half jested. "Is there anything else?"

"Nope, that should do it for now. Don't get too burned," Ty added and she could hear the smile in his voice.

"No worries about that. Fawkes has already slathered two layers of sunscreen on me," she tossed out, having a little fun at Ty's expense. Ty let out a not-so-silent curse. "Call you tonight?" she suggested.

She'd talked to him every day since she'd left Maine, but he had always called her and it had always been during the day, always when she was on duty. But what she'd just suggested was a private conversation, a personal one. When she recovered from this discovery, she found she more than liked the idea. She *wanted* to talk to Ty when she was alone, when he was alone, when they could talk about anything—the case, his friends, the weather—anything they wanted to, without having other people listening.

"You have my home number on your phone. Don't worry about waking me up," he answered.

Dani smiled to herself. "Got it, lieutenant," she answered. As soon as she hung up, Fawkes's voice interrupted her thoughts

"Ty and Dani sitting in a tree, K-I-S-S-I-N-G. First comes love— ouch! You have a mean slap, woman."

• • •

After another uneventful night and day, Buster, with Drew's permission, had pulled her from the surveillance team and given her a night off. Dani didn't really need it, but was enjoying it anyway.

"He's a good kid," Fawkes said, referring to Savendra as he leaned against the railing of the pier and looked out on the Pacific Ocean.

"You mean aside from joining a paramilitary militia," Dani pointed out, turning her back on the view and letting the fading sun hit her shoulders.

"He's misguided," Fawkes countered. Dani thought someone had to be a little more than "misguided" to join a group like Eagle's

Wing, but she couldn't summon the argument—she actually agreed with Fawkes.

"You'll be glad to get back tomorrow?"

Dani nodded. "It's a bitch of a flight, military transport and all," she shrugged in acceptance. "But, yeah, I'll be glad to be back."

"So, it's your last night here, sure you don't want to jump into bed with me?"

Dani shook her head and rolled her eyes at his shameless grin.

"Guess not." He gave a dramatic sigh.

"I'm trying to protect you. Ty would surely kill you," she bantered back.

"Yes, he would," Fawkes admitted with a smile. "But even if he wouldn't, you wouldn't sleep with me anyway. You two have it bad. Or maybe good, depending on the way you look at it. I'm inclined to think it's good, since it's Fuller and all."

Dani looked at Fawkes. "I have no idea what you just said to me."

Fawkes shrugged, like he'd just turned shy. Dani continued to look at him. She knew from experience that most men caved under her scrutiny. This big bad SEAL was no different.

"It's the real deal for Fuller. He's a good man. The best. And from what I can tell, I think you guys are a good match."

"What makes you think it's the 'real deal,' and what does that mean anyway?" Dani couldn't help but ask. She knew she shouldn't delve into such a personal topic, but the words were out before she could stop herself.

"See, if I was dating you, I'd make sure everyone on the planet knew you were mine," he cast her one of his trademark grins. "In every way, of course," he added. "But Ty doesn't say anything— other than to post big no trespassing signs."

Dani laughed, feeling a little uncomfortable. "Maybe that's because Ty has more respect for women than you do."

Fawkes straightened and gave her a wounded look as he placed his hand over his heart. "Trust me sweetheart, no one has more respect for women than I do."

Dani arched a single brow at him.

"It's not that. You're right, Ty was never one to kiss and tell—although there was a time or two I *really* wished he would have," Fawkes waggled his eyebrows at her. "But it's different with you. He knows I'm razzing him, but after he razzes me back he goes all silent on me. Not like an I'll-just-wait-Fawkes-out kind of silence. It's more like the silence that happens on horror movies right before the killer strikes. It's quiet and intense and deadly. Not that I think he'd ever actually kill me or anyone else—unless they deserved it, of course," Fawkes added. "But it's intense. Way intense," he emphasized. "I wish I was going back with you. It would be really entertaining to watch the whole thing unfold. Ty wants it. You, well, you want it too, but something is holding you back. And Ty is not a man who accepts half-measures. You're doomed, just so you know."

Not sure how to respond, Dani said "Did you just liken Ty, the man you claim is my boyfriend, to a horror movie slasher?"

"You're missing the point, woman," Fawkes retorted.

Dani watched families on the beach packing up their belongings, couples taking walks, and others out just enjoying the evening. Fawkes's comments weren't a revelation to her. Though she'd never let herself think about it, now that Fawkes had vocalized it, she knew it was true. And it was a part of what scared her. From almost the first moment they met, there was something different about Ty, something different about the way they were together. It had niggled at her conscience that first morning and had scared the bejeezus out of her when she realized it wasn't going to go away. For a while she wasn't sure if it would be worse if Ty didn't feel the same way, or if he did. And then she realized it wasn't worth worrying about—she *knew* he felt the same way. They just had to figure out what to do about it. She had to figure out what to do about it. But trusting him, trusting whatever it was between them, meant giving up control.

Dani sighed and turned toward the ocean. "No, I got your point, Fawkes. Loud and clear."

• • •

Ty lay back on his bed after hanging up the phone. He'd just finished a late-night conversation with Dani, for the second night in a row. He looked at the clock. Two in the morning. And his mind was racing. Talking to Dani did that, but the other reason had to do with the fact that he still couldn't figure out why in the hell Dani and her team were masquerading as DEA. It wasn't that the case didn't look like a DEA case—it did. And that was the problem. If it looked and smelled like a DEA case, it should be a DEA case. Why was the CIA interested?

Like good little DEA agents, their eyes were focused on the drug aspect of the case. They were keeping an eye on the weapons, for sure. And Getz was always on their radar; he would go down with the rest, that was a given. But their focus, as it should be, seemed to be on how the drugs were getting to the Eagle's Wing, who the contact was, what the channel was.

Ty's mind flipped through the people working on the case. He spent most of his time with Marmie and Cotter. He rarely saw Drew or anyone else on the team. Maybe he just *assumed* they were focused on Savendra and Sonny and the drugs. It was possible Drew had a whole team of people in the house researching the weapons.

But anything they were finding they were keeping close to the vest. Dani had talked a little about Getz during their conversation tonight. But her focus wasn't on the drugs or weapons, it was on how to get into Getz's place. She wanted to set up a mock-up of his house, with all the same security in place, and start running trials on how to get onto the property without triggering any of the underwater alarms. She wanted everyone ready in case they needed a silent raid. Which, given the set-up of the house, Ty thought was the best approach. They could go in with guns blazing but there were so many escape routes, people were bound to slip through the cracks. If they could get around the security and get the team in place, positioned over every damned inch of the peninsula, they'd have the best chance of bringing everyone in. Of accomplishing the goals of the mission—spoken and unspoken.

Ty sighed and rolled over, wishing Dani were there with him but knowing she wouldn't be, not for a while. Unable to sleep, and taking a gamble his friend would be awake, Ty grabbed the phone and punched in Jay's number. Jay was a devious bastard, maybe he would have some insight.

CHAPTER 14

DANI SNUGGLED BACK INTO BED. *Her* bed. Well, her bed at her sister's house in Maine, anyway. The flight home had been as brutal as she'd imagined. They had left San Diego at ten in the morning West Coast time and, with stops in Nevada, Texas, and Florida, she'd finally made it into Portland and into bed fifteen hours later, at around four in the morning East Coast time.

She knew Drew would let her sleep in as long as she wanted and, though she knew she wouldn't sleep late, she pulled the covers tighter around her and savored the feeling of her sister's sheets—sheets that had a thread count higher than most countries' GDPs.

She let out a little sigh of pleasure and rolled her head deeper into the soft pillow. She opened her eyes to judge the time of day based on the little bit of light coming in from behind the thick curtains and blinked. And blinked again. Then she let out another a little sigh.

"I'm not even going to begin to wonder why my spidey sense didn't start tingling when you walked in," she said, rolling onto her side and focusing on Ty, who sat less than four feet away, an ankle propped on his knee, watching her.

"I'm quiet," he offered.

"Have Drew tell you about how I saved his life once in Nicaragua. It involves a dark night, a tiny but deadly snake, and my spidey sense. Speaking of Drew, he would not be happy to hear about you visiting my bedroom." But even though she could understand why Drew wouldn't be happy about it, she was hard pressed to care all that much. Waking up to see Ty, well, there were a lot worse ways to wake up.

He smiled at her and she suddenly felt awkward luxuriating in bed. Throwing the covers off, she slid out from under their warmth. Ty snagged her before she could walk away and pulled her onto his lap. Titling her head toward his, he kissed her.

"Before you ask what that was for," he said. "It's called a welcome home kiss, or an I'm-glad-you're-back, or an I'm-happy-to-see-you, kiss. Take your pick, any will do."

Dani stared at him for a long moment. God, she wanted more. She always seemed to be wanting more when it came to Ty. But rather than respond, she rose from his lap and walked to the adjoining bathroom, knowing Ty's eyes followed her.

"Maybe you feel safe with me. Or at least your subconscious does." Ty's voice carried through the half closed door. "And if it makes you feel any better, which I'm not sure it will, Drew sent me." Dani turned on the water and didn't answer. She splashed some water on her face, dried it, then grabbed her toothbrush. There were too many implications to the last part of Ty's comment for her to think about before having a cup of coffee.

"We caught an interesting phone call, yesterday," Ty started talking again. "Savendra placed a call to his uncle from a pay phone in the airport."

• • •

Ty couldn't help but smile at the picture in front of him. Dani stood in the doorway of the bathroom, hair hanging loose over her bare shoulders, wearing an oversized tank top and a pair of boxers that did nothing to hide her amazing body. She had a toothbrush hanging out of her mouth and a look that told him he'd better start talking fast.

"He wants out of Eagle's Wing," Ty responded. He was about to go on when Dani held her hand up, telling him to wait, and disappeared back into the bathroom. He heard her finish brushing her teeth and then she marched back into the room.

"When did this happen and why didn't anyone tell me?" she demanded, her hands planted on her hips. For a brief moment Ty wondered what she would do if he grabbed her and pulled her back onto his lap. He wouldn't do anything else, just hold her. Probably. Not.

"Don't even think about, it Tyler Fuller." He looked up to her face, wondering if she could read his thoughts.

"You're transparent when you get that look on your face," she raised an eyebrow at him. That answered that question. He raised his hands in mock surrender. "Now tell me about Savendra," she continued as she began to gather up some clothes.

"It's not much. But, one of our guys inside the airport heard him talking to his uncle about Eagle's Wing and he wants out. Thinks they're 'really fucking wacko' were his exact words."

"How do we know he was talking to his uncle?" she asked, disappearing back into the bathroom, presumably to change. A shame.

"The power of the USA PATRIOT Act. We knew he was going to be there, he's suspected of terrorist activities, we put wires on the phones."

Dani popped her head out again, one leg shoved into her jeans, and stared at him. "Christ, how many wires did we use? And who the hell still has pay phones around?" she asked. All law enforcement was knowledgeable about the PATRIOT Act, which was passed days after 9/11. The act expanded the power law enforcement agencies had to fight terrorism both in the US and abroad. Even so, the sheer power it granted to them sometimes came as a shock. Like the ability to place wires on any communications device a person suspected of being involved in terrorist activities might use. This included home phones, work phones, computer communication lines, and, apparently, pay phones in the airport.

"Never mind," Dani said, shaking her head and disappearing back behind the door. "I don't want to know the answer to that."

Ty understood Dani's surprise, it still surprised him the stuff they could get away with under the Act. Not that he wasn't an advocate of better tools to fight terrorism. But it sometimes got hard to stomach when the fight included gross violations of innocent people's civil liberties.

"Yeah, so we know he was talking to his uncle. It looks like his uncle set him up with Bradley Taylor, the founder of Eagle's Wing."

Dani came back out, dressed in jeans and a t-shirt, and leaned against the door frame, a thoughtful expression on her face. "Why would a drug dealer want his nephew to get involved with an organization that is, for all intents and purposes, planning a terrorist attack on the US when everyone knows one of the quickest results of those kinds of attacks is a stranglehold on the drug trade?"

"Maybe the uncle doesn't know what Eagle's Wing is about," Ty suggested.

Dani thought about this for a minute before replying. "Maybe," she conceded. "But I'm not sure I'd buy that. Militias and foreign drug cartels don't make good bedfellows. It would make sense that the uncle doesn't know what Taylor is up to, but still—" she cut herself off, lost in thought. "What do we know about the relationship between Taylor and the uncle?"

"Marmie's looking into that," Ty answered, rising to his feet.

"So what did Savendra say?" Dani asked as they moved toward the door.

"Pretty much what I told you. He told his uncle that he didn't like it there. That he wanted to get out but didn't know how. He asked his uncle to talk to Taylor about letting him out."

"The kid was afraid." It wasn't a question.

"Yeah, and the uncle wasn't too sympathetic. He told the kid to grow some *cajones*. In much more colorful language than that."

"So the uncle wasn't opposed to Savendra leaving the group, he was just irked at being asked to help." She stopped at the door.

"Sort of the way it sounded, but Marmie's still looking into it," Ty agreed.

"And where is Adam?" Dani asked.

"He's on his way to Miami now. Sonny is expected to land tomorrow morning. It should give Adam some time to settle in and get to know the locals."

"I wish I were with him," Dani said to herself.

"I'm sure you do but, in the meantime, you still get to go swimming." He walked toward her, stopping a few inches away. Keeping an eye on her expression, he looped his arms around her. He expected her to pull away, to turn and walk away. For all her confidence, Dani was skittish when it came to him. But when she didn't move away, when she leaned into him a tiny bit, his reaction was instantaneous. His arms tightened and her head came to rest below his chin.

"Is that a gun in your pocket, Detective, or are you just happy to see me?" He could feel her smile against his throat.

"When this is all over, I think we should go somewhere where we can swim. Naked." His voice was gruff.

She sighed. "Sounds nice. But, in the meantime, in the real world, we need to track down our wetsuits."

• • •

Thankfully, they didn't need the wetsuits quite so early in the morning. Instead, Ty had arranged a little educational session so that they could all learn everything there was to learn, and probably more, about Getz's underwater surveillance system.

"Well, damn, look what the cat dragged in. We haven't had anything that gorgeous set foot in here in months," Jay commented as Dani and Ty walked into his office.

"He is pretty gorgeous, but you're not really his type," Dani quipped with a smile.

Jay tossed his head back and laughed. Ty rolled his eyes.

"Dani, Jay. Jay, Dani." Ty made the introductions once Jay stopped laughing.

"So you're DEA," Jay commented as he assessed her. She hadn't missed his initial male reaction to her, or his subsequent evaluation that, for a split second, as his eyes swept her body, conveyed doubts about her ability and about how she might have gotten to where she was. But when his eyes met hers in a gaze that didn't waver for a second, Jay nodded in acknowledgement of what she knew he saw there—intelligence, confidence, and the kind of wariness that came with seeing too much of the world and all its nasty bits.

"Well, that's that, then," Jay said, rising from his seat. "Did you bring the aluminum foil?"

Twenty minutes later, they stood with a couple of guys from Cotter's team in a small conference room in the building where Jay kept his offices. Sitting on the table in front of them were the Hunley and Abram. Both machines were the same make and model as those that surrounded Getz's peninsula.

"This is the Hunley," Jay said, placing his hand on the larger of the two machines. It was about two feet tall, a foot in diameter, and shaped like R2-D2. "It's the acoustic monitor Getz has around his place. If it picks up a certain kind of noise, an alarm will sound in the house and you can be sure that, within minutes, some of Getz's finest will be both on and in the water."

"What kinds of noises will trigger it? How does it differentiate between regular ocean sounds and abnormal sounds—sounds worth triggering the alarm?" Dani asked.

"It's a smart system," Jay began to explain to the group. "It goes through a two-week recognition period where it familiarizes itself with the surrounding sounds. It knows the basics when it's installed but it takes some time to learn the subtleties and the nuances. Once it picks up and stores information on the regular, everyday sounds, it will only trigger an alarm when it hears something else."

"Like what else?" Cotter asked.

Jay shrugged, "Anything, everything. Excess bubbles that

come out of a regulator, the sound of any kind of weapon being loaded, human sounds. Even the sound of oars hitting the water or scraping against a boat would set it off."

"Yeah, but aluminum foil will, uh, foil the system?" Dani's lips twitched at the bad pun. A couple of the guys laughed. No one could quite believe it.

"Yeah," Jay smiled back as he tossed each of them some papers detailing the specs of the system. "It's true, we tested it when we found out. But you still need to understand what might set it off, in case you lose your force field."

"Just how much foil are we talking about here?" Spanky asked. Dani heard a couple of the guys shift behind her. They were used to a lot of things: seeing a lot of things, doing a lot of things—ugly things. But not a single one of them relished the idea of covering themselves in foil.

"Not much," Jay answered and Dani heard a collective sigh of relief.

"How much?" Ty asked.

"We tested it a couple of days ago and a few bands in strategic places was enough."

"Will it cause the system to scramble or show any errors?" Dani asked, grabbing a cup of water from the cooler in the corner. The room wasn't meant to hold more than two or three people.

"No, that's the beauty of it. Something about the composition of aluminum foil makes the machine go deaf for a minute or two, only it doesn't know it."

"So what's the layout of these machines?" Cotter asked.

Jay nodded in acknowledgment and turned toward the back wall of the room. He pulled down a marine map of Getz's peninsula that showed a series of red and blue Xs surrounding the land.

"The blue Xs are the Hunley monitors. The red ones are the Abram monitors, but we'll get to those later. As you can see, the Hunleys are arced around the peninsula about twenty-five feet apart. It creates a basic 'wall' around the land."

"What's the range of detection?" Dani asked.

"On a good day, the range can be up to fifty feet."

"Getz chose this option," Jay said, motioning to the map behind him. "It looks cleaner, but from a security perspective, it's suboptimal because, once you get past the single line of machines, you're over the wall, so to speak. And we didn't feel like arguing with him," he added and cast a glance at two of his employees who were smiling and shaking their heads.

"Not that Getz's men could do anything to us that we couldn't do to them in half the time. We just didn't like the guy. Real prick. We figured if the system failed he'd get what he deserved anyway," he added.

Dani glanced at Drew and saw a wry expression on his face. He hadn't been too keen on bringing Jay in but Ty had convinced him. Dani could tell by the smile that tugged at Drew's lips that he was beginning to like the guy.

"Any more questions on the Hunley?" Jay asked. They shook their heads. "We've got it set up in a bay not far from here so we'll take some test runs this afternoon, but we need to go over the Abram system next." A couple of the guys took the opportunity to grab water as Jay moved toward the second machine sitting on the square table. Dani opted for opening a window. They'd gotten spoiled at her sister's place with all that space.

"It looks like something from the evil empire," Spanky commented as they all returned to the table. The Abram machine was smaller, shaped like a basketball. Black in color, it had an ominous look to it.

"It not only looks like something from the evil empire, it acts like it, too," Jay said.

"Meaning?" Dani prompted.

"This is one unforgiving bitch of a system," Jay shook his head, and stared at the machine, as if trying to puzzle out its motives.

"We've got people working on it, working on finding its weaknesses. We haven't found much but we do have two. And they're two substantial weaknesses.

"So, here is how it works," Jay started, moving in front of the machine and pointing to a small black window. "This machine is custom-programmed for use in a specific area. In other words, if you want to use it in Florida, it would be programmed to recognize sharks because they've got them there and you wouldn't want the system going off every time a shark swam by. And, knowing what we know about the area, we can give an educated guess as to what Getz's systems is programmed to recognize. So here's what we think," he moved back toward the marine map with the Xs as he spoke. "Given where we are, where Getz's house is, we're going to recommend that you assume anything over three feet long or two feet wide will be recognized."

"That's not very big and counts all of us out," Dani pointed out.

"Yeah," Jay agreed, "That's the bitch of the system," he moved back to the machine. "As I said, it has two big flaws, and we're going to need to count on those. See these?" he asked, pointing to a series of little black windows. "These are like infrared beams, like the kind you'd see in museum. And, like in a museum, unless you break the beam, the monitor isn't going to pick you up."

"How many are there on each machine?" Drew asked.

"On a standard machine there are eighteen. We didn't install them, but the guy who did installed the standard version. Which brings up a good point, we're working on the assumption he hasn't altered either machine. Given that Getz used two different companies to install the systems, it's possible he used a third to customize them. I don't think it's likely, there aren't many of us who can do this kind of work, but it bears mentioning. But, back to the Abram, the beams can pick up movement up to fifteen feet away."

"Okay, so we have some leeway in how we approach the monitors and I'm assuming we're going to run those trials today as well, so what's the second weakness?" Dani inquired.

Jay smiled. "The machines are completely unreliable." He paused for dramatic effect.

Next to her, Ty sighed. "How unreliable?" he asked.

"If they bump into anything they'll shut off. If a big storm comes and shakes them around, they'll shut off. If it gets too warm or too cold, they'll shut off. And when they shut off they don't raise an alarm. Don't get me wrong, if they shut off, whoever is monitoring the system at the house will know the machine is off, but it won't raise an alarm."

"And how often does this happen?" Dani asked.

"In the three hours we tested four machines, all of them shut off at least once for a time period of at least ten minutes."

"Hell of a system," Dani said. "Do they come back on automatically or do you have to reset them?"

"They come back on automatically in most cases, once the system readjusts or recalibrates, but we did have to manually reset one of the machines," Jay answered, pacing in the front of the room.

"So, if we can get a couple of the machines to shut off at strategic times, given the number of times something similar has, presumably, happened in the past, it's unlikely the guards are going to come running," Ty commented.

"One can hope," Jay gave them all a satisfied, if somewhat feral smile. "The machines have created their own 'cry wolf' situation that we can take advantage of. And," Jay added, moving back to the map, "looking at the placement of each system, I don't think it will be difficult to arrange for a machine or two to accidentally need to recalibrate."

• • •

"Christ, I'm cold," Dani swore to herself as she peeled the wetsuit off her body. Or at least she thought she was speaking to herself.

"It's because you have no body fat." Ty stood next to her, already sans suit. Reaching out a hand, he helped her step out of her own.

"Funny, I thought it was because the water is about sixty degrees," she shot back. She *hated* being cold. She'd soldier through, but she'd never like it.

Ty laughed at her disgruntlement. "We'll get dry suits next time. We should have had them this time."

"Yeah, no kidding," Dani grumbled.

"Dani, are you grumbling about the cold again?" Spanky came up behind her and collected her suit. Unlike her, Spanky was a polar bear, the colder the better.

"Not me," she gave him a toothy smile. "I'm being sweet as a peach."

Her colleague snorted in response. "Remember that time in—"

Dani cut him a look and he stopped mid-sentence.

"Right, I'll go wash these up and get you a dry suit for tomorrow." Spanky turned and walked away.

"That time when, what?" Ty asked with an amused look. He handed her a towel and a sweatshirt.

"It wasn't one of my better moments, I don't feel like reliving it right now," she answered, drying her hair. She pulled the sweatshirt over her shoulders and then stripped the top of her bathing suit down underneath it. The air outside was warm but she was still chilled from the water where they'd been training for the past two hours and needed the extra warmth of the sweatshirt. When it fell to mid-thigh, she glanced down and realized it was Ty's. She looked up at him. He shrugged.

"You looked like you needed it more than I did," he answered. "So, what does Dani Williamson look like when she's not having one of her better moments?"

Dani glanced around for her sweatpants before finding them under a pile of towels. They were a little damp, but better than nothing. She slipped out of her bathing suit altogether, safe in the coverage provided by Ty's sweatshirt, and pulled on her pants. It was a delay technique. She'd cut Spanky off not because he was about to reveal something about her, but because he was about to talk about a nasty operation they'd been on together in the Arctic Circle. Not a place your average DEA agent went. And Dani had no doubt Ty would pick up on that fact.

"Let's just say I get mean and could out-swear even the nastiest sailor." Dani remembered the operation. They had sat in sub-zero temperatures for ten days before the men they'd been waiting for decided to show up. She had been frozen for every minute of every one of those long days. It'd made her cranky and tired, and being tired had made her even crankier. She'd lost a lot of weight, which had made her body feel fatigued, which, shockingly, had made her *even more* cranky. But when the time had come, she'd single-handedly taken out nine of the ten heavily-armed men. "Of course, I also shoot really well when I'm cranky, so maybe being cold has its perks."

• • •

Ty walked into the big house and, for once, it was quiet. Marmie was at her computer, but she was reading. A book. Not a report or a computer printout. He didn't know where everyone else was, but it was almost disquieting.

"Hi Marmie," Ty spoke as he approached her. "It's quiet here this afternoon. Where is everyone?"

Marmie smiled and put her book down. Ty glanced at the title but couldn't make it out since it looked to be written in some sort of script.

"Cotter is out with his men and Jay, doing some more training. Adam's in Miami, the rest of my team is downstairs. Dani is up in her room reviewing some files and Drew is in the library," she recited with her usual friendly but perfunctory manner.

"And Spanky?"

Marmie shrugged but didn't answer. There was no way Marmie didn't know where he was, she just wasn't going to say.

"Dani might be in a good mood by now if you want to go check on what she's up to," Marmie suggested with surprising casualness.

"Any reason she was in a bad mood?" he asked, mulling over Marmie's curious change of approach toward him. He liked the older woman, but he'd always sensed a sort of protectiveness in her when it came to Dani. She sort of circled him like a mother lion trying to figure out if he was a threat to her cub.

"The cold. She hates it. She took a two-hour hot shower when they all got back. She claimed she was feeling human again a little bit ago when she came down for some coffee."

The information dump on Dani in those few sentences was more than he'd ever gotten from Marmie in all their previous interactions. Maybe she'd decided he wasn't a threat—at least not the kind she was looking out for. Dani, on the other hand, well, there was no doubt that she still saw him as a threat. But he'd wear her down.

But not right this minute. Right now he had something to discuss with Drew.

He excused himself from Marmie and made his way through the cavernous house toward the library, smiling all the way. He couldn't help it, something about the house always amused him. It was such a lavish place, filled with beautiful expensive things. But not filled the way a designer would fill a house. It was chock-full of stuff that looked like it was purchased merely because the purchaser liked it. There was no rhyme or reason, no matching pieces, no theme rooms, no continuous style. It was stuff that, though mismatched, seemed to go together. Probably because the person buying it, and Ty assumed it was Dani's sister Sam, had a strong personality and it came through in the things she surrounded herself with. Dani might think she and her sister weren't alike, but he suspected they were more alike than Dani would ever imagine.

"Come in," Drew called from behind the closed library door after Ty knocked. He walked in and closed the door behind him. If Drew was surprised to see him, he didn't show it. He gestured to a leather wingback chair and Ty took a seat—debating how to bring up the subject he wanted to address.

"It didn't go well this morning," Ty spoke, deciding on the abrupt, straightforward approach. Drew raised his eyebrows but didn't say anything, so Ty continued. "You know what I'm talking about. Your team is good and they dive better than ninety-five percent of the divers I know. I bet most have even trained under-water. But even so, they succeeded in getting past both machines only nine out of ten times." And the thought of Dani being in the water that one time it didn't work was the single thought driving this conversation.

"It was their first time out. They're still out there," Drew pointed out. Based on what Marmie had said, Ty figured Cotter and some of his team were still in the water, trying to rectify the numbers.

"And how are they doing?" Ty asked, knowing Drew would be receiving dive-by-dive reports—that he wouldn't wait for an end of the day recap. And, judging by the look on Drew's face, Ty guessed they weren't doing much better than this morning.

"Shit, Drew," Ty shook his head, forgetting for a minute he was talking to the team director. "It's not good enough and you know it," he looked the other man in the eye and held his gaze.

Drew's blue eyes studied him, unwavering for a long moment. His mind was sharp and intense, in stark contrast to his calm demeanor. Drew was taking his measure. Ty wasn't sure what Drew was looking for or if, when he looked away, he did so because he'd found it. But whatever was going on in Drew's mind didn't matter a bit to Ty—all he cared about was making sure the team director had the best people to do the job. He could never eliminate the risk to Dani, but he sure as hell would do whatever it took to reduce it.

Drew sighed and swung his eyes back to Ty. "What do you suggest?"

Ty looked at Drew, "I have a couple of friends from my SEAL days; bring them in. They can shut the machines down long enough to get the rest of the team through and they'll do it every time."

"They're military," Drew pointed out. Technically, US military wasn't supposed to use armed force on the US civilian population. Ty almost laughed—technically the CIA wasn't supposed to be operating against US citizens either. That Drew brought this up was amusing.

"They won't fire any weapons," Ty offered, knowing no

SEAL would willing go into an operation without weapons. They wouldn't be obvious, they might not even fire them, but they'd carry them. "But, if you're worried about protocol, one of our other teammates, Rani Khalid, formed a small securities company, Bright Line Security, when he retired. They could take a leave of absence and sign on with Rani. They'd be civilian." The setup wasn't quite that clean, but it would be clean enough to get away with.

"Bright Line Security," Drew cocked a brow. "Sounds like a day care center," he added.

"It does, but it's not. Rani picked the name as a joke since bright lines were hard to come by in our line of work."

"I know a little something about that myself," Drew replied. Ty studied the man and, for the first time, noticed that Drew looked his age. He wasn't old at thirty-eight, but if he'd entered the CIA right out of college, he'd been doing it for over fifteen years, and Ty knew how much gray a person could see in fifteen years.

"I suspect you do," Ty answered.

"And why would these friends want to do this?" Drew asked, bringing the conversation back on track.

"Because I'd ask them to," Ty responded. Drew's eyes never wavered from his and so Ty opted to continue. "And because they took a liking to Dani when they met her in San Diego. They'd be upset if anything happened to her."

"And you? Would you be upset?"

"Yes."

"Yes? That's all you're going to say?" Drew looked at him with something akin to amusement.

"What is it you want to know, Drew? That I care about Dani?" Ty countered and then continued when Drew remained silent. "You already know I care about her. And since you keep sending me to her room and turning a blind eye, along with the rest of the team, to what is obviously *not* a by-the-book working relationship, I'd wager you approve. Even if you can't outwardly support it." Ty studied Drew's expression. The director's jaw ticked and his eyes were carefully blank. He sensed that Drew had a lot to say on the matter, but the time and place wouldn't allow him to either confirm or deny Ty's assertion. So Ty took the opportunity to say what he wanted.

"So, yes, I do care about her. Very much. But the rest is between me and Dani. And if you're worried about me going off the deep end if something happens to her, don't be. I'm not going to lose it if something happens to her, but I sure as hell am not going to sit around and do nothing when I know how to reduce some of the risk both she, and the rest of your team, face." Ty wasn't convinced he was telling the truth about not going off the deep end, but he was saying what needed to be said.

"You've changed her," Drew said.

Ty shook his head. "Whatever she's doing differently is her choice. Maybe it's because of me, I'd like to think I might be affecting her in a good way, or maybe it's this case."

"Or maybe it's both. And as for being in a good way, well, we'll see. As her friend, I'd say yes, no doubt. As her boss, the jury is still out."

Ty was surprised that Drew allowed himself to comment on the matter, and he knew he should leave it at that. But he couldn't. He couldn't let Drew think Dani might let him down. "You should have more faith in her, Carmichael. Even if she's changing, or probably more to the point, letting herself change, she's not going to screw up her job. It's too much a part of who she is."

Drew raised an eyebrow in a *we'll see* gesture and turned away, ending any more talk of Dani.

"We don't know when this thing with Getz is going to go down, or even if it is going to happen here. It could be a big waste of your friends' time," Drew said, returning to the earlier topic.

"Fawkes hasn't taken leave in a couple of years, believe me, he won't mind coming to the house to hang around for a few weeks. If you don't want him here, he can stay at my place. As for Roddy, he and his wife just had a baby and her family is from a few miles south of here. He also has a lot of leave and his wife is already excited about spending some time with her parents."

"You've already talked to them." It wasn't a question. And Drew wasn't happy about it.

"They know enough about what's going on from when Dani was in town—when you authorized their assistance," Ty pointed out. Drew had approved using Fawkes and Roddy as backup, so to speak, for Dani. "They know I'd like them to come and work on the team but not what we'd need them to do. I've run the logistics by them. If you agree and bring them on, it's your show, it's your job to tell them what you want them to know."

Drew was silent again for a long while. He rose, ending the conversation. "I'll think about it," he said.

It wasn't what Ty wanted to hear but it was better than a flat "no" so he nodded in acknowledgement and left without another word.

• • •

Ty closed the door behind him, and Drew wondered if he was heading to Dani's room. For the first time in possibly forever, he liked one of the guys Dani was seeing.

Except protocol dictated that they not technically "see" one another.

Ty was a good man, and strong enough to handle Dani, which was saying a lot. But Drew also saw the little things Ty did for Dani, like giving her his sweatshirt earlier in the day and sending her restaurant recommendations when she was in San Diego. Things that made Drew understand that, while Ty recognized how strong and capable Dani was, she was still someone he wanted to take care of, still someone who could use a little TLC every now and then. And he did it without making a big deal out of it. Maybe that was why she seemed to accept his attentions—the most surprising development to Drew's way of thinking. It was good for Dani, but it meant additional stress for Drew as he tried to separate what he wanted for her as a friend and what he needed from her as an agent.

And he hadn't been lying when he told Ty that Dani was changing. She'd been the same woman for years—focused, determined, one of the smartest people he knew. And she hadn't changed in those respects. But there was something more to her now, an openness that wasn't there before. A willingness to look at the possibilities. And, as her friend, he did think this was a good thing. It could be a good thing as an agent, too. But because she was changing in new and different ways, and because it was happening in the middle of a mission, Drew didn't know how much he needed to account for the differences between the Dani he'd always known and one he saw her becoming.

Yes, there was no doubt it was causing him additional stress. But if anyone deserved a chance at happiness, Dani did. And so did Ty for that matter. Now all Drew had to do was make sure they got it.

CHAPTER 15

DANI CRACKED HER EYES OPEN and sighed.

"Good morning," she grumbled, snuggling deeper into her warm bed, ignoring the annoying fact that—yet again—she hadn't woken up when Ty had come into her room.

"Morning, sunshine," Ty answered. Dani could hear him getting comfortable in the chair next to her bed. She rolled over and faced him, pulling the covers up and enjoying the feel of the soft material on her bare neck.

"I'll get out of bed soon, I just want to stay warm for one more minute before we have to go out in that god-awful water again," she said.

"No worries, we're not going out in the water today," Ty responded. Dani studied Ty with a frown and wondered how he happened to be "in the know" so early in the morning. She flicked her eyes to the clock and realized that, if he'd already talked with Drew, he must have been to the house earlier than usual. And he didn't look the least bit tired, even though she knew he left late last night, or rather early this morning. She took in his dark eyes and black hair and smooth jaw. He was wearing jeans, a cotton t-shirt and pair of boots. He must have ridden his motorcycle this morning. His ankle was resting on his knee and he was watching her all but devour him with her eyes. His eyes glittered and a smile played on his lips. She'd been caught ogling.

Dani tugged the blanket over her head and groaned with a mixture of embarrassment and resignation. No wonder Drew was worried about Ty affecting her work, though he had been remarkably lenient. She hadn't given a second thought to what she might be doing today, she'd been thinking how much she'd like to run her fingers through Ty's hair. Amongst other things.

"Aren't you the least bit interested in what we *are* going to do today?" Ty teased, as if reading her thoughts.

She heaved a dramatic sigh, flipped the covers back and turned back to Ty. "Yes, and I'm sure you'll be able to tell me."

"We're going on a boat ride."

"And," Dani prompted as she sat up in bed, tossing the covers away.

"And we're going to cruise on by the compound, drop a few surveillance bubbles, and hang out for a while. We'll have to think of a reason to loiter at the edge of the bay, but I'm sure we can think of something."

Dani heard the words and even absorbed the meaning. She wasn't worried about being caught by Getz's henchmen, she wasn't worried about dropping the surveillance bubbles—they'd figure it out. She was wondering why he wasn't making a move to kiss her, like he had yesterday.

As soon as the thought formulated, Dani laughed at herself. Ty raised an eyebrow in question. Since when did she wait for what she wanted? She swung herself out of bed, placed her hands over his arms where they rested on the chair, leaned in, and kissed him. She felt the muscles in his arms flex beneath her hands as he shifted his body forward, trying to lean into her.

The kiss deepened and became almost desperate as Dani held him in place. There was something heady about keeping his arms locked on the chair. Keeping the focus on the kiss, on the way he felt against her mouth and the way he responded to her. For a moment, she was tempted to slide her hands up his arms and her body onto his. But she ended the touch and pulled back to look him in the eye. His eyes were impossibly black now.

"In case you were wondering, that was a good morning kiss," she said, her voice husky. She met his gaze and held it for a long time. They both knew where they wanted the moment to go.

But they both knew it couldn't, not now, not when the team was waiting for them. So Dani shoved away and walked toward the bathroom, shutting the door behind her.

• • •

"How's it going down there?" Ty called over his shoulder, keeping his binoculars trained on the coastline. The gentle wind picked up the ends of his unbuttoned shirt and they fluttered open, pulling the seams further apart and exposing his chest to the cool ocean air. He wore a pair of khaki shorts and deck shoes. All were high quality. All gave the impression of the leisurely wealthy.

"Good," Dani called back from below deck. "We've covered about half of it," she added.

"Any surprises?"

"No, it looks just like the picture Jay painted for us," she added and Ty noted the satisfaction in her voice. Dani and Jay had taken a liking to each other, despite, or maybe because of, their similar brusque attitudes. Ty knew Dani was going to take some measure of pride in the fact that the map Jay provided to her team, the map that contained detailed information about the location of each of Getz's underwater surveillance machines, was going to line up with the underwater mapping they were doing now.

The mapping was being done at Jay's suggestion with support from both Drew and Ty. Jay was ninety-nine percent certain his original map was accurate, but Ty knew, by the way Jay watched Dani, that he'd figured out Dani was, to use an inadequate cliché, special. And like a good friend, he'd stepped up and was being extra cautious. He'd shown up that morning with access to a sixty-foot yacht and several "bubbles" they could drop and use to scan the surrounding area. The scan would pick up rock formations and depths, but it would also pick up all the underwater surveillance machines Getz still had floating around his fortress.

"How close are we now?" Ty asked, his voice tighter than before. With good reason. Four of Getz's men were emerging from the boathouse in a pretty little sloop that looked like it could top about one hundred miles per hour. And if Ty wasn't mistaken, it was a gun they were tucking under one of the seats, out of sight.

"About ten feet further than we were last time," her sarcasm echoed up the galley.

"We have company, honey," Ty's answered. "You might want to come up and say hi."

"How many?"

"Four. Men. And at least one jimmy between them. Probably more."

"I'll be right up," she called back.

Ty watched the boat approach them. He watched the four men as they watched him. He knew how he looked. Relaxed, confident, rich, and casual. In short, he looked like all the other wealthy tourists that made their way to the southern Maine coast every summer. Only he was about two months too early.

He dropped the glasses and watched as the driver throttled back the engine and the boat slowed to a quiet drift.

"Everything all right, sir?" the man behind the wheel asked. All eight eyes locked onto Ty.

Ty smiled. "Of course, it's a beautiful day, I'm not in the office, and it's not often I get to see a betty of a boat like that," he added with a knowing nod at the smaller boat. "She's a beaut. Did you get her around here?" he asked, setting the tone of the conversation.

The driver inclined his head at the compliment. "From France," he answered.

Before he could ask Ty another question, Ty cut him off. "Hey, honey, are you coming up? You've got to look at this boat," he called over his shoulder, knowing Dani was going to wait until the timing was right to appear. "I'm out with my fiancé," Ty offered with a shrug and a grin down at the men below him. "We're getting married this fall and she wanted to check out some properties up here. She used to come up here as a kid." He looked up and down the coast with a deliberate look of appreciation on his face.

"Hey," he spoke, as if the thought had just occurred to him.

"You guys came out of that boathouse. It's a great house and nice piece of property. Any chance it's for sale or rent? We want something secluded and easy to secure for the wedding. Media, you know," he added hoping he could get away with claiming he was something of a celebrity, even if they had no idea who he was.

The men looked confused, glancing between Ty and the house behind them. The man behind the wheel, the man Ty decided to call Groucho for his big mustache, spoke.

"No," he said shaking his head. "You're looking for a place to get married from the water?" He wasn't disbelieving, but there was a healthy dose of skepticism in his voice. And Dani's appearance at his side was the perfect distraction.

"Hey, baby," she said, loud enough for the men to hear, as she sidled up to Ty in a skimpy bikini and her own unbuttoned shirt. She leaned in and gave him a playful nip on his neck as she slipped her hand under his shirt and slid a gun into the waistband of his pants. The feel of the cold metal on the skin of his lower back was almost enough to distract him from the sight of Dani in a bikini. Almost.

As if reading his thoughts, Dani quirked an eyebrow at him out of sight of the men and all but dared him to do something. So he did. He buried his fingers in her hair, tilted her head up and locked his lips over hers. She opened her mouth and he invaded, like he owned it. He could say it was all part of the ploy, but he didn't have any interest in lying to himself.

He thought he might stay there forever, too, kissing Dani, until he heard a cough from below. He pulled back and watched Dani blink a few times and shift her train of thought back to her role, the role they'd decided on before leaving the marina.

She flashed him a huge smile and gave him an overtly suggestive caress before turning to the boat. She gasped. Ty bit his cheeks to keep from laughing. It was such a vapid, dramatic, non-Dani-like gasp. It was the kind of thing most people would have expected out of someone who looked like Dani. And from the rapt attention on the men's faces, it was working.

"Oh, baby," she said, keeping her voice husky. "Look at that baby girl." With strategic absentmindedness, she patted his chest, her eyes locked on the boat. The men below didn't take their eyes from her breasts, which were now hanging over the railing.

"Ooo, she's gorgeous. What does she do?" she asked Groucho. It took the man a full ten seconds to recover from having her attention focused on him.

"One hundred around here. More if we can get somewhere calm," he managed to stutter. Ty tuned them out, knowing Dani was keeping them occupied while the machines clicked away below deck. His eyes surveyed the coastline. There was no sign of any of Cotter's men and he didn't expect to see any. He knew they were there though, taking in everything they could from the details of the boat to whatever they could see from the open boathouse door.

"Can I?" Dani asked, pushing away from the railing.

"Um," Groucho hesitated and then looked at his men—who all looked at him like he was crazy to hesitate. "Of course," he turned back to Dani and smiled.

"Ooo, you're the best," she spoke on an excited breath. "Baby," she said, turning toward Ty. "These nice men are going to let me take her for a spin. I'll be right back." Before Ty could protest, she'd planted a kiss on him that was long enough and hot enough to let the four men waiting for her see just how good she could be. It was an excellent distraction technique—no doubt they'd be thinking about what it would be like to be in his place, rather than what they were doing. It also distracted him for a split second. The split second it took Dani to slip from his side. Doing his best to hide his annoyance— and anxiety—he watched her go.

Not thirty seconds after she'd motored off with a roar of the powerful engine Ty felt his phone vibrate. Glancing at the number, he answered.

"What the hell is she doing?" Drew barked. Ty sighed. He could relate.

"I'm sure you can figure that one out, sir."

"Fuck," Drew bit out. "I don't suppose she's armed?"

"Her body and brains," Ty answered as he watched the boat disappear into the boathouse.

"I'm going to kill her. And then I'm going to hand her over to my mother who will kill her."

"Yeah, well you'll both be getting my leftovers," Ty answered. "Of course, even with just her brains and body, she's better armed than most of America," he pointed out. It was true, but it didn't make him feel better.

"What?" Drew's muffled voice came through. It was obvious the director wasn't speaking to him so he remained silent, focused on watching the boathouse. Willing the boat and Dani to reappear.

"She's got her camera glasses," Drew came back on the line.

"Huh?"

"Her sunglasses. Cotter says they have a camera in them. She's going to get pictures of the boathouse." Drew paused and Ty heard him take a breath. "She's so goddamned sharp, but I'm still going to kill her."

And that was the end of the conversation as Ty heard the distinct click of Drew hanging up. He thought about how much he had in common with the man when it came to Dani. She'd seen an opportunity and grabbed it by the horns. Not only was she buying time for the monitoring machines to finish the scan of the bay, she was going to get pictures of the inside of the boathouse. And whatever else Getz had in there. But despite all this, Ty knew he was going to have a rough time fighting the urge not to shake her when she climbed back on board. Which, he noted with a sigh of relief, would be soon.

The little vixen was on her way back.

Wearing a huge grin.

The four men in the boat probably mistook it for joy at driving their boat. Ty knew better. She was feeling proud of herself for having suckered them and gotten pictures of the inside of the boathouse. And she was going to gloat about it.

"By the look on her face, I can see what our first purchase will be when we head to Monaco next month," Ty spoke to the men as they pulled up and he reached out to help Dani back on board.

"She did take the name of the maker," Groucho answered with a slight nod and smile.

Ty pulled Dani up and wrapped an arm around her waist, anchoring her against him. It was a little too late, but still, he needed the feel of her next to him. They stood that way for a while, watching the boat turn, waving to the men, looking for all the world like a harmless, rich couple out for a day of sightseeing.

When the boat full of Getz's men turned back into the boathouse, Ty took Dani's hand and tugged her down below deck. The minute they were out of sight, he pressed her against the wall and kissed her. He didn't care that, through his touch, she would know how worried he'd been when she climbed aboard that boat. He didn't care that she could feel the tremor in his body when he thought about what could have happened to her in the boathouse. And he didn't care that the adrenaline coursing through his body was making him rough and demanding.

The moment he touched her, the only thing he cared about was the feel of Dani against his skin. His hand moved from her bare waist to her thigh, urging her leg around his waist. He needed to feel her, all of her. And when her leg wrapped around him, he pressed against her even harder, feeling her whole body against his. Need surged through him when a little sound escaped her and she pressed back against him, moving her hands from his neck, down his chest and to the button on his shorts. Her mouth was just as demanding against his. The dam had broken and everything they'd been keeping in check broke through in their every touch.

Or tried to. Her hands were on his zipper when his phone vibrated on his hip. They both froze and, for a long moment, their gazes locked. Ty was breathing hard, as was Dani, and he could still feel the heat pouring off of her. The boat rocked beneath them. The phone vibrated again.

Using more will power than he thought he possessed, he pulled back and answered the call.

"She's fine, we're pulling up the monitors," Ty said. "Dani held them off long enough that we've got a map of the whole bay now." He was surprised at how casual his voice sounded considering that not one minute earlier he'd been *that* close to burying himself inside Dani again.

"And it matches the map Jay gave us." Dani had moved away from him and was looking at the information on the computer screen in front of her.

"We'll head in now," Ty said, ending the call. He turned to find Dani watching him. A curious expression on her face.

"What?" he asked.

"For a moment there I thought you were going to tell me to never do what I did again. Leave, alone, unarmed," she clarified. Ty studied her face and knew she was trying to figure out what it meant that he hadn't. He knew it could mean anything from her knowing he trusted her to the possibility that he didn't care.

He let out a deep breath and moved closer to her. Reaching out, he stroked his fingers along her cheek, all that he trusted himself to do. "Believe me, I wanted to. But that would have been pretty stupid. I know you have a job to do, a job you do well, a job you've been doing for years before we met. I hated watching that boat disappear into the house. I hated not being able to see you. I think it took a few years off my life. And I wish you'd taken me with you. But I know why you did it and I even respect how you did it. You saw an opportunity and took it. I'd be hard pressed to tell you not to do it again."

Dani watched his eyes and then offered him a tentative but genuine smile.

"Of course, if you ever do something like that when we're not trying to stop a terrorist attack or bust up a major drug distribution chain, I can all but guarantee my reaction will be very different," he smiled back, stroking his thumb over her lower lip and then replacing it with his own lips.

"We should head back in," he said, pulling away. "It's not what I would like to do right now, but I do have a surprise for you when we get back."

"A surprise? I love surprises."

CHAPTER 16

"FAWKES!" DANI EXCLAIMED AS THE man himself swung her up in his arms, ignoring Ty's scowl. "When did you get here?" she demanded as he set her down, keeping his arms looped around her waist.

"Early this morning, only to find out you've run off with another man. Tell me I'm not too late, sweetheart," he answered, placing his hand over his heart in a dramatic gesture. "You know I'm the one for you," he added with a wink.

"The only thing I know about you, frogman, is that you may not last the day with the way Ty's scowling at you," she responded.

"Come with me baby, and we'll make a quick getaway. I've always been able to outrun Folsom and I'm sure I still can, even if I have to carry you," he teased as he swung her into a fireman's hold. She laughed and swatted him on the butt.

"I told you you're my kind of woman," Fawkes grinned at the gathering crowd in the kitchen.

"Put me down," she managed to say.

"Not until you say the magic words," he teased, oblivious to the stares.

"Please," Dani added.

"Not quite there yet, darlin'. Try again."

"You're the man for me and I'll run away with you?" she said, not quite able to keep a straight face.

"Such sincerity," Fawkes answered.

"How about put her down, Fawkes. She's federal law enforcement." Ty's voice broke through the fun. He knew Fawkes was harmless, but he still didn't like the fact that his hands were on Dani's thighs.

Fawkes laughed and slid Dani from his shoulder. "See, it's that intense serial killer thing I was telling you about," he said with a knowing nod and meaningful look at Dani—who rolled her eyes at him.

"Stop taunting the locals," Dani smiled at Fawkes as she slipped her arm through Ty's. "He's had a rough day."

Fawkes rolled his eyes. "Yeah, I can see how rough it was," he said with a pointed look at their clothes. Ty was still in his shorts and button down Cuban shirt and Dani was in shorts, her bikini top, and an open shirt.

"I, on the other hand," he added, making puppy dog eyes, "have been decked out in a dry suit and making mincemeat out of a certain security system."

Dani's eyes widened and went to Ty, who shrugged.

"You've been called in to help out?" Dani asked, all business now.

Fawkes picked up a couple of nuts from a bowl on the counter and tossed them into his mouth. "Yep, me and Roddy are here. You guys are good and all underwater, but what can I say? Roddy and I are the best. And certain people," he added with a wink and jerk of his head in Ty's direction, "suggested it might be better to have the best people on the job than to risk the people you have." Ty sighed.

"So what are you doing?" she asked as Drew entered the kitchen.

"Oh, Dani, Ty," he said in acknowledgment. "You're back. Good. We need to go over a couple of things. In the study, please." He included Fawkes in his line if sight before turning and leaving without waiting for acknowledgement.

"The king awaits," Fawkes said with flourish and held the door open as Dani and Ty preceded him through.

• • •

Dani cast a look around the room. Navy SEALs, Portland Vice, the CIA. It almost sounded like a bad joke. But there was an easy camaraderie already and, though Dani noticed it, it felt like something she shouldn't, or didn't want to, question. So she turned her attention to Drew.

"So, here is the plan for tomorrow," he began as he pulled out the map of Getz's bay. "Roddy and Fawkes have been testing the systems all morning in the mock-up Jay set up in the bay a bit further north. They nailed it every time." He gave a nod of acknowledgment toward Roddy and Fawkes, who both gave a sharp, businesslike nod back.

"We're confident they know their way around those machines and so tomorrow we're going to do a test run. Dani, Ty, you'll go out on the boat again tomorrow. You'll head north but drop Roddy and Fawkes in the water as you pass Getz's place. They'll swim in and have a look around as you two continue to head north. We'll give them about forty minutes for the initial pass. You'll have to swing around and pick them back up." He looked up from the map to make sure the four of them understood the plan. They all nodded back.

"I presume a moving pickup won't be a problem?" Drew asked, referring to the fact that she and Ty wouldn't be able to stop the boat during the pickup without calling attention to themselves. The question was directed at Fawkes, who glanced at Ty and then gave a simple shake of his head.

"Dani, Marmie's got the pictures you took of the boathouse with your sunglasses today?" he asked. Still displeased with her actions, his voice thinned a bit. Which she ignored.

She nodded and then pulled up the blueprint of the boathouse. "There's a door here," she pointed to a section of the wall that went straight into the cliff side. "And one here," she pointed to another spot. "There was a huge boat parked in the other bay so I couldn't get a good look around it to this wall," she said, drawing a line down the wall farthest from the bay. "But I think it's safe to assume this second door goes up to the house. I'm not sure where this first door goes but I'd bet some money there is a good dry storage space cleared out of the cliff right behind it."

"Intuition?" Drew asked.

"That and the door," Dani inclined her head, studying the map. "The door was a vault-like door. Steel, probably thick, and I could see the sealing—like they wanted to keep the moisture out. And there were a few locks on it. I saw at least three but I bet we'll see more in the pictures."

Drew nodded and turned to Ty. "We've got the maps finalized?"

Ty nodded. "The information was transmitted to Marmie from the boat. I suspect she's taking the information and overlaying it on the topographical map to get a better image."

Drew nodded and reached for his phone. Placing a quick call to Marmie, he confirmed that the detailed maps would be available within fifteen minutes.

"I'll make sure you get copies of them as soon as we do," he said to Fawkes. "Do you and Roddy need anything else? Any equipment, space?" he added.

Fawkes thought for a moment before answering. "Just a room would be good. We'll need to take a look at all the maps, find the best entry and exit points. It would be nice to be able to spread out."

Drew glanced at Dani. "The library is open," she offered. "So is the breakfast room."

"Isn't this the library?" Fawkes asked with a glance at the books surrounding him.

"This is the study. The library is on the second floor," Dani answered as she looked back down at the maps.

"Oh, well, yes, of course," Fawkes responded, done with business for the day.

"I could put you in the dungeon," Dani shot back with a small smile.

"You going to chain me up?" Fawkes shot back.

"Okay, kids," Drew broke in with sympathetic look at Ty.

"Time to get back to work. Dani, Spanky will be here in a minute, we need to go over a few things."

She didn't give Drew another look, she knew what they were going to be talking about. She stood and walked with Fawkes, Roddy, and Ty to the hallway and pointed them in the right direction. Ty gave her a questioning look that was more professional than personal, before he turned on his heels and headed up the stairs.

As she turned back toward the study, Spanky rounded the corner and together they entered the room where their director was waiting for them.

"Spanky?" Drew said without pretense as soon as the door clicked shut behind them.

"Keogh is definitely involved," he said, handing each of them a file. "All our intel indicates that Smythe doesn't have a clue."

"Which doesn't come as a huge surprise, though it's nice to know we won't be having to tell MI6 that one of their diplomats is an arms dealer. What about Nelly?" Drew asked.

"She's a different story." Spanky handed them photos of Keogh and Nelly together in various settings, including walking hand in hand through the cargo area of the airport.

"When was this taken?" Dani asked, holding up that last picture.

"Two days before the crate of weapons showed up in Smythe's staging area."

"Scouting mission?"

"That's my guess."

"Do we have anything more concrete?" Drew asked.

"We're trying to tap into the phones, but don't want to go through the regular channels, for obvious reasons." Which meant they were relying on satellite interceptions. The technology was good, but unless they had the funds, or power to keep it locked on a specific target, the intel they got would come in fits and spurts, as various satellites moved into, and out of, position to pick up the conversations.

Drew nodded, then glanced at her, before picking up yet another file. "Dani, I told Spanky about our conversation the other day. I had him dig to see if he could come up with any people who might possibly have the connections, access, and motivation to manipulate this situation."

"Any luck?" she asked. Finding that kind of connection was an almost impossible task. They *might* be able to find someone who knew Getz, Eagle's Wing, and Keogh. And they could probably find someone with the power and influence to set everything in motion. But finding someone with both?

"We're trying. And we're going to keep trying. We're working all the angles," Spanky responded.

"What do you think?" she pressed.

"About whether we'll find the link? Or our theory?" he asked.

"The theory," she clarified.

Spanky paced in front of her and ran a hand through his hair. "I don't like it. Not because I don't think it's a good fit, but because if it is, whoever is doing the manipulations is a powerful bastard. Probably more powerful than we can imagine."

"But you think it's possible?" Dani pressed.

Spanky frowned. "Yeah, I do. Drew and I talked about it a lot after he talked with you in San Diego. It's the only thing that makes any sense. Not only are some of the players involved natural antagonists, some are even directly at odds."

Dani didn't waste her time feeling gratified that her theory was looking to be true. Turning to Drew, she spoke. "So what do you want us to do now?"

• • •

Hours later, Dani and Ty were making their way up to her room. She was carrying yet another manila file filled with photos but she doubted she'd get to any of them tonight. She and Spanky had spent hours poring over possible links between the parties involved in the case, researching where and when they'd traveled, and then trying to connect the dots with known players who would have the kind of influence needed to orchestrate the operation. And, like she suspected, they could come up with a few potential links and a few potential names, but they could not get any of *those* to connect.

"It's two in the morning, you might as well sleep here," Dani commented to Ty as they climbed the stairs.

"Right after Drew kicks my ass twice, I'm sure I'd make a perfect bedfellow," Ty smiled.

"Twice?" Dani asked, tossing the file on the bed. A scattering of photos fell out and slid across the quilt. Dani ignored them in favor of brushing her teeth and washing her face.

"Once for professional reasons and once for personal ones," Ty raised his voice so she could hear him over the running water.

"You're growing on him," Dani replied, emerging from the bathroom as she dried her face with a towel.

"Yes, but not enough to let me sleep with his top agent—and quasi little sister—in the middle of an operation," Ty stood by the window and watched Roddy's car disappear down the drive. When Dani didn't answer, he turned from the window and seized at what he saw. Dani was standing at the foot of her bed, sheet white and shaking.

"Dani, Christ. Are you okay?" he asked moving to her side. Only he didn't make it. She turned on her heel and ran for the bathroom, slamming the door behind her.

Ty made it to the closed door before he heard the unmistakable sounds of someone getting sick. He hesitated for a split second, wondering if Dani would want her privacy, and then decided to hell with it and burst in.

"Go away," she managed to say between heaves.

"Not going to happen, sweetheart," he mumbled under his breath as he crouched beside her and held her hair as she retched again. Blindly, with his free hand, he reached over, felt around, and found the discarded towel. He dumped it in the sink, turned on the cold water and let it soak. Pressing it against the side of the sink, he squeezed a fair bit of the water out before dabbing it against the back of Dani's neck.

After a few minutes she seemed to be done retching, so Ty flushed the toilet and helped a still-shaky Dani to sit on the closed lid, head down. When she looked steady enough, he stood, grabbed a glass, filled it with water, and handed it to her. She looked up and then took the glass from his hand and took a sip.

"Are you okay?" he asked, kneeling beside her again. She took a deep breath, closed her eyes, and nodded.

"Um, out of curiosity, could you be pregnant?" Ty asked. That got Dani's attention. She looked up and gazed at his face, as if looking at a complete stranger, and then frowned.

"Why would you ask that?" she said, her voice quiet and hoarse.

"The sickness came on so fast. I remember my sister telling me about it. One second she'd be fine, then the next she'd be on her knees. And it has been a couple of weeks since that night. I know we used condoms, but they aren't foolproof," he added.

Dani looked at him for a long time, as if it were taking her a very long time to process his statement. And then she shook her head. "I get those shots, too. Four times a year. Between the two, I don't think I'm pregnant."

Ty took a deep breath and let it out, surprised by his lack of emotion at her response. If it had been any other woman, he would have been relieved there hadn't been an "accident." But with Dani, he wasn't relieved, nor was he disappointed.

"Are you okay? Do you think you can make it to the bed?" he asked, moving to stand over her.

"I'm fine...I just...I saw...oh god," she said before sliding off the toilet, flipping the lid, and retching again. Her shaking was so intense she couldn't hold herself up, so Ty curled behind her and held her steady. When she finished, she went limp in his arms and, if it weren't for the subtle fluttering of her eyelashes, Ty would have thought she'd passed out.

"Hold on, honey," he said as he slid from behind her, wrapped a towel around her shoulders, and propped her in the corner. Her head lulled back and Ty considered calling Drew for medical assistance. But then she closed her eyes and he could see her take control of her breathing again.

Working fast, he stepped into the bedroom, gathered up the photos and pulled the blankets back. Returning to the bathroom he handed Dani another glass of water and she dutifully took a small sip. He rinsed the towel again and used it to wash her face. When he was done, he picked her up, cradled her against him, and carried her to the bed.

"The pictures..." Dani mumbled.

"They're on the bedside table," Ty soothed as he placed her on the bed. Then he stripped down to his t-shirt and boxers and slid in next to her, pulling the covers up over them. Drew could do whatever he wanted, but there was no way Ty was going to leave Dani tonight.

"I need...Drew. To talk to Drew," she mumbled.

"Tomorrow, honey. Not tonight. You're not going to do anything tonight but rest." To add emphasis to his statement, he pulled her close against him, hoping some of the heat from his body would stop her shakes. Tucking the covers around them, he felt her resist and then, as he soothed her with meaningless words and gentle strokes to her hair, her body relaxed. All but a single hand that gripped his shirt throughout the night.

CHAPTER 17

"WHERE IS SHE?" TY DEMANDED as he flung open the door to the study. Drew stood at his desk, looking grim faced and pissed. Ty couldn't have cared less. It was eight in the morning and he had no idea how long Dani had been gone from their bed.

"Back off, Fuller," Drew replied. "This isn't about you."

Ty held back from decking the man. He knew something about Dani and like hell would he let Drew keep it from him. He advanced on Drew, who didn't back down. As Ty approached the desk, he glanced down and saw a photo with a red circle drawn around a man in the background. Ignoring it, he raised his eyes and met Drew's gaze.

"If it's about Dani, it has everything to do with me." His words were quiet but his tone made it *very* clear to the man exactly where he stood when it came to Dani.

Drew stared at him for long time. Ty watched the muscles tick in his jaw and saw the deliberation in his eyes. Drew wasn't happy about something but he didn't think it had to do with him or Dani, not directly anyway. He looked like a man who'd just had his plan shot to shit and was being forced to rely on plan B—when there was no plan B.

"Where is she," Ty repeated again.

Drew swallowed and, for a fleeting moment, Ty could see pain in the man's eyes. But then Drew shook his head and turned away.

"She said she was going to the shooting range. At least that's what her note said. I didn't see her this morning."

Ty didn't take the time to respond, he just turned and stalked out.

He found her where the note said she would be. He watched her for an hour. She stood three lanes down from his observation point, oblivious to the comings and goings around her. He'd never seen her quite like this before. Yes, he'd seen her intense and focused, but this—this was the stuff of demons. The target at the end of the shooting gallery had a face, if only in her mind. And Dani blew it away time and time again.

When he couldn't take it anymore, couldn't stand to watch her hurt all alone, he pulled on his ear guards and entered the range. The next time she stopped to reload, he stepped behind her, pulled both their ear guards off and out of the way, and wrapped his arms around her waist. For a split second, he could feel her gratitude that he'd come as she relaxed against him. And then, in an instant she pulled away and continued to reload.

"That's enough, Dani," he whispered in her ear.

"You have no idea," Dani shot back. Ty raised his hands and cupped them over her forearms, pulling them back down to her sides. She stood there, rigid in his arms.

"Then tell me, Ella," he whispered against her hair. And it triggered something in her. Her arms dropped to her sides, her head fell back to rest on his shoulder and her eyes closed. And he just held her.

"I'm so tired, Ty. Take me away somewhere." Her voice was nothing more than a whisper but it was etched with so many years of pain that even Ty had to close his eyes under its weight.

"God, Dani," was all he managed to say.

They drove for hours. Through country roads, along the coast, everywhere Ty could think of that might soothe Dani. She didn't talk for a long time and when she drifted off to sleep, Ty called Drew to let him know she was with him and that they wouldn't be back to the house for a long while. It was the first time in his life, and probably Dani's, that he'd put off his duty for personal reasons. He could argue that he'd pulled the two of them that day because

Dani wasn't fit to fulfill her duty and he'd be telling the truth. But it wasn't the reason. He was making Dani, and her health and mental state, the priority in his life and he felt, bone deep, it was the right thing to do.

He pulled into a deli, picked up a few sandwiches and drinks, and made a call, all while Dani continued to sleep. A few minutes later, he drove to the marina, parked, and woke Dani with a gentle touch.

She looked around and then asked, "Where are we? What time is it?"

"We're at a marina north of town, I have a friend who has a boat here. It's close to five and little early for dinner, but you haven't eaten all day. I thought we could just sit on the boat for a while and watch the water?"

Dani turned her gaze to the water, watched it for a while, then nodded and opened the door.

Twenty minutes later, Ty handed Dani a glass of iced tea and slid down to the deck of the boat where she was sitting, legs hanging over the edge, arms over the first rung of the safety railing, staring out at the Atlantic Ocean. She glanced at the glass and then looked up to study Ty. After a few minutes she mumbled her thanks and took a sip.

"How are your shoulders?" he asked. The amount of shooting she'd done that morning was bound to have an effect on her arms and shoulders. Not to mention the fact that she'd followed the spree with several hours of sitting inert in a car.

In response, she rolled her shoulders, testing them. "They'll be a little sore tomorrow, but I should be okay."

Ty let a few minutes pass before he asked. "Will you? Be okay?"

The silence stretched between them, but Ty didn't doubt she would answer. Finally, she spoke.

"When I was thirteen, my sister Sammy and I were supposed to have a sleepover at Lucky Adams' house. My mom loaded us up into the car and drove us down the road. It was summer and we were in the Hamptons, as usual. By the time we got to the Adams' house, I was sick as a dog. One of those sudden virus things, I guess." She paused, staring out at the harbor.

"Anyway," she resumed, "I came back with my mom, lying down in the back seat the whole time, I was so sick. When we got home, I went straight to bed. Sometime later, I don't know how long, I woke up and heard voices. I knew my dad was coming for the weekend, so I thought it was him. I wanted to see him. Even though I felt so sick, I still wanted to see him.

"I managed to crawl out of my bed and make my way to the top of the stairs. And then, I don't know what happened, instinct kicked in? Something didn't feel right. I was terrified but didn't know why." Dani shivered as a soft breeze blew across the boat. A bell rang in the distance.

"I froze in the hallway and listened. I heard my dad talking to someone and the tone of his voice scared me even more. He was angry. Not screaming and yelling angry, but the kind of angry you get when someone disgusts you. I didn't know what it was then, but after doing what I've been doing for as long as I've been doing it, now I recognize it. It's the kind if tone you use when someone is so disgusting that their mere presence on the planet is offensive. And I don't just mean people who don't bathe. I'm talking about traitors, backstabbers, turncoats, that kind of thing." She turned to Ty for acknowledgment. He brushed his fingers across her check, tucked a piece of hair behind her ear, and nodded. He did know the type. All too well.

"I was terrified, but wanted to know who my dad was talking to. After a few minutes, I gathered up the courage to peek around the corner." Dani paused and took a deep breath before continuing. Her face was pale and her arms were wrapped around herself, trying to stop her body from shaking.

"And I saw a man with a gun. I'd never seen a real gun before but I was old enough to know that's what he held in his hand. I don't know how long I stood there before I realized I needed to do something. I was shaking so hard that I was afraid I would press the wrong buttons on the alarm system. But some angel was looking over me that day. I crawled down the hall to the upstairs alarm pad. I pushed in the silent alarm code and then snuck into my parents' room and dialed 911. I don't remember doing all that, but I've been told it's what happened. I do remember telling the 911 operator there was a man with a gun in my house. I remember her telling me to stay on the line. And then I remember standing at the top of the stairs, holding the phone, watching.

"The argument was getting more heated in a quiet sort of way. My dad sat down and I thought it wasn't a good idea for him to relax around a man with a gun. In retrospect, I know he was trying to convey that he wasn't concerned about anything the man with the gun could do to him. Whether he believed that or it was a bluff, I have no idea. But then my mother walked in." Dani's voice broke. She closed her eyes again, took a few deep breaths, and then gathered strength.

"I can imagine he, the man with the gun, saw my mother as both a threat and an opportunity to prove to my dad that he was serious. My mom had about as much time as it took her to take in the fact that my dad wasn't alone before the man shot her. Execution style, in the middle of her forehead."

Ty swore under his breath and took Dani's hand in his. She didn't resist, but she didn't welcome him either. He didn't take this as a rejection. He knew she just didn't have the energy to do anything else but talk.

"Everything happened so fast after that. My father jumped up and the man turned his gun on him and shot my father in the same way. I must have screamed or something because he turned and looked straight at me. I didn't remember anything about his face but his eyes—until today. But his eyes were burned into me. Even from the top of the stairs I could see they were ice blue and expressionless. He looked at me like he'd done nothing more than take the trash out. No sign that he'd just killed two people. No sign that he cared or that the two lives meant anything to him. He just stared at me and raised his gun in my direction."

Dani stopped talking and gazed out at the ocean for a long

time. She shook her head like she was still trying to puzzle out what happened that day. "I don't know," she said. "The next thing I remember is coming to in the hospital with Sammy and Karen, Drew's mom, at my bedside. I guess I'd been conscious the whole time, but I was in shock. I don't remember why he didn't shoot me. I don't remember the arrival of the police, or even being taken to the hospital. Some sense of preservation must have kicked in and blacked it all out. I remember coming to and seeing Sammy and Karen, eyes red and swollen, and I knew it wasn't a dream."

"Oh, honey," Ty said wrapping his arm around her shoulder.

This time she leaned into him as the boat swayed beneath him.

"I can imagine that the police arrived right as he was deciding whether or not he had time to come after me. I must have run because the police report said they found me curled up on my parents' bed. Maybe he figured it wasn't worth the risk? I wondered for a long time if I was grateful for that decision or not." Dani pulled her legs up and curled them at her side as she leaned more fully onto him.

"I got sick after that. In two years, I didn't gain any weight. I was comatose but functioning. I don't know if that makes any sense, but I was physically fine, other than the weight—but I wasn't *there*. I ate, bathed, and did all the necessities, but I almost never spoke and almost never left my room. Karen and Andrew, Drew's parents, became our guardians and fought tooth and nail to keep me home with them. I guess the doctors wanted to put me in a hospital but the Carmichaels would have none of that. Karen homeschooled me as much as she could—as much as I would let her. Jason, who was still living at home, and Sammy did their best, too. I think the truth of the matter was, I had no will to live." The thought of a young Dani scared, locked into her own hell, alone, twisted his heart. He pulled her closer and, resting his cheek on the top of her head and closing his eyes, gave thanks that she hadn't given up.

"Finally, during the first weeks of summer two years after the shooting, Drew came home from his second year in college and got through to me. I don't remember how he even convinced me to take a walk, I just remember sitting on the boat dock with our feet hanging in the water and staying that way for a long time. Drew put his arm around me and said 'Talk to me, kid,' and I did. I cried, I talked, I told him everything I remembered. It had been locked inside me for so long that I think, once I started talking, I didn't want to stop. I must have told him the story a dozen times, crying harder and harder each time." She wrapped her arms around Ty and rested her head against his chest.

"By the time I was talked and cried out, it was almost dark. We stayed though, and watched the moon rise. Drew knew then that he wanted to go into the CIA, so he offered me a deal. Once he could, he would do anything he could to help find the man who killed my parents. In return, I had to get strong, physically and mentally.

"The deal worked and I regained my strength. I started with yoga, then moved on to Tai Chi, and then I worked my way through all the other forms of martial arts. When I was eighteen and could go to the shooting range without permission, Drew started taking me. And then I went on my own. By then, Drew was working for the CIA and he started to bring me pictures of anyone who might fit the description I'd given him. By the time I was twenty-three, I'd finished my bachelor's and master's degrees and entered the CIA myself. Drew was senior enough at that point that he took me onto his team—it was beneficial for both of us. Our families have known each other forever and our family businesses are intertwined enough that it's a great cover for us when we travel together. But regardless, we've kept our deal all these years—he still gives me pictures and information and I work on staying strong."

Dani smiled at this last statement. "At this point, I don't think it's much of a deal, but we stick to it anyway."

"And this morning?" Ty prompted, running a hand down her back.

"It was him," Dani's voice became stronger. "Sitting in a chair behind Sonny at some café in Miami. I was so shocked, after all these years, to see his face that I think I—well, you know how I reacted."

Ty pulled her closer and dropped a kiss on the top of her head. "And how are you now?"

Dani seemed to ponder this for a while before answering. "I'm good," she said, and Ty could hear the truth in her voice. "I was shocked and it took me back for a while there, but I feel okay now, relatively speaking. We can work on getting an ID on him and go from there. I won't ever be able to forget what happened, but at least I can work on bringing the man to justice."

He didn't answer, thinking that if it was justice Dani wanted for the man, she was much more forgiving than he.

"Ty?" she said after another long silence.

"Hm?" he answered, still holding her close, her head back on his shoulder.

"I've never told anyone, other than Drew, what I just told you."

Ty took a moment to digest this and then pulled her closer, resting her whole body against his. She didn't require an answer, so he didn't offer one. She just wanted him to know.

"You realize you blew your DEA cover by telling me that you're with the CIA?" Ty pointed out, after the moon had risen even more.

"We knew you knew," Dani answered.

Ty laughed. "We knew you knew," he mimicked, making Dani laugh, too. "Who blabbed?"

"Your brother. Who is a great guy, by the way," she answered.

"Yeah, so great he ratted me out," Ty said, but without malice.

"Not exactly, if it makes you feel better. I saw the email address on the information you gave to Drew, I recognized it and called him to check it out. I've worked with Cameron a couple of times over the last few years. I knew his last name was Fuller but there are a lot of Fullers out there so I didn't make the connection right away when we contacted them for information on Getz's equipment."

"Still, he didn't tell me he told you," Ty pointed out.

"You going to tell your mom on him?" Ty was happy to hear the relaxation in her voice.

"So, tell me why you guys are in on this operation? And I assume you had some idea the blue-eyed man was involved somehow with Sonny, which is why you pitched a fit about going to San Diego rather than Miami. And why Drew opted to send you to San Diego rather than Miami, come to think of it," he added.

"I did know, but not until we were onto Getz." And she told him about Jonathon Smythe, the weapons, and how the weapons led to Getz. This part of the story was new to him, but he knew the rest from the files he'd read the other day. Once they were onto Getz, they'd found Eagle's Wing and Sonny Carlyle.

"And when I saw Sonny's name in conjunction with the Eagle's Wing, I knew."

"How?"

"His dad did some occasional work for us," she explained. "He wasn't an agent or even a contractor. He kept his ears open and, on occasion, passed on interesting bits of information to us, but that was all. So, when he was killed, we knew. And we knew how he was killed before we ever knew about Smythe and Getz." She took a deep breath before continuing.

"The murder caught my attention because he was shot execution style and something about the scene was too similar to my parents' murders—and to a few other murders that have come to my attention in the past several years. I had kept my eye on it, more out of curiosity than anything else," she admitted before moving on.

"And you think the man who killed your parents may be the same man who killed Sonny's father?" Ty asked.

"I think it's too much of a coincidence to have two people in similar industries, killed in the same way, so yes, I think it's the same man."

"Which is why it came as such a shock when you saw him in the picture with Sonny. The last man you'd expect to see hanging around the son is the man who killed the father."

Dani nodded. "And, because he was there, it makes me wonder what else he might have planned. I know how vulnerable Sonny might be. And for a few days we've been thinking someone must be pulling all the strings in this situation. Maybe it's him?"

"You think the man who killed Sonny's father might have convinced him the government was behind his father's death and he should get back at them by joining the militia?" Ty asked, intrigued by this new information.

"Or that the government wasn't doing enough to solve his father's murder. I think either would be motivation enough for a young man, angry over his father's death."

Ty mulled this over. He didn't know enough about Sonny to say, but if he was a hotheaded kid, he could easily see this happening. Easily imagine someone manipulating him into action. The question was why. So he asked.

"I'm not sure why. I know this all must sound like a crazy web of similarities, but my gut says they're all connected."

"Okay, I'll grant you that. So, tell me why your instinct is telling you this?"

"The country my dad was working in was fine when he started his research. It wasn't rich but it was stable and experiencing moderate growth. Nothing crazy, nothing like the western countries experienced in the eighties, but it was slow and steady. After my father's death, a report was issued, from a different firm, stating that there were significant reserves of gold in the country. Lots of it. The country didn't have enough money to invest in the resources to extract the metals so they applied to the World Bank for a loan on the basis of this report."

"And let me guess, there was no metal?" Ty asked, though he knew the answer.

"None, or not much. You can imagine what that kind of debt did to the country over time. One thing led to another, one coup led to another, one rebel group to a counter rebel group. The country backslid and war broke out. It's been clawing its way out of poverty over the past decade. With the generous assistance of the

United States, of course," she added. Her caustic tone was mild but unmistakable.

"You think the US set the whole thing up?" Ty knew governments could do all sorts of things, and he wasn't blinded by his own allegiance to his country, but he had a hard time believing what Dani seemed to be insinuating.

Dani frowned and thought before answering. "See, that's the thing that I can't figure out. I *don't* actually think the US government is involved. There's no doubt they're benefiting from the situation. We offer debt relief, but in return we get to set up a puppet government—though, of course, we'll never admit that. But, I don't think the government has the patience to set up a situation like this. It would take too many years to see any benefit, too many terms, too many political changes for the US government to commit to that kind of scheme," she conceded.

"And?" Ty prompted.

"Sonny's father was in a similar situation. I think a man capable of executing people without hesitation or remorse might be capable of a lot of things, including arms dealing."

"Okay, so if this man who killed your father, and Sonny's, is involved, he must be in it for money and power. But why involve Sonny in this part of his plan?"

Dani took a deep breath and sighed. "I don't know, maybe he's setting Sonny up for something? Maybe the bombing plot we've been gathering intelligence on is going to be blamed on him?"

"How would that benefit him?"

Dani shook her head again. "I wish I knew, but I don't. I'd guess it has something to do with power and money and manipulation, but beyond that, I just don't know."

"I wondered if you all might get around to sharing information with me." He tempered his mild rebuke with a gentle kiss on her head. "But why all the secrecy?"

"Even though Smythe, as a foreign diplomat, is firmly within CIA jurisdiction," she clarified, "we still had to lobby for it. We wanted jurisdiction, we wanted to lead the investigation because of

Sonny's dad. We felt we owed it to him. Drew threw some fancy, if stretched, logic into his request that included Sonny's international travel experience, his multiple passports. Between those facts, the potential involvement of a foreign citizen, and arms trading, Drew was able to convince the powers that be to give us the lead."

"He wanted the case because you asked him to get it." Ty laughed when Dani gave him a chagrinned looked.

"Yeah, he did. We'd tracked the weapons and were about to hand the case over to the feds, but when Sonny Carlyle's involvement cropped up, I asked him to do this for me."

"But what started as a favor, may be what breaks the investigation." Ty offered. "Now we know the man who killed your parents is involved, and considering he might be the man manipulating everything from behind the scenes, I'd say that's a pretty good catch. A man like that, with those kinds of connections, needs to be stopped."

Dani sighed. "I haven't been thinking about much of anything since I saw him in that picture. But it's a thought. Drew is probably thinking along the same lines we are. My guess is we'll have all sorts of new information when we get back to the house."

Ty wrapped both arms around her and pulled her onto his lap. "Drew's a good egg, isn't he?"

Dani tightened her arms around Ty's waist, tucked her head against his neck, and nodded. "Although I'm sure he won't be happy with the delay I caused today," she added.

"Drew is more concerned about you than this case, but to put your mind at ease, there wasn't any delay. He sent Jay and one of the women who works for Cotter to drop Roddy and Fawkes."

"We're collecting a rather ragtag team," she commented on the number of people now participating in the investigation that weren't employed by the CIA. "How'd it go?" she asked.

"They're all contractors. It's all legal," Ty responded to her first comment. "As to the rest—good. Fawkes and Roddy made it up to the boathouse and back with no problems. They thought it was great fun so they made a second run this afternoon, only they went in from up the coast. One of Jay's places has a boathouse so they dropped there, swam down the coast, checked out the security again, scoped some areas, and then made it back."

Dani shivered in Ty's embrace, no doubt remembering the chill of the water. "Of all jobs, I'm glad I don't have that one."

"Me, too. I'd hate to hear what Fawkes would have to say after seeing you in a wetsuit," he mock shivered himself, making Dani laugh.

"He's harmless," she teased.

"I know, but it still bugs me," Ty said with affection.

"So, are we all set for the water approach?"

Ty nodded. "Fawkes scoped the shoreline and he and Roddy are drawing up a plan tonight to detail who will go where and when once they get the monitoring equipment good and fouled up."

"Any new information on the time frame?"

Ty shook his head. "Not since the last time I talked to Drew, which was a couple of hours ago."

Dani sighed. "I guess we have to get back," she said without much enthusiasm.

Ty could understand, he sympathized. He would be happy to sit there holding Dani long into the dark, quiet night. He didn't plan on letting her go, but he knew they'd have to change venue—they still had a job to do.

"Yeah," he agreed, resting his cheek against her hair. "Drew will want to see with his own eyes that you're okay."

"I don't want to leave you, Ty."

Dani's matter of fact statement had the same effect as a swift kick to the stomach. If he had any doubt before, he knew, in that moment, that he was in love with Dani Williamson and would do anything to protect her, to keep her safe, and to keep loving her.

He cleared his throat and swallowed. "Good, I'm glad, because I'm not going anywhere."

CHAPTER 18

DREW GLANCED UP FROM THE desk when Dani and Ty entered the room. There was a heightened focus emanating from them which Drew found interesting. They were two of the most focused people he knew. How they could increase that intensity was beyond him. Only it wasn't—not when he saw Dani glance at the folder with the picture of the man he now knew had killed her parents and then watched Ty unapologetically wrap an arm around her waist and direct her to a seat. Drew knew Dani had told Ty what, until that day, had only been known by him.

And he knew she wasn't going to lose it, she wasn't going to get sick like before. Now, with help from Ty, she was going to stay strong and centered on her goal. And now that her goal had an identity—and a name, thanks to some of their friends back in headquarters—she, and Drew, had at least a shadow's chance of finding the answers they'd sought for so long.

"His name is Nicholas Frey," Drew started, as soon as everyone was seated. "He's also known as Frankie in reference to Frank Sinatra and the similarity of their blue eyes," he added with a look at Dani, whose eyes followed his every movement.

"We don't have much on him after about 1976. But, prior to that, here are his specs," he said, passing around sheets of paper to everyone in the room, which included his core team of Spanky, Cotter, and Marmie, along with Jay, Fawkes, and Roddy.

"Born and raised in Podunk, Indiana. Small, rural farming town. Not much to offer in it. Good people, low crime, but poor, and there were few opportunities to get out. Nicholas enlisted in the army in '68 and was shipped to Vietnam. In the couple of tours he did, he never distinguished himself, but there were never any problems either. He did his job, was reliable and, by all reports, a team player. He was one of the few survivors of a small but efficient ambush by the Vietcong that wiped out most of his unit. After that, he was discharged and not a whole lot has been found on him since," Drew concluded.

"And why is he important to us?" Cotter asked. Drew looked to Dani who gave him a small smile, as if to reassure him she was okay, and then she spoke.

"Because he killed my parents," she said. Drew heard Marmie suck in a quick breath. All eyes swiveled to Dani, demanding an explanation but respectful enough to give her the space to decide when she would explain. Dani looked over her shoulder at Ty, who rubbed an encouraging hand down her back. She looked back at the group and told them everything.

When Dani finished, the men in the room all let out a string of swear words at various volumes and Marmie pursed her lips and shook her head. Not for the first time did Drew concede that Ty had been right to suggest bringing in Fawkes and Roddy. Drew was a pretty efficient fighter, but based on the way the two men looked right now, he wouldn't want to meet them in a dark alley. And Jay. Jay was a kind of scary-looking dude to begin with. Now, Drew wouldn't have been at all surprised if he let out a war cry and went on his own hunting expedition. Despite all the caged anger, Drew had to smile. Dani had a good team of people at her back. Not only would they watch out for her as a colleague, they would go to bat for her as their friend. Each and every member of the team was now personally invested in finding Nicholas Frey and, given what else he'd learned that day, finding Frey meant getting Getz and the Eagle's Wing.

"Drew?" Ty prompted when silence fell again. "What else did you find?"

"Like I said, not much. But enough to know that Dani's instincts were right on when she suspected he had something to do with Sonny's father's death and, based on what Adam is seeing down in Miami, he's probably involved with Sonny as well." Drew took a deep breath and launched into the additional information he'd learned in the last few hours. Information that more than suggested Nicholas Frey was their puppeteer.

"Our intelligence tells us Nicholas Frey was seen with Sonny's father twice before he was killed. The first time was when Sonny senior was visiting the site of the rumored oil reserves. Photos taken that day show the two men talking. We're locating the agent who was present to learn more about the actual interaction, but we do have confirmation the two men met. The second sighting was in London a couple of weeks later, which was also a few days before Sonny's father was found dead in his Virginia home. Again, we don't know much about the exchange since we didn't have anyone in the area, but we did catch Nicholas on the CCTV entering and leaving Sonny senior's hotel room. A few minutes later, Sonny senior made a call to his contact in the agency requesting a meeting. He didn't say why and he never made it. He was killed two days later."

"And Sonny himself?" Dani asked.

"I'll get there," Drew turned to look at her. He knew what he was about to say wasn't going to come as a shock but he also knew what it was going to do to her. He paused before going on. As if sensing what was to come, Ty reached forward and took her hand. With a glance at him, Drew continued.

"I also had them dig back as far as they could on the work your father was doing."

Dani frowned at this bit of information but waited for him to continue.

"His notebooks and files were all examined right after the murder but there wasn't anything in them at the time that raised any red flags. When my parents took the time to go through much of the stuff in your old house, just before it was sold, they asked me what they should do with those files. We had our deal," he said looking at Dani, who gave him a small nod. "And so I told them to box them up and send them to me. I put them in storage and hoped someday they might come in handy."

"I didn't know. I thought all the files were returned to the firm he worked for," Dani commented. Drew could tell from her careful tone that she wasn't sure what to think or feel about the fact that he'd had possession of her father's effects all these years and hadn't told her.

"Most were, but his personal files stayed in his office. Once we had an ID on Frey, I sent someone over to the storage locker to go through the boxes and see if anything synced up."

"And?" Dani prompted.

"There are several journal entries where your father mentions Frey."

"Did he say anything about Frey, about what he was doing in the area or what he wanted? Was there anything that would tell us anything about him?"

Drew took another deep breath before continuing. "Your dad seemed to like Frey. He didn't say a lot about him, but mentioned meeting him a couple of times on the site and then they met for dinner a few nights as well. He thought Frey was smart and they seemed to agree on the potential political issues their presence in the country raised. They talked a great deal about what effect it would have on the region if they projected high yields of the metal and what effect it would have if they didn't. Both seemed to agree that if the metal wasn't found the country would get by. It would continue to grow, just at a slower rate. They differed on what they thought would happen if metal was found. You're father wasn't so sure it would be the manna Frey seemed to think it would be."

Everyone in the room was silent when Drew finished. While it was more likely Dani's father was taken in by Frey, played by him, and killed by him for *not* going along with whatever game Frey was up to, Drew and, judging by the look on her face, Dani were unsettled by the fact that he'd known Frey well enough to share dinner with him. Drew wanted to believe that the man who was like a second father to him, the man who'd spun tales of exotic travel and political intrigue, tales that played a huge part in his own decision to join the CIA, wouldn't have become involved with a man like Frey in any way. A man who could kill and not think twice about it. But believing it wouldn't make it true. And so, for now, he had to at least explore the possibility that Dani's father might have intentionally walked into something that eventually resulted in his own death, as well as the murder of his wife.

Drew was glad when it was Marmie who broke the awkward silence. "Drew, even if Dani's dad was mixed up with whatever Frey was doing—which I don't think he was, especially considering what we know about Sonny," she added with blunt and honest look at Dani. "What does that have to do with Getz and Sonny senior and Sonny?"

"Maybe nothing," Drew admitted.

"But you don't think so," Ty interjected. Drew could take issue with his tone, but decided not to, knowing Ty was acting wary and defensive on Dani's behalf.

"I do think they're related, now," he added with a nod toward Dani, indicating her part in convincing him. "I think it's too much of a coincidence that we have two men, one a petroleum geologist and one a metallurgist, who both knew the same man, were involved in surveys with huge political fallout, and were both killed in the same way. Now, whether your father and Sonny senior were involved too, or knew what was going on, I don't know. But," he raised his voice to override the protest he knew was about to fall from Dani's mouth, "I have to consider the possibility, or I wouldn't be doing my job. None of us would," he finished, with a pointed look at everyone in the room.

Drew watched as Dani turned her back on him and looked to Ty for moral support. Drew saw no expression on the man's face but Dani was satisfied, or assuaged, by whatever silent communication passed between the two because, when she turned back, he no longer saw the look of denial in her eyes.

"And Getz?" she asked instead.

"And the drugs?" Ty added.

"We know Getz has the arsenal of weapons. We also know Frey has visited several of the countries where those weapons, and others, could have originated from or been transported through," he added.

"And the good news?" Fawkes joked.

Drew grimaced. "Believe it or not, it gets better," he shot back. "We don't know everything Getz has in his arsenal. But, if we take a look at the countries where Frey has been and work on the assumption that he is manipulating this whole thing, it's pretty fucking scary. As in, think about the top ten worst countries to work in, and we all know what those places are, and use that as your basis for guessing what kind of weapons Getz might have. If Frey is involved, and I think we're all thinking he is, we might have just stepped into a major clusterfuck."

The room filled with curses and utterances of disgust. Drew was silent, having already absorbed the fact that it was possible Getz, via Frey, had some of the ugliest, dirtiest, nastiest weapons—weapons most of the rest of the civilized world couldn't even imagine—sitting in his house in Portland, Maine. Sitting in his house, waiting to be handed over to an anti-US militia.

"And I'd bet it's the same for the drugs," Ty interjected.

"The man is ugly and knows ugly people," Drew responded with a nod. The group processed the information in silence. It was a shift in the investigation and everyone knew it. They were no longer just looking at Smythe or Getz or Eagle's Wing. Now they were looking for a murderer and arms dealer—a man with enough power and influence to make just about anything happen. A man who now had a name and a face.

"And Sonny?" Dani asked. "How would he be involved?"

"You said it earlier," Ty looked at Dani, though he spoke to the group. "If Frey is capable of dealing arms, making deals with drug cartels, and somehow dabbles in international politics, my guess is you're not far off on what he's done to Sonny. Now *why* he would manipulate Sonny, I don't know, but my guess is, he is," and looking for confirmation, he turned back to Drew.

"He is involved with Sonny and we're on the same page here. We don't know how, or why, but Adam just sent a few photos of the two of them together."

"You seem to know an awful lot about a guy you said you didn't know that much about," Cotter noted.

Drew looked at the older man—a man who had probably seen more ugly things than most of the people in the room put together. He sighed; *Christ the world can be a bad place*, he thought. "We know where he traveled and are tracking down where he stayed during his travels—and he does travel a lot. But beyond that, we don't know much. We don't know where he lives when he's here in the US. He's got a bank account but it's not that big. We don't know what he does or who he sees when he travels. In other words, we have the skeleton of him but no meat. He's never been on a watch list, never raised any red flags. He was just a guy who traveled for business. But now we're digging and we're digging deep and fast," he added.

"Great," Fawkes drawled. "We've got ourselves a grade-A mother-fucking psychopath arming a group intent on making an explosive statement somehow, somewhere, and that's all we know about him?"

"That about sums up the situation," Drew conceded with an annoyed shrug. He wasn't annoyed with Fawkes, but with the situation. It irritated him to no end that Frey had been operating for decades without so much as a by-your-leave from the CIA. It made his skin crawl thinking about all the things this guy might have done, might have been involved with. Things they might have been able to put a stop to had they put two and two together earlier. And while he hedged his bets with the team, there was no doubt in Drew's mind that Frey was pulling the strings and everyone, including Dani's parents, were nothing but puppets to him.

"And the plan?" Marmie asked.

"Now that we've got an ID on Frey, we've got someone on him," he began to answer.

"Are we confident he won't tag the guy?" Spanky asked.

"It's Kapitany," was all Drew needed to say to his team. They all nodded in approval. Ty, Jay, and the others looked to him for explanation.

"Ethan Kapitany?" Jay asked. When Drew nodded, Jay nodded back in recognition.

"Jay?" Ty said. Ty didn't say anything else, but he looked to his friend for assurance on Kapitany.

In response, Jay gave Ty a sharp nod. Drew saw Ty's shoulders relax and then send Roddy and Fawkes a single look. At this, they relaxed as well. Though Kaps was a company man through and through, it didn't surprise Drew that Jay knew of him. He was a legend among those who had ever touched his world—which, apparently included Jay.

"So what now?" Roddy asked.

"Now we rest. We wait. Cotter, I have a few things I'd like you to look into with respects to Frey's time in the army?" And, just like that, the meeting ended. Everyone but Cotter filed out and within minutes, Drew and the Cotter were alone.

When the door closed behind the last person, Drew turned and spoke. "Find out what the hell happened to him in Vietnam. He was a kid from nowhere when he went in and the minute he comes out he disappears and then shows up like this? Something happened, find out what."

It wasn't a request and, though he didn't often give Cotter orders, even though he had a right to, he did so now—without hesitation. Cotter studied him for a long period and then, giving a curt nod, he left, leaving Drew to contemplate what Frey was involved in and how he was going to keep Dani out of it.

• • •

By unspoken consensus, everyone but Drew and Cotter moved from the library to the kitchen. Drew had dumped a lot of information on the team and they needed some time to process it. Ty smiled, watching the team's personalities surface as they did so.

Marmie went straight for the pastries Fawkes had brought in earlier that day. Spanky proceeded to make some god-awful thing that
Ty supposed could, on a stretch, be called a sandwich.

Fawkes, Roddy, and Jay, as the relative outsiders, observed
the subtle actions from various places around the kitchen. Dani
touched Ty's arm and asked if he would like some coffee. He smiled
at her gesture, tucked a strand of hair behind her ear, and shook his
head. He was tired and he knew Dani must be exhausted.

He accepted a glass of water instead and leaned against the
counter, Dani at his side. The silence stretched and, though it
wasn't uncomfortable, there was a definite undercurrent. Then
Spanky tossed his sandwich down and swore.

"Christ, Mack," he said. "I had no idea. I'm so sorry," he
added. And then, taking everyone by surprise, he walked over and
gave Dani a hug—a hug she returned.

Marmie walked up and moved Spanky to the side. She gave
Dani a look communicating that she seconded his statement. "I'm
so sorry about your parents, dear," she said before enveloping Dani
in yet another hug.

Ty watched the team rally around Dani and he felt himself
relax. He hadn't even realized he was tense, but he had been, on
Dani's behalf. She'd been through enough today that he didn't
want her teammates to question her father's motives or actions or
give her a hard time about keeping something from them. When
they showed nothing but support, he allowed himself to let down
his guard a little bit. Not much, but a little bit. Still, he was ready
to step in and run interference which, judging by Dani's body language, he would need to do soon. She appreciated the support, and
even let herself be comforted, but he could see all the attention was
beginning to make her uncomfortable.

Fawkes must have noticed, too. "Fawkes, don't even think of
coping a feel," Ty all but barked as Fawkes stepped forward to offer
his condolences with a big hug.

Fawkes shot him and Dani an unrepentant grin. "A guy's gotta keep trying. Didn't you teach us that lieutenant? Failure is not an option?"

Ty rolled his eyes and Dani laughed. If nothing else, Fawkes had accomplished his goal. Within minutes, sensing Dani's need to be alone, her team had disappeared into their own little worlds scattered about the house. Jay and Roddy headed out and Fawkes dragged his feet up the stairs with one last offer to let Dani share his room.

When the kitchen was empty but for Dani and Ty, he put his hands on her shoulders and turned her toward him. He massaged her neck. Her head fell back in appreciation and she closed her eyes.

"How are you?" he asked.

For a long moment she remained silent.

"I'm tired, Ty. Just...really tired."

"You've been through a lot today."

"It's strange," she said. "I haven't told anyone about what happened in almost twenty years, and then to tell it twice in one day..." her voice trailed off.

"How did it feel?"

"Tough," she said. "It was tough. But it was also the right thing to do. It was time. Probably way past time, if you asked a shrink," she added with a small smile.

Ty pulled her against his chest and ran a hand down her back. They stood that way for a long time before either of them moved.

"I'm so tired, Ty," she said again, this time the sadness was thick in her voice.

"Go on up to bed," he replied, his voice quiet.

"What about you?" she asked.

"I have to run home and get a change of clothes. I'll be back as soon as I can."

"Good," she said, burrowing gently against him. "I don't want you to leave me."

"I'm not going anywhere. Not tonight." *Not ever* hung in the air between them, but he didn't say it because he didn't need to.

• • •

The house was quiet when Ty returned—showered, dressed in clean clothes, and carrying a small bag. It was quiet but he wasn't fooled. He had no doubt the house was buzzing with activity—well, silently buzzing anyway. If he poked his head downstairs, he'd see Marmie's team sifting and sorting through information. Cotter's men would be out watching the compound, and Spanky's team would be plugged into their electronics.

As he headed for the stairs, the door to his right opened and Drew stuck his head out.

"Ty," he said.

"Drew."

"Can I talk to you for a minute?"

Ty turned and walked into the study. He set his bag down and waited for the team director to speak. Drew's eyes went from Ty to the bag at his feet and back again.

"How's Dani?" he asked.

"Tired. I hope asleep by now," Ty answered, wondering why Drew hadn't asked her himself.

Drew's eyes flicked to the bag again.

"I'm staying, Drew," Ty said in response to Drew's unspoken concern. Drew studied his face for a long moment before sighing and turning back to his desk.

"The day's been hard on her," he said, pulling out a file. It was a massive understatement and Ty didn't bother responding.

"Here," Drew said, handing Ty the file. "That's the picture of Frey Dani recognized on top, and a few more that Adam sent today from Miami."

Ty flipped through the pictures, not needing much time to burn the image into his memory. He flipped the file closed and handed it back to Drew, waiting for whatever Drew needed to say next.

"He's on his way up here," Drew said. Ty raised an eyebrow.

"Booked himself a flight. He arrives tomorrow in Portland."

"And it's legit?"

"The ticket's booked. Whether or not he gets on the flight, we'll have to see."

"And if he does?"

"We've got a plane on standby. Kapitany will take it and make it here ahead of Frey so he can pick him back up at the airport." Ty mulled this over, knowing now why Drew called him into the office. He wanted Ty to break the news to Dani.

"And Sonny?" Ty asked.

"He's headed back to Eagle's Wing tonight. And they're all booked on a flight to Toronto tomorrow."

"So it's happening," Ty commented.

"In the next few days is my guess," Drew concurred.

Ty nodded and reached for his bag.

"When are you going to tell her?" Drew asked, the sadness and memories of all those years still heavy in his voice.

Ty sighed, "Tomorrow. She's tired, she needs a good night's sleep, and nothing can be done about it now."

Drew managed a half smile. "She's not going to like being the last person to know."

Ty chuckled, "I know. That's why you gave me the dirty job."

CHAPTER 19

Dani was relentless. But then, after knowing her for her entire life, this didn't come as a shock to Drew. But still, even he was surprised at the extent she interrogated Adam about his trip to Miami and every little detail he could remember about Nicholas Frey.

Dani was hovering over Adam's desk and, though Drew couldn't hear everything they were saying, he did catch the occasional "save me" glances Adam was throwing in Ty's direction.

Drew turned his attention to Ty and saw he was deep in conversation with Roddy, Fawkes, and Jay. All of Adam's pleas were going nowhere. Even when Ty did glance in the direction of Adam and Dani, all of his attention was focused on her.

As he approached Ty, Drew could hear the men talking about currents, drop times, swim times, and other SEAL-related topics. As he came closer, the men stopped talking and looked up at him expectantly.

"You need to call off the dogs," Drew said to Ty with a jerk of his head in Dani's direction. Ty smiled.

"No way. I did your dirty deed this morning and kept her from coming after you for withholding the information last night *and* the information about her father's files being in your possession. Don't think she's forgotten about that," Ty offered in warning.

Drew grimaced. She'd get over his little omission, he knew she would, but she wouldn't be graceful or gracious about it.

"Drew?" Marmie said, walking toward the group carrying a stack of files. "Ready?"

He nodded and moved to the center of the room. "Guys," he called. The room went silent. When Drew was sure everyone was listening, he continued.

"As you all know, Nicholas Frey arrived in Portland about an hour ago and made his way to Getz's compound. Sonny's schedule changed and he is expected to land in Toronto within the hour and several of his Eagle's Wing cohorts are already there.

"Martin Cassidy, the cousin in New Brunswick," Drew reminded everyone, "procured a couple of boats this week. Long range sport cruisers. The kind of boat that, if it launches tonight, will be down here by the day after tomorrow."

"Which means we go in tomorrow night," Fawkes interjected.

"Which means you go in tomorrow night. Early morning to be exact," he added, confirming the plan they'd already set. Fawkes and Roddy would lead the water assault by taking in a team in the dark hours of the early morning so they had a higher chance of emerging from the water onto the land without being seen. Once on land, the team would get in place and stay that way until the action started.

"What about the drugs?" Dani asked. "Do we know whether the Eagle's Wing has them, or if they are getting them somewhere on the way? And if they're getting them on the way, where?"

"They didn't have them when they arrived in Toronto," Drew answered. "Canada agreed to let us handle customs and we ran a couple of extra-high tech searches. Nothing came up, so we know they're clean for now. It's looking like Cassidy might have acted as the intermediary, receiving the goods and storing them until they are shipped down to Getz."

"Or?" Ty prompted. Drew didn't even bother to hide the fact that he hadn't wanted to share his own opinion on what he thought might take place. He didn't have any evidence to support his new belief, but his instincts told him it might not be drugs Getz was going to be receiving from the militia.

"Or," he started, taking a deep breath. "Or, it's not drugs they'll be exchanging at all. It's possible Sonny has something else, maybe information, they will be handing over instead. Something passed to him from Frey."

"What kind of 'something' and why wouldn't Frey pass it on himself? He's there already," Spanky pointed out.

"Manipulation," Ty replied. Drew nodded.

"For some reason, Frey wants Sonny involved with both Getz and the Eagle's Wing. Again, we don't know why, but he seems to be setting Sonny up for something. As for what that 'something' is, I'm not sure. But, a couple of months ago, Frey was in South America when the oldest son of a prominent drug lord, one of Getz's suppliers was killed. My guess is, he has information about this. Information Getz could use to secure access to more drugs and expand his growing empire."

"So Frey gives Sonny the name of the man who killed the kid and Sonny hands the information over to Getz and gets the weapons in exchange. In the meantime, Getz gets to take the information to the drug lord and use it as a bargaining chip to get cheap drugs."

Drew shrugged, knowing he didn't have any evidence to back up his claim, but also knowing chances were good he was right.

"Okay," Fawkes jumped in, weighing this new information. "So, if it's true, the boats that come in, probably won't have anything on them so there will be no drug seizure. They'll be light and fast until they're loaded with the weapons and then they'll slow down and burn through fuel like nobody's business." It didn't change the equation all that much but it needed to be taken into account.

"That's assuming the weapons are heavy," Spanky interjected.

Fawkes acknowledged the point but added, "We know they're big though or they wouldn't be bringing down two boats. So it could be light, it could be heavy, but either way, it's probably big."

"And either way, you drop as planned," Drew responded. "Once we confirm the boats are headed down the coast, we'll move forward. The current won't be good for swimming down the coast so Jay found us a fishing boat. It won't raise any flags with anyone watching if it's seen out in the early hours of the morning. You'll drop about a mile off shore at around three in the morning, swim in, and set up." Drew pulled a map out of one of the files Marmie had handed him and tacked it to the wall.

"You'll have a team of five with you, so that gives us seven on the ground, including yourself," he said to Fawkes. "And you," he added with a nod to Roddy. "Now why don't you take the rest of the team through your plan." Drew stepped away as Fawkes moved toward the map.

"We'll drop here," he pointed to a spot off the coast. "And swim in this way," he marked the path with his finger. "Roddy and I have already been in a couple of times to scope the area and this is our best bet. It's not great for staying deep but it puts us out here," he pointed to a spot on the shoreline that was about four hundred yards from the house. "There are a series of boulders here that will provide cover for our exit. We'll be able to strip and set up out of sight from the house, but still be close enough.

"We'll be taking a couple of people from Cotter and Spanky's teams, people we've been training with these past few days," Fawkes continued. "Based on the reports we've been receiving regarding the activity at the house and the movements of the security guards, we're not expecting any problems."

"You've done a trial run?" Dani asked.

"Trial enough. Trust me, this is a piece of cake compared to some of the things we've done," he added when she flashed him a skeptical look. Drew had to fight a smile when Dani, as she had the day before, turned to Ty for some sort of guidance. Ty gave her a quick nod.

"You sure?" she asked, concern etched in her voice.

"Yes," Ty responded without hesitation. She accepted this with a nod and turned back to Fawkes.

"You're hurting my feelings darlin'. You don't trust Fawkes," he said. Dani rolled her eyes and everyone laughed. No doubt his plan.

"So, that's the plan for us. We've got our gear, we'll be in place and waiting for your orders," he concluded, turning the floor back over to Drew.

"Once the boats have made their way into the bay, we'll move into place," Drew took up talking as he looked at his assembled team. "Even though drugs might not be the currency of the day, we're still treating it as a raid. Spanky will keep monitoring the situation from the control rooms. Cotter's team will be the first to go in," he said with a nod to the older man who responded with his own curt nod of understanding. They'd made a deal earlier in the day that no one else knew, or would know, about. Cotter was going after Frey. His team would secure the area and stay focused on Getz and the militia members. But Cotter, with all his experience, was who Drew trusted the most to bring the man in, in whatever way he could.

"Dani, Ty, Adam, and Cotter's team B," he said, referring to the secondary team Cotter led, which included agents who had combat experience but who usually sat on Spanky's team, "will come in second, plugging any holes. Between Fawkes's water team covering the boats and the shoreline, and the two teams coming in by land, we should have the place covered."

Everyone in the room nodded. The information they'd gone over wasn't new to anyone, each team had developed their own plan with Drew coordinating efforts, but it was the first time they'd heard the orchestrated results.

"Folks," Drew raised his voice a bit to be heard over the growing din of conversation. "I know I don't need to say this, but please keep your eyes on the targets." He knew Dani would take the comment personally, as a warning to her to stay focused on her job, regardless of Frey's involvement. And, in all honesty, it was. While he wanted Frey as much as everyone else in the room, with the possible exception of Dani, he didn't want to lose their chance at Getz or let the Eagle's Wing slip through their fingers. He'd promised Getz to the DEA in exchange for letting his team take over the investigation. He would lose credibility if he didn't deliver, and the man would still be on the streets pushing his drugs. Drew hoped like hell that if drugs weren't being exchanged, there were at least enough on the premises to deliver on his promise.

As for Eagle's Wing, he didn't know what their target was, but just knowing they intended to target something was enough. He wanted them taken out of the equation. Now that they knew who Frey was, tracking him would be easier and, with his mobility reduced, his effectiveness would decrease. If they didn't get him now, they'd get him soon.

He waited for Dani to comment on his parting words. "Coward" wasn't a word he used to describe himself, except for when it came to situations like this, so he kept his head down, focused on collecting papers from the desk rather than on Dani. But curiosity got the better of him when, after a few minutes she said nothing, so he glanced up. To his surprise, she seemed not to have noticed his comments at all—or rather, not to have taken them too personally. She and Ty stood head-to-head, Ty's hand wrapped around her arm as they talked. Dani nodded at something Ty said, his grip on her arm relaxed, and his hand slid down to grasp her fingers. Cradling the tips of her fingers in his, he leaned forward and said something into her ear that made her smile. She whispered back. Drew couldn't hear it but could guess the topic when Ty gave her a single focused look before laughing. Her smile broadened and she moved away. Ty watched her go and then turned to find Fawkes. As he scanned the room, Drew caught his eye and Ty walked over.

"You're not planning on going against my orders, are you?" Drew asked. He didn't think so. He was almost certain the little exchange he'd just watched wasn't a plot to go after Frey, but he wanted to hear it from Ty.

"Feeling a little paranoid?" Ty laughed.

"It happens when Dani doesn't respond the way I'm used to her responding. It makes me nervous."

Ty laughed again. "No, we're not plotting to go after Frey ourselves. As tempting as the idea is, I think I've convinced her you must have a plan. Which," he added, with a little tilt of his head, "I imagine you do. And I can even understand why you're not telling Dani about it. But, I'll give you fair warning—if you are keeping something from her, it's one more thing she'll hold against you and, sooner or later, you will need to deal with it."

The advice was half personal, half professional, and wholly unnecessary. Drew knew that by keeping the information to himself, he was causing a rift in the working relationship he and Dani had so carefully developed over the years. On a personal level, she might be able to forgive his omissions, but professionally, she'd have a much harder time accepting his decision. She'd see it as sign of faltering trust between the two of them. It could pose a problem down the road. Drew knew this—had calculated the risk and chosen his course of action. He'd have to deal with it when it was all over. "I'll consider myself warned."

• • •

Dani stirred as Ty slipped under the blankets and pulled her next to him. She wrapped an arm around his chest and sank back into the pillow, enjoying the feel of him beside her.

"Is everything okay?" she mumbled.

"Yeah, Fawkes and his team are in. They should be on shore and in position within the hour," he answered, moving his hand down her arm.

"They'll check in?"

Ty chuckled, "Yes. Between me and Drew, I don't think anyone is going anywhere outside the lines on this one."

"Because of me," she said.

"Yes, because we care about you. We want to get Frey as much, or almost as much, as you do. But also because every player in there—Getz, Taylor, the militia, Frey—needs to be taken off the streets and out of action. Everyone knows how unstable the situation is, from drugs, to bombs, to arms dealing. We'll all sleep a lot better knowing all the players are accounted for."

Dani rested her head against Ty's arm and thought about what he'd said. She knew it was true. She knew everyone on the team, hers and the assorted others they'd collected along the way, was loyal and committed to the United States and had pledged their lives, at one point or another, to protecting it. She didn't doubt everyone wanted all the bad guys off the streets, but she also knew, in her heart of hearts, that everyone would go the extra for her. As she would for them. And she knew Ty was only trying to do some preventive assuaging of guilt. If anything happened to anyone on the team because of something they did that was above and beyond the call of duty, but was done for her, it would be hard to live with.

Intellectually, she accepted they were all adults and each person out there made their own decisions, but emotionally, well, there was no doubt in her mind she would feel responsible if something happened to someone. Ty was reminding her that she wasn't the only reason they were going after Frey—that there were other, very valid reasons they were going into this mission.

She didn't think this reasoning would work if someone actually did get hurt, but she appreciated his effort.

Dani turned her head and glanced at the clock. "An hour," she said. That was all they had before they needed to be up and preparing for the raid. Everything was in order. All the equipment had been checked and double checked, but she would check it again in the morning, as well as go through all the scenarios with Cotter and Spanky one more time. They'd review their "shit list"—the list of the worst scenarios they could think of and prepare for—a few more times. And during the night, someone would have come up with a few more scenarios to add to it.

Ty murmured something and his hand slowed its progress up and down her arm. For a moment, her mind went back to that first night. But then she realized his movements had stopped altogether. And judging by his breathing he was close to falling asleep. Dani sighed and tucked herself in closer.

They hadn't had sex, or made love, or whatever it was they were going to call it, since that one night a few weeks ago. If asked that Monday morning when she'd walked into the Portland police department what they'd done, she would have unequivocally said they'd had sex. It had been a mutual giving and taking of satisfaction with no promises. Neither had asked or expected any more. But now, now if they did what they'd already done, she wouldn't be able to call it sex. Physically, that's what it would be, but emotionally, it was more. Much more.

But the thought of rolling over and saying "let's make love"— well, she couldn't even think it and keep a straight face. Maybe it was the newness of it, the idea that she'd never before put herself on the line enough to even consider what she did with a man as something with the word "love" in it. Something about the term made her think of Michael Bolton and all the power ballads of the late eighties.

But all the giggles aside, she admitted to herself that being with Ty now, physically, would involve love, or something like it. Never having been in love before, never having even contemplated she would ever be in love, she wasn't certain what she did feel for Ty was love. But she was certain that, with every day, he meant more to her than anyone other than her family ever had. He'd broken down walls and boundaries that were so thick, she wasn't even aware they existed. She knew she was a better person for having met him and was a better person with him in her life. His steady presence calmed her, like a port in a storm that was her life. He made her laugh and held her when she cried. And no one had ever looked at her quite the way he did.

So, given that she knew this, why wasn't she turning to him and suggesting they use this hour to get reacquainted with each other? The gung ho part of her personality cheered her on to do just that. But a new, steadier side of her was urging her to wait until they were alone. Wait until they had more than an hour. Wait until there were no other distractions, nothing to take them away from each other. Dani didn't think she would always need the kind of focus she now desired, but once she'd identified this new feeling, she knew she wanted their first time back together to be more than a quicky in her sister's guest room with a house full of CIA agents just outside the door and a ticking clock to a major raid sounding in their ears.

And, as if reading her mind, Ty's hand dropped to her behind and he gave her a little pat. "We'll get there," he mumbled and then dropped off to sleep.

CHAPTER 20

"I'VE GOT A CLEAR SHOT." One of Cotter's sharp shooters checked in.

Dani glanced up at the monitor in the back of the van where she, Drew, Ty, and a couple of men from Cotter's Team B sat. The monitor showed the boats rounding the bay and heading toward Getz's boathouse. The wheelhouses weren't visible on their small monitor, but Dani knew Marmie and company would be enhancing the images, looking for weapons or other little surprises, even before the boats reached the dock.

"Here comes number two," the voice came through again and, on schedule, the second boat made an appearance.

"I've got one," came another sharpshooter.

"Covering two," answered the voice of the first.

"Four in one, six in two," came Roddy's voice as the boats moved closer to the boathouse.

"Sonny's in two," Fawkes added. "Taylor and his cousin are in one."

"Marmie?" Drew prompted.

"Shoulder holsters on four of the six in two. Sonny's not armed. Can't ID the weapon but at least we know it's not a rocket launcher," she added with almost a hint of sarcasm.

"Good to know," Ty interjected.

"And one?" Drew asked.

"All four in one are armed."

"Guys?" Drew prompted Fawkes and team.

"They're going in. Getz's men are there. Everyone on the boats is handing over their weapons," he supplied. "At least the visible ones," he added.

"Okay, Fawkes, ready?" Drew prepped.

"Ready."

"Cotter?"

"Ready."

"Good. Fawkes, on your call," Drew directed.

Thirty seconds passed and then they heard the call, "Now." Dani's heart pounded in her chest and it wasn't because of Getz. Over the years, she and Drew and their team had taken care of people far worse than Getz in situations far uglier than this idyllic bay in Southern Maine. Not that she didn't have a healthy sense of self-preservation, but this raid was chump change compared to some of the things she'd done in the past. No, the pounding in her chest and anxious energy that was making her jumpy was because of Frey and what he might tell her—what she might learn after all these years.

From her position in the woods along the driveway, she heard Cotter's men calling out, warning those inside the house that law enforcement was present and that they were being busted. She heard the distant roar of an engine and a single shot followed by the sound of the engine dying and more shots being fired.

In a crouched run, Dani made her way up the drive, sending a little prayer upward that no one on her team had been hurt by the shots. With Ty at her side, she made her way to the front door, rammed open by Cotter's team moments ago.

As efficient as she knew Cotter to be, even she was surprised to find a number of Getz's men already gathered in the kitchen, unarmed and flanked by two of Cotter's men and their weapons. Getz's men didn't look like they were interested in putting up too much of a fight and most just stood there, waiting to see what would happen next.

"Manny? Are we clear?" she asked one of Cotter's men, standing with his gun trained on the group.

"Clear upstairs, and we got this," he replied with a jerk of his head toward the men. She nodded and her heart gave a little skip.

She would have stayed if he'd needed her help, no question about it, but the fact that he didn't and she was free to continue through the house put her that much closer to Frey. Dani moved past the kitchen and recognized the sounds of the helicopter they'd arranged for and the additional police support now arriving up the drive. She ignored both and focused on her next move.

She and Ty came to the top of a set of stairs that led to the lower part of the house and then down to the boathouse. She called out her name and agency, giving anyone at the bottom a heads up, and then began to make her way down. She glanced out a window and saw Roddy, gun in one hand, his other hand wrapped around an unhappy Getz, headed back toward the boathouse. It looked as if the man had tried to cut and run. He'd been shot in the knee and, from the look on Roddy's face, Dani could tell Getz was complaining about it. A smile flickered across her face knowing that at least one of the three men they sought was accounted for. She gave another quick scan and saw Cotter skirting his way along the rocks, running with an agility that shouldn't have surprised her, but did. She wondered for a brief second who he was after, but then turned her attention back to her own descent.

They made their way through the rest of the downstairs, searching for people, knowing a more thorough search for drugs and weapons would follow once the house was secure. Finding no one unaccounted for as they finished the search, Dani's heart rate began to beat a steady pulse. The house was secure, she could hear the police upstairs taking care of the men in the kitchen. There was no one downstairs. Which meant everyone else, including Frey must be in the boathouse.

Stopping to take a moment to collect herself, she glanced at Ty, Ty who had been at her side almost since she set foot in Maine. He was studying her face and, no doubt, reading her thoughts.

"Ready, Ella?" he asked. She took a deep breath and then nodded.

Ty took the lead and called out their entrance before stepping through the open door of the boathouse, gun ready. Dani followed, close on his heels, and took in the scene. Getz was propped up against a wall looking like the condemned man he was. He wasn't shouting or protesting but was huddled, hands tied, leg bandaged, scowling.

Ten members of the Eagle's Wing group were kneeling in a line, hands tied and silent. There was something eerie about their silence. Getz's silence was that of man who knows it's best not to speak, whereas the militia members' silence had a martyred air to it, like they would almost be happy to die at the hands of the government, if only to prove a point.

Dani scanned the faces and her eyes came to rest on Sonny Carlyle. She didn't know what she expected, maybe to see a fraction of the grief that had ripped her apart when her parents had been murdered. But whatever it was, it wasn't there. He knelt with his colleagues, staring straight ahead, not acknowledging anything going on around him.

Despite his look of misplaced pride, Dani felt a wave of sympathy for him. She didn't know what his relationship with Frey was, but she'd bet, hands down, that Sonny had been played.

She walked in front of the group, measuring her pace, until she stood in front of Sonny. She stared at him and wondered what he was thinking, what he was feeling. She wondered if he'd been close to his father, if he missed him. As if feeling her scrutiny, his eyes flickered up and caught hers. And held.

And in that moment, Dani knew Sonny had loved his father and that whatever he was doing with the Eagle's Wing wasn't who he really was. That Frey had made him into something he wasn't.

"Nicholas Frey killed my parents." She saw the recognition in his eyes. "Gunshot, to the head. I was thirteen. I watched him do it," she added.

Sonny opened his mouth, then closed it. She didn't know what he saw in her eyes but his gaze wavered, then turned down.

"Do you know where he is?" she asked, her heart in her throat.

It hadn't escaped her notice that, of all the men under armed guard, Frey was nowhere to be seen. He couldn't have gotten far, not on the peninsula, but she wanted to set her own eyes on him.

Sonny's eyes darted to the open boathouse doors and then back again. Dani didn't bother following his gaze, whatever was out there, whoever was out there, would have run right into Fawkes, and she knew Fawkes would never let Frey get past him.

She repeated the question and Sonny's face turned down as a few of the militia members began to shift, warning him against speaking.

"Has anyone seen Cotter? He hasn't checked in," Drew entered the boathouse and demanded.

Dani kept her eyes trained on Sonny who, unlike everyone else who had turned at Drew's entrance, kept his gaze on Dani. Watching her, he let his eyes travel back in the direction they had the first time she'd asked him Frey's location. Realization dawned and she glanced out the door. There was nothing there, no one around, and no sign anyone had been there.

And then she remembered the flash of Cotter's movement she'd seen earlier. He'd been running along the rocks, toward the mouth of the bay, chasing something. He would have been out of sight of both of the men posted at the entry to the bay. Cotter would have been shielded from view by the rocks on one side and tucked too close to the cliff side on the other.

"Drew, you need to see this." Roddy caught the director's attention as the room filled with the backup support. "Ty, come take a look. I haven't seen some of this kind of stuff in years," he added. As the men moved toward the room behind the heavy door Dani had photographed earlier, she used the whirlwind of activity to make her own escape. She didn't think, she didn't stop, she just left.

Bolting out the door, following the path she'd seen Cotter on, she ran. Keeping her gun drawn, she forced her sense of panic down. Cotter caught up with him, she told herself over and over again. They couldn't lose him.

Dani ran, keeping as low as possible as she scrambled over the rocks. She ran until she couldn't run any farther. A big boulder blocked the tip of the bay and, unless she had gear to climb it or gear to swim around it, she wasn't going further. The tide was on its way in but not that fast. Cotter and Frey had come this way less than ten minutes earlier. The water would have been lower but still not low enough for them to make it around. Which meant Cotter and Frey were somewhere behind her.

It didn't make sense. She'd kept her eyes open the whole time and hadn't seen a thing—no cave, no boulders big enough to hide behind. But then again, she remembered the ledge Ty had shown her, maybe she wasn't looking at her surroundings in the right way.

She began to backtrack, sticking as close to the cliff wall as possible. If there was a cave or hole in the cliffs, it wouldn't be big. It would be small enough to go unnoticed at a casual glance. About a third of the way back, she found something that looked promising. A small crack, not a large entrance, but big enough for a man to slip through. Dani paused and looked. It could go nowhere, which meant she might waste precious time. Or, it could lead her to Frey and Cotter, which would be good, but she was beginning to get a bad feeling about the situation.

She didn't have a light and didn't like entering a cave, if it was in fact a cave, without one. She'd be a sitting duck while her eyes adjusted to light. If someone were sitting inside, she'd never even know it. On top of that, it wasn't feeling right that Cotter hadn't checked in yet. She had her earpiece in and she would have heard. But she hadn't. And she didn't like it.

Giving the side of the cliff another quick sweep with her eyes, she decided to bite the bullet, hopefully not literally, and step inside. She turned sideways and scooted in a few feet. It was a tight fit for her, it would have been difficult, though not impossible, for Cotter.

She wiggled a few more feet and the fit got tighter. She was about to begin to wiggle out, thinking that if it got any tighter, Cotter wouldn't have been able to make it through, when the for-mation opened out into a large cave. Stunned at the sudden space around her, Dani dropped to a crouch and waited for her eyes to adjust. And when they did, her heart jumped into her throat.

"Cotter!" she called in a whisper and then swore. He was lying a few feet in front of her, sprawled on his back. She crawled over to him, feeling sick to her stomach that he might die because of her and her obsession with Frey. She reached out a hand and felt for a pulse. She took a deep breath when she felt one, steady under her fingertips. It was slow and weak but steady. She ran her hands over his head and felt nothing unusual. She did the same to his body and had the same experience. Nothing seemed to be wrong, he hadn't been shot and wasn't bleeding, at least that she could see, but he was hovering between life and death.

She reached into his pocket and activated his GPS and then turned her microphone on.

"Drew?" she whispered, knowing the sensitive equipment would pick up her voice. Silence. And then he was there.

"Shit, Dani. Where the hell are you?" he demanded.

"Cotter's down and needs an assist. He went after Frey and now I'm going to follow his lead."

"Where *are* you?" he demanded again.

"Can you pick up Cotter's GPS signal?" she asked already moving away from the man and deeper into the cave. A couple of beats went by where Dani imagined Drew barking orders at Spanky.

"Got it," he came back on.

"It's a cave and there is a tiny crack of an opening. The crack is about eight feet in length but once you get past that it opens up. Don't send anyone big, it's a small opening. I'm not sure how you'll get Cotter out—"

"We'll take care of that. You stay with him," Drew ordered.

"Too late, Drew," she said. She heard him swear and issue the order one more time before she took off her earpiece and shoved it into her pocket.

She made her way down the cave, using the wall as a guide.

It was dark but if she used her peripheral vision, she could make out shapes and the contours of the walls. About fifteen feet in, she began to notice that the cave walls were intermittently damp. She stopped at a wet spot and ran her fingers through the dampness. Touching the tips of her fingers together, she tested the texture. Blood.

She felt a fleeting sense of relief knowing Frey was injured enough to be bleeding on the walls—he must have bumped into them as he made his way down the cave. It would slow him down, make him easier to track. It would also, in all likelihood, make him panic. Humans were fight-or-flight animals. When Frey's flight response was diminished, his fight response would kick into high gear.

Tucking this bit of information away, Dani continued making her way down the cave. She paused every few feet to listen for recognizable sounds and feel for any air current. The fourth time she paused, she felt a whisper of a breeze on her face. A few more feet down the cave she felt it again, and heard a hint of water making a soft lapping sound. She slowed her pace even more but kept it steady, no longer stopping. If the cave ended at the ocean, it was possible there was another escape and Frey had slipped through their fingers.

Then she spotted the water and, though the tunnel was still dark, she could see faint light making its way through the darkness. She paused one last time, right where the cave seemed to open out to a small, inland beach. From her vantage point, she could see about ten feet of sand and ocean water but nothing else. She needed to step away from the security of the cave wall to see the whole area. She stood, silent, debating what to do when she caught the scent of fuel. It wasn't strong, a boat engine hadn't been started in the last few minutes, but the smell was distinct and clear. Dani knew that when she stepped away from the wall, she'd find the boat responsible for the scent still sitting in the water of the cave. What else she'd find she didn't know, but judging from the tracks she was beginning to make out as her eyes soaked in the filtered light, she guessed Frey would be on the other side as well.

She stood silent for a long time, waiting for him to start the boat. If she could get him on his way out, she could disable the boat and have him at an advantage. Which, given that she was alone, held great appeal.

But, after what seemed like ages, she still heard nothing but the lapping of the water, so she decided to take her chances. Stepping away from the wall, she swung her gun up and stepped into the opening.

And, for the first time in twenty years, she laid her eyes on the man who'd killed her parents.

He was leaning against the boat. Trying to stop the blood flowing from his upper arm by gripping it tight with his other hand. She couldn't make out the subtleties of his features but the lightness of his eyes burned in the darkness.

"I was wondering how long I would have to wait for you to come away from the wall," he said, as if he'd been wondering what time of day it was.

"Move away from the boat," Dani commanded, gun still raised.

Frey eyed her with complete and utter disregard. "I've been waiting for you so that we can get this over with. I wouldn't want to turn my back on you now, would I?" he said, acknowledging that he'd be forced to expose an Achilles' heel if he started the boat, turned his back to her, and headed out of the cave toward the sea. He raised the palm of his injured arm and started to lean back.

"You killed my parents." The words were out of her mouth before she could stop them and he paused in response. She wanted the answers and she wanted them now. Not in an hour or two when he sat in some interrogation room but now, in this dark cave, when it was just the two of them.

Then his expression changed to one of pleased surprise. "Ah, yes. I remember you. The little girl at the top of the stairs. I always regretted not being able to kill you. One of the few loose ends I've ever left lying about," he commented with an airy gesture of his hand that was incongruent with the blood seeping from his bicep. "And then you were so protected, well, I didn't feel you were worth the risk."

His matter-of-fact admission startled Dani. She'd been expecting some sort of protest, some sort of denial. Even though she knew he had killed her parents, hearing the words from him came as a shock.

"Why?"

He sighed, as if feeling put upon, then gazed at the boat before propping himself up on the edge. Dani thought about telling him not to move but stopped herself. She could disable the boat if need be. Frey didn't appear to be armed and he wasn't going anywhere fast with his arm bleeding the way it was.

"It was all quite simple. I wanted your father to write a report saying that he found gold. He didn't want to write the report, we got into a scuffle, he lost." The words were delivered so carelessly.

"Why did you want the report? Why did it matter to you so much?" she demanded.

"Money, my dear. It's always just money," he repeated, almost sad. "Well, maybe there is a little fun in it," he added.

"Your money or his?"

"Ah, yes. I thought he was another poor sap like me, slogging away in the hellhole that is central Africa. I had no idea your father had the kind of resources he did. That he wouldn't be swayed by the money we could make if he falsified the report. I don't make mistakes often, my dear, but I'll grant you, that was one of them."

"Why would you want him to falsify a report?" she demanded, struggling to understand.

Frey shifted and his tone took on an almost professorial intonation. "I told you, my dear, money. It's almost always about money and when it's not about money, it's about power and politics. Coming from the world you come from, the world of the elite and privileged, the world of the old boys' network and junior leagues, you should know this."

She did know this, all too well. But, unwilling to grant him anything, she pressed on, "How would a report bring you money or power?"

"Simple really, my dear," he said. "If a country receives confirmation of something like a significant presence of gold inside their borders, they can obtain a loan to begin the extraction process, sinking the money into the new industry. The problem is, the country usually doesn't have the human capital to do the work, so most of the loan goes straight into the hands of the subcontractors. Subcontractors who pay fees to the brokers of the deals. I arrange for the report to say what needs to be said in order for the loan to go through and then I broker the agreements. Like I said, a rather simple plan."

He paused and glanced down at his arm. Now that Dani could see better in the darkness of the cave, she could see the blood seeping through his fingers.

"Do you have any idea how much money flows through to the subcontractors in the extraction industry?" he asked, looking back up. "Hundreds of millions of dollars every year. Sometimes billions. A nice tidy profit," he added with a small satisfied smile.

"And what happens when the resource isn't there? When the country spends all that money and has nothing to show for it?"

He smiled again. "Ah, well that's the fringe benefit. I had no idea starting out that there would be so many political benefits. You see, I only wanted the money. I only wanted to crawl out from the pit I grew up in. But the political benefits, well, that's just icing on the cake."

She still didn't understand. She didn't understand what kind of benefits could possibly come about from running a country into bankruptcy. She'd worked in a lot of countries riddled with this kind of debt, debt they couldn't possibly pay back, and it was never pretty. Famine, violence, civil unrest, and often wars prevailed. And the politics of those countries were so unstable—any benefits were purely circumstantial. And then it hit her and her stomach dropped.

"Our political benefit, not theirs," she said.

He all but beamed at her. "The US does like its puppet governments. It's rather like watching a waltz when we step in as the benevolent benefactor when a country can't repay a loan we helped them obtain. And then, in the name of preventing a crisis, we back certain leaders and, if only for a moment, we bring stability to a country. Our leaders look good, their leaders look good, and all is right in the world. At least until the country becomes tired of being a puppet," he conceded with a hint of anticipation.

"And then there's war."

"And then there's opportunity," he corrected. "Don't ever forget the importance of financial benefits."

"Yours?"

"Of course. All those defense contracts come with finder's fees too," he answered. "But don't forget who is usually granted those contracts. US companies, and hence politicians receive their fair share as well." He paused and let out a sigh that Dani would almost call dreamy. "There is so much potential, so many opportunities, and so little time," he concluded.

"And when you can't find someone to write the report you want them to write, you kill them? Just like that? People who don't want to lie, people who don't want to be responsible for the downfall of a country? People who don't want to be responsible for all the poverty and war? All of this is for your commissions?" Dani asked, struggling to understand how this man could be so flippant about the role he played in so much death—not just her parents' but also the victims in the countries he'd helped devastate through bad loans.

Frey's eyes slid toward the open sea before returning to hers. "There was too much at stake for too many people, Ms. Williamson. So when your father wouldn't write the report, when he threatened to report me to US officials, I had to tie up the loose end."

Dani was speechless. To call him a sick man was a gross understatement—even *she* was stunned by his callousness. And having met some of the people she'd met in her line of business, this was saying quite a lot. It was all about money. All about power. There was no remorse, no second guesses, no regrets for the thousands of lives lost because of his actions. He was a sociopath in every sense of the word. And he'd killed her parents.

But Frey didn't seem at all bothered by her judgment. He just cast her a pitying look. And sighed. "Be that as it may, I think my time has come to go. I believe your friends are about to arrive," he made a vague gesture toward the cave.

Against all her training, Dani turned her head toward the opening of the cave where she could hear distant voices. And just as she made out Ty's voice calling out to her, a shock wave rocked her body and turned her world to black.

CHAPTER 21

DANI TRIED TO FORCE HER eyes open. Her body felt like it was glued to the bed and her limbs like they were growing roots. Her eyes fluttered open, but just as quickly closed against the bright light as she absorbed what her senses were telling her. The feel of the cloth against her skin was rough and the pillow behind her head, thin. The light was artificial and the smell was antiseptic.

Realization of where she was came swiftly and she squeezed her eyes shut, fighting back a wave a grief. She was in the hospital. She had let Frey win.

She forced herself to open her eyes and, when she did, she saw her sister, Sammy, sitting on the bed facing the window. Dani's hand lay in Sammy's lap and she was reaching for something. When her sister leaned back, she picked up Dani's hand and held it. Dani would have laughed if she'd been able. Leave it to Sammy to give her a manicure when she was in the hospital. Of course, Dani wasn't fooled; her sister was just trying to occupy herself. She recognized the jerkiness of Sammy's movements, it mirrored her own when she was feeling stress or anxiety.

Dani shifted her gaze to her left and saw Ty. He looked awful in a great way. He hadn't shaved, his eyes looked red and his clothes were rumpled. He looked like a man who'd been sitting by her side for a very long time. He was staring at her hand that lay between his hands, tracing her fingers with his fingertips.

Summoning her energy, Dani flexed her fingers and tried to curl them around Ty's. The movement must have caught him by surprise.

He stilled and stared hard, as if trying to decide if what he'd seen was real. When she did it again, his head jerked up and he looked right at her.

"God, Dani," he said in a strangled voice as he leapt to his feet, gripping her hand. Sammy spun at his movement and tears sprang to her eyes.

"Sam?" Ty spoke.

"I've got it," she answered still clinging to Dani's hand with one hand as she hit the call button for the nurse with the other.

"Ella," Ty whispered, tracing the contours of her face with his fingers. And, as if unable to stay away any longer, he bent down and buried his face against her cheek.

Dani turned toward him, offering him the only comfort she was capable of at the moment.

"God, you scared us," he rasped, before pulling back and staring at her face.

"Dani?" Sammy said. Even in her weakened state, Dani could hear the tension in her sister's voice.

"I'm okay. I'm just," she paused trying to find the right word. "Tired?" she said, knowing it was such an inadequate description of the bone weariness she felt.

"I'm sure you are," came a voice at the foot of the bed. A doctor had entered the room and was watching her closely. "I need to talk to Dani, if you don't mind," he added with a look at both Ty and Sammy. Both of them looked like they minded a lot but left anyway, after another quick look at Dani to reassure themselves she was truly awake.

"How are you?" he asked when they'd left the room. "Really?" he added, picking up her wrist and feeling for her pulse.

"Really, I feel okay. Stiff, but mostly really tired. I didn't get shot did I?" she asked, confused about what had happened. "And where am I?"

"You're in New York. A helicopter brought you in about thirty-six hours ago. No, you weren't shot." He stopped talking but continued with his physical exam of her.

"What happened?" she asked when he'd removed the stethoscope from his ears. He gave her a puzzling look and then perched on the edge of her bed.

"You suffered a massive heart attack," he said.

"Excuse me?"

"A heart attack," he repeated, which annoyed her. She'd heard what he'd said the first time.

"I'm not old enough for that. And I get regular physicals. I just don't see that happening. What *really* happened?"

He looked at her again, opened his mouth, shut it, and then shook his head. "I don't know the particulars, but I suspect your boss does. And maybe Detective Fuller too."

Dani narrowed her eyes at the doctor and then gave up. If he knew something, which she wasn't sure he did, he wasn't going to tell her.

"So, what's the prognosis?" she asked, closing her eyes.

He sighed. "If this were a normal heart attack, I'd say you should be up and moving around within the next few hours to prevent any further clotting."

"But?" Dani prompted.

"But you didn't have a normal heart attack. There is no clogging of your arteries, no plaque beyond what we would expect in someone of your age and in the shape you're in. Your attack seems to have been brought on by some sort of massive stress. As if something interfered with the beating of your heart. I don't even like calling it a heart attack, but that's about as close as we can get to putting a name to what happened."

Dani blinked. The stress part she could understand but what brought it on? Was it meeting Frey for the first time since her parents had been killed? Was it what he'd told her? Or was it something else?

"So, what does that mean?"

"That means we keep you hooked up to that EKG," he said with a nod toward the machine. "When you feel up for it, we'll get you up and see what happens. That's all I can say for now. Once we see how you react to being on your feet, we can do another assessment and make a plan from there."

"What if I'm ready to get up now?" she asked.

The doctor raised an eyebrow at her.

"Okay," Dani said. "I admit, I'm not. It's an effort to breathe. But when will I know?"

"Let's continue to rest for at least a few more hours. You can try stretching your arms, flexing your legs and, if that goes well and you feel up for it, we'll try to get you out of bed sometime tonight."

It wasn't what Dani wanted to hear, but then again, she didn't feel like getting up, so maybe the doctor wasn't too off base. She nodded in acquiescence.

"Let us know if you need anything," his features softened when he spoke his final words.

Dani gave him a smile and he turned to leave.

"Oh," he said turning back, holding the door handle in his hand. "You've had a lot of people hanging out to visit. So far, your sister and Detective Fuller have run everyone away. I'd let them keep running that interference until you feel up to more." As if on cue, Sammy and Ty all but fell into the room when the doctor opened the door.

Dani bit her cheeks to keep from laughing, it wouldn't do to laugh at the two people who meant the most to her in the whole world. The two people who looked like they had sat by her side since the moment of her arrival. For Ty, it had probably been even longer than that, assuming he'd come on the helicopter with her.

The door hadn't even closed when Sammy and Ty made it to her side. They looked at her, so relieved they were unable to speak. And then they both started speaking at once.

Which made Dani laugh. It wasn't a strong laugh, or a belly laugh—her chest felt too heavy for that—but it was real. And it made her think everything would work out fine. She didn't know how, but she knew it would.

"How are you?" her sister asked when Ty graciously stopped talking.

"I'm tired. Really tired," she answered. They deserved her honesty. "And sore. But other than that, I'm feeling okay. Glad to be here," she added with small smile.

"You have no idea," Ty muttered and squeezed her hand.

"Can I get you anything?" Sammy asked.

"Maybe some water?" Instead of Sammy getting it, Ty stood and poured her a cup from the yellow plastic pitcher that stood on the bedside table. After placing a straw in it, he held it to her lips.

Dani looked at the straw and then summoned more energy than she thought she had to raise her hand. Once she'd pulled it off the bed, she found moving it wasn't so hard. Still, she didn't think she could hold the cup on her own so, rather than take it from Ty, she wrapped her fingers around his and took a sip.

When she finished, he placed the cup on the table and perched on the bed next to her, taking her hand between his and setting it in his lap.

"Do you want to rest?" he asked. Dani thought about this for a long minute. The idea of closing her eyes and slipping back into sleep sounded heavenly. It would be so easy. But her sister's anxious expression and Ty's furrowed brow, along with her own curiosity, weighed heavier on her. She shook her head.

"Tell me, what happened?" she asked Ty. She watched as Ty and Sammy exchanged a look and waited. "I let him get away, didn't I?" The moment she spoke, she knew it was true. She'd had the chance to disable him and the boat but she hadn't done either. No, she had wanted answers and because she let her own needs interfere with the mission, she had let the man who'd killed her parents get away.

"It was a weapon," Ty said, answering her first question. "It's at the weapons lab. You can be sure Drew is driving the forensics. But it's about the size of a chestnut and it caused a shock wave to travel through your body and interrupt your heartbeat."

Dani frowned. "It must have been short range, because I wasn't the only one in the cave. I heard you. I assume Drew was nearby. And Frey—he was there, too."

Ty's eyes slid toward the window and Dani could see he was weighing what he should tell her. "Ty," she said in warning. In response, he and Sammy exchanged yet another look.

"It hit me, too," he said as he exhaled. "Not as much as it hit you, but I could feel it. It felt like what you would imagine it would feel like. I felt my heartbeat become erratic, breathing became hard, and I had to slow down for a minute to get my bearings. Drew was far enough behind me that he only felt a moment of dizziness. And as for Frey, the only thing we can figure is that he'd ducked behind the sides of the metal boat.

"By the time I made it to you, all I could see was the wake of Frey's boat and your body lying on the beach. I'm sure I don't need to tell you what my priorities were at that time."

Dani closed her eyes and absorbed the information, telling herself over and over again it would be okay, that Ty was there. He was fine. She opened her eyes and looked at him.

"You're okay?' she said, mostly to make herself feel better. He nodded, raised her hand to his lips, and gave her a gentle kiss.

"What about Cotter?" she asked, remembering with a start that she had come across him in the cave, unconscious and barely breathing.

"He's fine," Ty answered, reaching out to stroke her hair. "He's down the hall. He was already regaining consciousness when we got to him in the cave. He's even been in here to check on you."

"And everyone else?"

"Everyone is fine." Ty said. "We got Getz and his men. We confiscated a lot of drugs and a lot of arms. Sonny and the Eagle's Wing group are all being held as well. I don't know the specifics because I've been a little preoccupied," he gave her a half smile before continuing. "But, I know Drew is chomping at the bit to see you, and he'll have more information."

"But I let him get away, didn't I?" she repeated.

Ty pressed his lips together.

"I don't know, Dani," he said. "Like I said, Drew will know

more. I wish I had more to tell you, but I don't. I've been more concerned about you than about Frey, but Drew will be here soon."

"Jason and Karen and Andrew are all waiting, too," Sammy jumped in. "I've had to kick them out more than once," she added, her grip still tight on Dani's hand.

Dani looked at her sister. Looked at the face that mirrored her own yet seemed so different. There was always a kindness, a softness that Dani knew she didn't possess. Sammy's face was always welcome and open, ready with a quick smile, whereas Dani knew her own eyes communicated a distance, a warning to others to stay away. But still, she admitted to herself, while she couldn't have changed the events of all those years ago, she could have handled it differently. She could have talked to her sister or to Karen. She could have asked for help rather than turn it away every time it was offered.

Looking into her sister's face, Dani knew Sammy had been told about Frey. She could see it in her eyes. But she also knew neither Drew nor Ty would tell Sammy the whole story. And it was time that she and Sammy talked about it.

Dani switched her gaze to Ty and, as if reading her mind, he shook his head. "Dani, you're tired. You should rest."

She didn't disagree but she needed to talk with her sister even more. "I need to, Ty," was all she said. He studied her face for a long moment, then swore to himself and stood.

"Promise you won't push yourself," he said, stroking her cheek.

She gave him a small, private smile and nodded.

"I'll be outside," he said as he brushed his lips against hers and then again against her cheek, where he paused for a second. "Go easy on yourself," he added as he was leaving.

"Dani?" Sammy prompted, concern etched on her face. Dani took a deep breath and answered.

• • •

Twenty minutes. That was how much time Ty decided he'd give Sam and Dani. He didn't doubt they needed more—Dani had years of memories to talk about—but it was all he was going to give them. Dani needed to rest. He'd never seen anyone who was so full of life, so ready to take on the world, look so pale. He couldn't keep his anxiety in check when he remembered finding her in that cave less than two days ago. Just thinking about it, and the intervening hours, caused his heart rate to kick up and he had to remind himself to take deep, calming breaths.

The breathing did get his pulse under control, but still, the niggling sense of panic he felt when he stepped away from Dani wouldn't leave. He knew he was acting like a mother hen but, as much as Dani needed to rest and be taken care of, he needed to know she would be okay. So he hovered by the door, not near enough to hear what the two women inside were saying, but close enough to hear the timber of Dani's voice.

It was there that the Carmichael family found him. Ty spotted Drew first and shoved aside his instinct to tell the man to go away. He liked Drew, knew Drew was here as Dani's family, not her boss, but he also knew Dani would press Drew for information about Frey. Next came Jason, Andrew, Sr., and Karen. They were a formidable family. All of the men clocking in at over six feet and Karen just a sliver shorter. All were attractive and had the look of the elite about them. Not arrogant or forced, but poised, confident, and self-assured of their place in this world.

Ty greeted the family as they approached, but he stopped Drew from opening the door to Dani's room. In response, Drew raised an eyebrow in question.

"Sammy called a few minutes ago, I thought she was awake?" Karen asked, concerned.

"She is. The doctor was in. She seems to be okay, seems to have pulled through okay, though she's tired. So tired she can hardly move."

"Then we'll be quick," Drew responded, moving toward the door again.

"She's talking to Sam," Ty spoke, holding Drew's gaze. After a few seconds, Drew got the message and swore as he let his hand fall from the door.

"Drew?" Karen prompted.

Drew shook his head and took a deep breath. "She's talking to Sammy about the day Nicholas Frey killed their parents."

Karen frowned and glanced at her husband who looked just as concerned. "I thought she didn't remember any of that day? Did it come back to her?"

Drew shoved his hands in his pockets and studied the floor before answering. "She remembers. She's always remembered," he said.

Ty watched the elder Carmichaels absorb this bit of information and, when the truth of the matter hit them, he heard Karen suck in a quick breath and Andrew mumble something.

"But why didn't she ever say anything? Why didn't she come and talk to me? To anyone?" Karen's voice sounded both hurt and concerned. And when Drew didn't answer, Ty saw her eyes narrow on her elder son as she realized the truth. "She did tell someone. She told you."

Drew nodded. "When she was fifteen. Two years later, she told me."

"And you didn't tell anyone, son," Andrew responded.

"I thought it was for the best at the time. She'd been so sick for so long. I thought if I kept her secret, as long as she was getting better that was the important thing," Drew defended himself, though it was clear to Ty that, even now, the man doubted the wisdom of the decision.

Dani had been a young girl, hurting, sick, and trying to come to grips with the brutal murder of her parents when she'd spoken to him. She wasn't the woman she was now. She wasn't strong and capable. Had he hurt her more by not trying to convince her to talk to someone, anyone else, about what she had seen? He had worked on getting her physically better and mentally stronger, but what about emotionally? How much had he helped her build that wall around herself?

Ty wasn't the only one who witnessed the internal struggle playing across Drew's anguished features. Karen sighed as she stepped forward and hugged her son. "We all did the best we could. We all did what she would let us. Maybe we all could have done a little more, but maybe not. If she's in there talking with Sammy now, it's a start."

"How long have they been in there?" Jason asked. Ty couldn't help notice that not only was Jason concerned about Dani, but also that he was now worried about his wife as well. About what she was hearing behind that closed door.

Ty glanced at his watch. "About fifteen minutes," he answered. The five of them shared an uneasy silence for a few more minutes before Sam opened the door. Her eyes were red but she also wore a tentative smile.

Ty felt a moment of envy when her eyes sought and found her husband.

"You okay?" he asked, stepping forward and wrapping his arms around her. Sam nodded against his chest, sniffed, and then pulled back.

"She's tired," she started. "But I know she wants to see everyone, if only to make you all feel better." Sam's grin was broader this time. "I think it will be too much if everyone goes in so Karen and Andrew, why don't you go in first. I'll stay out here with Jason and Drew." Then turning to Ty she added, "I don't think I need to say this but she asked that you go back in first. And stay. With her," she tacked on. Ty wasn't going anywhere and he wasn't going to let Dani exhaust herself to make everyone else feel better.

"Give me a few minutes?" he asked as he reached for the door. He saw the family open their mouths to protest but Sam cut them off.

"Of course. I'll send Karen and Andrew in a few minutes." The smile she gave him was affectionate and knowing and he didn't have to wonder if she knew how he felt about her sister.

"Ty?" Dani's voice was weak in the dim light of the room.

"I'm here," he replied stepping forward and taking her hand. He sat next to her on the bed and they looked at each other.

"How do you feel?" he asked. Dani took a deep breath and let it out. He wasn't asking about her physical health and they both knew it.

"After so many years of not talking about what I saw that day, it was hard to tell you. But it was harder to tell her. Not only does she now know what happened to our mom and dad, but now she has to live knowing I kept a secret from her all these years." Ty squeezed her hand in support and she looked back at him.

"We're close. I know we're supposed to be close because we're twins and all, but we're even closer than most, I think. Our parents' deaths might have had something to do with that, but I think we were like that even before they died. I just always remember telling her everything, of us being there for each other. Once I got over being sick, once I decided to rejoin the land of the living, Sammy and I rebuilt our relationship. She knows everything about me, but still, I held that part of me back. I didn't trust her enough to tell her." The sadness in Dani's voice was palpable. Wanting to make it better and needing to be beside her, Ty shifted her and slid onto the bed. Wrapping an arm around her shoulders, he held her with her head tucked against his chest.

"I think you did what you thought was best. You didn't want her to hurt like you did," he said.

"I know. But she did. She did hurt. I thought she wouldn't be able to handle what I would say, so I decided I was *protecting* her by not telling her. But all along I was protecting myself from not having to confront both what happened that day and my own feelings. And in the meantime, she's spent years wondering what happened."

"But you told her now," Ty said, stroking her hand that lay flat on his chest. "It's a start."

Dani sighed and moved closer to him. "Yes, it's a start. She wants us to 'see someone' together." Ty felt Dani smile at this statement. "She said it's time to stop living in an 'emotionally barren world.' Her words, not mine."

Ty chuckled at this. Dani and Sam were more alike than not. If the situation was reversed, Ty had no doubt Dani would be not-so-gently prodding her sister to do the same. Given the details of what Dani was dealing with, Sam's insistence might seems callous, but Dani had been living with everything locked up long enough, the time for babying her was long over.

"How do you feel about that?" he asked. Dani thought about this for a long moment, tracing unseen patterns with her finger across his t-shirt.

"If she'd said something like that a month ago, I would have laughed at her. But now," she paused, looking for the right words. "But now, I know she's right because, up until about month ago, I *was* living in an emotionally barren world. Meeting you has changed me, I'm not sure why, but I do know how. It's made me realize how much I've cut myself off from other people."

"You don't know why?" Ty teased, knowing this conversation wasn't easy for Dani and not wanting to press her. "It's not my stunning good looks?"

Dani laughed and raised herself up to look him in the eye. "Well, you *are* easy on the eyes, Fuller," she said with a smile. "But in all honesty, I've been with other good looking men, smart men, capable men and, before that frown becomes permanent," she grinned at his scowl, "not a single one made me want to look at my life and see what I'd been missing. Not a single one made me acutely aware of my emotional deficiencies, and not a single one ever inspired me to change them. You do. So, I guess I can see her point," she continued, reflecting on Sam's comments. "My life *was* emotionally barren. Now I think I might be getting there. Or at least letting myself contemplate getting there. With you."

Ty studied the woman who held his eyes. She was the same strong, capable woman he had met a few weeks ago in the bar. The same woman he'd taken home. The same woman he had spent that one amazing night with. But her eyes were now different. They were open and exposed and showing him her vulnerability. Her vulnerability and her desire to start trying to live a different life. Not altogether different, but different enough to allow him—to allow herself to want him—as a part of it.

"Ella," was all he could say as he framed her face and brushed his lips against hers in a gentle promise.

"I see you're not quite as immobile as I was led to believe." Drew's dry voice startled the couple apart.

Rather than rolling back onto her back, Dani tucked herself on her side next to Ty and grinned. Drew was eyeing Ty, no doubt debating whether or not to suggest Ty leave so Dani could rest.

"How could I possibly be immobile with this hunk of manliness lying next to me," she shot back, making Ty laugh aloud and Drew roll his eyes.

"I take it you're here for the long haul?" Drew asked Ty.

Ty stroked Dani's back through the blankets and looked at her. "I don't know, am I here for the long haul?" he asked with a smile playing on his lips. In response, Dani snuggled even closer.

"Definitely here for the long haul," she answered. Ty raised his gaze to Drew, who was watching Dani as if he'd never seen her before.

"You heard her. And we all know what Dani's like when she wants something," Ty grinned at the look of confusion in Drew's expression. Not confusion about him and Dani, but about how he should react. He could see it in Drew's face, the need to protect her like an older brother, the role he'd had for so long, warring with the realization that maybe the best way to help her was to encourage her to open up with someone else.

Drew made a noncommittal grunt and sat down. "Sammy decided I should come in first. I think she figured you wouldn't have as much time to assault me with work questions with my mom and dad waiting to talk to you."

"So, talk quick," Dani prompted, though her body was feeling the strain of fatigue. Drew must have seen it too because he hesitated before starting.

"I'm sure Ty gave you the basics of the weapon Frey used. It's still at the lab and the lab techs are having a field day with it. You know Cotter is fine. Getz and the Eagle's Wing folks are all locked up. I'm heading up there tonight to do some follow up."

"Any update on Sonny?" Dani asked, her eyes closed but still following the conversation.

Drew shook his head, and then added, "No," when he realized she couldn't see him. "He wasn't talking when I left this morning. I'm going to see him again tonight. We'll see."

"Tell him about my parents, Drew." When Drew didn't answer, she continued. "I told him already. When he was in the boathouse. I told him Frey had killed my parents. He must have seen the truth in my face because he's the one who showed me where Frey had gone."

"He what?" both men demanded at the same time. Drew sitting up and Ty drawing back to get a better look at her.

"He told me," she said over a yawn. "Well, he showed me, with his eyes anyway," she corrected, and then told them how Sonny had pointed her toward the cliff where Frey and Cotter had taken off.

"Interesting," Drew said, relaxing back into the chair.

"Sounds like he was beginning to crack," Ty added, lost in thought, exploring the possibilities in his mind.

"Tell him everything, Drew. I think if you tell him everything, and I do mean everything, he'll come around. Tell him about my parents, about what Frey said to me in the cave, about his father and the work he did for us. Don't leave a thing out. He's a smart kid, he'll know if you're only giving him partial information and he's been played enough that he'll back off if he senses it."

"I don't know what Frey said to you in the cave," Drew said, hesitant to even raise the point when Dani had just regained consciousness.

"Drew," Ty warned. Dani sighed and patted his chest.

"It's okay. I'm tired but as long as I don't move much, I think I can tell you everything."

"Dani," Ty switched gears in protest.

"Just give me a minute," she said closing her eyes and taking a minute to rest before telling them everything Frey had told her. When she finished, she opened her eyes and looked at the two men. She looked pale and exhausted, and Ty felt a wave of irritation that Drew had let her talk herself into that state.

"That's enough," Ty cut Drew off as he was about to say something. Ty didn't know what he was going to say but, whatever it was, it could wait. He saw a muscle twitch in Drew's jaw, but Ty couldn't have cared less about how pissed off Drew might get.

Drew gave a curt nod and stood. Walking over to the other side of the bed, he bent and kissed Dani's cheek. Dani grabbed his hand as he straightened away. "I know I let him get away." The raw emotion in her voice tore at Ty. Drew looked at her, a moment of confusion crossing his expression, and then he frowned and shook his head.

"No, Dani. There was nothing you could have done short of shooting him on sight. Judging by where the weapon fell, we think it just tumbled out of his hands. He had it ready and the moment you made any move toward him, he was ready to set the weapon off. I don't recommend talking to people like Frey," he commented with a wry smile, "but in this case it was the right thing to do. He was going to do what he was going to do. This way, we at least have some additional information about him."

Ty watched Dani study Drew, looking for any falsehoods. She gave him a soft smile. "Thank you."

"Get better, Danielle Gabriella," he ordered. "I'll send my parents in," he added as he stepped out.

CHAPTER 22

Two days later, Dani was sitting in her bed after her morning walk when Cotter strolled in, looking fit as a fiddle, Dani noticed. A young woman followed him in and, when the door closed, they both stepped forward.

"Dani," he smiled at her.

"Cotter, I'm glad to see you," she smiled back and eased herself back up onto the bed. She'd sent Ty out to get some real coffee and pastries and so, for the first time, was attempting to climb into bed on her own. And Cotter stood watching. Somehow he'd convinced hospital staff to let him wear sweatpants rather than the hospital gown, though it was clear, from his wristband and the nurse hovering out in the hall, he was still a patient.

"You look annoyingly healthy," Dani grumbled.

Cotter grinned. "Guess who's more fit now?"

"Dad," the young woman said, stepping forward to help Dani with the blankets. "You know you looked this bad a few days ago, too," she chastised.

Dani looked at the woman who handed her the blankets and stared. "I, uh, I didn't even know you had a daughter, Cotter," she managed to say. She'd worked with the man for five years and had had no idea.

"Not many people I work with do," he answered. It wasn't a slight on either his daughter or the people he worked with; Dani could understand wanting to keep your private life separate from your professional life, especially in their line of work. Hell, she'd done the same thing.

"Josie, this is Dani, Dani, Josie." He made the introductions and Dani shook the younger woman's hand.

"Are you keeping him in line?" Dani asked with a smile.

"As much as he'll let me," Josie answered.

"Ha," Cotter barked. "You say that like I'm giving you a hard time. I've been nothing but a pussy cat since I've been here."

"Which has been all of three days," Josie rolled her eyes. She held up her hand to halt his further protest and talked over him. "I know you wanted to talk with Dani about something, so once you sit your butt down, I'll leave you to it."

Cotter eyed his daughter. "Bossy little thing, ain't she?" he asked, even as he followed her orders and sat down.

Dani grinned watching Cotter and his daughter; it was unlike anything she'd ever seen from the man.

"I'll be back in twenty minutes," Josie announced and then turned and left.

"She seems like a good kid," Dani commented when the door shut.

Cotter's eyes softened. "She is, she's the best. It's one of the things I wanted to talk to you about."

"Your daughter?" Dani asked, eyes wide in interest.

"Sort of. I'm leaving," he announced. Dani looked at him and then the meaning of his words sunk in.

"You're leaving the CIA?" she asked. He nodded.

"It's been a long time coming. I left the army when my wife died and joined the CIA figuring it would be a little safer than what I had been doing."

Dani didn't even bother to wonder what he had been doing that would make the work they'd done seem safe.

"Josie was seventeen when her mom died ten years ago. I was away so much that, even though we were close, all of us, I still missed out on a lot. I decided it was enough, and I didn't want Josie to be left alone, so I left the army and joined the CIA. It's been fine, what I thought it would be. But then this happened and, well," the man paused and a lost look flickered in his eyes.

"I don't like thinking I might never see my daughter again. Oh, I know," he waved a hand in front of him. "I know I could get hit by a bus tomorrow, or she could, for that matter. But then it would be an accident. Not something I chose to do, and we both know the mortality rate for folks in our job is higher than the average."

Cotter took a deep breath and let it out. "So, there you have it. I wanted to tell you and thank you for coming after me that day. I don't know what would have happened if you hadn't come by. Well," he stopped and chuckled. "I do know what would have happened if you hadn't come by, which is why I decided to leave."

"So, what now?" Dani asked, not sure what else to say. To say it was a shock to hear Cotter's plan would have been a huge understatement. She never imagined there would come a day when he would not be there, be a part of the team. Then again, she hadn't known about Josie or even how the pull of love and family could become stronger than the desire to work.

"I'm going to retire to my little cottage on Chesapeake Bay. Spend some time with Josie—she's a teacher in DC. Maybe catch up with some old army buddies."

"Do you think you'll get bored?" Dani asked, curious. Cotter laughed.

"Maybe, but don't tell Josie I told you," he lowered his voice to conspiratorial whisper. "She and her husband—he's a good man, a professor—are expecting their first baby. She's only about ten weeks along so doesn't want to tell anyone yet. But, I think she told me as way to get me to move away from the light, if you know what I mean."

Dani laughed. The thought of Cotter as a doting grandfather was *not* an image she would have come up with on her own. But now she couldn't see him as anything else—it was an oddly perfect fit.

"Dad?" Josie's head popped in and she pointed to her watch. Cotter gave a dramatic sigh and stood.

"They're letting me out tomorrow," Cotter announced, stretching his legs.

The realization that she would never work with Cotter again—may never see him again—made her catch her breath. He must have noticed because he stopped and gave her a gentle smile.

"We'll keep in touch. Trust me," he said. Dani smiled back, comforted by his words.

"Oh hey, Cotter," she called him back as he moved toward the door. "Since you're on your way out, tell me about your handle."

"I'm leaving the team and all you want to know about is how I got my handle?" he teased, but stepped back into the room with Josie by his side.

Dani gave him an unrepentant grin and nodded.

He glanced at Josie. "I don't think you've ever heard this story either," he looked at her, affection clear on his face, and she shook her head.

"It had to do with your mother, my wife," he added, looking back to Dani. "I fell in love with her the first time I laid eyes on her."

"How old were you?" Dani asked.

"Five. Mrs. Morgenstern's kindergarten class. I was new to the town. Angie sat at the desk beside me. When the bell rang that first morning, she turned and smiled at me and I fell right then and there. The town was small and when we got to high school there wasn't a lot of dating going on. Instead, Angie and our friends all just hung out together. It didn't mean I didn't try for more, because I did. I'd been telling her from day one that I was going to marry her. I told everyone I was going to marry her. I got into the habit of referring to her as 'the girl I was going to marry.' Everyone in town knew the whole story, but when I was drafted, the guys in my platoon thought I was crazy to be holding out for a girl who hadn't even kissed me on the lips when I shipped out. But we wrote to each other every week and, pretty soon, everyone was rooting for me. Every time I got a letter from her everyone would ask if she'd said yes yet."

He shifted and looked at his daughter. "When the letter came, the letter that said she'd marry me as soon as I got home, everyone cheered. I don't know who started it but someone started chanting 'caught her, caught her,' which was shortened to Cotter. I think, in retrospect, my courtship with Angie was one of the only bright spots of our deployment."

"What took her so long?" Josie asked, her love for her father strong in her voice.

Cotter smiled. "I asked her that and for years she never answered. Finally, she told me that I'd had my heart set on her for so long that she was afraid she'd disappoint me. She thought it would be easier to avoid me than to risk disappointing me. I'm sure you'd know something about that," Cotter turned his attention from his daughter to Dani.

"But," he continued, "when you realize you love someone, that you well and truly love someone, you realize that you could never be a disappointment. I thanked god every day that Angie learned this. I suspect you will, too, Dani," he added.

Dani smiled, touched by Cotter's words. "Thank you," she said. He smiled back as Josie took his hand. "And good luck," Dani added.

"I'll be in touch. Oh, and tell Drew to tell you about Frey and Robertson," he responded with an overhead wave as the door closed behind the pair.

Just moments after Cotter left, the door swung back open and Ty came in with two take-out coffees and a bakery bag.

"Who was that I saw with Cotter?" he asked.

"His daughter," Dani replied, still testing the concept.

"Daughter?" Ty said, just as surprised. He handed her a coffee and spread the pastries on the bag on the table. "I didn't know he had a daughter."

"Neither did I. I also didn't know he was quitting the CIA and retiring to his cottage on Chesapeake Bay as soon as he is released tomorrow," she added with no little bit of envy in her voice. Then she frowned. Cotter might be choosing to leave the CIA, but what if he hadn't? Given what had happened, would he have been able to return to the field? Would she?

"Chesapeake Bay," Ty mulled this over as he took a bite from a scone. "It's nice there. We should go on vacation there this fall." He hadn't noticed her sudden discomfort, and she was glad. It wasn't something she was ready to think about yet.

"If they ever let me out of here," Dani grumbled as she pulled the top off of a blueberry muffin and popped it into her mouth.

"Oh, I didn't tell you?" Ty spoke with mock surprise. "I ran into your doctor in the hallway on my way in here. He said that if you stay on track today, and if I promise not to let you overdo it, you can go home tomorrow."

Dani stopped chewing and stared at Ty. "You're not kidding, right?" she said over a mouthful of muffin.

"Believe me, honey, that's *not* something I would joke about," he smiled and touched his thumb to her lip, catching a crumb.

Dani swallowed and smiled. "Have I told you that I love you?" she blurted out, surprising even herself with the veracity of the statement.

Ty smiled, "Aw shucks, you just said that 'cause I'm springing you from this joint," he answered. Dani knew he was trying to lighten the moment, giving her an out if she wanted it.

"I did, but I do," she said, suddenly certain she wanted Ty to know her feelings for him were real, and strong.

"You did, but you do?" he asked, confused.

"I did say it because you're springing me, but I do love you," she clarified. He searched her eyes for a long moment before placing his coffee and scone down. "I mean, that's just how I feel, you don't, well, you don't have to," her backpedaling came to an abrupt stop when he covered her mouth with his in a long, slow kiss.

"I can't tell you how glad I am to hear that," he said when he pulled away. "Because I do too. Love you, that is," he clarified and then emphasized it with another kiss.

That ended with the sound of someone clearing his throat. Ty glanced at the door over Dani's shoulder as she rolled back against the raised bed. Spanky stood in the door, grinning. Drew stood next to him, hands planted on his hips.

"Do you wait for me to show up to do that?" Drew asked rhetorically as he moved into the room. On reflex, he went to look out the window. Spanky stopped midway and picked up a scone without asking.

"Drew," Dani said, picking up her coffee and taking a sip. "Cotter said I should ask you about Frey and Robertson."

Drew turned and stared at her. "You sure don't need any warm up do you. You just jump right in," he responded, taking the empty seat near her bed.

"That shouldn't come as a surprise to you, Drew, but in this case, I have no idea what I'm jumping into. I know who Frey is but not Robertson or why we should care."

Drew glanced at Spanky, who swallowed the bite of scone, took a sip of water, and then proceeded to fill them in. "You do know Robertson. William Robertson," he started.

Startled, both Dani and Ty put their cups down and stared.

"Yeah, that was about the same reaction we had when we found out Frey and the fricking President of the United States, William Robertson, were army buddies. Turns out that ambush we knew Frey survived," Spanky paused to give them time to remember Frey's dossier that Drew had passed on to them in Portland. When both Dani and Ty nodded, he continued. "Well, it turns out Robertson was the only other survivor of the same ambush."

"An ambush, I might add, that was recorded in a couple of contradictory reports," Drew interjected.

"I'm sure there are a lot of contradictory reports from that time period," Ty pointed out.

"And do they make a difference? Did anyone benefit from the discrepancy?" Dani asked.

"Not any of the other nine men who were killed that day," Spanky muttered in disgust.

"Robertson's report is kind of interesting. He says he was told the area was secure and advanced on orders only—it's bare bones. But Frey's report extols Robertson's leadership when they came under fire. Frey says he was told they might encounter enemy combatants, but no one expected the ambush and that Robertson was cool under fire and did the best he could, given the difficult situation. Nine men died but, according to Frey, Robertson managed to get all the bodies out so they could make it home for a proper burial."

"Maybe Frey was just thankful Robertson got him out alive and exaggerated the situation a little bit?" Dani asked, doubt clear in her voice.

Drew seemed to agree with her. He shrugged and shook his head. "I doubt Frey's motivations were that generous. But, Robertson was awarded for his actions that day. It was big news that the son of a prominent senator had fought so valiantly. He campaigned on it in his first election and, of course, his record has been a point of discussion in every subsequent election, including his presidential election."

"So you're thinking Frey sets him up for an award and then starts calling in favors?" Ty put the question out to no one in particular.

"But why would Frey think he deserved favors if Robertson did what he did in terms of getting the bodies out, staying strong and all that," Dani interjected.

"Unless of course, Robertson didn't do any of it and Frey lied," Ty answered, cynicism clear in his voice.

"My guess?" Drew started. "I think Frey led the march right into enemy territory. I think Robertson, followed along because he wanted to prove himself to his father. I think when the bullets started flying Robertson probably ducked for cover and Frey did all the dirty work. How much of the dirty work did he do?" Drew shrugged. "I wouldn't put it past him to have killed his own men in order to ensure no one questioned the events of the day. So, at the end of the journey, we have an injured Robertson, who knows the truth about what happened in the jungle that day but is already being lauded as a hero and praised by his father. And we have Frey, who may or may not have set him up, but also knows the truth and has joined the canonize-Robertson contingent."

Drew rose and walked to the window. Dani cast a look at Ty, who was staring off into the middle distance.

"As the only other survivor, Frey's voice carries a lot of weight," Drew said.

"And Robertson crashes into victory in his first run for public office on the laurels of his actions. Most Vietnam vets weren't given quite the same welcome as the vets from World War II, but Robertson is from a conservative state," Ty added as he sat forward and took Dani's hand.

"I can buy Frey being involved in the death of so many men, no problem, but I don't get why Robertson was involved. Why Frey wouldn't just take the credit? And does this have anything to do with what he told me in the cave?" she questioned.

"As to the first, because Frey was a down-on-his-luck nobody trying to claw his way out of poverty," Drew answered, repeating, essentially, what Frey had said when talking with Dani in the cave.

"And as for the second question, Robertson was his ticket," Spanky supplied. "Even before Robertson enlisted, he was a golden boy expected to follow in his father's footsteps. What better way for someone like Frey to climb out of poverty than to have something to hold over someone like Robertson. Someone who can give him access and contacts."

"So where does that leave us?" Ty asked.

Drew sighed and Spanky looked pained. "That's part of the problem. Or rather, it's part of the puzzle Marmie is trying to work out. You see, we know they were together in Vietnam. But ever since then, since the late seventies, there have been no known interactions between the two. *At all*," Spanky added with emphasis.

"What about the extraction companies? Does Robertson have any link to them? Maybe that's the connection?" Dani suggested.

"Marmie's looking into that," Drew answered. "Robertson does hold a fair bit of stock in a variety of extraction companies, but so do a lot of other people. It doesn't mean it's the connection between the two."

"But it doesn't mean that it's not either," Dani pointed out. "Who else is working on this?"

"You're looking at it," Drew answered.

"And Marmie," Spanky added.

"Right, I'm sure it's better to keep the team small, given the potential situation," Ty interjected.

Dani swore under her breath and all three men concurred. If the president were involved with someone like Frey, they'd be fighting an almost impossible battle. Because, while the American people seemed to revel in White House scandals involving sex and money, a White House scandal that involved duping the American people for decades and the murder of innocent people would be resoundingly crushed by all the powers that be, along with all the people involved. Neither party would want a sitting president to be impeached and tried for murder, it would rock the political foundation too much.

So, not only were they fighting to find Frey and bring him down, they would be fighting for their jobs and possibly their lives as well. While this truth escaped none of them, no one in the room looked interested in walking away. If anything, as Dani scanned the faces of the three men, they looked even more intent on their objective—finding Frey and stopping him.

Just as Dani opened her mouth to ask about Drew's interrogations of Sonny and the captive militia, he cut her off.

"I think that about covers it for now," Drew said, moving toward the door. Spanky looked surprised but fell in line after a quick look at Dani.

"We'll be back tomorrow. My parents are coming by again a bit later," Drew added as the two exited the room.

"Wow," Dani said into the silence that followed. "I must look bad. Drew ran away faster than a scared cat."

"You look pretty good to me," Ty said, handing her another piece of pastry. "I think he wants to make sure you keep it up."

"And he thinks withholding information will help?"

"I think he thinks I'll remind you that whether you know

whatever it is he knows today or tomorrow, it isn't going to make a difference. There's not much you can do until you're back on your feet."

"What about my enormous brain power?" she asked with a cheeky grin. "I can think about things."

Ty rolled his eyes. "You can, but then, when you realize you can't *do* anything about what you're thinking about, you'll start to get all twitchy and moody and demanding, and the next thing we'll know, a half-healed Dani will be checking herself out of the hospital against doctor's orders."

"I would not," Dani shot back. Ty quirked a brow. "Okay, maybe I would," she conceded with a sigh. "I guess you're stuck entertaining me then?"

Ty laughed, "I can think of worse things, honey."

CHAPTER 23

FOUR DAYS LATER TY AND Dani walked into her apartment off of Central Park. Dani paused in the hall, looked around at the familiar setting, sighed, and dropped her purse onto the hall table. Because the doctors had never seen an injury like hers, they had been extra cautious, holding her for more days than she'd wanted. But she was out. And now she was home in her spacious fourth-floor, two-bedroom, renovated apartment in the vintage building she'd fallen in love with ten years earlier.

"Good to be home?" Ty asked, moving past her with her small bag in hand. She smiled and nodded as he headed for the bedroom. He dropped her bag and re-emerged to find her looking out the windows in the living room. It was June, and a hot one in the city. Ty could see people carrying iced drinks in shorts and t-shirts, probably headed to the park one block over.

"Are you hungry?" he asked. Dani turned and smiled at him and then he saw her eyes take in the subtle evidence of his presence in her apartment.

"I never even asked, but I assume you've been staying here?"

"Your sister gave me a key when they stopped letting me stay overnight with you. I hope you don't mind?"

Dani glanced around, then met his gaze and gave him a chagrinned smile. "I should have thought of it. Of course, I don't mind."

Ty walked up to her and looped his arms around her waist. "You had other things on your mind."

"Still, you'd think I would have thought to ask you if you needed a place to stay."

"You didn't need to, your sister took care of it. As long as you're happy I'm here, then we're good."

"I am and we are, aren't we?" she asked, resting her head on his shoulder.

"Yes, we are. Now, do you want something to eat?"

"Shower first and then something to eat," she mumbled. Ty frowned. She was doing much better, but there was no doubt that the taxi from the hospital to her apartment and the general excitement of the day had made her tired.

"Why don't you shower and rest while I make something."

"Mmm, sounds good," she said.

Ty stood and listened to her enter her room and then the attached bathroom. When the water started running, he moved into the kitchen to see what he could scavenge. He'd been staying there but had been spending almost all of his time at the hospital, trying to keep Dani from jumping out of her skin with so much inactivity.

He opened a few cupboards and found them stocked, which was a surprise, given the fact that Dani hadn't been home in more than a month. He opened the refrigerator and was even more surprised to find milk, yogurt, and few other perishables, all recently purchased. Sam. Ty smiled. He should have known. Sure enough, when he checked the freezer and the pantry, it was all stocked. The fridge even had some prepared food from the local grocer.

"Ty?" Dani called from the shower. Her voice was faint. He froze, not sure he'd heard her at all.

And then he heard her call his name again.

His heart stammering in worry, he ran to the bathroom. "I'm here, honey. Is everything okay? Are you okay?"

Dani stood in shower, soaking wet, smiling at him. "You were worried?" she said with faint surprise.

"Umm, yes," he managed to say. Now that it was obvious nothing was wrong, he couldn't help but be distracted by the image presented to him. It had been over a month since he had last seen Dani naked and his body was reminding him of just that fact.

He cleared his throat and dragged his eyes back to Dani's face. "You are okay, right?"

Her expression softened even more and Ty saw a hint of vulnerability in her eyes. "I'm fine. I'm lonely."

"You want company?"

She nodded. "Yes, please."

Twenty seconds later, he was in the shower, holding her in his arms, stroking her back, and kissing her neck.

"I've missed you, Ty," she said in his ear. In response, he kissed her deeply. She pressed against him, against his arousal, and let out a little groan of appreciation.

"Don't mind that," he said, thinking she was too tired to do any more than what they were doing.

"But I miss *that*," she said, reaching down between them.

"Dani," he caught her hand and drew back to look her in the eye. "You're still recovering."

She smiled and wrapped her hand around him. "The doctor said all heart attack victims should exercise with someone else, once released."

"Dani," he hissed, losing his will to say no.

"Please, Ty. Make love to me," she whispered. He looked her in the eye and saw the need. The need to be held, to be loved, to be alive, and his resolve vanished. He kissed her, taking his time, remembering how they were on that first night together. Showing her how thankful he was that she was here, that they had this chance. Shutting off the water, he grabbed a towel, dried them off, and led her to the bed. Lying down beside her, he skimmed his hand along her body from her hair down to her knee and back again, absorbing the moment and the feel of her. He glanced at her face, her eyes closed, just focusing on the feel of his hand on her skin.

He palmed her breast, tracing gentle circles with his thumb around her nipple. She gave a little shiver and then relaxed even more. Turning her on her back and easing her legs apart in the process, he moved his hand down to her stomach. He heard her breath catch in anticipation. He still wasn't convinced she was up to making love, but he could at least give her some satisfaction.

To his surprise, she opened her eyes and met his gaze with an intensity he felt in every fiber of his body.

"You, Ty. I want you," she said.

He thought about asking if she was sure. About pointing out that it might be too soon. But he didn't. He took one look at her expression and found that he needed her as much, if not more, than she needed him. He moved between her thighs and slid inside. Dani let out deep sigh of satisfaction and didn't move, feeling him as he lay, unmoving inside her, memorizing her.

"Ty," she managed to say on deep breath. The sound of her, speaking his name as he lay buried inside her, released a surge of love the likes of which he'd never felt before.

"God, Dani," he said against her neck as he began to move inside her. She whispered his name and they moved together, rediscovering the passion that first brought them together. Passion made stronger by time and love.

* * *

Ty paused in the entryway of Dani's apartment to listen to the debate occurring on the other side of the door.

"They're holing up," Sam's voice drifted through the closed door.

"They're what?" Drew's somewhat confused and exasperated voice answered. Ty had kind of the same reaction.

"Holing up," Sam repeated and Ty could all but hear her eyes rolling. "As in, not talking to anyone, spending time together, lots of it in bed is my guess."

"So, what are you doing here?" Drew asked, sounding like an older brother.

"I," Sam said with great self-assurance, "am just dropping this basket of food at the door. I'll text Dani and let her know it's here to grab whenever they have a chance. I suggest you leave too, and call before showing up next time. If you want to talk to either of them."

"You're saying I shouldn't knock on the door and tell Dani what she's been asking me about for days because she and Ty might be having sex? Which, by the way, is *not* an image I need in my head. You guys are like sisters to me, and the thought of either of you having sex isn't something I need to talk about."

"Drew, I'm married to your brother. We have three kids. Do you think they came about through immaculate conception?" Sam chided.

"I don't want to talk about it," Drew grumbled back. On the other side of the door, Ty smiled to himself.

"Are they talking about us?" Dani asked as she sidled up to Ty in the entryway. He wrapped an arm around her shoulder and nodded.

"Drew wants to talk work. Sam's telling him not to bother us because we're having sex," Ty grinned.

"She's not!" Dani protested with a laugh. Ty chuckled in response. "Good lord, Drew is going to have his own heart attack just thinking about the possibility of us naked together."

Taking pity on Drew, Dani moved to the door and opened it. Two sets of eyes turned. Sam stood with her arms crossed across her chest, basket in hand, and Drew stood with his hands jammed on his hips. Both looked at Dani with startled surprise.

"We're not having sex, so you might as well come in," Dani opened the door wider and gestured them in. Both stood there staring.

"What?" Dani demanded.

Ty came up behind her and rubbed her shoulder. "They might believe you if you were wearing more than a sheet," he laughed.

Dani glanced down in surprise, forgetting that she was, indeed, wearing nothing but a sheet.

"Good lord," she rolled her eyes and marched back to her room.

"Since you're here," Ty said, gesturing them in.

"I just came to drop off some more food," Sam said, handing Ty a basket.

"Dani will want to say hi," Ty protested.

"Then Dani can call. She deserves a few days without family bugging her. She deserves a few days to hole up and spend time with you."

"You're very understanding," Ty replied with a smile.

"I have three kids; believe me, I understand how important *alone* time is with your partner," she added the emphasis and a pointed look at Drew, who ignored her. Before anyone could protest any more, she waltzed down the hall and disappeared into a waiting elevator.

"They're a lot alike aren't they?" Ty mused as he closed the door.

"You have no idea," Drew responded with a shake of his head, no doubt thinking of all the years he'd known the two women.

"No idea what?" Dani asked as she entered the room wearing a pair of Ty's boxers and his shirt. It wasn't much better than a sheet but, of course, Ty thought she looked good either way.

"Nothing," Drew answered. Dani shot him a suspicious look, then changed tactics and started pawing through the bag of food.

"Sammy left?" It wasn't a real question so no one answered. Satisfied with her perusal, Dani grabbed an apple and then plopped down on her sofa and looked at Drew. "So, what's up?"

Ty watched indecision flit across Drew's face and hid a grin. He'd probably never seen Dani looking so relaxed, so happy. It threw him off. Drew cast a look at Ty who shrugged, grabbed his own apple and perched on the sofa behind Dani.

"Maybe I should come back later," Drew spoke.

"You're here. You know I'm not going to let you leave before you tell me what you came to tell me," Dani replied.

Drew eyed her for a long minute, looking like he was debating whether to take her at her word or not. Deciding on the former, he sat down and told them everything he'd learned from Sonny Carlyle. "A few months after his dad was killed, Frey approached him. At first he wasn't sure what Frey wanted, but because he seemed to know so much about Sonny's dad, Sonny listened to him, even sought him out after a while. Sonny learned from Frey that his dad sometimes did work for the CIA. Nothing huge but enough that he earned some good friends and allies. But then, Frey told him, one of the allies switched allegiances and, when Sonny's dad confronted him, he killed him. Sonny said Frey told him that we, the CIA, knew who killed his father, but chose not to do anything about it because we needed the rogue agent more than we needed his father."

"We needed a rogue agent?" Dani repeated.

"Frey convinced Sonny that this agent had enough valuable information, even though he was playing both sides of the coin, that we planned to overlook his father's murder."

"And this agent is?" Ty prompted with a drawl.

"Fictional," Drew replied. "Carlyle only had contact with three agents. All three have been checked out, just in case. All three are clear."

"So Sonny thought the government his dad tried to help was protecting the man who killed him?" Dani surmised.

"Pretty much about sums it up," Drew shrugged.

"So, what was Frey's solution?"

"Sonny wasn't very clear on this. He said that Frey suggested talking to Bradley Taylor, the guy who runs Eagle's Wing and maybe Taylor could help him 'work through it.' Taylor's not talking, but when we raided the Eagle's Wing compound, we found detailed maps of the IRS headquarters, along with security information and potential weak points."

"Put it together with what we know they were collecting from Getz and we can assume they were going to target the tax man. Somehow that seems appropriate for an anti-government militia. But why Sonny? Why wouldn't Frey facilitate the transaction through both Getz and Taylor?" Ty asked.

Drew took a deep breath and let it out. "This is Adam's theory and, though he's the newbie, I think it has some merit." Drew paused and looked at both of them. Ty had slid down onto the sofa and was sitting next to Dani. "We know Frey and Robertson know each other. We know Frey helped Robertson get elected and we know Frey has worked with a lot of companies Robertson and his cronies own or control. We also know Robertson's polls are low, some of the lowest in history, and there is an election coming up in a few months—"

"Drew," Dani sat back and warned as if she could stop Drew from saying what he was going to say next. Drew cast her a sympathetic look, like he'd give anything not to have to say it as well.

"We also know Sonny holds a Saudi Arabian passport. He's not a dual citizen, since it's not allowed. He was born in the United States but applied for a Saudi Arabian passport based on his mother's nationality. He isn't a dual citizen, but he has possession of both."

"Shit," Ty breathed. Drew looked like he concurred.

"You think Frey was orchestrating an attack on the IRS headquarters as a favor to bolster Robertson's polls and that he needed Sonny, or someone like him, because he wanted to be able to lay the blame at the feet of foreign terrorists. Even though Sonny isn't foreign," Dani added.

"It's what Adam has suggested," Drew replied.

"And you agree?" Ty asked.

"And what would happen when Eagle's Wing claimed the attack? How would they get around that?" Dani interjected.

"I'm not sure whether or not the attack would take place, but the effect is still the same. If it *had* been successful, Robertson would reinvigorate the war on terrorism, call on the country to come together, and, lo and behold, we have a second-term president. But, even if the attack was foiled, it would still bode well for Robertson. He'd be able to sell his success to the press, point out that we're still at risk and that we need leaders like him to keep us safe, and, bang, we have the same result, he gets re-elected," Drew replied with a mix of cynicism and anger. "As for Eagle's Wing, I hate to say it, but who do you think the people will believe capable of such an act? A militia no one has ever heard of before, or a young man with ties to the Middle East?"

"And, of course, the fact that Sonny has a foreign passport provides the added fodder and saves the president from the embarrassment of having to admit that some terrorists are home grown," Dani finished in disgust. "But why Sonny? It seems that any number of people could have performed the same function."

"We're working on that," Drew responded. "There might be a reason, or it might be chance. Either way, we'll find out."

"So, where does that leave us?" Ty asked, after a long silence during which they had digested the information.

"We've got some feelers out to try and figure out how involved Robertson is. We still want to go after Frey, we still *will* go after Frey, especially now, knowing he's involved in arms dealing as well as a planned attack against a US target. The question is whether or not we'll have Robertson's support or if we'll have to wheel and deal." "You think we'll get his support?" Dani asked, curious.

Drew shrugged. "I don't know. I don't know how involved Robertson is in this. We know Frey is a master manipulator. If he's been manipulating Robertson all these years, Robertson might be glad to have a chance to get rid of him. On the other hand, if Robertson and Frey are in it together, we'll have to use another route."

"Such as?" Ty prompted.

"Extortion," Dani supplied.

Drew looked at her and cracked a smile. "Such an ugly word don't you think?" he responded. "And it wouldn't be extortion, it would be blackmail."

"You let us go after Frey and we won't tell the public you're an accomplice to murder and attempted terrorism," Ty interjected, disbelief palpable in his voice. "If he's involved, I'd say that's a pretty small price to pay."

"True," Drew conceded. "I think we'd make sure he never ran for public office again. And once he was out of office, we probably wouldn't let things lie, but we wouldn't go public."

"What? You'd sic the IRS on him or something?" Ty said.

Drew chuckled, "You'd be surprised how effective the IRS is at destroying a man's life."

"What's the timeline?" Dani asked.

Again, Drew shrugged. "Hard to say, a couple of weeks maybe? Hopefully sooner rather than later, given that the election is coming up in less than five months."

"You'll let us know?" Dani asked.

Drew nodded and stood. Dani and Ty followed suit. "Dani," Ty said, looking at Dani. "Can you go heat up some of that pasta Sam brought?"

Dani shot him a look and let her gaze travel to Drew. She shook her head and laughed. "Yes," she said, going up on her toes as he ducked his head down to kiss her. "But if you wanted a chance to talk to Drew without me in the room, all you had to do was ask."

"And you would have listened?" He asked in earned disbelief.

"Probably not," she said over her shoulder. "You just got lucky this time that I happen to be hungry, too."

The men watched her leave and then Ty gestured Drew toward the door. When they were out in the hallway, he spoke. "I want to know everything, whenever you have it," he said.

"Revenge is a nasty beast, Ty," Drew said.

Ty stared back.

Drew nodded. "Right, of course," he said with a sigh.

"I'm serious, Drew," Ty cut in. "This man killed Dani's parents and god knows how many others and, more importantly to me, at least, he almost killed her. He knows who she is now, he knows where she works. He's a man who knows a lot of nasty people and I'm not willing to take the chance that he might know someone who would take care of her for him. And we both know she won't be able to go."

There was a long silence during which Drew studied Ty.

"How deep do you want to go?" Drew asked, finally.

Ty knew Drew was remembering the conversation they'd had earlier that summer—remembering Ty's own internal conflicts and why he left the SEALs. If Ty joined forces with Drew on this mission, he'd be going straight back into the lion's den.

"As deep as it takes to get him out of her life permanently," came his fast reply.

"It's been a while since you've been active," Drew pointed out. And they both knew what he meant. Active in the military, active on foreign missions. Active with the kind of skills and training he'd had when he was a SEAL.

"I'll take care of it," was all he said, already planning a training regimen.

Drew studied him for another long span of silence before giving him a curt nod and turning away.

"Make sure you do, because Dani will kill me if anything happens to you," he added over his shoulder as he disappeared into the stairwell.

Ty stood for a moment in the silence of the hall, contemplating what he'd just promised. He hated the idea of leaving Dani to go after Frey, though he knew he would have to. He would hate being away from her and he would hate knowing she would, at some level, begrudge him his involvement. She would want to go herself, but there was no way he or Drew would let her. She would be pissed, but she would understand it wouldn't be safe to take her, wherever they ended up going. He wasn't worried that Frey would get her— though there was that. But it wasn't likely, given the extent of her injury, that she would ever be the field operative she was a month ago. He knew it, Drew knew it, but Ty didn't think Dani had even thought about this yet. When Drew refused to let her go after Frey— and Ty knew he would—it would be like slapping her in the face with this fact. Not only would she have to deal with her involvement with Frey and her belief, as misplaced as it was, that she let him get away, she'd also have to start coping with the fact that her career as she knew it was over.

Ty sighed and turned back toward the apartment. The time would come soon enough when Dani would have to confront her uncertain career future. In the meantime, he would spend his time working on their future.

CHAPTER 24

"WHERE'S DANI?" DREW ASKED AS he stepped through the door Ty held open.

"Shopping with Sam. Picking up some clothes for the kids, or so I'm told," Ty answered, closing the door behind Drew and moving toward the kitchen. It was hard to miss how bad Drew appeared, including the look of relief that crossed his face after finding out Dani wasn't home. His eyes were red with fatigue, his usually immaculate clothes were rumpled—his shirt was even untucked— and his facial hair was growing in, making him look almost scruffy.

"I'd offer you a beer," Ty said, opening the fridge. "You look like you could use it, but you also look like it might put you to sleep."

Drew eyed him as he pulled out a chair at the kitchen table and didn't answer. Ty pulled out a bottle for himself, popped the top, and leaned against the counter, knowing Drew would talk when he was good and ready.

A half a beer later, in which time they'd done nothing but sit in the quiet, Drew rubbed his hands over his face, swore, and asked for one himself. Ty handed him a bottle and then sat opposite him as Drew took a long pull.

"Robertson's done," he said.

Ty blinked. "Excuse, me?"

"He's out."

"Out, as in out of reach? Out of the dealings? Out of what?" Ty prompted, leaning forward, listening.

"Out of the election," Drew said under his breath. Then, taking another deep breath, he spoke louder. "He's not going to run. He's withdrawing from the election."

"It's four months away," disbelief and shock clear in Ty's voice.

"I know. It's the only compromise we could come to," Drew closed his eyes and let his head fall back. They remained quiet for a long time until Drew lifted his head and met Ty's gaze.

"This is the story and you're not hearing it from me," he said with a pointed look. Ty nodded and Drew continued. "Robertson admitted to knowing Frey, admitted to helping him by giving him contacts in the extraction and industrial construction industries in the seventies. He told us everything he knew about what happened in Vietnam and it's about what we thought."

"Frey set him up and then called in favors?"

Drew nodded. "Robertson says Frey had a video of that day. A video showing him cowering behind a tree as Frey took on the Vietcong. Robertson was hit and did get knocked out which is why he didn't remember any of it until Frey showed him the video—after he won his first election."

"Hold on," Ty held up a hand. "Frey had the whole ambush recorded? Who would do that—and for what purpose?"

"From what Robertson remembered, Peterson, one of the other officers involved, was the cameraman."

"Only Peterson didn't make it out."

"Robertson doesn't remember what happened, but he said he wouldn't put it past Frey to have killed Peterson too."

"So we've got Robertson not remembering the ambush and Frey feeding him lies about how courageous he was. So, Robertson goes home, campaigns, wins, and then Frey presents him with the video and starts calling in favors?"

"That's about how it started, according to Robertson," Drew added.

"Okay," Ty nodded, soaking in the information, the confirmation that the sitting president was involved with a man like Frey. "So then what?"

"Robertson didn't hear from him for years, and then one day George Collier, a friend and major contributor to Robertson's campaign, mentions Frey in a conversation. Robertson says he was surprised to hear Frey's name after all the time that had passed, but not surprised to hear it in conjunction with some shady arms dealing that was going on in South America at the time. He claims it was Collier who suggested they use Frey to orchestrate the arming of a guerilla group interested in overthrowing a certain dictator that wasn't very friendly to the current US administration."

"And thus started the slippery slope." Ty sat back in his chair in disgust.

"Pretty much," Drew admitted. "Frey kept his regular business going, but from then on, he would do favors for Robertson and vice versa. Collier was always the intermediary, which is why we have no record of Robertson and Frey being in the same area since the seventies."

"And Sonny? And Dani's parents?"

"Collier had a meeting with Frey a few days after Sonny's dad was killed. Robertson claims all he knew was that Collier was going to talk to Frey about doing something to increase his, Robertson's, approval ratings."

"Like orchestrate a terrorist attack and blame the kid," Ty provided, his voice flat.

Drew wagged his head. "Robertson claims he had no idea what Collier or Frey had in mind."

"You believe him?"

Drew was silent for a minute. "Yeah, I do. I don't think he knew what Frey was planning. He all but got sick when we told him about the weapons Eagle's Wing was going to collect from Getz and that we'd found plans to the IRS headquarters in their compound."

"He could be faking it," Ty countered.

"He could be, but I don't think so. He didn't tell us anything until we fed him that piece of information. After he realized what

Frey was capable of, he started talking." Drew pressed his lips together.

"And offered his resignation."

"And offered his resignation," Drew nodded.

"So, what else did you get? Anything on Frey?"

Drew let out a heavy breath. "We think it was just in the timing that he targeted Sonny. Sonny was on Frey's mind when Collier talked to him. Frey needed a scapegoat, and who better to manipulate than the grieving son of a former CIA informant. The man's a damn puppeteer, the way he manipulates people," Drew swore for emphasis.

"But what about now? Did Robertson know where Frey might be?"

Ty watched a muscle in Drew's jaw tick as he sat forward and began to pick at the label on the bottle. It had been a long couple of days for Drew and Ty felt for him.

"Africa," Drew spoke. Ty glanced up and met his eyes. "He owns an island off the coast of Sierra Leone. He also owns islands in the Caribbean, the Mediterranean, and a few other places, in case you were wondering what he's done with the money he's collected over the years."

Ty didn't, not really. What Frey did with his money was irrelevant at the moment. He studied the man across the table and absorbed what he wasn't saying. They were going after him. And by the looks of it, soon.

"When do we go?" Ty asked.

"Ty," Drew warned, but more out of duty than anything else. "You don't need to go. You can stay here with Dani. The rest of the team is going."

"I know," he responded, not moving his gaze from Drew.

"Dani's not going to like it," Drew tried again.

"I know," he replied again. Drew swore and raked a hand through his hair.

"We leave in two days," he said, resigned.

"We?"

"Me, a couple of folks from Cotter's team, Roddy, Fawkes, and Jay. Of course Cotter wanted to go, but, like Dani, he's out."

"Roddy, Fawkes, and Jay?" Ty asked, not bothering to hide the surprise in his voice.

Drew nodded. "You were right, they took a liking to Dani," he added with a tired smile.

Ty let the information sink in. Never in a million years did he think he'd be out on another mission with his former team. And he'd never been more grateful for their friendship. It was going to be a shitty operation, and he was relieved beyond reason to know his friends would have his back when he went for Frey. And they'd all understand that Frey would be his, without question. Aside from wanting to deal with Frey for what he did to Dani, he also knew that Dani, once she accepted she wouldn't be going after Frey herself, wouldn't truly trust anyone but him to do it. Well, that wasn't entirely accurate. She'd trust Drew to *try*, but Ty knew she wouldn't trust that Drew would tell her the truth if things didn't go as planned; that was a burden, or honor, he knew only he carried. And the only way confirmation of Frey's death would truly come from him is if he took care of Frey himself.

Ty stood and dumped the rest of his beer down the sink. He didn't drink all that much and had only had a few glasses of wine with Dani since she'd come home from the hospital, but now, well, now he wasn't about to put anything that might impair his ability to function into his system until after the mission was complete.

"Where do I need to be?" he asked. Drew looked up and Ty could see the debate still warring in Drew. "It has to be me and you know it," Ty said. "It can't be her and she won't trust anyone else."

Drew closed his eyes and then gave a slight nod before pushing out of his chair. "Tonight we go to DC. We'll have a debrief there and then head out." Ty nodded.

"What about Dani?" Drew asked. "She's getting stronger, but I don't want..." he let his voice trail off.

"She'll have to face it sooner or later," Ty replied with a regretful sigh. Frey hadn't killed her, but had taken a good agent out of commission.

"You'll tell her?"

"You chicken?" Ty offered a smile, trying to lighten the moment.

Trying to pretend they weren't talking about the end of Dani's career. Drew smiled back. "Hell, yes."

Ty sobered as they moved toward the door. He reached for the knob and pulled the door open with a sigh. "Yeah, I'll tell her," he replied, the weight of the information hanging heavy on his shoulders.

After Drew left, Ty sat in the armchair and waited for Dani to get home. His bag was packed, his flight was booked, and all that was left to do was talk to Dani. He didn't bother trying to suppress his anxiety about taking part in the mission. He was more in shape than he was a few weeks earlier, but nowhere near where he'd been when he was at the top of his game, when he was an active duty SEAL. Still, it wasn't this that made the thought of deploying so difficult. It was Dani.

He'd deployed so many times during his time as a SEAL, but this was different. It was even different than leaving Carrie because, while he didn't belittle what he and Carrie had once felt for each other, what he felt for Dani was different. Not only was he was older and more aware of what he wanted out of life, but he had a different appreciation for how unique and fragile life, and love, could be. And in those hours, as he waited for Dani to come home, he gained a whole new respect for the men and women of the armed forces who left their spouses and loved ones behind.

He heard the door fly open and slam shut. By the sounds of Dani's movements, by the way she kicked off her shoes and tossed her keys on the entry table, he knew she already knew something was going on. He stood and waited for her to enter the living room.

She rounded the corner and, when her eyes met his, he felt as if someone were ripping his heart out.

"You're going," she said, so quietly it stopped his breath. He moved toward her, but she put her hand up to stop him.

"I heard on the radio that Robertson is withdrawing from the election. Some 'private medical condition that may interfere with his presidential duties,'" she repeated what he assumed she'd heard. Ty hadn't bothered to watch or listen to the news, Robertson was now inconsequential to him.

"His party held an emergency meeting and has given the nomination to the vice president. He knew about Frey and knows where he is and you're going after him," she rambled. Ty stayed where he was, wanting desperately to hold her, but knowing she needed some time.

"Don't go for me, Ty," she pleaded. Her voice broke. "Please, don't go for me."

"Oh, Ella," he said, as he moved to her, unable to stay away any longer. He wrapped his arms around her and pulled her close. She tucked her head against his shoulder and held on. He leaned his cheek against the top of her head and breathed in her scent— fresh and subtle with hints of honeysuckle that reminded him of his childhood. "I'm going for me," he said. "I'm going for us," he added, holding her tighter.

"But not for me," she repeated. He shook his head. In truth, he was going in part for her, for all the reasons he'd talked about with Drew—mainly because she wouldn't trust anyone but him to give her a truthful account of what would take place on Frey's little island. But she didn't need to hear this and he didn't need to say it. And it was just as true that he was going for himself. *He* needed to know Frey was either dead or so under the control of Drew and his team that he wished he was dead. He wanted Frey out of their lives, without any doubt. Without any regrets.

"I wish I could go instead of you," she stated. His heart felt like it was going to burst from his chest. The honesty of it was clear in her voice and her body as she leaned against him. She would take his place if meant keeping him safe.

But that wasn't possible.

"Honey, you know—"

She placed two fingers over his lips and stopped him. Pulling back to look him in the eye, she spoke. "I know," she said with a calm acceptance. "You and Drew have been tiptoeing around it since I was in the hospital. Why you would think I wouldn't figure out that my days as a field agent were over, I don't know." She gave him a sad smile.

"Maybe because we didn't want to accept it either," Ty offered, running a finger across her cheek, pausing at her lips and then replacing his finger with a light brush of his lips against hers.

"So, when do you leave?" Her voice hesitated on the last word.

"My flight is in six hours." She held him tighter for a moment and then, with a sigh, seemed to accept whatever the fates would bring them.

"Will you lie with me until you have to go?"

Ty cradled her against him as they walked toward the bedroom. "Anything, Dani. Anything you want."

CHAPTER 25

"No," Spanky said. "Absolutely not," he added for emphasis. Dani didn't move from her spot.

"Dani, you *know* I can't," he tried a different tack. She raised her eyebrow at him. It was a lie and they both knew it.

"Well, I can't," he tried again. "Not with them in the room," he added with a gesture toward Sammy and Jason, who stood behind her in the little room that held some of the best audio equipment owned by the CIA.

"Drew authorized it," Dani countered, holding out a printed copy of an email that was addressed to her. That it was sent from Drew's private computer, which anyone with any training could hack into, wasn't missed by Spanky who gave her a you-can't-be-serious look. But she was. Serious. Very serious.

She wanted to listen in on the mission that would bring Frey down. She wanted to know it was going as planned and, most of all, she wanted to know that Ty was okay. The email wasn't official, and they both knew it, but it would be enough to cover Spanky's butt if anyone ever questioned him about having the three of them in the room.

"Mack, it's not a good idea," he pleaded again, this time more concerned than anything else.

"I know," she conceded. "But still, I'm here. And still, I want to listen in."

Spanky stared at her for a long time. Technically, he could throw them out. He could call security and they'd be out of there faster than they could say "goodbye," but she was banking on loyalty now. On their years of work together. She was asking him as a friend.

"Dani," he sounded pained, but she wasn't going to change her mind. "Shit," he said, in final resignation. She almost smiled in triumph, but he turned his gaze on her and pinned her to the spot with the deadly seriousness in his eyes.

"I'll let you stay, Dani, but you know as well as I do that this mission could go any number of ways. We all want it to be easy in and easy out, but we both know things can go from sugar to shit in a heartbeat. Are you ready for that? Really ready?" he demanded.

He was asking her if she was ready to listen to Ty die. No one expected it to happen, no one expected anyone to die on this mission. But it was always a possibility.

Taking a deep breath and willing the panic the thought caused to subside, she nodded. For a moment, it didn't look like he believed her. With good reason, since she didn't believe it herself—how could anyone be ready to hear someone they loved die? But, it wasn't going to change her mind. She wanted—she needed—to be there.

Spanky threw up his arms and made a vague gesture to the empty chairs in the room. Dani sat, giving Spanky a wide berth, given that he wasn't too happy about her presence. Sammy sat next to her, with Jason behind them. Dani must have looked as nervous as she felt because Sammy grasped her hand and offered a reassuring squeeze. She squeezed back and they both held on.

They were still sitting like that, several minutes later, when the audio synced up. She could hear Drew orchestrating the mission from the Navy boat anchored off Frey's island. She heard Roddy and Fawkes and, after what seemed like an eon, she heard Ty.

Closing her eyes, she focused on his voice. On the little snippets of information he passed on, location, status, visuals—all standard operating procedure. And every time she heard him, she gave a little prayer of thanks, and one of pleading, pleading to bring them all home safe.

Her mind raced with every second that went by in silence

and she sat still, so still, as they listened to the mission unfolding thousands of miles away in the dark of the night. The only movement was the occasional squeeze from Sammy when they heard Ty checking in.

And then they heard the shots.

Even though the sound was expected, Dani jumped. Her heart rate accelerated but, even knowing she was still recovering from a heart attack, she ignored the sensation and leaned forward, aching to hear Ty's voice through the now near-constant sound of weapons being discharged.

She gripped Sammy's hand and sensed Jason's hand on her shoulder as she listened to the sound of a gunfight that felt like it was never going to end. Voices shouted across the airwaves, but there were too many, there was too much chaos, to pick out Ty's.

Once or twice Spanky cast her a concerned look, but she ignored that, too, always focusing on the sounds and trying to sort through everything she was hearing. And then it was silent. The shots stopped, no one spoke. No one in their tiny room moved.

"The target's down. The area is secure," came Ty's voice, loud and clear. Dani, who hadn't cried in years, felt the tears tracking down her cheeks.

"He pulled a knife on me," Ty continued, sounding almost amused.

"He hit you?" Fawkes's voice carried through to the room.

"Yeah, in the arm, but I'm fine," Ty answered.

Dani sat back and let out a choked breath.

"We're clear here," Ty spoke again.

"We've got the backup, clean up team on the way. ETA ten minutes," Drew answered. "Casualties?" he added.

"Everyone's accounted for here," Ty answered. "I'll need a stitch-up when I'm back on board, but other than that, no one else was dumb enough to get in the way of a knife or bullet."

"Glad to hear it, Fuller," Drew responded. "And the target?"

"Down, out of commission. It was self-defense on my part,"

Ty added and Dani could hear the smile in his voice. "There are two guards on the beach and six in the house."

"Anything we need to worry about?" Drew asked.

"You'll need to do a sweep of the jungle behind the house when you get here. We've got people posted back there and they haven't seen a thing, but when the backup gets here, they should do a more comprehensive search."

"Roger," Drew answered. "Take your team and head back to the boat."

"We're on our way," Ty answered as the lines went silent. It was hard to believe the end of such a horrible mastermind came in less than ten minutes. But it was over.

Dani closed her eyes and sent a silent prayer out to whomever, thankful that the team was okay. That Ty was going to be home soon.

"Dani?" Spanky spoke. "You okay?"

She opened her eyes and smiled. "I'm fine. Better now. Thank you, Spanky." He still didn't look convinced that he'd done the right thing, but he nodded and glanced at Sammy and Jason, who looked as relived as she felt.

"Better, baby?" her sister asked, brushing a strand of hair from her face. Dani nodded and squeezed her sister's hand. She'd gone through hell, but she had the love of her family and Ty, and things were going to be better. She knew it, she could feel it.

She opened her mouth to say just that when the audio crackled behind them. Startled by the sudden sound, Dani swung her gaze back to the console, only to find Spanky looking just as surprised.

"Shit, we've got incoming," Fawkes's voice rang through the static. The tension in it was unmistakable.

"Get back to the boat, now!" Drew ordered.

"We're on our way," Ty answered as the sound of an explosion rocked the room.

"Ty!" Fawkes shouted.

"Ty, Fawkes, what's going on out there?" Drew demanded, the panic in his voice carried straight into Dani.

"Shit, we've gotta swim. The boat's sinking," Fawkes answered. "Ah, shit!"

And another sound of something exploding echoed.

"Ty!" Fawkes called, panic and fear clear in his voice.

"Get back to the boat, now!" Drew's demand was met with silence. "Fawkes? Ty?" He called again.

"Can't…need to find Ty…" Fawkes's voice faded and then the audio went dead all together, muted by Spanky.

Dani stared at the console, at the speaker that Ty's voice, moments ago had come through. And refused to believe what she'd just heard.

"He's not dead," she mumbled, shaking her head. "He's not," she repeated.

"Honey," Sammy's voice shook next to her.

Dani raised her eyes and looked at her sister. "He's not," she insisted. "They'll find him. Fawkes wouldn't let anything happen to him. I'd know if he were dead. I'd just *know*," her voice raised. "Spanky," she demanded, turning to her colleague. "Turn the audio back on. Get on the phone to Drew and tell him to send the search boats out. They have a helicopter, use it dammit! It must have a spotlight. The damn Navy boat probably has one, too. Make them use it!" She pounded her fist on the desk.

"Dani, you know Drew is doing everything he can," Spanky responded. But still, no one was moving, they just watched her, doing nothing.

"Do something!" she screamed at Spanky as Jason's arms came around her from behind. She struggled against him, fought him, refusing to believe what had happened. Even as she sank into darkness, she still refused to believe.

CHAPTER 26

DANI STOPPED HER CAR AT the bottom of the long driveway and looked up at the adobe house perched at the other end of the drive. It was late fall in Taos and the landscape looked barren and harsh. Beautiful and rugged. She could see why people would like it here. She could even see Ty, as a young boy, hiking around the jagged mountains, exploring the unusual terrain.

Three months, Dani thought to herself as she sat in the idling car. Three months since Ty had disappeared into the waters off Africa. Three months since she'd fled the city and all that reminded her of everything they'd had together. The chance they'd lost.

She still had a hard time accepting that he was dead. His GPS had been found on a bit of the boat that was pulled from the water. There hadn't been a body, nothing to prove if he'd lived or died, nothing to say goodbye to.

She glanced at the house and wondered if she was doing the right thing. Would Ty's parents want to be reminded of their lost son? But looking at the house, the question vanished, replaced by the memory of Ty's voice telling her about his family, how close they were, and how much they loved each other.

And it was for Ty that she was here, waiting to gather enough courage to introduce herself to his parents. She could have gone a lifetime without this meeting, without the reminder of what would never be, but she owed it to Ty. And herself.

And their baby.

She placed her hand on her belly. It was the one good thing to come from her injury. The sound waves that caused her heart attack had affected other parts of her body, rendering the birth control shots she received unreliable. They hadn't known then. And for that she was glad, because if they had, they would have taken extra precautions and she'd have nothing left of Ty.

She put the car in gear and slowly made her way up the driveway. When she reached the top, she turned off the engine and, before she could chicken out, opened her door, slid from her seat, and closed the door behind her.

Pulling her jacket tight around her, Dani made her way to the front door. It opened before she knocked and an attractive woman, who looked be in her sixties but with eyes like her son, stood before her.

"Is everything okay, dear?" she asked. "I saw you down on the drive. It's not a great day to be out. Come in," she beckoned. Speechless, Dani followed.

The door closed behind her and a man appeared in the hallway.

"Is everything okay, Jeannie?" he asked, his eyes on Dani's. Dani blinked at the man who so resembled Ty his face was like looking into the future, at what could have been, and then she suddenly found herself embraced in a tight hug from Jeannie Fuller.

"It's okay, dear. It will all be okay," she soothed. Dani took a few deep breaths only to find herself crying in the arms of this stranger. And then something broke and, after months, she let the grief take hold.

She didn't know how long she cried, or how long afterward she slept. But, when she awoke, she was lying on the couch, in front of a roaring fire, wrapped in a quilt. Jeannie was knitting in a chair beside her and Ty's father was reading the paper. He looked so much like an older version of Ty that she couldn't help staring.

"How are you feeling, now? Can I get you something to drink?" Jeannie's voice cut through the haze. Dani glanced back to the woman and then, embarrassed by what had happened, she swung her legs off the couch and began to stand.

"Sit, Dani. It's okay," Ty's father spoke.

Dani stared at the couple, easing back down onto the couch, before she found her voice. "You know who I am?"

"From the moment you stepped out of the car," Jeannie answered. "You look a little different than the photo Ty sent all those months ago. But I saw the resemblance. And then, when you looked at Christopher," she added with a nod to Ty's father. "We knew it was you."

"Ty sent a picture?" She knew she must sound crazy or stupid, but it was news to her.

Jeannie smiled and nodded. "He loved you."

Dani blinked to keep the tears welling in her eyes from falling. "I—" she stopped and cleared her throat. "I love him, too," she managed to say.

"And that's our grandbaby?" she asked with a nod to Dani's barely-there stomach. Dani nodded in response. And Jeannie smiled.

"Well, Christopher," she said, turning to Ty's father. "What do think about another grandbaby?"

Christopher Fuller smiled at his wife, and then turned to Dani. "I can't tell you how glad we are that you've come."

Dani swallowed back another set of tears before she spoke again. "You know what happened, right? You know he went after a man because of me?" Somehow it was important to her to say what she was going say, to make sure they *knew* that Ty's disappearance was her fault.

Christopher frowned. "Did you tell him to go?" Dani shook her head. "Did you force him to go?" Again, she shook her head. "If Ty hadn't gone after this man, would he have come after you or done something else awful?"

"Someone else would have gotten to him first," she answered. "It didn't have to be Ty."

"But would he have? Would this man have come after you or someone else?" Christopher pressed. And Dani nodded.

"Then he went because he needed to," Christopher pronounced.

"But—" Dani started to protest, but stopped when Jeannie's hand touched her arm.

"Dani, he loved you. He did what he thought was best for both of you. It's not your fault. It's not anyone's fault but the person who killed him. Do you understand?" Jeannie fixed her with a look and, though Dani wasn't yet convinced, she found herself nodding.

"Good, now that we have that out of the way, what are your plans for the baby?" Jeannie sat back and took up her knitting again.

"I don't know," Dani hesitated. "I've been driving around for the last couple of months. Wandering. Trying to heal, I guess. Or run," she added with a self-deprecating smile. "I haven't been in touch with anyone but my sister. She wants me to come back to the city, but I don't think I'm ready for that."

"What about your parents?" Christopher asked.

"They're dead," Dani answered, able to say it for the first time without a sense of panic. "They were killed when I was thirteen by the same man Ty went after in Africa."

Both Jeannie and Christopher looked up at this bit of information.

"You saw it?" Jeannie asked. That she already knew the answer was clear in her voice, but Dani nodded.

"And did Ty get him? This man?" Christopher asked. Again, Dani nodded as the two exchanged a look.

"Good then, I think it's settled," Jeannie spoke.

"What's settled?" Dani asked.

"You'll stay here with us," Jeannie spoke. It was a statement, but when the older woman met Dani's eyes, Dani saw the question there, saw the woman's hope for her grandchild, her love for her son, and her desire to have what was left of him.

"If that's alright with you," she added. Dani's eyes went from Jeannie to Christopher and then swept the room. As she nodded in agreement, a feeling of how right the decision was wrapped around her like a blanket. Almost everything had been taken from her, her parents, Ty, even her career. But looking at Ty's parents, she knew this was a gift, that the baby was a gift. And she could all but hear Ty saying "Take it, you deserve it. *We* deserve it."

And so she did.

CHAPTER 27

DREW LOOKED OUT THE WINDOW into the gray day. It was early March, spring was on its way. It was supposed to be nice, but nothing in the weather, or his mood, lent itself to "nice." If he were honest with himself, he'd admit that he hadn't had a day that felt anything other than tolerable since that night, seven months ago, when Ty Fuller didn't make it back from the mission to destroy Nicholas Frey. That they'd succeeded in ending Frey's reign of terror and even backtracked his movements and brought several more people to justice—in more ways than one—wasn't enough to get him to think back on that day as a good day in Agency history.

He hadn't spoken to Dani in months. She kept in touch with Sammy, but that was it. She'd called on Thanksgiving and Christmas, but told no one where she was or what she was doing. He'd even tried tracking her credit card statements to at least get a general idea of where she was, but she hadn't used any in a long time—long enough for Drew to get the hint that she was hiding. And after a few months of no obvious leads, he'd decided to respect her privacy and let her tell him when she was ready.

"Drew?" his assistant's voice buzzed through the intercom.

"Yeah," he replied, already dreading the phone call. He didn't know who it was, he just plain wasn't interested in talking to anyone.

"Call on line one," she said. When he didn't pick up she added, "It's the consulate in Côte D'Ivoire, he says they have a Tyler Fuller in their office."

Drew's heart slammed into his chest as he hit the connect

274

button as fast as possible. "This is Andrew Carmichael," he barked. He was both terrified and convinced that it must be some hoax and praying it wasn't.

"Drew, get me the hell out of here. I want to come home." Ty. Ty's voice. Ty's voice on the phone. Ty, alive and talking to him from the Ivory Coast. "Drew?"

"Jesus Christ, Ty. I'm having a heart attack here. Are you okay?"

Ty chuckled. Drew did not. He rubbed a hand over his face, pinched the bridge of his nose and, for the first time in many, many years, fought back tears.

"I'm fine. I'll tell you about it when I see you, but I want to come home. Can you arrange it?"

"Yes." Drew had to clear his throat but he didn't hesitate, already making the arrangements in his head. "I'll have a helicopter to you within the hour. You'll have to go through Germany and then back to New York."

"I don't care, I just want to be home. Tell me about Dani? Is she okay?"

Drew hesitated for a split second before lying. "She's fine. She didn't take it too well when, well," he hesitated again before Ty supplied the rest.

"When everyone thought I was dead? But she's okay, right?" Ty continued.

"Yeah, I'll find her and let her know you're on your way home."

"Find her?" Ty didn't miss the slip. "Where is she?" he demanded.

"Just get on the helicopter. I'll talk to you when you get to Germany. I'll have your documents waiting for you when you get back to New York."

"Drew," Ty warned.

"Just get on the helicopter. We'll talk about it when you call from

Germany," Drew ordered.

Ty grunted his assent and the two hung up. The line was dead for two seconds before he started barking orders. Not the least of which were orders to find Dani.

• • •

Drew raked his hand through his hair and rubbed the hair growing on his chin. It was late, or rather early morning, and he'd been in the office longer than he should have, but he wasn't going to leave. Not until Ty was on his way back the US and not until he could find Dani. Which was proving more difficult than he'd imagined.

He glanced up as his computer beeped, indicating a new email message. Swinging back to the monitor, he clicked open the message and attachments and started reading.

Two fractured femurs, a couple of crushed ribs, a lacerated Achilles tendon, a broken collar bone, and a broken arm.

But nothing long term, nothing to keep Ty from living a long and happy life. As long as Drew could find Dani.

He walked back to his desk, picked up the phone and punched in some numbers. "Drew Carmichael," he said as someone picked up the line. "I need to speak to Dr. Sinha." It was close to five in the morning in DC, which made it well into the workday in Germany, and he was on hold less than thirty seconds before the doctor picked up.

"He's good to go?" Drew asked, without preamble.

"He was good to go the minute he walked in here," the doctor answered. "He had an amazing recovery considering he had no experienced medical care. His bones are healed fine, he'll have a limp, but it won't stop him from doing anything save running a marathon."

"And the blood work?"

"Everything looks good. No infections, no foreign antibodies, nothing to indicate his return to the US will pose any problems."

"Good, is he there?"

"About to yank the phone away from me," the doctor chuckled.

"Drew?" Ty's voice came strong through the phone.

"I've got a transport waiting for you. It will leave in twenty minutes," Drew answered the unspoken question.

"Where's Dani? Is she there?"

Drew took a deep breath and braced himself. After everything Ty had been through, he didn't want to deliver the message, but there was no way around it.

"She's not here. She left New York a month after you went missing. I don't know where she is, but I'll find her." His statement was met by silence. Ty's tension was palpable, even through the phone.

"You don't know where she is?" he repeated.

"I know she's fine," Drew rushed to answer. "I spoke to her on Thanksgiving and Christmas. Sammy talks to her every other day. She just needed to be on her own and we needed to respect that. If I'd known you would come back, that you were okay, I never would have let her go without giving me some way to contact her, but we did let her go and now I just need to find her."

"Use Sam," Ty spoke, not bothering to hide his intensity.

Drew sighed. "I plan to, but she is currently on a flight to Singapore. We have people waiting for her at the airport. Dani bought herself a new phone when she left New York six months ago and Sammy is the only one with the number."

"What about caller ID from when she last called you?" Ty demanded.

"She doesn't use the cell and usually calls from a blocked number. As soon as we can reach Sammy, we'll get Dani's number and, in the meantime, we're trying to back trace the call she placed over the holidays to see if we can unblock the number. And I have folks checking credit cards, ATM usage, and all the usual channels."

"When was the last time she used them?"

"She used a gas card about four months ago near Albuquerque. There hasn't been any activity since then. Judging by her spending, she was steadily heading west."

Drew heard Ty take a deep breath, then let it out. "Fine, okay," he took another breath. "Can you get me transport to Albuquerque once I land in New York?"

"You're going to look for her in Albuquerque? She could be anywhere by now, Ty. You need to come here first and we'll work together."

"I'm going home, Drew. My parents live in Taos. I'm going to go there, let them know I'm not dead, and then I'm going to contact my brother and have him put everything he's got into helping me find her. You may be good, but he's better."

Drew absorbed the information in a split second and agreed that Ty's plan was the best, even though he'd prefer to have Ty come to DC for a debrief.

"I'll have your papers waiting for you in New York and a jet waiting to take you to New Mexico. There's an airport closer to Taos, if you want to go there?"

"Can you arrange it?"

"I can arrange almost anything," Drew replied with a small smile. Sometimes it paid to have personal wealth. He'd arrange a private jet for Ty, not for the luxury, but because it was the fastest way to get him home, and he deserved to be home. More than anything, he deserved to be home.

"Thanks, Drew," Ty said, some of the tension gone from his voice now that there was a plan in place.

"It's the least I can do considering you're going to become my almost brother-in-law once we find Dani. Right?"

"If I have any say in the matter."

Drew relaxed, hearing the affection and fidelity in Ty's voice. It would be okay. He'd make sure of that.

• • •

Ty paid the taxi driver with money Drew had made available to him and closed the door behind him. Swinging his duffel bag over his shoulder he paused at the bottom of the driveway to his parents' house and took it in. It was the same house he'd grown up in until the move to Maine, and the same house he and his brother and sister always came home to for the holidays. Only now it looked like a haven.

He started up the drive, his left leg still bothering him. When he reached the top, the family dog raced out and barked once before it realized who it was and then subsided into wiggles and pleas for head scratches.

Ty dropped his bag and knelt to give the dog a good rub. After months of living in a tiny village in the jungle, petting his parents' dog was a simple pleasure. As he rubbed the dog's belly, he glanced around. His parents' car wasn't in the drive, but he could hear music coming from the back yard. It was an unseasonably warm day, maybe his mom was out starting her garden. He had thought about calling, about letting them know right away. He had even tried to call them from New York. But when the phone rang and no one picked up, he took it for a sign of what he already knew about them. They would be happier to see him in person, to know he was fine, to see for themselves. So here was, about to show up on their doorstep.

Rising from the ground over protests from the spoiled pup, Ty headed around the back of the house. He knew being here was the right thing, but he wasn't sure of the best way to approach his parents. After all, it wasn't every day that a son came back from the dead.

He thought about knocking on the door rather than appearing in the back yard. But since their car wasn't in the drive maybe they weren't even home. Ty hesitated at the side of the house before rounding the back, not wanting to startle anyone. He would look to see if his mom or dad were in the back yard and, if so, he would then go back around to the front and knock on the front door, rather than appear out of nowhere.

He took a deep breath, bracing himself for the sight of his parents, and walked to the corner of the house. He glimpsed around the corner and his knees almost buckled.

Dani.

His heart slammed into his chest and he reached out, putting a hand on the house to steady himself. Closing his eyes and taking a few deep breaths, he opened them again. And she was still there. He blinked back the moisture rising in his eyes and drank in the sight.

She was wearing a loose-fitting cotton dress, a sweater, and sandals. Her back was to him and she was hanging laundry on the clothesline. Her hair was pulled back into a low ponytail and she was swaying to the gentle music playing on the radio.

He watched her move along the sheet, straightening it and fastening it into place with clothespins. He couldn't have moved if he'd wanted to, he was so overwhelmed with emotion. He stood, locked in place, staring.

And then she turned.

The sweater and dress were stretched around her rounded belly. A belly that held, he knew, their child.

He must have made a sound because her head shot up. He saw her blink a few times and then she reached out with a strangled noise. In a flash he was beside her, gathering her in his arms. More for him than for her, he picked her up and carried her to the bench swing his parents loved so much. He held her so close he couldn't see if she was conscious or not and so, fearing for the baby, his baby, he pulled back enough to see her face. Enough to feel her hands grip him and hold him, enough to see the silent tears streaming down her cheeks.

He buried his face in her hair and held her, whispering words to soothe and love her. Words to reassure them both that everything would be okay.

Finally Dani pulled back and looked at his face. She raised a hand and touched his cheek. Her eyes closed and she sighed.

"Ty?" she managed to speak. He took her hand in his and kissed the palm.

"I'm okay," he answered the question in her eyes. "I was rescued by some local fishermen. They took good care of me. I was pretty banged up and out of it for a long time. When I started to pull through, I realized I was in a village that had no phone, no satellite, no lines of communication. I needed a long time to heal and then I had to walk to the nearest city. They were in the middle of a civil war so, between that and my legs, the walk took longer than expected. I made it to the Ivory Coast and called Drew yesterday." He needed to get it all out. There was so much more than the bare bones he was telling her now, but he needed her to know, more than anything, that he was okay.

"He got me home, but didn't know where you were. I came here to see my parents and was going to have Cameron start to find you," his voice gave out, choked on emotion.

"Oh god, Ty," she whispered and then raised her head to brush her lips against his. It was the sweetest kiss he'd ever experienced.

When it ended her face had more color and he could see the edges of happiness creeping into her eyes. She was starting to believe he was really there, with her.

He smiled and placed his hand on her belly. "Is this why you came to my parents?"

She placed her hand over his and gave him a watery smile. She moved it to the side and he felt the baby kick. He swallowed hard.

"His name is going to be Tyler, after his father."

He stared at her belly, wondering what he ever did in life to be this lucky. "A boy." He repeated, rolling the words around his mind.

"Due in a month," she added.

He looked at his hand, resting on Dani, covering their baby and then looked at the woman resting in his arms. He raised his eyes to meet hers and then smiled a smile full of hope. A smile full of promises for their future. A smile full of love.

"Then I guess I got back just in time."

ACKNOWLEDGMENTS

BOOKS MAY BE WRITTEN IN solitude but they certainly aren't published that way. I'd like to thank my first introduction into the world of professional writing and editing, Andrea Hurst of Andrea Hurst & Associates, Sarah Martinez (who is one of the most positive, encouraging writers and editors around) and my editor, Julie Molinari (who must have "who said this?" on auto-populate for me).

Now on to the personal acknowledgements. Saying thank you to my family, who somehow manage to let me have blocks of hours to write but can't let me brush my teeth without needing something, seems so inadequate. You make me laugh, keep me grounded, encourage me, and remind me every day of what is really important. I am also grateful (and lucky) to have a number of amazing women in my life. Special thank yous go to Sarah C and Angeli, you may be thousands of miles away at any given time, but you're never far. And to Lisa, because you never let me doubt myself, Sarah A, because you're my partner in crime, and Jere, because under that fabulous Nicole Miller is one of the strongest women I know. And last but not least, to my parents who instilled in me both a love of reading and the knowledge that while there are some things I shouldn't do, there is very little I can't do if I decide I want to.

Keep reading for a preview of Tamsen Schultz's

A TAINTED MIND
WINDSOR SERIES BOOK 1

OBSESSED with her job as a medical examiner and lead consultant with the FBI, Dr. Vivienne "Vivi" DeMarco is a woman running from her own demons. And finding the remains of a body on the side of a road in rural upstate New York wasn't part of her plan.

FRUSTRATED that the ghosts from his past won't leave him alone, Ian MacAllister makes for a reluctant Deputy Chief of Police of Windsor, New York. But as more victims are discovered, all women that bear a shocking resemblance to Dr. DeMarco, he knows he'll need to call on all the skills he learned as an Army Ranger if he wants to keep her safe.

DENIED over and over again the one thing he desires most, a killer may have finally reached his breaking point. The only question that remains is, will he take Vivi and Ian with him?

CHAPTER 1

VIVIENNE DEMARCO GUIDED HER CAR onto the shoulder of the country road and peered out through the windshield into the black night. Her eyes skirted to the side windows as she tried to see something, anything. When that failed, she turned her gaze to the rearview mirror then let out a long, slow breath. There was nothing. Nothing but the darkness and the deafening sound of rain hammering her car.

It was a dark and stormy night, she thought to herself with a rueful sort of inevitability as she loosened her grip on the steering wheel. Here she was alone, in the dark, on a deserted road, and in the middle of a torrential spring downpour. Her life had become a series of clichés lately and tonight was no different. As if in a bad movie, she'd been felled by a simple flat tire.

She craned her head forward and looked up through the windshield again, debating whether or not to risk the pelting rain. She knew storms like this moved on as fast as they came in. And so, after listening to rain drops the size of New Hampshire lash at her car, Vivi put her faith in experience and opted to wait.

Still, as she sat listening to the metallic sound of her roof taking a beating, the cliché-ness of the situation—of the past year—did not escape her. She was just a woman who'd thrown herself into her job after a searing loss—a job that had propelled her to the brink and finally catalyzed a meltdown of epic proportions. A meltdown that drove her away from everything she knew in an effort to find herself again. Honestly, all Vivi needed now was the urban legend hitchhiker scratching his hook along her window. But at least the hitchhiker would make a good story. As it was, her life story was all so prosaic that, if it were a book, it would never make it past an agent's slush pile.

With a sigh, she pulled her mind from her uninspiring existence and glanced at her GPS. Judging by the tiny map, she wasn't all that far from her destination, a place her aunt had been telling her about for years. Windsor, New York, was a small town in the Hudson Valley and, having been in her fair share of small towns, Vivi figured that if she saw anyone on this night, he or she was more likely to stop and help than to stop and slit her throat. But either way, the storm was letting up and she wasn't going to sit around and wait for help, or anything else, that may or may not come. She knew how to change her own tire.

However in the dark and wet, what should have taken her no more than twenty minutes took forty and, after tightening the last bolt, she needed to stand and stretch out the kinks in her back and shoulders. The now gentle rainfall had soaked her clothes, and water was running under her jacket's hood, down her neck, and onto her back. At least the job was done.

With the smell of wet earth hanging in the humidity, Vivi paused. Taking a deep breath of the heavy air, she inhaled the cleanness of it, the purity of the scent. No pollution, no smells of the dead and decomposing. And knowing Windsor would have somewhere she could stay for the night, Vivi ignored how uncomfortable she was for a moment and savored the peace as a sense of calm settled over her.

But as if to object to her enjoying such a small luxury, an owl screeched in the night, jarring Vivi back to the here and now. Gathering her flashlight and tools, she tossed the jack into the car, wiped the grease from her hands with a wet rag, and shut the trunk. She turned toward the driver's door as a sound behind her, muffled by the dense air, caught her attention. Vivi stilled and cocked her head. It wasn't a car and it hadn't sounded like footsteps either.

There, she heard it again. Vivi frowned. Judging by the gentle thuds and cracks, it was nothing but a few rocks tumbling down the shoulder behind her. But there wasn't much wind to speak of now that the storm had reduced to a drizzle, nothing strong enough to move rocks around. Shining her flashlight onto the water-soaked road, she realized that it was possible the runoff from the storm was stronger than she thought and that the rain had dumped enough water to loosen the soil under the asphalt. Or maybe there was something else causing the disruption.

This thought came out of nowhere and disturbed her more than the sound itself. Despite her experiences, despite her job, she was *not* one of those people who saw danger or evil everywhere she looked. And, more to the point, she didn't ever *want* to be one of them. So, forcing herself to come up with some alternate logic for her errant thought, she remembered her aunt telling her that bears were endemic to the area. Maybe one had come out for the night, dislodging the earth as it made its way into the field across the road?

Yes, a bear—or maybe even a deer or a fox. That made more sense than anything else out here on this quiet road. This option gave her a small sense of relief until she realized that, while she might know how to change a tire, she knew nothing about bears. What did someone do when encountering a bear? Run? Stay still? Vivi's mind had just started spinning when she brought it to a purposeful halt. She was getting ahead of herself. She had no idea what, if anything, was out there. And so, with some trepidation, she made a half turn and swept her flashlight across the road. Nothing.

She glanced to her left. A forest of elm and birch trees lined the road. Even if she shined her flashlight in that direction, which she did, she couldn't see more than a few feet into the dense woods. To her right, and steeper than she had originally thought, the side of the road dropped down about ten feet before leveling out onto a cornfield filled with stalks about a foot high. Curiosity got the better of her, and she moved a step away from her car. She'd seen lots of deer in her time, but she had never seen a bear, or even a fox, in the wild. As long as she knew an animal wasn't right next to her, she wouldn't mind catching a glimpse of one moving about in nature.

She pointed her light along the line of corn at the edge of the field, looking for some sign an animal had disturbed the crops. After two passes, the only thing she saw were neat rows of baby stalks, their tops and leaves battered by the heavy rain. Vivi should have felt comforted by the lack of wildlife, but she didn't.

As she took another step away from her car, the night encompassed her. Steamy fog was rising from the road, casting eerie shadows that drifted in the weighty air and made the hairs on her neck stand up. She thought about getting in her car and driving away;she hadn't gathered up the courage a few weeks ago to take a much-needed leave of absence from all the violence of her work only to step right back into the thing she was trying to get away from.

But it wasn't in her makeup to let fear guide her response, so Vivi took a deep breath, moved away from her car toward where she thought the sound had originated, and stopped. Standing silent and still, she let the night become familiar. After a few moments of hearing nothing but cicadas and frogs, Vivi directed her beam down the edge of the road as far as the light would go. But the fog and shadows blended with the black of the night and the darkened roadway, so it was hard to see much of anything.

Rather than move farther along the road, she redirected the light down the side of the slope to the field's edge, the contrast of the lighter dirt making it easier, just a bit, to see any anomalies. Starting below where she stood, she swept an area in a straight line away from her as far as the beam would go. Then, shifting it up a foot or two, she brought it back toward her, searching the area in a grid-like way, looking for what might have made the noise.

Standing on the side of the road, wet and exposed, combing the area for something unknown, Vivi couldn't ignore the reality that, to her dismay, she *had* become one of those people—one of those people she never wanted to be. She no more expected to find a simple little rock slide than she expected to see Santa Claus. The pain and death and evil she worked with every day had filtered into her life and colored her experiences.

The irony of her situation did not escape her. Whatever was compelling her to stay and find answers on the side of this country road was the same thing that had gotten her here in the first place. She didn't like to let things go, and because she couldn't let things go, she had almost destroyed herself with her last case. She'd taken to the road to escape, maybe to find some balance. If she were to hazard a guess, though, she'd say that whatever balance she'd found in the past few weeks was about to be tipped.

And, as if to give weight to the direction of her thoughts, about fifteen feet away from her position and about halfway down the embankment, her light landed on a small collection of rocks. No, not rocks, pieces of road that had broken away from the winter-weakened, rain-pummeled lane and tumbled down to rest a few feet away.

Vivi kept her beam trained on the pile as she walked closer. Tracing a line up the embankment, she could see an approximately two-foot by one-foot section of the road cracked and starting to cave in, the edge beginning to break away.

As she contemplated the small sinkhole illuminated by her flashlight, a gust of wind picked up. Her wet jeans pressed against her legs, her ponytail lifted, and her skin broke out in bumps from the sudden chill. Another piece of the road cracked and tumbled down the slope.

And there, at that crumbling edge, barely visible in the dark and shadows, was the unmistakable form of a human hand.